THE RESURRECTION

Part Three in the Day-Walker Saga

Elle Brice

THE RESURRECTION

The Resurrection
Copyright © 2016 by Elle Brice

All rights reserved. No part of this book may be reproduced or transmitted in any form or by any means without written permission from the author.

ISBN: 978-1522861492

Printed in USA by CreateSpace

Image from shutterstock.com

ELLE BRICE

Other books in the Day-Walker Saga

Angel of Darkness
Demon Unleashed

Coming soon...

Redemption: Part One

Prologue

Sacramento, February

"Ah, yes. I can see now. Your boss really appreciates the work you do," Ajala said as she trailed her hand over the man's palm. "If you keep it up, you may get a promotion."

"Really? You hear that, Kate? I'm gonna get promoted?"

The man's girlfriend rolled her eyes. It didn't hurt Ajala's feelings. She knew very well that she didn't have a real gift of foresight; just very strong intuition. A gift she'd been blessed with her entire life. Fortune telling wasn't what she'd imagined doing day to day, but it earned her money.

The two people left and she got up to find more incense to burn. The cinnamon sticks were completely blackened and she could barely smell them anymore. She loved that scent. It reminded her of home. Her husband would bring a large batch whenever he came to visit with their son. It was hard being away from the family but necessary. At least she had her brother there to fill that space.

She heard someone enter the tent, so she hurried to find the sticks then grabbed a lighter from her desk drawer. She liked to allow the visitors to admire the trinkets first before she would approach them.

It helped her earn a little extra money by selling homemade blankets, tea mixes, and herbal remedies. There wasn't a single time that she had to
pack up what she hadn't sold. Having to replenish her products kept her busy in between shows by giving her something to do.

Five minutes passed before she stepped out from behind her privacy curtain. The visitor was alone and it was a man. He was dressed in blue jeans, a blue thermal shirt, and brown boots. For this time of the month, his clothes weren't exactly weather appropriate. He had a fedora that matched his shirt.

"Good afternoon," she said in her fortune teller voice she'd practiced for years. "How would you like to have a glimpse of what is to come?"

"Thank you but ..." The man turned around and removed his hat, his crimson hair tumbling over his shoulders. "I would rather tell you *your* future."

She dropped the plate of incense and began to tremble. Though she had only seen him in a painting, his face was burned into her memory. Her entire life, she'd lived in fear that one day, he would appear to her and now that he had, she was frightened to the point of paralysis. His alabaster skin; the eerie blue eyes; this was undeniably Lucian Christophe.

"I'm...sorry, sir," she managed to say. "I don't know what you mean."

"Oh, I think you do."

He stepped closer to her and she tried to calculate how long it would take her to get to the exit. He was immortal, so running would be pointless. If someone were to be interested in her exhibit, this would be the perfect time. He wouldn't kill her in front of someone ... right?

"You are the one who gave Lela my blood," he said. "I remember from her memories. If it were not for you, I probably never would have been resurrected."

How could this have happened? Her family had worked so hard to keep him dead and now he was here to reap vengeance. She wondered if Melody knew about this. Ajala had promised to call her if anything like this were to happen but she didn't have time.

"Who killed the vessels?" she asked

"No one. They willingly brought me back. Lela was murdered and the other two brought me back to try and save her." The menacing gleam in his eye softened a bit. "There is only one left."

Ajala swallowed. "Why are you here?"

The dark expression returned and he smiled. "I learned a bit of information during my travels. I learned that the coven isn't what it used to be. The founding families scattered and are now living normal lives.

Except ... they still pass down their stories. Their rituals ... their ... secrets." He glared at her. "Only one vessel needed to die, am I right?"

Ajala started hyperventilating. That had been one of her biggest regrets. Lying to Samil was one thing but lying to Lela was cruel. She had only been following the instructions of her ancestors; deceive any threats into thinking resurrecting Lucian was a difficult task and discourage it. But Samil wouldn't relent. He stopped at nothing to achieve his goal and he'd succeeded.

"Yes," she admitted. "All you would need is some of your blood and then human blood to replenish yourself."

"And now three people are dead because of you. Not to mention my daughters and my wife." He chuckled. "I do not care so much about Florence. I do feel, though, that the others deserve to be avenged, don't you?"

Lucian rushed up to her and grabbed onto her throat.

Ajala tried to scream, but his grip was too tight. Gasping for air, she attempted everything she could to rouse attention from people who were passing by. She knocked a lamp off the table then tried to push some bottles over but then he released her and

bit onto her throat.

"They...." She tried to speak, resorting to breaking her first and solemn vow. "They're alive."

Lucian stopped drinking from her. "What did you say?"

"They're ... alive."

"Who?"

Her will to live slowly dissipated as her body became weak from blood loss. She no longer had the energy to speak. Her heartbeat slowed and he dropped her to the ground. Now all she could do was think of her family. She hadn't been able to say goodbye.

He must have been spooked by something because he hurried behind her privacy curtain. Sure enough, her brother walked in. He had been planning to meet with her for lunch that afternoon. If only he had come sooner.

"Ajala?" He said in shock. "Sister no! No!"

"Run!" She said in a breathy voice. "Go!"

The warning had come too late. Lucian came out from behind the curtain and attacked her brother. As she lost consciousness, she could hear the yells of her brother being murdered right in front of her. His agony was the last thing she heard and she regretted not being able to save him.

Chapter One

Italy, April

I wasn't really sure what death was supposed to be like. I had been taught all my life that we would first enter purgatory and then receive the final judgement. I didn't expect the never ending void of darkness. I waited and waited for a bright light, or any sign that I had crossed over into the next life, but it never came.

I began to hear things; familiar voices. At first I thought I was getting closer to crossing over, but the voices began to mention names that I could recognize and I knew that something much more extraordinary was going on. I assumed that I was trapped in my mind, just as Lucian had been when I was alive. Had we simply traded places?

The voices started out sounding muffled like the teacher on Charlie Brown, but as more time passed, I could hear everything that was being said. I didn't always hear them, though. They would cut in and out like a phone with bad reception. I listened to a snippet of a conversation and figured out that David was talking to someone.

David, what's going on?

I tried to speak, but I couldn't find my voice. It was the most frustrating thing, but I kept listening all the while. I wasn't sure, but it sounded like he was leaving. Was Samil letting him go? Had he decided to let David go free because he'd gone against their agreement to keep me alive? I doubted that Samil was that fair, though I didn't really care how or why David was leaving. He was safe and that was all that mattered.

Come on girl, what is the name? I heard someone say. It took me a minute to figure out that the person was talking to me. Was it Lucian? Was he communicating with me? If he was, I couldn't decipher what he was asking me exactly.

The restaurant. What is the name?

He must have been referring to the restaurant Lydian had taken me to. I remembered the sign, but I probably pronounced it wrong in my head. Why would he want to know that? Did he plan on enjoying foreign cuisine? That didn't seem like something he would be interested in.

For a while after that, there was just silence, and I began to feel discouraged again. I didn't mind being in the darkness if it meant that I could hear what everyone was saying. I was starting to get bored in my nonexistence

Suddenly, I felt something, which I never knew was possible; pain. I felt as if I was being beaten with a baseball bat. Someone was hurting me. I felt each blow from my invisible attacker.

Ow! Quit it! I thought to myself. It was probably pointless since no one could hear me, except maybe for Lucian. If Samil was beating my dead body, that would be reaching a new low.

I felt someone kick me really hard, right in the stomach.

I said stop!

The pain left shortly, and I was comfortable once more. As comfortable as I could be while trapped in a black void. I wasn't even sure what comfort was anymore. I couldn't feel my body, but I could feel pain. It was as if I only existed in a spiritual level. But if I was only a spiritual being, then why could I feel someone hurting me?

Finally, after what felt like forever, the voices came back. This time it was Gallard's. I tried to call out to him, but failed every time. He sounded angry about something and I longed to know what it was. I finally figured out who he was yelling at when I heard,

THE RESURRECTION

"Is this how she suffered? Huh? Is this what she felt before she died?"

"I'm so sorry, Gallard. I didn't mean—"
"Shut up Lydian! How could you do that to her? She cared about you, and you left her to die!"

The talking sounded more distant than usual as if they were speaking several yards away. Was he going to kill her? I hoped that he wouldn't. Lydian may have betrayed me, but she hadn't been the one to end my life.

I hoped that my questions would be answered, but the voices stopped again. I waited for them to come back, but when they did it was just Gallard. He was telling someone, whether it was Lydian or not I was not sure, that he was going to kill them. I could tell that he was taking my death very hard, and I longed to comfort him.

And then someone spoke to me again.

Lela, say something. Anything! He needs to be convinced or he is going to kill us!

This time, I was sure the person was Lucian. He wanted me to say something to convince Gallard that I was alive. I began to speak again, this time with more confidence.

Gallard! I love you, old man! Don't do this, I'm still here! Please tell me that you can hear me.

Everything went silent again, but I felt something. A kiss maybe. It had to be. Gallard must have heard me, and I started to get some hope.

There were even longer gaps of silence after that; almost twice as longer than usual. By that time, I was getting used to being alone with just my thoughts. The moments where I would hear voices became like that of holidays. I saw them as something to look forward to like Christmas or the Fourth of July.

Once, I heard a yell which I recognized as Aaron and I wondered what had hurt him. Another time, I heard a familiar voice say, "Lucian! You deceitful little bastard. How are you here? How are you in Lela's body?"

I kept listening for someone to explain, but the conversations were so vague that I couldn't piece together the whole situation. Someone mentioned the name Solomon and I became a bit excited.

Had they found him again? If so, would he help us this time? Maybe that meant that sooner or later I would be able to wake up.

I had been enjoying the silence when suddenly I heard a loud hammering sound. I wanted to cover my ears, but I had no ears to cover. It went on and on for what felt like hours and I tried to yell for it to stop, but it kept on going. This was the longest time I had ever heard anything, and I was angry that the sound I had to be hearing so long was that of a jackhammer, which I'd assumed it was.

Suddenly, in the middle of the sound, I felt pain again, and with the pain came the sudden stopping of the hammering noise. It was like someone had stabbed me in the side. I wanted to cringe, but there was no body to move. Another stabbing sensation came in a different spot and I yelled inside my head. The pain was more intense than the last time and it lasted longer.

"Lucian, enough!" I heard Gallard say.

Wait, what? Lucian is hurting me? That asshole! How dare he, after all I've done for him!

The hammering started again but it wasn't annoying to me anymore. I took everything I heard as a sign that I was alive.

The silence returned, and I wondered what everyone was doing. I tried to come up with reasons for why they would be using a jackhammer, but everything I thought of sounded ridiculous. Whatever they were up to, it had to be important. More than anything, I longed to hear Gallard's voice. He seemed to be the one constant in my nothingness. I heard his voice more than anyone else's and it was soothing like a lullaby even when he was sounding angry.

Sometime later, I was awoken from my daydream by the sound of multiple voices speaking. For the first time, they were crystal clear and not muffled. It was as if I were hearing everything with my own ears instead of through a speaker.

"Lela! Don't do this to me! I can't lose you! I can't!" I heard Gallard say.

You won't! I'm here! Can't you hear me?

Suddenly, for the first time, I saw something. Gallard must have opened my eye because for a short second, I saw a flash of his face before the darkness returned. I tried to move; to open my eyes and show him that I was alive, but nothing worked. I was paralyzed.

THE RESURRECTION

"She was never alive, was she?" I recognized this voice as Solomon's. "You deceived them. You had them believing in a lie so that they would help you!"

As much as I didn't want to defend Lucian after he'd stabbed me, I had to speak up. My life depended on it.

No, he isn't lying! I'm alive!

"She can't be dead. If she's dead, then Lydian died for nothing! And her own father ... David ... he died for nothing!" I heard Jordan say.

What? David and Lydian are dead? No! This can't be happening, they're lying! My father can't be dead, I just got him back! And what happened to Lydian? Why is she dead?

"They died for love. They died for hope. I would have gladly died too if there was a chance that it would bring her back," Gallard spoke again.

This darkness, this paralysis was just too much. Two of my closest friends were dead, for real this time, and I could do nothing but listen to the others lose all hope.

I finally realized what was going on. I wasn't unconscious or in a coma, I was dead. And this was hell; my own personal hell. I was doomed to have to listen as my friends suffered while I could do nothing. Doomed to listen to the man I loved be in agony and not be able to console him. I suddenly wished that hell had been like what they'd taught in church; an eternity of fire and physical pain or torture. Anything would be better than what I was experiencing.

Gallard, Jordan, and my brothers made their decisions about what to do with my body and what story they were going to tell everyone. I wept internally as I listened to the sorrow in their voices. They exchanged very few words from then on, and I hoped that the voices were going to disappear altogether eventually. They said very kind things about me, and I assumed that they were giving me a funeral.

Besides the few times I felt pain, I hadn't felt anything else up to that point. I started to forget what it felt like to be touched; to feel someone else's skin against mine. I'd heard that babies had died from not having enough physical contact, and I hadn't believed that until then.

Suddenly, out of nowhere, I felt something; someone was

kissing me again, and I could actually feel it more clearly this time. I didn't have to guess who had done it. I knew those lips like I knew my own.

I love you Gallard. I'll miss you, and I hope you find joy in your life.

It became quiet for a final time, and I knew that I would never hear the voices again. I wallowed in self-pity, wondering what eternity would be like without ever hearing Gallard's voice again; without seeing my baby brother or Robin or Aaron and Jordan again.

The silence continued on, and I kept myself sane by replaying the past four years over and over in my mind like a film reel. My memories were the only thing I had left, and were a small light in my bleak existence.

When the memories hurt too much, I would imagine an alternate reality. One where my mother and David raised me together. We would have lived in Orlando, and I would have met Lydian in college where we would be roommates for four years until we both graduated. Then, I would meet Gallard and we would get married and have five children. Soon, it didn't matter how great my alternate realities were because my real one sucked too much.

The ache in my heart grew worse as more time passed. The memories of what had been and the thought of what would never be drove me into a depressive state. I could no longer handle it. They were a painful reminder that I couldn't hold Gallard anymore; that I wouldn't see my sister grow up; that all the suffering I had endured was for nothing. What was the point? Everything that had happened from the moment I drank that blood from the gypsy woman had culminated to this.

I went back to that moment. I envisioned myself lying on my bed and sleeping through my alarm. If I had never woken up, I would have forgotten the blood in my drawer. I rarely ever went through my desk drawers. I probably wouldn't have found it for months. By then, I would have lost interest. My parents would have come home and I would have gone to church and come home and eaten lunch as usual. Life would go on.

Then I felt a flutter. I wouldn't have noticed it had I been wallowing in my misery but now that I was in a better place, I became completely aware. The flutter returned again, only this time

THE RESURRECTION

stronger than before. I had almost forgotten what a heartbeat felt like ever since I plunged into this terrible nightmare, so I was confused at first. Warmth followed, and I could feel the heat pulsing throughout my body as my heart began to pump blood. My limbs tingled as they regained circulation.

Finally, my lungs expanded, and I took my first breath. I breathed hard and quick at first until the fire in my lungs dissipated and then I decided to try and move. I started with kicking my foot and then wiggling my fingers. The sensation was so surreal that I thought I was dreaming; that I had finally lost my mind. I waited for this miracle to end but it never did. I was alive. The only thing I had to do now was open my eyes.

I opened my eyes with excitement hoping to see the sky, but my sight was greeted with horror as I saw nothing but darkness. I reached up in front of me and my hand came in contact with a rough surface. I brought up both hands and felt around before pushing up. The hard thing would not move. I started panicking and began beating on it over and over with my fists with no progress. I was running out of air, and nothing I did seemed to work. It was then that I realized what was happening. I was buried alive.

Chapter Two

I began to panic when the realization of my current situation began to register. Was I far below the ground? Was I six feet under? Each possibility made me panic more and I began to beat on the roof of the coffin with my hands. Nothing happened and it didn't budge. I tried to punch my way through but the surface was hard, like stone. I could feel my knuckles were bleeding and my fingernails were broken as I tried to claw at my surroundings.

"Help!" I shouted. "Somebody please!"

Tight spaces never used to bother me until now. I was getting more and more claustrophobic by the minute and my heart rate picked up. I had lost air long ago, but I never had trouble breathing. I should have. Mortals couldn't survive without air. I was weak too. My pounding became less forceful and my arms tired from use. I screamed again, this time getting more and more high pitched. I was never a screamer before and this was the best time to start. My voice cracked and my throat felt raw, as if I hadn't used my vocal cords in a long time.

A noise in the distance caused me to stop screaming and I listened. Whatever the sound was had been amplified as if it were playing on a speaker. I didn't used to have crisp hearing like that. I

THE RESURRECTION

recognized thesound as footsteps. They were coming towards me. This inspired me to start yelling again.

"Hello? Is someone there?"

"*Dove sei?*"

I didn't understand that language. It sounded like Spanish, but I couldn't tell. Truthfully I didn't care. All I wanted was for this person to find me and help me get out.

"I'm here! Can you hear me? I'm inside the coffin!"

The person spoke again and I discerned it was a man. I then heard the sound of stone scraping against stone. He must have been trying to open the lid. I waited patiently since I assumed it was very heavy. It didn't seem like he was making much progress. He might need more help.

As if he'd read my mind, I heard him run off and I took a deep breath, trying to calm down my nerves. I wasn't in a panicked state anymore but I was eager to get out. Not five minutes later, I heard more footsteps, this time belonging to more than one person and I heard them push on the lid. It had shifted and I smiled. Soon, it was moved enough that I could see light streaming in and then they created a space big enough for me to crawl out.

Three men were standing above me and I looked up at their faces. They were all tan with olive tones and had dark hair. One was older while the other two were maybe in their thirties. They stared at me for a moment, probably equally as confused as I was, then one of them took me in his arms and lifted me out. He set me down and I planted my feet on the ground, but nearly fell over from the lack of use of my legs. He caught me just in time.

"*Attento!*"

"Sorry, sir. *No habla Español.*"

The three men exchanged a glance. They had on coveralls and old grey shirts. There were a few shovels nearby and I guessed they worked in the cemetery.

"You are American?" The older one asked. He looked down at my clothes. "Alberto?"

I frowned then looked down as well. I was wearing a light blue jumpsuit with a nametag that indeed said *Alberto*. Why was I wearing this? And why were they surprised that I was American? I was Caucasian with blonde hair and blue eyes.

"Yes," I finally said. "My name is Lela Sharmentino. I live in Florida."

"Florida? That is very far from here."

I wasn't quite steady yet, so I used the coffin to keep my balance. My legs were incredibly stiff and I was still tired from trying to get out.

"Where am I?" I asked.

"Roma, Italy," the one in the brown coveralls said.

My eyes widened and I felt even weaker than before. I was in Italy. I had no idea how I had gotten there or how long I had been there; how long I had been in the coffin. It felt like not too long ago my brothers and Gallard had given me a funeral. I had no idea I was so far away from India.

At this point, the smartest thing to do was probably to call the police. They would be able to help me get back home and then I could find my family and friends. No doubt they would be in for the surprise of their life. I still couldn't believe this miracle had occurred just when I had reached the lowest I had ever been in my life.

"Thank you so much for helping me," I said. "Um ... would you mind taking me to the police?'

"Yes, of course!" the older man said.

With support, I was able to get through the cemetery and rode in the backseat of their car. It was a new experience driving on the left side of the road. The scenery was beautiful, and I couldn't believe that I was really in Italy. I had always dreamed of traveling there, but never thought I would get the chance to. Even if the circumstances of my not-so convenient location were a mystery, I figured that I should enjoy it while it lasted.

We arrived at the station, and I thanked them once more before going inside. I figured there would be a translator available and sat in one of the chairs in the waiting room. There were a few other people around, some fighting and some looking beaten. I hadn't had a chance to look in the mirror, but I probably didn't look so great. I could feel that my hair needed a good washing and brushing. It was longer than I remember, which was to be expected.

"*Ill prossimo!*" the man at the desk yelled. By then it was my turn, so I stood up and approached the desk.

"Do you speak English?"

THE RESURRECTION

"I speak English, French, Mandarin, and Russian." He set his papers down and sighed. "How can I help you?"

"I just woke up in a coffin."

"All right...so how did you get there?"

"I don't remember. I was here with my fiancé celebrating..." I tried to think of a holiday it could be. I had left for India in mid-February. "Valentine's Day. We drank a lot and I must have blacked out."

He picked up the phone and hit a button. He spoke with someone in Italian for a moment then hung up. "Go into the office and find cubicle seven. Officer Camillo will see you...Alberto?"

"Lela. Thank you."

I went further into the precinct and was grateful that the numbers were numerical and not in Italian. They were attached to the cubicle walls and I quickly found seven. I got a few weird stares from people as I walked by but I ignored them. I couldn't help what I was wearing. Whoever had put it on me either had a weird sense of humor or it was the only convenient clothing.

Officer Camillo was typing something on the computer when I approached him. He smiled at me then closed out of his tab. "Hello, miss. Please sit."

I thanked him then sat in the free chair across from him. He too had an olive complexion but he seemed younger than the men who found me. His hair was shiny from product and he had a neatly trimmed mustache.

"How can I help you today?" He asked.

"Well, I'm trying to get back to America. It seems that I am having trouble remembering the past few weeks. I don't remember how I got here."

"I see. What is the last thing you remember?"

"I was in a bar," I said. "My fiancé and I were having some drinks."

"Was there anyone suspicious there? someone lingering around you longer than necessary?"

"There could have been." I hated lying but I couldn't straight up tell him that I had been murdered by vampires. That would get me a one-way ticket to an institution. "Yes, there was a man. He was Indian. He kept asking where we were from, how long we were staying; intrusive questions like that. I never thought anything of it. He uh...offered to share his taxi."

"Now we're getting somewhere." He started writing this down. "So this man conversed with you now you're in Italy with no memory of what happened after. How long ago was this?"

"Maybe a few weeks? It was February." I cleared my throat. "February seventeenth I believe."

"What year?"

"Two-thousand fourteen."

He looked up at me and stared for the longest time. He put his pen down and folded his hands on the desk.

"Lela...what year do you think this is?"

"Is that a trick question?"

His expression became sympathetic, and I began to worry.

"The date is April eleventh, two thousand fifteen."

The sick feeling returned, and I hung my head between my knees. That much time couldn't possibly have passed. I remembered being in the warehouse like it had just happened. I hadn't been in the dead for that long. How could I have been gone for a year and not know it?

The officer continued talking, but I couldn't hear what he was saying. I began to shake, and he got out of his chair and walked across the room to fill a cup of water from the water dispenser. He came back, handing it to me. I took it but didn't take a drink. I wasn't sure if I could stomach it.

"I know this might be a lot to take in," he said. "But I promise you that we will do everything we can to make sure you are returned to your family. Is there anyone you can call? Your parents maybe?"

My state of shock passed over, and the idea of calling someone perked me up. If I had been gone a year, my friends would probably want to hear from me.

He instructed me on how to make a long distance call then he gave me some privacy as I dialed. The phone rang once but then an automated message said the number was disconnected. That had been Aaron's, but my call got ignored. That made me annoyed. Gallard didn't have a phone or if he did, I wouldn't know his number. Kevin didn't have one either. There was always Jordan but in that moment, I couldn't remember his number.

THE RESURRECTION

My last resort was calling the Curtis. He was the kind of guy who liked to keep it simple. He kept the same navy bedsheets for years until he finally bought a newer set of the same design. He also bought the same brand of toothpaste and socks and everything else. Aaron always made fun of him for it, but it was convenient now because he probably kept the same cell phone number.

The phone only rang three times before going to voicemail. Voicemail was better than being ignored. I didn't speak right away since I wanted to be delicate about what I would say. He wasn't expecting me to contact him, so he would probably be a little shocked, especially if he'd been told I was dead.

"Hello, Curtis," I said. "It's Lela Sharmentino. I know this may be hard to believe, but it's really me. I couldn't get ahold of anyone else. I don't know how I got here but…I'm in Rome. If you could call me back on this number, I would appreciate it. Hope you get this."

I hung up and ran my hands through my hair and was disgusted at how grimy it felt. I wanted to wash it more than anything, so I decided to ask Camillo when he came back.

"Is there any way that I could take a shower?"

He called a female officer over to us then spoke to her in Italian. He explained that she was going to take me to the women's locker room, so I followed her.

As I went into the shower room, I turned on the water and let it wash over me. It was so soothing and all my worries seemed to wash away with the dirt down the drain. As I washed off, I looked at my entire body. I was still slightly bony from being sick the year before. When I examined my torso I found several healed wounds as well as two puncture marks with signs of scar tissue. It must have been the result of the wounds I'd felt before.

The memories of everything I had experienced; everything I had heard while I was unconscious came rushing back to me. I remembered that Lydian and David were dead and that they had died to save me. If it hadn't been for them, I would never have woken up. The pain in my heart overwhelmed me and I began to sob. I trembled so much that I could no longer stand and I kneeled on the floor wrapping my arms around myself as the water continued to pour over me. I ached for my dead friends, and longed to be in Gallard's arms; to disappear into his comforting embrace.

When I finished showering, I dried off. On the bench, just outside of the shower, were a white t-shirt and a pair of grey sweats. I assumed they were for me and put my underwear on before donning the donated clothes. It felt good to be clean again.

I happened to pass by a mirror and I glanced at my reflection as I walked on, but backed up to take a longer look. I nearly shrieked when I saw my appearance. My hair was blonde, but throughout my locks were random streaks of black. What shocked me most of all were my eyes. One of them was blue while the right was dark grey.

I couldn't handle any more weirdness, so I went back into the hallway. I saw that more police had arrived only they were dressed semi-casually instead of in uniforms. I walked towards the same desk I had been sitting at, expecting to be questioned again about what had happened in the park, but instead, I got a completely different greeting.

"Lela Sharmentino?" Asked a tall, gruff-looking cop. He was extremely tan with dark, slicked-back hair and thick eyebrows.

"Yes, I am she."

The officer spoke again and a woman translated for him.

"We were informed that you've been in Italy for the past couple of years and we're here to help you get back home. Since you don't remember anything from the time you've spent in this country, we are assuming that you don't have
the necessary papers to leave?"

I nodded.

"It may take some time, but we will assist you in anyway we can. For now, we will give you a place to stay and provide you with any needs."

This was a start. Curtis hadn't called the station back yet so there was nothing else I could really do but rest. I was still tired and extremely hungry while feeling sad and lonely and scared at the same time. I had a year of my life to make up for and I wanted to start as soon as possible.

Chapter Three

Evelyn McAlister flinched when she heard a knock at the door. It had been over a year since her brother was killed and still she got nervous whenever someone would visit. She put a hand to her heart and tried to catch her breath before setting down her dust rag. Cleaning was one way she liked to take her mind off of her fears and anxiety.

Though Evelyn put her own touch on her brother's house, she couldn't bring herself to change anything major. She kept the same mocha leather couch that Mark and Sheila purchased the year Lela went missing. The large oak dining set had been a wedding gift and was in Mark's will to go to Aaron, so that wouldn't be going anywhere.

It was still strange sleeping in the master bedroom, though she and Jeff brought their own bed from Texas. Her sister-in-law's bedspread, curtains, and clothes had been boxed and taken by Sharon Lockfield. Evelyn didn't really mind, but she wished Sharon had asked instead of just staking a claim. She never understood the strange bond between the woman and her brother. Evelyn always thought something was a little off about her.

Once she'd calmed down a bit, she went to answer the door.

Solomon had left to pick up Robin from school and Jeff had left for his shift at the hospital. She hoped it was her nephews coming for a visit. She hadn't seen them since Christmas, and Robin had been asking about possibly going to stay with them a few days for spring break.

Opening the door, she found her prediction wasn't anywhere close. It was Mark's college friend Simeon Atherton. She hadn't seen him in so long. He hadn't been at the funeral and only received a brief phone call giving his condolences. She thought it was odd that Mark's closest friend hadn't gone to his memorial service.

"Evelyn." He smiled at her, flashing perfect white teeth. "Look at you all grown up and gorgeous."

Evelyn forced a grin. The last time she'd seen Simeon was when she was barely seventeen years old. The few Christmases he'd spent at Mark's she'd been with Jeff's family. They were very adamant about him spending holidays there, and she sometimes wished she'd put her foot down and told her in-laws that she was going to see her brother for a change. She didn't have that option anymore.

"Hello, Simeon. What brings you here?"

"I thought I should check in on my best friend's baby sister. He would have wanted me to make sure you're doing all right."

Somehow, she could sense he wasn't telling the whole truth. Nothing was ever simple with Simeon, and he gave her the creeps. She always made sure she was never alone with him.

"Well, that was kind of you. I'm fine. Jeff, Robin, and me; we're all fine. Taking one day at a time."

Something moved behind Simeon and she was greeted by the faces of a little boy and girl, probably around the age of five. They had dark brown hair and eyes the color of mint leaves. The boy and his sister were mirror images of each other, except the girl had long hair in two braids and the boy had coveralls while she had a jumper.

"Oh! Who are these precious children?" She asked.

"This is my boy Desmond and his twin Dominique." He rested a hand on the boy's head. "Kids? Can you say hello to the pretty lady?"

The little boy gave her a shy wave and she smiled. She had no

THE RESURRECTION

idea that Simeon had any children. Mark never mentioned it. She knew Simeon was somewhat of a womanizer but never thought he would father a child. He didn't seem like the fatherhood type.

"I thought maybe Robin might like someone to play with. I know she doesn't have many friends in school."

The smile left Evelyn's face. How would he know that? The only ones who knew Robin's personal life were her, her husband, and Solomon. The exception was Gallard who would visit at least once a month and that always made her day. His visits would turn her mood around for weeks and just when she was going back into her funk, he would come again. She couldn't thank the man enough.

"How do you know if Robin has friends or not?" Evelyn asked.

Simeon gave her a wry grin. "You are not the only one Mark asked me to look out for. I don't know if you're aware, but I have Mark's will." He reached into his pocket and took out a folded piece of paper. "I think this might interest you."

He handed the paper to Evelyn and she began to read it. Most of it was familiar to her since the family lawyer went over it with her, Lela, and Jeff after her brother died. In the event of his and Sheila's death, custody of Robin would go to Evelyn and Jeff. The house was theirs as well until Aaron decided to sell it, and Robin would receive her inheritance upon reaching the age of eighteen.

She read further and found what Simeon had been trying to show her. Nearly in fine print, there was a section that stated that if anything were to happen to Jeff and Evelyn, custody of Robin would go to Simeon. Evelyn clenched her jaw in frustration. Why had Mark done this? There were several people who would have been more capable than this creep. Yes, he was a father, but that didn't mean he was the best candidate for a guardian.

"Why are you showing this to me?"

"I think we both know why. It's been a year and that so-called private investigator hasn't even come close to finding those responsible for killing your brother and Sheila. My concern is only for Robin's safety."

"She is safe. Solomon checks on her periodically while she's at school and we have a top of the line security system."

"I don't think you understand the nature of how dangerous this situation is. Witnesses reported that up to fifteen men were sighted the night they were killed. Do you think your guy is capable of taking on that many men by himself?"

Evenly narrowed her eyes. "Are you trying to scare me?"

"Is it working?"

"No, I think you're just being a bully. How dare you come here and threaten to take Robin away!"

Simeon chewed on his lip. "Is that how you're taking this visit?"

"Why else would you be here? You show up with my brother's will and make hints at my safety like you're so sure I'm going to be killed at any second. Of all the times you could have visited, why now?"

His expression changed and became solemn. She'd never seen him genuinely sad before. He was always hard to read and she couldn't tell when he was serious or not. Whether he was lying or telling the truth.

"My wife recently died," he said. "Left me alone with a teenage daughter, three boys, and two five-year-olds."

Evelyn's hostility softened. She had no idea Simeon had been married either. Then again, he wasn't usually the topic of conversation when she spoke with her brother in the past. A teenage daughter? He must have been married a long time. She thought at one point he had been involved with Sharon. Maybe he was just a big flirt.

"I am so sorry," she said. "How long were you married?"

"Five years. She's not the mother of my other children, but they did love her like she was." He lifted the two kids into each of his arms. "I'm here because I know how precious life is. The people we love are here one moment and gone the next. I just wanted you to know that you never have to worry about your niece. She will always have someone to look out for her."

A black Cadillac Escalade pulled into the driveway at that moment. Solomon was home with Robin finally. It made Evelyn nervous leaving Robin at school even though she knew Solomon would be watching over her. Solomon got out then proceeded to help Robin out of her booster seat. Once she was out, he carried her pink backpack for her and they headed for the house.

"Hello dear!" Evelyn said to the little girl.

"Hi, Aunt Evie! Uncle Solomon bought me lunch!"

THE RESURRECTION

Solomon chuckled then looked up at Simeon. When the two men's gazes met, she could suddenly feel a strange tension. Solomon's jaw grew taught and he wasn't his usual friendly self.

"Um...Solomon, this is a friend of Mark's. Simeon, this is—"

"Solomon Schaech." Simeon held out his hand. "Pleasure. I hear you're solving my friend's case?"

"Attempting." Solomon quickly took his hand back. "You know Mark long?"

"Oh, about twenty some years. He was like a brother to me." Simeon set his children down. "Hey Des, Dom, you see this adorable little girl here? Her name is Robin. How would you like to play with her?"

Solomon put his hands on Robin's shoulders, suddenly going into protective mode. Evelyn had seen this side of him before and it was very intense. Kind of how Mark would get whenever men hit on Sheila. It was very apparent that Solomon had grown attached to Robin.

"I think Robin would like that," Evelyn said. "Simeon, why don't you three stay for dinner? Jeff won't be home 'til late, but Solomon and I would love the extra company."

Simeon gave Solomon a look that Evelyn couldn't read. "I would love to."

———※○☾———

Gallard walked into the apartment and threw his keys on the counter before taking a blood bag out of the fridge. He'd finally put in his two-weeks notice as he'd planned and was glad to be done working at the night club. This shift seemed to drag on and he couldn't wait to get home, away from people. He didn't like people much these days, aside from Jordan. Everyone else was just a face in a crowd, none of which who were her.

It had been over a year since he'd left her in Italy, though it felt like it had just happened yesterday. Every second of it haunted him like a vengeful ghost, forcing him to relive it every day after. She'd been so cold in his arms. He'd cried out to her over and over, begging her to open her eyes and look at him; to wake up and make a corny joke about his age. He'd loved her jokes. And now he would never hear them again.

As he finished the blood bag, he looked around at all the boxes in the living room. Almost everything was packed up, so it was almost time to move on. He and Jordan had decided it was best that they find somewhere else to live. The apartment contained too many memories for the both of them. Memories of Lydian and Lela.

It had taken several months to save enough money to afford to live elsewhere because he'd relapsed and gambled away quite a bit of his savings. Bodoway found out and stopped sending checks as an attempt at intervention. It worked, somewhat. He still hit the occasional slot machine when Jordan was out hooking up with strangers. Their combined earnings weren't as much as they'd like, but they would make due.

Jordan came out of the women's room carrying a tub of Lydian's things. They had decided to save their room for last since it hurt too much to go in there. The rest of the apartment was done, save for the necessities such as clothes and bathroom items.

"How was your night?" Jordan asked him. Gallard guzzled down the last bit of blood before tossing the bag into the trash. He hadn't really been hungry. It was just a habit to drink after getting off of work. That's how he'd survived the past year; getting into the habit. If he didn't have a routine, he would go mad with grief.

"Long," he mumbled. "As always. I'm glad that I'm finished there."

"I guess we're all set to leave then. There's just one more thing we need to do."

Gallard knew exactly what that thing was. Packing up Lela's half of the room. He didn't know how he was going to be able to do it. He'd put it off for so long because he'd hoped that the day would never come when he would need to. Jordan was stronger than he was. He'd lost someone that he loved as well, but he found the will to clear out Lydian's half. How he did it, Gallard could not comprehend.

He stopped leaning against the counter and walked over to the bedroom. He hadn't been in there in months and always had a feeling of dread as he passed by it. The door was cracked, so he pushed it open all the way. He sighed as he slowly walked in and stopped in the middle of the room. It was exactly the same as when she'd left; flowered bedspread with two white pillows and the picture of her and David from the dance on the wall. He wasn't sure why the room had sentimental value to him. It wasn't like he hadn't seen her long after she'd left and gone to live in Tampa.

The place that had real sentimentality was India. It was the place where she'd told him that she loved him and when he'd admitted that he reciprocated her love; where they'd finally kissed each other. How he'd loved her kisses. He'd counted them. She'd kissed him a total of seven times before Lucian had possessed her body. Seven had not been enough. He'd thought that it would be seven hundred and maybe even more. But that was not so.

Being in the room was too much for him so he quickly left slamming the door behind him. He needed some fresh air so he headed for the front door.

"You all right?" Jordan asked.

Gallard turned around and said, "I couldn't do it. Not tonight. I need some more time."

Jordan put a hand on his shoulder, giving it a sympathetic squeeze. "If you want, I could do it for you."

"No, I can do it. I'll do it tomorrow for sure. I just need one more night."

"Okay. By the way, Robin called. I told her you were working and that you'd call her back."

He checked his watch. It was around two-thirty so that meant it was about three-thirty in Miami. He would have to wait until they were on the road so he wouldn't wake anyone in the house.

"Would you mind if we dropped by there? I would like to see her in person. It's been a while since I checked on her."

Jordan smiled. "I don't mind at all. I miss the kid. She said she liked my cooking."

"I think everybody likes your cooking."

He went out the door and down the hallway. Sitting out by the pool seemed like a good idea. There were hardly any kids in the complex so it was bound to be free of people. He took the elevator down to the bottom floor then walked through the glass doors leading to the back. The smell of chlorine blasted him as soon as he stepped outside. The tenants had been complaining for months about the smell, yet nothing had been done.

Gallard pulled one of the lawn chairs from the grass onto the concrete then sat down. The moon was crescent tonight so it wasn't very bright. It didn't matter. He wasn't out there to enjoy the scenery; he was there to clear his head. There could be a celestial being rising into the sky with doves and a chorus of angels singing and he wouldn't care.

He'd been sitting for about fifteen minutes when he heard someone else come out to the back. He turned to see who it was and gave a half smile upon seeing her.

"Mind if I join you?" she asked. It was Kathleen Oaks. A forty-year-old widow who also lived in the apartment. She was pretty with wavy brown hair and light green eyes. She was probably the only other person he could stand to talk to these days. They'd bonded over their common situations and he would often talk with her about things that he couldn't with Jordan.

"I don't mind at all. Pull up a seat," he said. She did then leaned back in her chair, a glass of wine in one hand and a bottle in the other.

"Want a drink?" she asked. He shook his head. As much as he wanted to drown his sorrows away with alcohol, he couldn't. It wouldn't even give him a buzz.

"So a little bird told me that you and your brother are moving out pretty soon," she said.

"Would that little bird be Hallie?"

Hallie was the landlady who knew everything about everyone. She was a sweet person, though. She'd even stopped by to personally give her condolences about Lydian and Lela's passing. They'd told her that it was a car accident. If only she knew just how much worse it was.

"Where are you headed?" she asked, filling her glass once more. He didn't know how to answer. They hadn't chosen a specific destination yet. Anywhere other than Nevada, Texas, and Florida were fine with him. They could go to Iceland for all he cared. He was just glad to finally be in a position where he wasn't running from someone. Lucian was still out there somewhere, but Gallard wasn't on his target list. Solomon had assured him that he would look out for Lela's family, so he didn't have to worry about them. He wouldn't have minded just the same. Gallard would have done anything to make sure Lela's family was safe. He would have done it for her.

"Not quite sure. We're thinking we'll just pack up and drive. Eventually, we'll get somewhere."

"Well, I'll be sad to see you go. I've enjoyed our late-night talks."

She put her hand on his and began running her fingers along his knuckles. This wasn't the first time she'd flirted with him. She'd made it clear a while ago that she was interested, yet he didn't give in to her advances. He couldn't, knowing that he was still in love with Lela. He was in love with a ghost and no one, not even a beautiful woman like Kathleen could make him forget her.

"I want to thank you," he said, breaking the awkward silence. "For everything. You listened to all of my problems and were there when I needed someone to talk to. I appreciate it."

"I guess I listened because I wished I had someone to talk to when Jackson died. It makes the grieving process so much easier."

It did make it somewhat easier. Jordan and Kathleen had been the only ones keeping him sane and he was grateful to the both of them. Especially Jordan. He'd been the rock of the two of them, making sure that only one of them was an emotional mess. Gallard couldn't understand how Jordan could be so strong. Then again, Jordan was very much like how Gallard's mother had been. She had been the strength and the core of the family while his father had been the provider. Gallard never knew who he was more like. He'd figured that he was a mixture of both. Kathleen had stopped stroking his hand and wrapped her fingers around his completely.

"Why don't we go up to my place," she said. "We could get lost for a few hours; forget about our troubles." Their chairs weren't that far apart, so she was able to lean over and start kissing his neck. As she did, she slid her hand beneath the buttons of his shirt and massaged his chest. "Have I ever told you how sexy I think you look in your job attire?"

As much as he wanted to feel something, he didn't. It would have fixed all of his problems if he could bring himself to be attracted to her in that way, but he wasn't. He gently pushed her away and said, "I'm sorry. I can't do this with you."

"Is it because of her?" She asked, disappointment in her voice.

"She would want you to be happy, Gallard. Wouldn't you want the same if your places were reversed?"

"Yes, yes I would. But they're not. And I'm not ready to move on. I'm flattered, really. I just can't have that kind of relationship with you."

She sighed and leaned back in her chair. For the rest of the night, they just stared out at the view of the city and watched as the sun began to rise. He didn't know what else to say. He'd just rejected her for the hundredth time and didn't know how to start a conversation after that without feeling like a jerk. She was right. Lela would want him to be happy. He just couldn't imagine being happy with anyone but her.

"It's beautiful, isn't it?" Kathleen asked.

The edge of the sun framed the horizon like a golden halo. It was very much like the sunrise he'd watched with Lela the last time they'd sat together on the very same patio. He remembered the smile on her face as she took it all in and said how beautiful it was. And he, not even noticing the sunrise, had said to her, *"Yes, very beautiful."*

"I should go," he said. "There's something that I need to take care of. It won't be easy, but it needs to be done."

"And what is that?"

He stood up and looked at the horizon one last time before replying, "I'm going to pack up her room."

As he went back inside, he kept thinking about what Kathleen said. She was right about Lela wanting him to be happy. He knew because he would have wanted the same for her. It wasn't healthy to keep hanging onto the past but how could he let go when he had wanted her in his future? One day, he would move past it; one day he could think about her without falling apart. Until then, he would push forward and be there for Jordan. Gallard hadn't forgotten that he had lost his love too. Entering the apartment, he saw Jordan was standing in front of the window and talking on the phone. He must have been really focused on the conversation because he never turned around when Gallard approached him.

"How can you be sure?" he asked. "Has anyone..." he lowered his voice, "has anyone been over there? Me? Don't you think that...yes, I agree. Go with him? Yeah...I guess I could do that. Would he mind? Perfect. I'll call you as soon as I know anything."

THE RESURRECTION

Jordan hung up then turned around. Gallard waited for him to explain what the call was about but instead, Jordan went into the bedroom. Puzzled, Gallard followed him and leaned against the doorframe as he watched Jordan begin taking clothes out of one of the boxes and putting them into a bag.

"Who was on the phone?" Gallard asked.

"Uh…Solomon. He thinks he may have found Lucian and he wants me to check it out. See if it's a legit lead."

"Well, then I'm coming with you."

Jordan zipped his bag. "No, you stay. It's probably nothing, but we can't take chances right?"

"I'm not staying here in this depressing apartment while you run around playing hero. I'm going."

Jordan sighed then dropped his bag. "Gallard, I'm going to say this in the most loving way possible. You are a mess. I have to monitor your meals or you won't eat. You can't pack up Lela's room, and you're gambling again. The last thing we need is for you to see Lucian again to stir up old memories and send you over the edge."

"Send me over the edge? What do you mean?"

Jordan hesitated before speaking. "I called Bodoway. I knew you'd been through this before and I wanted some advice. I know that…back when you got the phone call you went crazy. I was afraid you wouldn't snap out of it, but you did. I am just trying to prevent you from going on another killing spree."

Gallard's frustration began to grow. Yeah, he was a mess but wasn't feeling murderous. And why would anyone care if he went *Man on Fire* on Lucian? Didn't they want him dead anyway? His demise shouldn't have mattered.

"How would you rather me get over losing her, huh? You want me to be like you and sleep with every woman I come across just to feel something?"

Jordan looked hurt and he regretted saying that. It wasn't his business that Jordan was channeling his pain into a series of one-night stands. It seemed to be working for him since he wasn't holed up and falling apart at every turn. He kept his back to the wall and slid down until he was sitting on the floor.

"I'm sorry," Gallard said. "I'm so sorry. You're right. I'm a mess. Worse even."

Jordan knelt down beside him.

"You're done working. Just take this time to focus on yourself and let's see if, by the time I get back, you have the room packed. And if not, that's okay. We're not in any hurry to go anywhere. I'm just going to go check out this lead and I'll be back in a few days tops."

Gallard nodded then forced a smile. "Go. Find that *fils de salop* and crush him."

"That's the spirit, uncle!"

Jordan grabbed his bag once more and left the apartment. Over the past year, not once had Jordan chided him or given him a pep talk and Gallard was starting to think it was long overdue. It was just what he needed to bounce back to reality. He would always love Lela and his heart would always have a space only she could fill, but maybe he could really start to move on.

He walked to the bedroom for the second time and took a deep breath. He thought back to the day he'd dropped Lela off at the airport to see her parents. Lydian had started talking to him the moment he came into the door, flooding him with suggestions about room trading and though at the time it was annoying, the memory made him smile. It was those moments that he needed to focus on; the times when they were all together like a family and watched each other's backs. Not the sad memories of betrayal and death. He could do this. With this thought, he began gently laying Lela's items in the first box.

Chapter Four

I hated being alone in the hotel, but it wasn't like there was someone to keep me company. It was more than generous of the people who paid for my stay anyway, and I couldn't have asked for a better gift. I probably would have ended up sleeping in the streets. The only downside was that I hadn't heard back from the police if Curtis returned my call.

The TV was on and I tried to pass the time by a lame attempt at catching up on the times. Since two-thousand fourteen, the iPhone six had come out and had colorful backgrounds, the Seahawks won the Super Bowl but then lost February of the current year, and there were rumors that *X-Files* was coming back. I got all of that in five minutes of commercials.

I didn't care about any of that stuff. I wanted to know what my family was doing; how Robin was holding up with losing her parents and recovering from her traumatic ordeal. I wanted to know if Kevin decided to get his GED or get a job. Did Aaron go back to medical school? I also wondered what Gallard and Jordan were doing. How Jordan was handling losing Lydian.

Sleep and hunger began to overwhelm me. I had eaten something from room service, but I wasn't satisfied. I was so hungry that I could barely think straight, but I was also tired. I couldn't fight it any longer, and I drifted off to the sound of the *Law and Order* theme. Sleep was peaceful at first. I was afraid that I would be reminded of the coffin, but instead, I was relaxed.

Then the nightmares started. I was in a dark room and the floor was hard. I was lying on an old mattress. I looked down at myself and saw that my clothes were ripped and bloody. Then Matthew came into the room and started torturing me. It was as frightening as experiencing it in reality. Every second of it was exactly the same except for how it ended. In my dream, I wasn't able to fight him off.

I woke up and remained frozen in my spot. The dream lingered in my mind for several minutes and nothing I did could make it fade away. Of all the things that had been done to me, that near assault had by far rattled me the most. Men didn't use to intimidate me because I had grown up in a house full of them. Not including the four years I'd lived with Gallard and David after only knowing them a few days. I had recovered from Simeon's attempt, but Matthew had shown me a side to them that I never thought I would see again. The perverse and forceful side.

The phone rang and I wiped my eyes so I could answer it. I pushed my disheveled hair out of my face as I got up and removed the phone from its cradle.

"Hello?"

"Miss Sharmentino, this is Lacey from the lobby. There are a couple gentlemen here to see you, and I wanted to make sure you were expecting them."

"What are their names?"

"Curtis Taylor and—"

"Curtis! Yes, I know him. Please send him up. Thank you!"

I didn't have to ask about the second person. I assumed it was either my brother or maybe even Gallard. I was disappointed that I didn't have time to shower, so I combed my hair with the brush I had gotten from the store down the street and threw on some sweats and a t-shirt. The clothes the police had given me were too big so I had taken the liberty of buying some new ones. Just to get me by for a few days until I would go home.

Someone knocked on the door, and I could barely contain my

excitement. I quickly straightened the room then went to answer the door. I had to take a moment to prepare myself before opening it. When I did, I was greeted by Curtis' familiar face. His hair was longer and he was very handsome.

"Curtis!" I threw my arms around him. "You have no idea how glad I am to see you. I've missed you."

He didn't hug me back at first, but when he did he held me tightly then pulled back and stared at me. I figured he needed some time to process. It had been over a year, after all.

"Lela?" He finally said. He hugged me again, slightly swaying from side to side. "You crazy girl. Do you know what you've put us through?"

A tear escaped my eye. "I can imagine."

"This year has been hell. When I got your message, I nearly passed out."

I realized I'd forgotten someone was with him. I stepped into the hall and when I saw Jordan I hugged him as enthusiastically as I had Curtis. This was such an awesome welcome party. He hugged me back and even lifted me off the ground a little then set me down and smiled at me.

"You have no idea how happy I am to see you," he said.

"Aw! You missed me?"

He hugged me again in his big, muscled arms. "Yes. You're the sister I never had and losing you was like losing family. I'm so glad you're back." He frowned. "Whoa…your eyes! And your hair!"

"I know. That was my reaction when I saw myself. I have no idea what it means."

We went into the room and I sat on the bed while Curtis and Jordan sat in the chairs at the small table. I studied their faces for a while, trying to see if they'd changed. Jordan's hair was longer but not as long as Gallard's and Curtis was looking more mature. He clearly wasn't the dopey boy I'd grown up with. It was more than just the way he dressed but how he carried himself. He'd overcome a heroin addiction, graduated from college, and now had a successful career.

"How's the job, Curt?" I asked.

"You're supposed to have been dead for a year and you're asking me about my job?" he asked chuckling. "When Aaron called and told me that you'd been murdered, I couldn't believe it. And the fact that we didn't have a body to bury made me suspicious as well."

I looked at Jordan. "You didn't tell him?"

"Yeah...I kind of hoped that we could go with the witness protection story."

"Sure. Because if I was in witness protection, I would totally call Curtis from a police station in Rome."

"You could say it was the Italian Royal Guard!" He shrugged. "You're right. We should tell him. At this point, he's already involved. He deserves the truth."

I didn't know how to approach the subject of my death. It wasn't hard telling Kevin about my vampirism, but Curtis was different. He'd never been a believer of anything supernatural like Big Foot or ghosts or anything.

"What if I told you that I *had* been dead?" I asked Curtis. "That I was killed but came back to life."

"I would say that you're crazy and ask what you've been smoking," he replied, laughing at me.

I gave him a serious stare to show that I wasn't joking around. After a while, his smile faded into a confused expression.

"What are you saying? That you were resurrected like Jesus or something?" he asked.

"No, not like Jesus, like—"

"Like a vampire," Jordan interrupted.

Curtis laughed again, harder this time until he was almost crying. I had to wait for him to compose himself before I could continue telling my story. I didn't blame him, though. Five, or actually six, years ago, I would have laughed too.

"Lela, come on. You're saying that you died and came back as a vampire? That's laughable. Tell me what really happened? Were you in witness protection?"

"I'm telling you the truth!" I insisted. "The last thing I remember was someone snapping my neck and the next I woke up in a tomb in the middle of Italy."

"Someone broke your neck? Who did this?"

I wanted to tell him all the scary details of what had been going down the past few years but suddenly decided not to. I would tell him about my being a vampire, but not about my brothers or friends. Especially not my enemies.

"The same man who killed my parents. He had Robin, and Gallard and I were trying to make a trade of some sort to get her back. The man traded her for me but when he got impatient with my not giving him what he wanted he…killed me."

Curtis looked shocked, but he wasn't showing any signs of doubt anymore. The more I spoke, the more he seemed to believe what I was telling him. I was being extremely vague with the details, but getting the point across.

"How do you know you were dead and not just in a coma?" He asked.

"I doubt that someone who is comatose can survive a year in an old cemetery without food, water or life support, Curtis. I woke up in a coffin for crying out loud. By medical standards, I should have died from suffocation."

"By medical standards you should have died from cancer a year ago, yet you survived. You never told me how you managed to cure yourself."

Curtis' questions were making it too hard to beat around the bush, so I decided to go ahead and tell him everything starting from the very beginning. I told him about the circus and how the gypsy had given me vampire blood, which resulted in me turning into one. I also told him about how Gallard was one as well and how he'd let me join him on his search to find others like ourselves who could walk in the day.

I told him about Samil and his followers who wanted to use our blood to bring back one of the first day walkers ever known in history and how Samil killed my parents in retaliation to being tricked. I told him everything that had happened up to the point when Samil broke my neck. I didn't want to tell him about what I'd experienced in the darkness. That was private, and not something I wanted to reminisce on.

When I finished my story, I observed to see how Curtis would react. He'd sat hunched over with his hands folded in his lap and didn't say a word the entire time. I couldn't get my hopes up too much. Not everyone would react like my brother had. Kevin was a special case. Anyone else would probably freak out and run away like Tyler.

Five minutes passed before he stood up from the chair. He looked upset and I held my breath. I had a feeling he wasn't taking it well.

"I...I need a minute," he said, standing up.

"Curt, wait. Before you take this all in, please just tell me now if you're afraid of me. Or that you never want to see me again or you want me to stay away from you. I know it's scary and unbelievable, but I would rather you be honest right now."

He came over to me and hugged me then kissed the side of my head. "I would never not want to see you again. Understand?" He let go of me and smiled. "I'm going to go and call your brother. You want any food?"

"Yes! Lots of food, preferably greasy."

"You got it. I'll be back soon."

Curtis left the room and I could see that Jordan had visibly relaxed. It was very hard to be around people who didn't know our secrets and now we could talk openly. If Curtis turned out to be okay with everything, then we wouldn't have to start monitoring our conversations.

"You know Gallard is going to kill me when he finds out I came here to get you without telling him."

"Jordan!" I stared at him in shock. "You didn't tell him? Why?"

"Because I didn't want to get his hopes up! You should have seen him, Lela. He's been through the ringer. For weeks after he left you here, he kept having nightmares about you being trapped in that coffin. If he knew that his nightmares were real, he would never forgive himself."

I could see his point. If I had found out that Gallard was buried alive and that I had put him there, I would have felt extremely guilty. But it wasn't his fault. There was no way he could have known that I was alive. Even I didn't know I was.

"What about you? You must miss Lydian like crazy. I know I do, despite everything. I wouldn't be here today without her."

He leaned back in his chair. "I have my own ways of coping. It helps that I'm a good actor. I'm good at pretending everything is okay."

"Why? Why pretend?"

"It's easier. I made the decision that only one of us should be

THE RESURRECTION

allowed to fall apart and I let it be Gallard. Now that you're back, he'll be happy again. And if he's happy, I'm happy."

I couldn't imagine what he was going through. How selfless he was being. I also thought it wasn't good for him to bottle everything up so much. Eventually, he was going to unleash all that grief he was holding in and I wanted to be there for him when that happened. Lydian gave her life for me and in return, I would make sure the man she loved was taken care of the way he had taken care of mine.

Chapter Five

Charity awoke suddenly as her cell phone began to ring. She swore loudly as she scrambled to find it amongst her covers. She finally found it and slid her thumb across the bottom of the screen just in time before it would go to voicemail.

"Who the hell is this?" she asked angrily. "Do you have any idea what time is?"

"Ah...four-thirty?" the person answered.

"Exactly, it's four-thirty! You better have a damn good reason why you're calling so early!"

"I'm calling to answer your ad in the paper; *Woman Seeking Vampire*."

Charity sighed and rubbed her eyes. She knew this call was important, but wasn't in the mood to deal with the situation at this ungodly hour. She wasn't particularly a morning person, which was why she'd taken a job that went from eleven to seven. Her normal wake up time was nine-thirty, and anyone who woke her up before that would be subject to her wrath.

"Right, the ad. Let me ask you a question, Mr. uh..."

"Abernathy. Sean Abernathy."

"Sean, are you a wannabe?"

THE RESURRECTION

"No."

"Are you a poser? Or one of those so called *psychic* vampires that feed off people's energy or some phony crap like that? Because if you are, I am going to be extra pissed off that you called me before sunrise."

"I assure you that I'm not a poser. I am immortal, just like you asked for in the paper."

She reached blindly over to her nightstand to retrieve a post-it then got a pen from the drawer.

"Good. So, what time do you want to come to my place for the uh…interview?"

"The sun sets at seven. Does that work for you?"

"Make it seven-thirty and it works for me. I'll see you then."

She hung up the phone then fell back against her pillow. She was glad to get that over with and was eager to sleep at least a few more hours before work.

After a half an hour went by, she found herself wide awake, and decided to get up and go for a run on her treadmill. She hardly ever used it, but had bought it a month before so she wouldn't have to get a gym membership. She didn't like to deal with people if she didn't have to, so whatever she could do at home, she did it.

Charity slipped into her workout clothes then set the treadmill to cardio mode and started to run. As she worked out, she thought of all the errands that she had to run for her boss. Being a magazine editor's assistant wasn't her idea of a dream job, but it paid the bills. She was supposed to have received a ton of money from her inheritance, but it had been frozen since she hadn't come forward to claim it. She planned to eventually, but for now, she would have to get by with a day job. The fact that she loved Chicago made her job all-the-more bearable.

When she'd had enough of the treadmill, she used a towel to wipe the perspiration from her face as she walked into her bathroom. Eager to shower, she stripped down before she even walked through the door then turned on the water and got in. She didn't mind waiting for the water to get warm. She was already hot from the workout, and the cool water felt soothing.

She finished her shower then began her daily morning routine. She didn't like to wear makeup, but it was a requirement for her job, so she forced herself to make an effort while still applying the least amount as possible. She never used mascara though since she had naturally long eyelashes. Her flawless alabaster skin was a blessing and a curse, and she had to apply rouge daily in order not to look sickly.

Once she was finished, she took out a contacts case and put them in, making both of her eyes green. She hated that her eyes were spotty and preferred covering them up. She wanted to be as unnoticeable as possible and if wearing contacts would help, she would suffer through the discomfort.

As she went through her day, she kept thinking about her anticipated meeting with Sean Abernathy. She wondered how old he was and what kind of life he lived; if he had a family or friends. She wasn't usually so vague with her questions when it came to her meetings, but that particular day she hadn't been in the mood for chit-chat.

A coworker walked up to her desk and folded her arms. Charity snapped out of her daydream when she saw her out of the corner of her eye.

"Charity, did you stay out late again?" her coworker asked.

"No Penelope, I didn't. Why do you ask?"

"You look tired and distracted."

She groaned inwardly. She usually could tolerate Penelope's nosiness, but she was feeling extra irritable that day. In fact, she felt irritable most days. She'd tried therapy, but that had only put her in a worse funk. It was because she couldn't reveal what was really bothering her. There were some secrets that she couldn't share, not even confidentially with a therapist.

"I just have a lot on my mind," she replied.

"Does a guy have anything to do with it?" Penelope asked, going into gossip mode.

"Sort of."

"Charity, why didn't you tell me you had a boyfriend? Now you have to tell me all about him!"

Charity rested her foot against a rung on the bottom of her desk and used it to rock her office chair from side to side. She wished that her problems involved a boyfriend. It would be much simpler than her reality.

THE RESURRECTION

"He's not my boyfriend. I haven't even met him yet."

"Wait, it's a blind date? Please don't tell me you found him on the internet."

"Newspaper actually."

"Char! You answered one of those man-seeking-woman ads? Are you crazy, he could be a psycho! Your answering a back-page ad is going to earn you a spot on the front page, the headline being, *'Red-head Hacked Up By Blind Date.'*"

"Don't worry, Penny, I can take care of myself."

Charity looked at the clock and saw that it was six fifty; about time to go home. She was glad that the day was over. She longed for the comfort of her peopleless apartment.

"Well, I'm going to clock out now. I need some time to find something to wear and clean up the apartment."

Penelope raised her eyebrows. "You're already planning on bringing him home? You must be really desperate."

Charity decided to ignore that comment and packed up her things. She said goodbye to Patty before grabbing her purse. She swiped her card through the scanner then headed out the door and into the elevator. She was glad that she only lived five minutes from her job, so she would have plenty of time to get ready.

When she entered her apartment, she took off her heels before straightening up her living room and taking a broom to the kitchen. She hadn't swept in weeks, and the floor was very dirty.

After she got everything looking decent, she quickly headed to her bedroom to find something to wear. She settled for her burgundy knee-length dress with the black belt and frilly straps and matching flats. She then went to the bathroom to pin her hair up into a simple, yet elegant style.

Five minutes later, she heard a knock at the door, and she took a deep breath before going to answer it.

"Good evening, Miss Toffee," the visitor said.

"It's Too-fay, actually. And good evening to you, Mr. Abernathy."

She stepped aside to let him in, but he just stood there. She frowned in confusion then realized what he was doing.

"I know that you don't have to be invited to come in, you're not the first vampire I've met, you know."

He chuckled before walking in past her. "And here I thought I could trick you in to believing that cliché."

She closed the door behind him before motioning to the living room for him to sit down. Sean Abernathy was taller than her, but not extremely tall; about five-ten to five-eleven. His hair was black and slicked back and his eyes were dark grey. He was very slender, but in a lean sort of way. He wore a dark pair of jeans and an olive green long-sleeve button-up shirt.

He chose to sit on the couch, so she sat across from him on the love seat. They sat in awkward silence for a few moments before he spoke.

"So, when do you want to do it?" he asked.

She pretended to be offended by scoffing. "You get right down to the point, don't you?"

"I meant when do you want me to turn you?" he clarified.

"Oh!" she said, embarrassed that she'd taken what he'd said the wrong way. "I think you have the wrong idea of why I asked you here. I don't want you to turn me."

"Then why am I here? You're not looking for a relationship, I hope."

"Believe me, that's the last thing I want. I don't do relationships. However, I do like the no-strings-attached thing."

She got up from the love seat and sat next to him on the couch. He smiled and moved closer to her. She was surprised when he kissed her, but she let him. It helped her get closer to what she really wanted.

"Why don't we move this interview to the bedroom?" she asked.

"Ah, I see. You're one of those. You like em cold, don't you?"

She leaned close to his ear. "Like a popsicle."

He stood up and she took his hand, leading, him towards her room. Normally, she wouldn't do this, but it had been a while since she had the company of a man. He was very attractive which was a plus. For the next few hours, she decided to enjoy this part of the meeting. He helped her loosen up and release all that pent up irritability she'd been holding in for the past several days.

Her internal clock woke her up at exactly nine a.m. She yawned and stretched and when she turned over, she accidently nudged Sean. It startled her at first because she'd forgotten he'd stayed

THE RESURRECTION

over. The memories of the previous night came rushing back and she grinned to herself. Totally worth it.

"Morning," he said. He leaned over and kissed her. "I was wondering when you would wake up."

"Sorry. I forgot that you don't sleep."

"That's all right, baby. I didn't mind keeping you company."

He started kissing her again and she knew that it was time. She hadn't meant to prolong this meeting, but she'd really needed a good time for once. She moved so that she was lying on top of him and felt as her fangs came out and she quickly changed from kissing his lips to his neck.

When she knew that she had him completely distracted, she bit down and started draining his blood. He yelled and tried to push her away, but with the fresh blood in her system, she was getting stronger by the second.

He ran to the door to try to escape, she beat him to it and bit him once more. He tried fighting her off, but failed. She pinned him to the floor with her knee then continued drinking his blood until he started to shrivel in her grasp into a heap of skin and bones. She released her bite, wiping blood off of her chin with the back of her hand then nonchalantly stepped over his body and went to put on her robe.

Once she'd wiped the excess blood off of her face, she wrapped his body in the blanket she always used for her meetings and dragged him into the living room. The sun was always shining brightly through her window at this time, which was why she'd planned this kill so carefully. He tugged him to just the right spot then took off the blanket. Instantly, his body caught on fire and she watched as he burned to a pile of ash. If only dinner could be less taxing.

While she was dumping the last of the ashes into a garbage bag, her cell phone rang. She looked at the screen to see who it was, and gasped in surprise. When she answered it, the person on the other line spoke before she did.

"Cherish! My darling sister, how do you fair?"

She was surprised at first. Nobody had called her by her real name is years and she barely recognized it anymore.

"Melody, seriously, when are you going to stop talking like we're still in the fifteen hundreds?"

"Somebody's grouchy. Love the accent, by the way. You almost sound like a real American. How have you been?"

She instantly dropped the accent and used her own. "I'm all right, I suppose. I just finished my breakfast actually."

"Who was it this time, a gorgeous newbie? No, let me guess; a lonely, brooding ancient looking for companionship?"

"The first one. We both know I'm always the brooding ancient in the equation. He was good in the sack, though. Why are you calling me?"

"Can't I call my sister and not have a reason?"

"Melody—"

"You're right. I have a reason. A bad reason actually."

Cherish tried to think of what her sister was about to tell her. There were only a handful of things that could be considered bad news. She and her sister had agreed to only call if there was an emergency, and she hadn't heard from Melody in almost six years. The last time she had called was to let her know that the last bottle had been drunk.

"How bad?" She finally asked.

"Our father is back."

Cherish nearly dropped the phone. The scenarios she had come up with in her mind were not nearly as bad as what her sister had just said.

"What, how? Don't tell me that that idiot Samil managed to outsmart Ajala!"

"Ajala is dead, Cher. Our father killed her. That's how I learned that he was resurrected. Her husband contacted me, desperate for help. Apparently he's out for the blood of the gypsies that descended from those involved in his death...*our* deaths."

"Again; did Samil have anything to do with this?" Cherish was beginning to get impatient. She didn't want to know all the extra details; she wanted to know who was behind it and whom she would need to kill in return.

"Samil is dead as well. Someone killed him too. Rumor has it that *Solomon* is the one who brought our father back."

"Why would he do that? He killed our father because of..." she stopped before finishing that sentence. It was always a touchy

THE RESURRECTION

subject and she and her sister hadn't spoken of it in years. "Why would he bring him back?"

Cherish had never forgiven Solomon for letting her and her sister die. Melody, on the other hand, had convinced her to let it go and spare him since he was keeping their father from coming back. She was always so forgiving. But if he was responsible for their father's return, then the rules were going to have to change.

"So, what are we going to do?" Cherish asked her sister.

"Before Ajala's brother died, he asked one of the circus people to pass a message. He said that Father Dearest is bent on killing Solomon's descendants. Solomon cares about his family line more than anything. Where the Sharmentinos are, Solomon will be. They reside in Florida, so pack your swimsuit and shorts, because we're going to the hottest state in the country."

Chapter Six

Evelyn sat on her bed, reading a magazine while she waited for Jeff to get home. He had just transferred to the hospital in town and was already being swarmed with patients. This was the fifth night in a row that he had called saying he would be home late. She didn't mind though. She was glad that he was adjusting to his new job. It had been hard for him to leave the hospital back in Denton, Texas since he'd worked there since after he'd graduated med school.

What helped her uneasiness was having dinner with Simeon, and his kids and Robin seemed to hit it off. The three were reluctant to part when Simeon left. Solomon remained civil through the dinner, but he seemed wary of Simeon.

Her door opened and she looked up as Robin came into the room, rubbing her eyes. It was quite late, and Evelyn wondered if she'd had another nightmare.

"What are you doing up so late?" Evelyn asked. Robin crawled under the covers next to her and rested her head against Evelyn's shoulder.

"I can't find Spock," she said.

"Well, why don't we go look for him?" Evelyn suggested. They both got up from the bed. Taking the girl's hand, Evelyn led Robin back to her own room and turned on the light. There were stuffed animals everywhere, but she knew exactly which one Robin was talking about. The bear in the *Star Trek* uniform.

"Where did you last have him?

"I was holding him when I went to sleep. I woke up and he was gone."

This made Evelyn even more puzzled. She checked under the bed to see if Robin had just simply dropped him but found nothing but some crayons and a Barbie doll. As far as she knew, Robin didn't sleepwalk, and she and Robin had been the only ones in the house all day. Simeon's children couldn't have taken it. It would have been obvious.

She then noticed that the window was open and her heart skipped a beat. She had distinctly remembered closing and locking it after tucking Robin in.

Immediately, she picked up the little girl and ran to her bedroom. Setting Robin down, she grabbed the phone, quickly dialing Solomon's number. She was glad that he answered almost right away.

"Hey Solomon, are you up? Would you mind coming over here? I think someone was in the house. No, I didn't hear anything, but Robin's window was opened even thought I locked it. All right, thanks."

Evelyn hung up and locked the two of them in the master bedroom. She tucked Robin in once more before going to the closet for the taser. Jeff had gotten it for her after they had moved in case the men who killed her brother's family decided to make a surprise appearance. She'd hoped that she would never have to use it, but if her life was in danger, she wouldn't hesitate.

Since Solomon was coming, she decided to change into something more descent than her night gown. She went into the bathroom and quickly threw on some black leggings and one of Jeff's old t-shirts. It was extremely baggy on her since she was quite petite, but it was better than what she'd been wearing before. She then clipped her seemingly untamable curly light brown hair up before walking out.

Five minutes passed and then ten. She still didn't hear anything downstairs, but she kept quiet just the same. It helped that Robin had fallen asleep so she wouldn't have to deal with the fear that Evelyn was feeling. She was nearly terrified out of her mind, and her hands were clammy as they hung onto the taser.

A door opened downstairs, and her heart began to pound in her chest. She held her weapon in front of her and waited to see what would happen. As she heard footsteps coming up the stairs, she quickly turned out the lights. The person drew closer and closer and she stood her ground, ready to fight the assailant.

The doorknob began to turn and she walked towards the door so that she would get a better shot with her taser in chase the person had a gun. She held her breath and the door slowly opened, and as the man walked in, she lunged forward, pressing the button as hard as she could and shocked him.

"Solomon! I am so sorry, I thought you were an intruder!"

"It's quite all right, that was my mistake. I should have announced my presence before barging in here. I must have had you scared to death."

Evelyn placed the taser on the dresser next to the door. When she turned around, she saw that Solomon was recovering quickly from the tasing. In fact, she didn't remember him reacting at all.

"How are you still standing?" she asked. "I had this on the highest setting, and you're acting like you only suffered from static shock."

Solomon shrugged and replied, "Maybe it's broken."

"My husband just bought this for me, it can't be broken."

"You said that a window was open, could you show me which one that is?" he asked.

Evelyn was a tad annoyed that he'd deflected her question but led the way out of the room anyway. She walked into Robin's room and Solomon examined the window.

"You were right to call me. The lock is broken. By the look of the break, whoever was in here got in from the outside," he said. He inhaled deeply and Evelyn almost thought that he was smelling the room. The idea was too weird, so she brushed it off.

Evelyn then felt her stomach turn and she wrapped her arms around her middle. The thought of someone being in her niece's room made her sick, and she didn't want to think about what he'd been doing during his unwanted visit.

THE RESURRECTION

"It's been a year," she said. "Why would they wait a year before coming after us again?"

"I don't know. It could have just been a burglar who backed out when he saw that he'd gotten into a child's room." Solomon crooked his mouth. "What if it was Simeon?"

Evelyn looked at him. "Simeon? Why would he break in here? Into Robin's room of all places?"

"Who knows why he does anything? I wanted to speak with you earlier, but felt it inappropriate considering the children were here. I don't think you he should come here around anymore."

She scoffed. "Oh really? He's my brother's oldest friend. The man was just checking in on us."

"The way he checked in on Lela?"

"What the hell is that supposed to mean?"

Solomon folded his arms. "I spoke with Gallard. He was sharing information that Lela gave him concerning what she went through while she was gone. She claimed that Simeon attacked her the night she disappeared."

Evelyn covered her mouth in shock. She always thought Simeon was off, but nowhere near this dangerous. She thought he was a harmless flirt. Could the same Simeon who would make her laugh at family dinners have done this?

"I...she never said anything." She swallowed. "Is that why she left?"

Solomon shrugged. "I think there were many reasons why she left, but I don't doubt that was one of them. She could have been afraid. The reports say Simeon struggled with the man who took her. I think the man helped her get away."

"Oh God." Evelyn pressed her back to the wall. "No wonder you were so chilly towards him. That bastard. He made it seem like he was all about looking out for this family and he helped Mark search for her when she went missing." She needed to calm down. Problems from the past weren't going to help the present ones. "You think this break in was personal?"

"If it were a burglar, he would have at least looked for something valuable in a house this big. It doesn't look like anything has been taken."

"But whoever it was *did* take something. Robin's favorite

stuffed animal is missing, and she swears that she had it in her arms when she fell asleep."

Evelyn couldn't hold back her tears any longer and began crying. Solomon cautiously put his arms around her, and she buried her tear-stained face into his chest. She liked his hug. It reminded her of the hugs she would get from her father. In fact, almost everything about Solomon reminded her of her father. For some reason, she felt deep down that he was more than just a private detective.

Solomon had said he was thirty-eight; three years older than she was and that he was an Italian native. He never said why he'd moved to the states, but she didn't question it. He'd so devotedly helped her family for the past year and she grew to trust him more and more as time passed. His presence was comforting and would bring her peace whenever Jeff wasn't around. It was nice having another man around to watch over her and Robin during the day.

She ended the embrace when she heard the front door open and the two of them headed downstairs. Jeff had finally come home and would want to know what had transpired that night. She told him about the broken lock on the window and how Robin's stuffed animal was missing. As she recounted all the details, she began crying once more and could barely get a hold of her emotions. Jeff on the other hand was furious and ready to take action.

"We need to call the police. That psycho was in our house, and that means he's in Miami. If we report it now, they could catch them before they try to skip town."

"I *am* the police," Solomon said. Jeff's lips tightened and he gave Solomon an accusing look.

"Okay, then why haven't you found the men responsible?" Jeff asked. "It's been a year and a half and you have done nothing. Someone was in the house and threatened my family!"

"They threatened my family too!" Solomon shouted. "If I'd come around sooner, none of this would have happened. Lela would be alive and—" he suddenly stopped and looked away, like he regretted what he'd said.

"Oh my God," Evelyn said. "You're...you're not a detective are you? You're Lela's father."

Solomon opened his mouth to speak, then decided not to. His

expression confused Evelyn. Was he afraid to admit to it, or was this something else? Whatever he was conflicted with, she knew he was hiding something.

"I'll do a quick sweep of the house," Solomon said. "If you hear or see anything else strange, don't hesitate to let me know."

"Hold on," Jeff said. "Was she right? Are you Lela's father?"

"She meant something to me, but…that is all I can say. Now if you want, you can look for Robin's missing toy while I do the search. If it's gone then we'll know for sure who we're dealing with."

Solomon and Jeff went upstairs and at the same time Evelyn went into the kitchen and started making herself some chamomile tea to calm her nerves. Her stomach was still in knots from the scare Solomon had given her, and from his reaction to her theory. She hoped that the tea would help her fall asleep later on.

After she filled the kettle and put it on the stove, she pulled on a light sweater and walked out onto the back porch. She needed some fresh air and some time to herself to calm down. She sat on a white-painted wooden bench. She smiled as she remembered all the Fourth of July barbeques she'd spent on that very bench talking with Sheila. Her sister in law had been like the sister she'd never had. Mark was her only sibling, and with both of them gone, she'd developed a hole in her life.

She tensed up as she remembered what Kevin had told her about Sheila's infidelity. She wondered what had gone so wrong that had driven her away from Mark and into the arms of another man. She also wondered what Sheila had seen in such a dangerous man as Timothy Fox. The thought of Lela having lived with his son for four years made her shudder, and the idea that Solomon might be Timothy Fox frightened her more, though he'd never given her a reason to feel unsafe around him.

What bothered Evelyn most was the fact that Lela's body had never been found. They'd had a gravestone made for her, but she wasn't really there. Her death never really had closure in Evelyn's heart, and she felt that she had been cheated out of a proper burial.

A loud whistling sound came from inside, and Evelyn knew that her water had finished boiling. She stood up to head back into the house when she saw a slight movement in the corner of her eye.

She turned her head towards the yard and screamed just as a dark figure ran across the grass and leapt over the fence. Jeff and Solomon ran out of the house just as the figure had disappeared and she finally stopped screaming.

"What happened?" Jeff asked. Evelyn clung onto him and pointed to the fence.

"There was someone in the back yard! I think he was watching me. He jumped over the fence into the front yard!"

"Did you see his face?" Solomon asked. She shook her head.

"It was too dark, and he moved so fast."

Jeff ran over to the fence and jumped up, barely being able to grab onto the top. He wasn't the most athletic guy, but he was still pretty strong. He hoisted himself up then looked around before dropping back to the ground.

"You said he jumped over the fence, did you mean that he climbed up *then* jumped over?" he asked when he came back to the patio.

"No, he *jumped* over, in one try," she replied. "Like some kind of animal."

"That's not possible, Evelyn. The fence is nine feet high at least."

"I know what I saw, Jeff!"

Solomon tried to usher them back into the house.

"Well, whoever it was, you were lucky that they didn't hurt you," he said. Jeff took his phone out of his pocket and began dialing.

"I've had enough of this, I'm calling the police."

Solomon grabbed the phone out of his hand and hung up.

"No. No police. They aren't equipped for this situation."

The two of them started arguing and Evelyn went back into the living room to use the house phone to try and get a hold of Aaron. She felt that if Lela's killer had been at the house that he would try and go after her nephews next, and she wanted to make sure they were all right.

Before she could dial, she heard light footsteps coming from upstairs, and she watched as Robin sluggishly came down.

"Sweetheart, what are you doing up?" Evelyn said, setting the phone back in the cradle. Robin yawned and rubbed her eyes before coming to a stop on the second to last step.

"I heard a scream. I thought Samil was back."

THE RESURRECTION

Evelyn picked the child up and carried her over to the couch.

"Who's Samil, baby?" she asked. This was the second name that Robin had brought up that night that Evelyn didn't recognize and she was starting to get the feeling that Robin knew something that she wasn't telling her.

"He killed mommy and daddy then took me away," Robin replied. Evelyn stopped breathing and froze.

"Robin, who are you talking about? Are you saying that you know the name of the man who hurt your parents?" she finally asked. Robin nodded her head but didn't say anything more. "Please, honey, if you know something that would help Solomon, I need you to tell me."

Someone knocked on the door and Evelyn jumped. The fear from witnessing the intruder from the yard came back. It was too much of a coincidence that not moments before, a dark figure hopped the fence and now someone was at the door. She picked Robin up and ran into the back yard where the two men were still fighting over the whole police thing.

"There's someone at the door!" she whispered harshly.

Their fighting ceased and Solomon walked passed her and into the house. Jeff and she followed in a formal line, but she stopped in the kitchen and waited in case she would need to make a run for it. She trusted Solomon to protect them if there was a threat, but he never carried a gun so there was a chance he might not be able to defend himself.

"Hello, Solomon," she heard a female voice say. The woman had a British accent, which startled Evelyn. Then again, Solomon had an accent as well, so it wasn't too farfetched that someone who knew him would be from a different country as well.

"*Maria Madre di Dio!*" she heard Solomon say. It was silent for so long that She almost contemplated going to see if he was still alive. "*Accarezzare*? Melody?"

"Yes, it's us," another woman said. "Don't worry, Solomon. We're not here to kill you. We want to help."

Curious, Evelyn walked further into the house to see this guest. It turned out that the guest wasn't alone. There were two women, one being shorter with hair the color of wine and the other taller with shoulder-length curled sandy hair. There was also a man with them, but he didn't appear to be a part of their group because the redhead had him by the arm and her grip looked tight.

The woman threw the man into the house and he groaned in pain. Evelyn noticed he was bleeding as well from a wound on his neck. He tried to get up but the redhead kicked him, keeping him from standing. Evelyn gasped and covered Robin's eyes. Violence made her very uncomfortable.

"We found this asshole trying climb into one of the bedroom windows," the redhead said. "Good thing I'm faster."

"Sister, watch your mouth! There are children present."

Evelyn held her breath as the two women moved their gazes towards her and she stepped into the living room. Solomon still hadn't said a word but kept staring at the two women with a silent fear. For the past year, he had always been so put together and calm. This was the first time she'd ever seen him act afraid. Where these women dangerous?

"Who are you?" Jeff asked. "And what are you doing with this man?"

"Like we said," the tall one spoke. "We showed up and caught him trying to break in. We took the liberty of bringing him to you." She held out her hand. "Melody Davis."

He shook it. "Jeff McAllister. You know Solomon. Are you private detectives too?"

The women shared a glance then the redhead spoke again. "Let's just say we have a common enemy." She kicked the man on the ground. "We have reason to believe this man is working for the person who is threatening your family."

"Is this true?" Solomon asked the man, finally speaking. "Do you work for…him?"

"He asked me to watch." The man shifted so he was supporting himself with his forearm. "I am to learn your routine so he can know when to strike. I only did this because he threatened my family."

"That doesn't surprise me."

"Please, I won't report to him if you help me disappear. I swear I wasn't going to harm anyone in this house."

The redhead shoved him onto his stomach then started digging in his back pocket. She pulled out his wallet and slipped through it.

"Dan Peterson, born nineteen sixty-three. Lives on four-two-

THE RESURRECTION

seven-oh Evergreen Lane, Winter Haven, Florida." She smirked and used her foot to move him onto his back. "Your fake I.D. handler is good, but not as good as mine. Tell us who you really are."

The man glared at her and she stomped on his kneecap, causing him to cry out in agony. Robin whimpered and Evelyn was tempted to take her upstairs, but she had to hear what this man was going to say.

"All right! I have no family. I'm Daniel Pavlovich. He offered me a sum I couldn't refuse."

"How much?" Solomon asked.

"Six hundred grand. Three in advance and three more when I return with satisfactory information."

Solomon picked up his bag by the door and pulled out a checkbook. He quickly wrote on it, tore the check out, and then held it out to the man. "Here's double for your silence and a location." The man reached for the check but Solomon jerked it out of reach. "Your boss may be a dangerous man, but I can be worse. I'm a holy man with no qualms over killing greedy men the likes of you."

"He's staying in a hotel," the man said after a while. "The Sheraton."

Solomon then let the man take the check. "Now get out of my sight. Don't come near my family again or I will do to you what I once did to the man who sent you."

Melody opened the door and the man pocketed the check before limping out and she closed it behind him. Evelyn thought that the tension it he room would dissolve with his absence, but the entire encounter had only raised more questions. Solomon had spoken as if he knew who was trying to hurt them and he'd referred to them as his family.

"Start talking," Jeff said through clenched teeth. "Or I will call the police and tell them that *you* are a threat to us."

"We'll give you some privacy," Melody said.

The two women went outside and Evelyn became conflicted. She wanted to speak with them and thank them. If it weren't for them, that man would have succeeded and they could have been in much more danger. So instead of listening to Solomon's explanation, she followed them outside.

She found them sitting on the porch swing and she set Robin down so she could pull one of the chairs over. They stopped talking and Melody gave her a warm smile.

"I'm sorry we didn't get to officially meet," Evelyn said. Once Robin was in her lap, she extended her hand. "Evelyn McAllister."

"Melody Davis. This is my younger sister Cherish—"

"Just Cherish, thanks."

Evelyn shook her hand as well. The more she stared at Cherish, the more she noticed something that made her heart ache. This woman was very lovely with alabaster skin and green eyes. It was the bone structure of her face that was familiar.

"I'm sorry but...you look a lot like my niece," she said. "If she were to have red hair of course."

"The one who died, right?" Melody said. "Not to sound creepy, but I did some reading up on your family before we came. I wanted to know who I would be protecting."

Robin lifted her head from Evelyn's shoulder and looked off into the distance. Without a word, she leaped to the ground and bounded off into the yard. Evelyn didn't even have time to stop her and she chased her.

"Robin! Where are you going?"

She nearly called for help, but then she saw what had caught Robin's attention. She was in the arms of a man whom Evelyn had seen several times since moving to Florida. Gallard had stopped by for another visit. Usually he would call, but unexpected guests were a given today.

Chapter Seven

Gallard felt so much better as he held the little girl in his arms. It was like having a piece of Lela with him and he knew that making a trip to Florida was just the thing he needed. As Jordan suggested, he'd packed up Lela's things and took everything to storage. It was a bittersweet event giving Hallie the keys to the apartment, but it was time to move on.

Since he didn't have a phone yet, he decided to get one. He texted Jordan his plans then made a spontaneous non-stop flight to Miami. He didn't know when he would get another chance to visit Robin and he wanted to leave his number with her in case she ever needed to call him, day or night. He didn't sleep so he would be available twenty-four seven and he wouldn't stop visiting until she asked him to. He wouldn't be prepared for the day when she would outgrow him.

"What are you doing up so late?" He asked. "Shouldn't you be asleep?"

"I was but then a bad man tried to come into the house and then some really nice ladies helped us. The short lady made the bad man cry."

He didn't know what to say to that. Robin wasn't exactly a

creative child. She was more practical and honest. She wasn't one to make up stories or misinterpret situations. All of these things must have happened and it sickened him that he hadn't been there to help.

Evelyn waved at him from the porch and he waved back then walked over to her. The lights were on in the house so there must have been a lot of commotion.

"Hello, Evelyn," he said. "Is everyone okay? Robin told me what happened."

"We're shaken up, but no one was hurt. Thanks for asking. What brings you here other than little Robin?"

"Just checking in as usual. I know you have Solomon, but it gives me peace of mind to know you are doing all right."

Glancing at the porch once more, he noticed two women were sitting on the swing. They were staring at him and he stared back. One, in particular, was very familiar and when it registered who it was, he was stunned.

"Cherry Pop?" he asked.

The woman came out to the yard and when she saw him she laughed.

"No way! Gallard D'Aubigne? What the hell are you doing here?"

He set the little girl down then hugged his old friend. Gallard had met Cher back in the eighties and they had gotten very close. She basically gave him an intervention when his life was spiraling out of control and changed his life forever. He wouldn't have been the man he was today without her, and he was forever grateful. They'd parted without saying goodbye when she suddenly left town and he'd always wondered what happened to her.

When he released her from the hug, he held Robin's hand once more.

"I am very confused right now," he said.

"So am I! How do you know this family?"

Gallard forced a smile. "I was longtime friends with the older daughter. We were...involved before she died."

"Oh no." Cherish looked like she was going to cry. "I can't believe you're going through that again. How are you handling it?"

"One day at a time. Unfortunately, I have relapsed. That's mostly why I'm leaving Vegas. Too much temptation and too many

THE RESURRECTION

sad memories." He picked Robin up once more. "This little one has made it easier."

The other woman joined them in the yard and held out her hand. "Pardon my rude sister, but she has failed to introduce us. I'm Melody Christophe-Davis."

"Christophe? As in *Lucian* Christophe?" Gallard asked. He glanced at Robin. "Sweetheart, would you mind going inside with your aunt? I need to talk to these nice ladies for a bit."

"Will you promise to be here when I wake up?"

He kissed her forehead. "I promise."

Evelyn then took her from him and they said goodnight before going in. Gallard then turned his attention back to Cherish and her sister. This explanation for her presence was beyond what he'd imagined. He couldn't believe the connection.

"Solomon told me that you were killed almost four and a half centuries ago."

"Or so he thought," Melody said. I saw Cherish roll her eyes, probably annoyed by her sister's cliché remark.

"Long story short," Cherish started, "Solomon broke into our house that night and killed our parents while the gypsies killed Mel and me. Nearly six months went by before we both came back from the dead. During that time, we were just trapped inside our dead bodies, unable to move or speak. Finally, we found the strength to awaken and I dug myself out of my coffin before I did the same for Melody.

"When we learned that our mother was killed and that our father had been incapacitated, we went into hiding. For centuries, we have been keeping tabs on Solomon and staying in contact with the gypsies and their descendants to make sure that my father would not be brought back. Now that he has been, we've returned to put an end to him for good."

"You said you died and came back...how?"

"We've spent years searching for answers and came up with nothing," Melody said. "We assume it has something to do with our paternity. Our father was a vampire and we must have been born with the gene. The strange thing is, we function like mortals and our source of nourishment is..."

"What?"

"Vampire blood," Cherish said. She shrugged. "Don't know anything about that either. It kind of lets us off the hook, though. We don't have to harm innocent human beings to survive. But that also makes it harder to get meals. I lure them to my apartment with ads in the paper."

He smiled. Cherish was always hands on in everything she did. She wasn't afraid to throw a punch if it was needed and she always spoke her mind. She wasn't emotionless, per se, but she didn't ponder on consequences or how something would make her feel in the future. She lived in the present and her motto was no regrets. She also had the ability to be kind and fun at the same time. It made for some pretty crazy antics when they spent time together in the past. She had no fear and was up for anything.

"You know the reason Lucian wants Solomon's family dead is because of what happened to you two," Gallard said. "If he knew you were alive, do you think he would call off the hit?"

"It's possible," Cherish said. "But then again, our father has always been erratic. Angry one moment and forgiving the next. I can't tell you how many times he's threatened to kill people and didn't fall through. He has a bad temper. I will tell you this; he doesn't drag things out. If he wants someone dead, he'll kill them where they stand, just like he did with the gypsy who gave Lela the last blood bottle. Whatever he's up to now is a mystery."

"That spy of his gave us a location," Melody said. "We're going to check it out, but I'm not approaching him. If he's there, we'll fill you in. If not…we'll find another way to locate him."

They spoke for bit, and then Melody expressed being tired. Cherish gave him her number then the sisters left to go to follow their lead. Gallard went inside to speak with Solomon and give him a follow up of what he'd just learned. He saw that Jeff and Evelyn had gone to bed, which was understandable. Solomon was sitting on the couch, holding his rosary and praying silently.

"Solomon?" Gallard said. Solomon opened his eyes and smiled.

"Hello, Gallard." He stood up and shook his hand. "Evelyn told me you were here. You couldn't have come at a better time. But…I don't know why you're here and not with Jordan."

"He asked me not to come. He was right to do so. I'm not really in a good state of mind to be chasing leads across the globe. I thought I might be of better use here."

THE RESURRECTION

Solomon gave him a funny expression. "You seem so calm. You're doing better than I am." He sat down once more and Gallard joined him. "I nearly had a heart attack when Accarezzare and her sister walked through that door. All these years I've carried the guilt of their deaths. I should feel relieved. Instead, I feel like a fool."

"You didn't know. They stayed hidden out of fear and probably anger. I know Cherish can hold a grudge like no other."

"You know Cherish?"

Gallard nodded. "She went by a different name back then, but yes. We were friends almost thirty years ago. I had no idea she was Lucian's daughter at the time."

"She's like her father in that way. Not as extreme, but her wrath is not something to be tested." He looked at Gallard again. "You will never guess who showed up today."

Gallard had a few ideas but didn't think they would be right. "Who?"

"Simeon. That man you said went after Lela all those years ago."

Gallard could have sworn his blood heated at the sound of that man's name. He couldn't shake the notion that Simeon had planned Sheila's complications so he could get Lela alone. Men like that deserved castration or worse.

"What did he want?"

"He claims he wanted to check in on Evelyn and Robin. He brought his children to play with her and he stayed for dinner. Something about him is…I don't know. Very little frightens me. He as all the makings of a sociopath. Anyway, he asked if Robin and his children could have regular play dates. Has two kids her age. Don't worry, I took him aside and told him all visits would be supervised by me. He laughed. I don't think he took me seriously."

That gave Gallard peace of mind. Though Simeon was a complete prick, he didn't want to deprive Robin of a friend. She often told him she didn't talk much with the children at school because they would ask questions about her parents and make her cry. They would sometimes talk about her sister and how people thought Lela killed them. That particularly pissed him off.

"What's your secret?" Solomon asked.

"Come again?"

"How are you handling your own revelation?"

"About the daughters? I don't know. It's strange...yet at the same time, I've seen weirder. Who knew that some vampires could possess another body?"

"Gallard, I'm not talking about Cherish and Melody, I'm talking about...." He frowned. "You don't know, do you?"

"Know what?"

Solomon put a hand on his shoulder. "Gallard...Kevin called me two days ago. Curtis Taylor received a phone call from Italy, and I sent Jordan to go with him to respond to it."

Gallard's stomach tightened. "A phone call from whom?"

"From Lela. Gallard, Jordan confirmed it. She is alive."

Gallard nearly fell over. This had to be a joke. Either that or he heard Solomon wrong. Unless he'd finally lost it and was beginning to hear things because of wishful thinking. He had to stand up and walk away in order to get his bearings. Why were they doing this to him? He was already on edge enough and now they were throwing this on him?

He thought back to what Cherish had said. She and her sister were killed and six months later they woke up. They believed it had something to do with their DNA. He covered his face with his hands. David had fathered Lela while he still had Lucian's blood in him. She was mortal when she died and that could have meant that she had the ability to come back as well. If that were true, then his worst fear had been confirmed. He'd had nightmares for months about it and Jordan had to try and convince him that he was just finding something to worry about.

Now all that fears from the moment he left her in the coffin came rushing back. She'd woken up in there. She had probably been trapped there for hours; days. Or weeks; maybe even months. This thought brought him to his knees and he began to tremble. Images of the woman he loved screaming and pounding on the inside of the coffin sent him quickly spiraling.

"I left her," he said. "I left her in there."

Solomon stood up. "No. You are *not* doing this to yourself! We all left her there, Gallard. It was a mutual decision."

"I knew something was wrong. Her body never started decomposing. She never went into rigor mortis. She was...it was

THE RESURRECTION

like she was asleep. Solomon, she was in there this whole time! She was probably trying to talk to us." He turned his head. "I heard her, you know. When Lucian was asleep, she spoke to me. It was why I agreed to help him. I knew she was still alive and that's why I couldn't move on. She was probably trying to talk to us when we left her there and we couldn't hear her!"

Solomon knelt down beside him. "We won't know for sure until we see her. Jordan is bringing her home but he didn't say where."

"How could she forgive me? I was the one who sealed her in. She could have been calling out to me and I had no idea."

Gallard pulled out his phone and dialed Jordan's number. He wasn't going to wait for when Jordan thought he was rational enough to handle the news. He needed to know where she was so he could go to her right away. The phone went straight to voicemail, which meant he was probably on the plane.

"I know," Gallard said. "I'm not going to yell at you or get angry; I have better use for my time. But if you don't tell me where you are...where she is, I just might find you and throttle you."

He hung up and looked to the stairs. Robin was peeking at him from through the bars of the stairs. He should have known she wouldn't have been able to sleep with all the commotion going on. She stood up and padded down the stairs then he scooped her into his arms. He didn't want Evelyn to be mad that he was keeping her up, so he carried her back to her room and tucked her under her covers.

"Why are you sad?" she asked. "We're not supposed to be sad. Lela made me promise."

"I know, sweetheart." He hugged her tiny frame. "What if I told you that we don't have to be sad for much longer?"

"Are you moving in with us?"

He chuckled. This was pretty big news for her and he wasn't sure he even believed it just yet. He wouldn't be sure until Lela was in his arms, alive and breathing. Until then, he would hold off on telling Robin. If this was a hoax, he wanted to keep the casualties to a minimum.

"No, I'm not. But I promise you will be seeing more of me. I just need to take care of something." He looked into her eyes. "I promise you I will come back in a couple of days."

"Okay." She sat up and kissed his cheek. "You always keep your promises so I believe you."

"I appreciate that. Now go to sleep, sweetheart. I'll see you soon."

She buried herself under her covers and he started to get up when he noticed something. She always slept with her favorite stuffed animal. Always had since her Uncle Declan bought it for her at a gift shop in Virginia.

"Hey, where's Spock?" he asked.

"The bad man took him," she said in a groggy voice.

"The man who tried to break in tonight?"

She shook her head. "A different man. I thought it was a dream but I remember now. He had red hair like that lady."

THE RESURRECTION

Chapter Eight

We landed in Tampa around two in the morning. I hadn't gotten any sleep, but I wasn't tired. I was very hungry, though. I had eaten a whole order of spaghetti that Curtis picked up as well as half a loaf of garlic bread. I shouldn't have wanted to eat for days. The hunger was familiar, yet I couldn't figure out what I was craving. I kept feeling this burn in my throat.

Jordan and Curtis only had carry-on bags, so we were able to quickly leave. Curtis drove us in his car, and we headed to the house. I was glad that he was still living there. It was a cozy little place, and I had loved the neighborhood.

When we arrived, I noticed that the tenants from last year were still there. They had quaint lawn furniture and Solo cups lying everywhere. They were still partying people. I didn't mind it because I was used to the neighbors in Vegas throwing parties.

I looked down at the potted plant then picked it up. There was a key underneath it, and I shook my head.

"Really?" I asked.

"I didn't like keeping it in that board space on the deck. It kept getting stuck."

"If I were you, I would come up with a safer spot so no one

breaks in and murders you."

Both men's expressions darkened. I realized how bad my comment had sounded. That was exactly what had happened to my parents. I had been there when the horrible men killed my parents right in front of me and my younger siblings.

"Let's go inside," Curtis said.

He opened the door and we filed in. When he turned on the light, I was met with evidence that everything was exactly the same, only I then noticed there was a lounge chair that looked familiar. It was Mark's.

"Where did you get this?" I asked.

"Aaron gave it to me. He didn't want it for some reason, so I took it. Losing Mark was like losing an uncle. I wanted a keepsake I guess."

I thought it was strange that Aaron didn't want the chair. He was Mark's favorite son and the two of them were closer than any of us were with our father. Mark and I might not have always gotten along most of the time, but he was the man who raised me.

Curtis showed me to my room and I admired the silver and blue décor. I had put a lot of time and effort into painting those walls. All my furniture was still there, but my clothes and belongings were packed away.

"Did you ever get another roommate?" I asked.

"Yeah, actually. Kevin. He was living with Aaron, but he got tired of hearing his brother going at it on the other side of his wall. We've been roommates for almost a year now."

"That's great! I'm glad he's here. You're a good role model for him."

"Gabby stays here sometimes too," he said. "She missed you as much as I did."

"How is she?"

"She's good. She had her baby. Get this, she had twins! That sneak didn't tell us she was expecting two little ones until she sent a picture from the hospital. Identical girls. I love those kids to death." He shoved his hands into his pockets. "I'll let you sleep. Jordan will be in the extra guest room if you need him, and I'm still in the room at the end of the hall. Don't hesitate to wake me up."

He left and I contemplated what I would do. I was extremely

hungry, but I also needed a shower. I couldn't decide if I wanted to be clean before I ate. I sat in the chair in front of the vanity, and when I saw how awful I looked, my reflection helped me make my choice. I found all of my toiletries in my bag then went to look for the bathroom.

The light was already on, but the door was open so I went inside. When I saw Jordan standing there and shaving with his shirt off, I chuckled.

"Sorry. I thought it was vacant."

He rinsed his razor then smiled. "It's okay. I'm used to you walking in on me."

I rolled my eyes. "It's your fault! Don't you know that people close the door when they shower?"

"You don't like looking at my body?"

Jordan winced and I saw that he'd cut himself on the side of his jaw. He set the razor down and as he dabbed at it, my throat began to burn. It was like in that moment, my hunger intensified. I couldn't take my eyes off of the cut. As I stared, I felt a familiar pain in my gums. The pain worsened and I whimpered.

"Something wrong?"

"I...ow!" I slid my tongue over my top teeth and as I did, I cut my tongue as well. My entire mouth hurt now. "What the hell?"

"Look at me." He cupped my chin in his hand. "Open your mouth."

I did as he asked and he studied me teeth. He then raised his eyebrows and let go of me.

"Your fangs came out." He said. "I don't understand...you were mortal when you died."

"I know! I'm completely confused right now." I stood next to him in front of the mirror and used my finger to lift my top lip. He wasn't lying; there were definitely two fangs poking out where my regular teeth used to be. "You've got to be kidding me."

"Maybe you're like Lucian now. He was a day-walker who could eat food. What if when you died and came back, you changed into something like him?"

That was a plausible explanation. I had stopped being surprised by weirdness from the moment I first realized I was a vampire. I had contacted a dead person, been possessed by said dead person, and then died and came back.

"You're hungry," Jordan said. "You ate everything the flight attendant gave you but you're unsatisfied, correct?"

"Yeah...I probably need more than just food."

"You need blood. Unfortunately, I don't have any with me. I didn't think to pack." He finished rinsing his face then motioned for me to follow him. "Come with me."

He tugged on a shirt then took my hand and pulled me outside. I was had a feeling I already knew what he had planned for me. He wanted me to hunt. I was completely against that. Taking a life back then had been hard for me and it would only be harder now that I was a year and a half clean from being a murderous vampire. I didn't want to break that streak.

We didn't speak as we walked down the street. It was mostly quiet and there wasn't very much traffic. Though it was inevitable, I hoped that he wasn't taking me out to kill someone. A neon sign came into view. I recognized it from when I had been there before and I thought we were going to pass it when he opened the door and motioned for me to go inside. I stopped on the edge of the sidewalk.

"Seriously? You dragged me out in the middle of the night to get drunk?"

He laughed. "No. I dragged you out to find you a victim. We'll go in together but I'm not going to sit with you. Men won't approach you if they think you're with someone. I'll be across the bar."

This sounded like a terrible idea, but I went along with it anyway. I couldn't believe I was doing this. Scoping out victims in a bar. It felt sleazy and I had already done this whole thing in Miami. The poor man at the nightclub thought he was going to get lucky when instead he met an early end. That night marked the end of my taking a life for nourishment. Until now.

As promised, Jordan sat about eight seats down and pretended not to know me. I felt completely out of place so I sat on the first stool I laid eyes on and studied the drink menu. Drinking alcohol sounded like the worst idea, considering what had happened the last time. The bartender finally approached me with tired eyes and leaned against the counter.

"What'll it be?"

THE RESURRECTION

"Just water, thanks."

He turned the sink on and filled a cup before handing it to me. I thanked him then sipped it as I looked around. Jordan hadn't really given me time to prepare for this. I was still wearing clothes I had gotten at a convenient store and they didn't exactly make me a guy magnet.

To step up the game, I rolled my shirt up so that my midriff was exposed then tied it back with a hair band I had around my wrist. I then pulled my pants down so that they rested slightly below my hips. It wasn't perfect, but an improvement.

A couple sitting at the bar caught my attention and I watched as the man whispered into the woman's ear and then led her away into the men's room. I shuddered, having an extreme case of déjà vu. I had a feeling that I'd seen this before. I turned my seat in the direction they'd just gone and waited for them to come out. Something about the whole situation felt fishy.

Not long after I saw them come out of the bathroom. the woman had wrapped a scarf around her neck. They didn't even seem ashamed of their trashy behavior. He walked with a lilt in his step, and I wrinkled my nose, trying not to imagine what had gone down in that bathroom. This entire night was turning into a joke.

I stared at him for a bit until I realized where I'd seen him before. It was Andre; the vampire that almost killed me back when I was still human. I was surprised that he'd stuck around, considering I'd survived his attack and could easily have told the police about his identity.

He didn't see me as he walked by, so I waited until he was out the door before I followed him. Once I was outside, I looked around to see which direction he'd gone. I spotted him just as he rounded the corner and I ran after him.

"Hey!" I called to him down the alley. He stopped in his tracks and turned around. He looked the same as before, only his eyes were green instead of dark blue.

"Oh no, not you again!" he groaned. He walked towards me and came to a stop about five feet away. "I thought you would have been dead by now."

"What can I say? Life isn't done with me yet," I said, feeling very cocky. An amused laugh escaped his lips.

"Either you're dumb or you just have a death wish. You may taste disgusting, but that won't stop me from killing you this time around."

"Go ahead. Kill me. I've been killed before, and that didn't stop me."

He lunged at me, but I ducked out of the way just in time then kicked him onto the ground from behind. He rolled over and chuckled. "Well, well. Look who broke their promise," he said. "What happened to not turning back like your boyfriend asked?"

"It's complicated."

He stood back up then slammed me against the wall. I expected it to hurt more, but it barely phased me. I kicked him in the ribs and he punched me in the jaw. I could feel it break. I popped it back into place and within seconds, it healed.

He lifted his foot to strike me again, but I grabbed it, twisted him around then shoved him away from me. He recovered quickly then latched his right hand around the back my neck, swinging me around in a half circle and rammed my head into the garbage can, creating a huge dent. It rattled me a bit, so I wasn't able to get up right away.

"All right, a fight!" I heard someone say. A small group of guys had congregated at the other end of the alley and were cheering like they were at a boxing match. I prepared to stand up, but Andre kicked me in the ribs over and over. I couldn't believe they were enjoying watching a man beat up a woman. I could hold my own, but it was still disturbing to me.

"Are you gonna take that?" shouted another guy, "Get up!"

He kicked me again and I felt blood rise into my throat. I swallowed it, determined to win the fight and looked something I could use to fend him off until I could stand on my feet again. I found a broken beer bottle, and just as he was about to kick me again I stabbed it into his leg. He yelled then stumbled backward and I pulled myself up using the edge of the dumpster.

"This chick fights dirty!" said another person from the group. Andre was still trying to pull the bottle out of his leg when I got to him. I didn't want to kick him while he was down. I wasn't going to bring myself as low as he was. Besides, I'd drawn blood. That meant that I won.

But when I smelled the blood from his leg, something in me

THE RESURRECTION

went wild. I became very thirsty, and I could think of nothing but tasting it. I was so distracted by it that I didn't have time to react when he pulled the bottle out and stabbed me in the stomach.

"You know, I was going to let you walk away," I said grimacing from the pain. "But now you're pissing me off!"

I pushed him away then yanked out the glass from my torso. He tried to come at me again, but I stopped him by sinking my teeth into his neck. I bit down as hard as I could, allowing the blood to flow freely down my throat. I couldn't get enough, it tasted so delicious and I was sucked into a euphoric trance. I drank until I could no longer feel him struggling then dropped his body to the ground.

When I was in my right mind once again, I turned to look at the group that had been watching. They were staring at me in utter horror, their mouths agape. I'd forgotten they were there, or else I would have ended the fight differently.

"Get out of here or you'll be next," I said in the most threatening voice possible.

The group ran off, bumping into each other as they went and disappeared around the corner. I started assessing my wounds to see how much damage I had that I would have to explain to Curtis. The wound on my stomach had healed, but it left a bloody hole in my shirt. There were several shoe marks on it as well and my sweats were covered in Andre's blood. My lungs hurt, possibly from being punctured by my cracked ribs. His blood was helping me heal, though. In no time, I would be back to normal.

"Oh yeah," I said. "It's good to be back."

Someone started clapping and I turned around to see Jordan.

"Hot damn, you are incredible!" Jordan said. "What did he ever do to you?"

"A lot. First, he tried to force me to turn then he fed on me, only to tell me I was disgusting then he tried to strangle me." I took a deep breath to try to calm down. I was feeling extra irritable and pounding on Andre had kind of helped vent my building frustration.

Jordan glanced at the body. "Did...did you feed on him?"

I nodded. "Yeah, I...I did feed on him."

He knelt down and turned the man over onto his back. I didn't see the point in checking for a pulse. He was undeniably dead.

"Lela...this man was a vampire."

A breathy laugh escaped my lips. I hadn't even thought about the irony of the situation until after the fact. His blood had smelled so good and all I could comprehend was how much I wanted to drink it.

"Oh great! So now you're telling me I'm a freak? I'm a freak vampire who feeds on her own kind. That's just perfect!"

"No, that's a good thing. It meant you didn't kill a person. I was hoping you would fight him, which you did, but...I never thought you would drink his blood."

I hadn't either. The scent of his blood was still fresh in my memory and I could taste it on my tongue. It was utterly delicious, and I wanted more. Though fighting him had been my way of establishing my comeback, I wasn't up for taking another life.

We walked back to the apartment, and I was feeling more energized than ever. Andre's blood had been just the thing that I needed to satisfy my hunger. At the same time, it had left me feeling more confused as well. I wasn't a vampire since I didn't crave human blood, and I wasn't human because I had all the abilities of a vampire. I didn't know what I was, and I had no idea who would be able to give me the answers I was looking for.

Using the spare key, we went inside. I was now too wired to sleep and since Jordan didn't need to, I asked if we could talk. After I showered and changed into clean clothes, he caught me up on what I had missed. Aaron and Kevin were in Orlando and my Aunt and Uncle had gotten legal guardianship of Robin. Everyone was well. It was nice getting to spend time with him again.

"Jordan," I said just as he was about to leave.

"Yeah?"

"When can I see him?"

He closed the door then walked back over to me. I didn't need to say a name for him to know who I was talking about. I understood that he hadn't originally told Gallard about me to protect him but now I wanted to see my best friend; the man I loved.

He lay on the bed but was sitting upright against the headboard.

"Soon. I promise you I won't keep you away from him. We just have to be delicate about the situation. You're going to have to decide whether you want to reveal yourself to your aunt and uncle and especially Robin. Your return will put some big changes into motion."

"What about Lucian? We need to find him and make sure he doesn't hurt anyone. I'm not letting what happened with Samil to occur again."

"We won't. But you should sleep." He kissed the top of my head. "We'll talk in the morning."

I expected him to leave but he didn't and I was glad. I didn't want to be alone again. I slowly drifted off to sleep with the anticipation of seeing my loved ones again.

One last lock of hair fell in the sink as Lucian finished cutting, and he looked into the mirror to admire his new appearance. He had cut almost all of it off in order to be discreet and was somewhat taken aback by how short it was. He hadn't had his hair that short since he was a young man, and it felt weird not having his hair passed his shoulders.

"Well, what do you think?" he asked the young woman who was cowering in the corner of the bathroom. She whimpered as she held a towel to her bleeding wrist, but managed to quietly answer him.

"It looks good."

He smiled then looked back at himself in the mirror. He didn't really care for her opinion but engaged in conversation for his own amusement. He liked the fact that she was afraid of his every move. He had held her captive in his motel room for the past five days in order to have easy access to a food source. He figured that since she was a prostitute, no one would miss her for a while.

"I'm starting to look like a modern man," he said. "If only I could get better clothes. Jeans are not really my style." He turned and looked at the woman. "Why don't you procure me some? Only shop at the nicer places. Nothing from that horrible store…oh what was it. It had something to do with a shade of blue. Old something..."

"You mean you'll let me leave the motel?" She asked, suddenly more articulate.

"For the time being. But you must return to me post haste or I will hunt you down myself and do more than just take a little from your wrist."

He grabbed her by her hair and she yelped as he pulled her up off the floor.

"And if you tell anyone where you've been, well...you get the point," he snarled. He then let go of her hair and she ran out of the bathroom and out of the motel room.

Once he was alone, he began cleaning up the hair that had fallen all over the sink. He held one of the long, burgundy locks in his hands and suddenly thought of his youngest daughter, Cherish.

Unlike her sister, she had inherited most of his features, including his hair color. She had been like him in so many ways; smaller than other children her age and had a tremendous temper. He could only imagine what chaos would have lain in her wrathful wake if he'd been able to turn her. She'd died before he could finish his work.

After all the hair had been properly disposed of, he went into the bedroom and looked at the stuffed toy that lay against the pillow. He picked it up, smiling at the memory of when he had taken it. It had been almost too easy to climb into little Robin's room and watch her as she'd slept. He had even been bold enough to stroke her hair and pull the covers over her exposed arm. He hadn't done it out of affection, but out of a twisted way of bragging to himself how close he had been able to get to Solomon's descendant without his knowing.

He wasn't ready to take any lives. Not just yet. He wanted to make them feel helpless not knowing when or where he would strike. It was only a small part of his plan of revenge.

The door opened and he turned around to see one of his recruits had returned from spying. It had been easy finding waste-of-space immortals who needed some extra money. After finding all of the money he'd hidden years ago, he was able to properly fund all of his needs. He had a lot of money, and he used some of it to pay people to do things for him.

THE RESURRECTION

"Well?" he asked.

"We have a problem," the woman, Kendell said. "Daniel skipped town."

The smile left Lucian's face. "What do you mean?"

"I guess he was caught in the act. Solomon paid him double what you offered then Daniel took the money and got on a bus."

This was a damper in his plan. He wanted to be able to know what time of day was best to act, but now he would have to send someone else. Someone less greedy than Daniel. Even Kendell would do. One night of seducing her and he had her doing all of his biddings. He hated that he had to stoop to his late wife's tactics, but they proved to work. Lust ensured loyalty.

"Then I will have you act as my spy instead," he said. "You are more reliable anyway."

She smiled at him then walked up to him so that she was inches away from his face.

"What do I get in return?"

He pressed a kiss to her lips then pulled back. "You will earn your reward tonight. For now, watch for that prostitute to return with my clothes and once she is back, leave at sundown."

After she left the room, he set the toy back down before walking over to the window and staring out at the street. He would carry out his next move very soon, and he could hardly contain his excitement. It was going to be bigger and more sinister than just lurking around the Sharmentino house. They would never be prepared for what was going to hit them next.

Chapter Nine

That night I dreamt of Gallard. We were back in India and it was when he first told me he loved me. He then laughed and to me it was the most wonderful sound in the world. The more I stared at him, the more he became irresistible. He had the same kind eyes and this smile that gave me goosebumps. I wanted to kiss him so badly, and I was going to when he did first. I could feel everything that was happening as if it were real.

As suddenly as the moment escalated, I was jolted awake by a ringing phone. Groaning I sat up and looked over to see that Jordan was asleep. The phone hadn't woken him up, so I looked around for the source of the ringing. I found the phone in his back pocket and checked the I.D. It was an unknown number, but I wanted it to stop so I answered it.

"Hello." I cleared my still scratchy morning throat. "Who is it?" It hadn't helped much.

"Who is this?"

"I asked you first," I somewhat snapped. I wasn't too happy

that I had been woken from such an amazing dream because for a moment I forgot that I was a vampire again. Not only that, but I was screwed up and fed on the blood of my own kind. This day didn't have that great of a start.

"Let me guess; you and Jordan hooked up last night?" The caller said.

"Excuse me?" My voice slightly shrilled.

"Look, I'm going to be honest here. He's only doing this to get over someone so if I were you, I would get out while you still can. He'll treat you like you're something special when in reality, he's going to be with a different woman tomorrow. So I'm telling you this in the nicest way possible. Get up, walk away, and don't waste any more of your time."

"Who do you think you are, assuming you know…" Now that I was more awake, I realized who I was talking to. I knew this voice. I had fallen in love with this voice, and I couldn't believe I was really talking to him. "Gallard?"

Jordan, who I thought was asleep suddenly sat up and took the phone away from me. I tried to grab it back, but then he tackled me and pinned me to the bed in a way that I couldn't move.

"Hey ugly!" Jordan said. "Sorry about that. The very charming uh…Stacy doesn't know any boundaries. I told her not to answer my phone. What? No…of course not!" The nervous smile left his face. "Who told you? Solomon? I should have known. He's a priest; he can't lie." He looked at me, and I tried to bite him but couldn't reach his arm. "Yes. It's her. Yeah, I don't think that's a good idea. Because reuniting over the phone isn't romantic."

"Yes, it is!" I shouted. Jordan tried to cover my mouth and I used that as my chance to bite him.

"Ow! Damn, woman!"

"We're in Tampa!" I shouted. Jordan gave me an exasperated look and I smiled.

"Well, that very stubborn cat is out of the bag. Or in this case out of the coffin."

I glared at him again and he winked.

"I guess we'll be seeing you. Bye Gallard."

"I love you!" I shouted right before Jordan hung up. I glared again. "Why didn't you let me talk to him?"

"Don't you think it would be better to talk to him in person?"

"Oh, I get it. You don't want him here because you want me all to yourself!"

Jordan rolled his eyes and I laughed. He was always joking around about me flirting with him, so I figured I could do the same and show him how ridiculous he sounded.

He got up and let me move again. I could have put up a better fight but chose not to. The only thing that mattered was that my best friend was coming and I couldn't wait to hold him and kiss him. I also wanted to see my brothers too. I couldn't be kept hidden away at Curtis' forever.

Jordan got off of me and picked his shoes up from the floor. He left the room, and I did the same so I could get dressed. Curtis must have still been asleep because he wasn't in the living room or the kitchen, so I took the liberty of looking through his fridge. He had plenty of ingredients and I used eggs, some vegetables, and cheese to make an omelet. Andre's blood had taken away the burning in my throat so now I just felt regular hunger. I was stoked that I could still eat food.

"You should be resting," I heard someone say. I turned to see Jordan next to me. He was good at sneaking up on me. His hair was wet from the shower as well.

"I've been resting for fourteen months. I don't think I need any. I'm more hungry than anything. Is Curt up? I want to make some for him too."

"He left for work an hour ago. He told me to tell you not to go anywhere."

"I don't plan to. I'm staying put until Gallard comes."

"Good." He nonchalantly pushed me aside and took my spatula. "Let me finish this."

"What for? I'm perfectly capable of making an omelet."

He gave me a patronizing smile. "You may think you are, but you aren't. You have the stove on way too high. You're going to burn the egg before it's even flipped. Not to mention you were going to flip it too early. Trust me, I'm an expert."

I decided not to fight Chef Jordan and let him take over. While I stood there, I suddenly felt a slight pain in my lower stomach. I winced, startled by the uncomfortable sensation, but it was oddly familiar. It lingered for a few moments before leaving, only to return again. That's when I realized what it was; cramps. That explained the irritability and my appetite. PMS always made me hungry.

"You okay?" he asked, concerned as always.

"Yeah. Just girl problems." The cramps returned, only worse this time. This situation seemed urgent, so I asked, "By any chance could I borrow ten bucks? I need to make a run to the store."

"Not by yourself. You're going to have to wait until tonight because I can't go outside until the sun goes down."

I frowned. "Why not? I think I proved last night that I'm not helpless. Jordan, I'm a woman. I can't just put my feminine ways on hold until it's convenient."

He sighed. "Okay fine. Promise me that you won't make any extra stops. Just go in, go out, and come back. Understood?"

"Yes, dad."

He then dumped the omelet in the trash and I gasped. "You screwed this up. There was no saving it. I'm going to make you a complete breakfast for when you get back. My wallet is in my bag in the front zipper. Take the twenty."

I thanked him then left to run my errand. I was actually a little excited to see what Jordan was going to make so I wanted to be quick. The store was very small but had a decent variety of items, including freezer dinners and nurse scrubs.

I found the aisle I was looking for and tried to narrow down my choices. While I browsed, I realized that I hadn't done this in a long time and not in the sense that I was dead for a year. I held a box of Kotex in my hands and suddenly I had a flash of a memory.

"What about...protection? Do I even need it?"

"It might be best if you did...but technically, you wouldn't need it. After you became a vampire, you lost the ability to – "

"Get pregnant?"

"That and contract diseases. But anyway, whatever you decide to do or not do, just be sure to guard your heart. Even if we are immortal, we still have feelings."

"David said the same thing yesterday."

"Well, he was right. We both care about you very much and would hate to see you get your heart broken."

That had been when I was a regular vampire. If I was really experiencing PMS and all the symptoms, did that mean I could have children? That was another question that I had no answer to.

I went inside and put the change back into Jordan's wallet. I zipped it closed then listened for any movement. I didn't see anyone, but I sensed that someone was in the house. This was a different feeling like there was an ominous presence.

I tiptoed into the living room, looking in each corner and checking behind me once in a while. I didn't want to be caught off guard from behind. I heard movement from the rooms in the back and rushed towards the sound. I ran so fast that I accidently bumped into someone and they grabbed me, pushing me against the counter. The blow caused me to drop my sack.

"Aaron!" I shouted. "You scared the hell out of me, what were you doing sneaking around here?"

"I should say the same to you, little sister. Last I checked you were supposed to be dead!"

He backed off, allowing me to move away from the counter and I studied his face. He was exactly the same. His eyes still had a passiveness about them and his expression was nearly blank, like his soul had been sucked out of him. If it had been Kevin, I would have been crying and hugging him because I'd missed him. But with Aaron, I couldn't bring myself to feel that way. His demeanor was colder than ever.

"Curt called Kevin who then called me," he said. "I hear he knows about us and what we are. Now all the Taylor kids know."

"All? What do you mean?"

"Well, let's just say Gabby and I had a little moment a few months ago. Long story short, she knows too. She has the marks to prove it."

"You fed on her? How could you do that, she's our friend!"

Aaron rolled his eyes and put his hands on his hips. "Here we go again. Listen up everyone; Lela's about to give a self-righteous speech about the rules of immortality."

My anger boiled over to the point where I couldn't control my actions. This was probably due to my sudden PMS, but that didn't stop me from punching him in the shoulder as hard as I could. He

THE RESURRECTION

stared at me in shock then slapped me across the face which I then retaliated by kicking him as hard as I could in the groin. He doubled over then grabbed me by my hair, but Jordan jumped in to play referee before it got out of hand.

"All right, enough!" he shouted. "Aaron, I don't ever want to see you hit your sister in my presence. Got it?"

"Yes, sir." Aaron turned to me. "You think it's funny tricking us like that? Do you get off on other people's pain? Because we were *all* in pain, Lela. Your death was a hard blow and we're still reeling from it."

Even though his face didn't show it, I could tell that he was genuinely upset. The old Aaron was speaking to me now and all the anger I felt towards him from his slapping me went away. I hugged him around his waist and he returned it. It was like old times for a minute. The times when we'd been incredibly close and had the best relationship a brother and sister could have. Our bond was incredibly dysfunctional now, but he was still my brother and I loved him.

"I'm sorry I slapped you," he said. "I was devastated when you died, and I was just angry, maybe at myself for not doing a better job of protecting you. I'm your older brother. I should have looked out for you."

I pulled back and forced a smile. Normally I wouldn't have forgiven him that easily, but I'd missed him, so I was willing to put our differences aside for the time being. I didn't want our reunion to be filled with fighting and violence.

Jordan went back to the room so he could give us some time to talk alone. I had a lot of questions for Aaron. I'd been away for so long that I needed to catch up on the current threats, issues, and possible plans to resolve said threats.

"How are Kevin and Robin?" I asked.

"Kev is fine. Ditched me to live here with Curt. Robin is with Evelyn and Jeff at the house. We try to visit her when we can, but it's hard since we can only come out after sundown."

My heart went out to him. I couldn't imagine what it would be like to be a slave to the darkness. I'd been a day-walker so I hadn't been forced to give up my ability to walk freely during the day. This had made it so easy to blend in. Even now I could go outside, whatever I was. I would never understand the woes of being a regular vampire if that was the appropriate term.

"Gallard's coming too," I said. "Almost the entire clan will be here now."

Aaron gave me a sly smile. "I knew you would be asking about him sooner or later. As your brother, I should be concerned that you're banging someone who's so much older than you, but I'm surprisingly okay with it. You've inspired me. Believe it or not, but I found myself an older woman. She helped me get here actually."

I groaned in disgust. "Nobody's *banging* anyone Aaron. Do you have to be so crass?"

"Whatever, Lela. You can't hide it from me. I saw that steamy make-out session in the kitchen. Something went down between you two in India, and there's no denying that."

Something had happened, but not what Aaron was hinting at. I'd stopped it before it would go any further, hoping that maybe we could be together once all of our problems were solved. But it didn't turn out that way. I was unexpectedly killed and was dead for over a year before we could even start a relationship.

"So, who is this supposed older woman you speak of?" I asked.

"We're not exclusive. And she doesn't like people to know about us."

"Is that code for she doesn't exist?" I jabbed. I wanted to get back at him for that comment about Gallard and me.

"Ow, burn!" Jordan said as he came into the room. "I wouldn't push your sister's buttons if I were you. She's kind of vicious."

"Lela *vicious*? I'm so sure."

I punched him in the arm again and he grunted. When we were kids, Aaron used to wrestle with me and I actually got pretty good at it. I was the only girl and wanted to be treated like one of the guys. I never could beat him, though. He had four years on me. I was sure I could take him on now.

We sat at the table so I could eat my food. Jordan was an amazing cook and I savored every bite. I didn't speak much but listened as Jordan explained to Aaron what went down in Italy. I chimed in every now and then, but he had most of it right. I finally learned the story behind my "Alberto" jumpsuit, which was kind of morbid and funny at the same time.

THE RESURRECTION

Jordan was interrupted by his phone ringing. He answered it. "Hello? Solomon, what's up?" His expression darkened. "How long? We're coming right away."

"What is it?" I asked once he'd hung up.

"Your aunt and uncle left the house with Robin without saying anything. Lela, Lucian seriously wants your family dead. Without protection, they're a moving target."

I pushed away from the table and stood. "Well then let's go!"

"You'll have to drive. Aaron and I will need to be covered. Do you know the way?"

"Of course."

I didn't even bother thoroughly packing. If my little sister, Evelyn, and Jeff were in danger, I wanted to get to them as soon as possible. The only thing I did was grab the sack of items I just bought as well as a change of clothes, throwing it all together then wrote a note to Curtis.

Emergency in Miami. With Aaron and Jordan. Don't worry. Will give update ~ Lela

Chapter Ten

When they merged onto the Dolphin Expressway, Evelyn was finally able to relax. It hadn't been easy packing up and leaving while the others were downstairs. She thought that they were never going to get a moment alone, and with more people showing up for secret meetings with Solomon, she and her husband had had enough with being kept in the dark.

Evelyn felt her phone buzz, and she took it out of her pocket to see who it was. Solomon had already called five times and left five messages. Each one had been the same, a warning that she was in danger and a plea for them to come back. She started to answer his sixth call when Jeff shook his head.

"Don't answer that, Evie. We can't trust anything he says. I don't trust that Solomon character as far as I could throw him. I think he knows something about Mark and Sheila's death that he isn't telling us. Right now, our best option is to trust the police."

Evelyn nodded in agreement then turned her phone off. If she didn't hear the calls, then she wouldn't be tempted to answer them. Soon, they would be at the police department and getting the protection that they needed.

THE RESURRECTION

Robin was in the backseat, coloring obliviously with her new crayons. They were mostly doing this for her. She was their priority and they needed to do everything to keep her safe. Evelyn felt she owed it to her brother.

"What are you drawing, sweetheart?" Evelyn asked.

"The man from my room."

Jeff looked at Evelyn, and she saw the color drain from his face. Robin never mentioned seeing a man in her room and she'd thought that the two women had stopped the intruder. Then again, Robin's stuffed animal was missing. That only meant one thing; someone else had been in the house that night.

"What man, honey?" Jeff asked.

"The one with red hair. He looked like the pretty lady named Cherish. I think he took Spock."

Evelyn's blood ran cold. The little girl had seen the person who had taken the teddy bear and she'd kept quiet about it. Had the man threatened her if she said anything? If so, then Robin was braver than Evelyn gave her credit for.

She was about to give in and call Solomon back when she looked up and saw a man step into the road in front of them.

"Jeff, look out!" Evelyn shouted.

Jeff swerved the car since he didn't have time to hit the brakes. The car hit the guardrail and flipped into the air before rolling into on-coming traffic. An SUV tried to dodge them but hit the fender causing it to spin three times before slamming into the rail and coming to a stop. The rest of traffic had been able to avoid the accident, but only a few stopped completely.

Evelyn coughed as she tried to push the deflated airbag out of her face. The car had landed right-side up, thankfully, and she turned her head to look at her husband. He was unconscious and there were shards of glass protruding out of his face and chest. His airbag had not deployed, probably since it was such an old car.

"Robin?" she coughed. "Honey, are you okay?"

"Yes!" the little girl wailed. "The seatbelt hurt my tummy, though."

Evelyn was relieved that Robin was fine. For the most part, she felt that she had minor injuries, herself. She could move her legs and nothing felt broken. When she turned around to face the front, she was startled by a man popping up next to her broken window.

"Are you all right, Ma'am?" he asked.

"My husband...he's hurt and he needs an ambulance," she finally managed to say.

The man nodded then turned his attention back to her. "What about you, are you injured at all?"

Evelyn started moving all her fingers and limbs to see if she was paralyzed but was grateful to find that all she felt was a bit bruised and disoriented.

"I think I'm okay," she said.

The man then smiled and said, "Good."

He reached into the car and started choking Evelyn. She grabbed his hands and tried to pry them off, but he was too strong for her. She let out a light yell, but it was cut off when he pressed harder and crushed her larynx. She wanted to cry out in pain, but no longer had the ability to do so. Her lungs ached for air until finally the pain stopped when everything went dark.

I speeded the entire way and thanked God that I didn't get pulled over. I made it to Miami in three and a half hours flat. Jordan's phone had been ringing constantly, but it wasn't within my reach and I didn't want to stop in fear that
I would be killing time.

I probably looked like a maniac on the road but I didn't care. I got into an area that my family had driven through several times and I was able to turn off the GPS.

The house came into view and I parked in front then grabbed Jordan's bag and ran to the door. I knocked urgently then waited for someone to answer. Jordan said that Solomon had been staying there to watch over my family and I hoped he was still there. I knocked again with no answer, so I tried the door. It was locked.

THE RESURRECTION

My next option was the garage and when I typed in the code, it opened. I nearly tripped over everything inside, but I managed to get to the door and slipped inside.

"Hello! Is anyone here?"

I checked the kitchen, the dining room, and the living room. I could see that someone had been there in the past few hours because the dishes in the sink were still soaking. I set the bag down and unzipped it so Jordan and Aaron could get out and they transformed. Jordan then checked his phone. I tapped my foot anxiously as I waited for him to listen to the message.

"Oh no," he said. He turned his gaze to me. "Lela...something's happened."

"Please...just tell me."

"There was an accident. Jeff and Evelyn's car flipped on the Dolphin Expressway. Jeff was dead on the scene."

Stunned, I slowly walked into the dining room and sat down. This shouldn't have shocked me. I was used to burying people that I loved. First my parents then David and Lydian. Now Jeff was dead.

"What about...Evie and Robin?" I asked.

"Evelyn is in critical condition and Robin only has a few cuts and bruises. They're in the University of Miami hospital. Lela...they say that someone tried to kill Evelyn. Witnesses saw a man try to strangle her. She survived and she's very lucky."

I stood up from the chair and headed for the backyard. The pool was always the place I would go whenever I needed time to think. I admired the yard and smiled when I saw that it was very similar to when I left. The grass was as green as Mark liked to keep it and the pool was cleaned and blue. I sat on the edge, taking my shoes off and put my feet in. Closing my eyes, I thought back to what had happened that terrible night.

"You know something! The gypsy would not lie. A Sharmentino has the body and you will tell me where it is! Unless you want to watch me torture your family, starting with your wife's bastard child."

"All right! I have a name, but that is it. He contacted me fifteen years ago. His name is Solomon Sharmentino. I don't know how he's related to

me or where he is. I swear that is everything I know. Just don't hurt my family."

I trembled as the images began forming in my mind. There were several men in the house and they were holding my family hostage. My mother had Robin in her lap and a man was standing behind her. Mark's head was bleeding and a dark man was speaking with him. They'd looked so terrified and I hated that I couldn't do anything to help them.

"That's what I like to see; cooperation," Samil said. "Your information is much appreciated." He looked at one of the men standing by the door. "Take him out back and finish him off."
"No!" I'd shouted. "Please, I'll...I take back what I said! You can have my blood. I'll do everything you need to find Lucian's body. Don't kill him!"
"Why do you wish to save him? He isn't even your real father. He's nothing to you!"
"You're right, he isn't my real father. "That doesn't mean I wouldn't die for him."
"I am amazed by your ability to care so much. It is your downfall, unfortunately. But it doesn't matter. It's not your blood I want, it's Gallard's. I have an old score to settle and he will be sacrificed." He turned to the man holding Mark. "Take him outside."

I started hyperventilating as the rest of what happened played out. The man drank Mark's blood and when I tried to fight back, they stabbed my mother. I was then shot several times then all of my family was dragged to the backyard. They forced me to drink Kevin's blood then they left us to die in the yard, taking my little sister with them. Killing Samil was supposed to make my family safe again but now there was a new threat.
"Lela?" I heard Jordan say. He must have been standing in the doorway to keep from getting sun exposure because his voice sounded far away.
Wrapping my arms around my middle, I began to sob violently. It was about ten minutes before my sobs began to lessen and I could finally breathe again. I wasn't feeling despair anymore. It would be

easy to sink into depression and want to give up, but I couldn't. I was angry.

I used to think it was my fault that my family had suffered but now I knew better. I wasn't the one who killed them. We'd fought against these threats and now there was a new one. Lucian Christophe. He killed Jeff and nearly killed Evelyn and my sister. He was a dead man.

Standing up, I went back into the house. Jordan and Aaron were waiting for me, and I could see they were concerned.

"I'm okay." I wiped away the stray tears. "I want to go see my aunt and sister."

"You'll be fine alone?"

"Yes. Have you called Gallard?"

He nodded. "He's picking up Kevin in Orlando then heading here."

I gave Aaron a hug before going out to the car. I knew which hospital Evelyn and Robin were in because my mother had been there before. The drive was longer than I wanted it to be but I arrived around four-thirty. The receptionist informed me that they were on the second floor so I took the elevator up.

As I neared the room, I noticed a man was sitting in a chair in the hall. He looked up at me and when we made eye contact he smiled at me.

"Lela! I cannot believe you're here!" He walked over to me and took my hand in his. If anyone else had done this, I would have thought it was creepy, but I recognized him. "I am Solomon Sharmentino. We've met once before, but our meeting was very brief."

"It's nice to meet you again. You're the one who sent us money, right? And you helped…bring me back?"

He nodded. "I am sure Jordan told you the news. My thoughts and prayers are with you in this time of loss. I know you were close with your Uncle."

"Thank you, that's very kind. So I hear Evelyn is in ICU?"

"Yes. I am still waiting for an update. You can sit with me if you like."

Solomon paced the hall while he prayed. He had a rosary in his hands and his expression was full of despair. I was surprised at how upset the news of Jeff's death had made him. For being such a distant relative, I wouldn't have assumed he cared so much about his family. I had obviously been wrong.

The doctor finally came out and the two of us stood up.

"She's going to be okay," he said. "She has a crushed larynx and is unable to speak, but we've given her notepad to write on. Your aunt is extremely lucky."

"That's saying something, considering she's a Sharmentino," I said to lighten the mood. The doctor smiled.

"I've worked with her husband for a year now. He was a great addition to this facility, and I am sorry to hear of his passing. I enjoyed working with him."

I nodded in thanks then Solomon and I followed him to Evelyn's room. He decided to let me go in alone and I had no problem with that. I needed to speak to her in private. I couldn't thank her enough for taking care of my sister while I was away. I owed her so much.

When I went in, her eyes were closed. The only sound was that of the heart monitor and the compression of the machine that was helping her breathe. There was a long tube attached to her throat and it made me want to cry. I hated that she was in danger by association but glad that Lucian failed to take her away. I didn't want to lose any more people.

"Aunt Evelyn?" I said in a quiet voice. Her eyes fluttered then she opened them and looked at me. Her eyes widened in what I thought was fear but the more I looked, I saw it was surprise. Maybe joy? "It's me...Lela."

A tear fell down her cheek and she waved me over. I sat down in the chair by the bed and took her hand in mine, bringing it to my lips. Her grip tightened and a smile formed on her bruised lips. She pointed at the notepad on the bed and I moved it closer to her so she could write. She scribbled a little then handed it to me.

You're alive! It said. *Where have you been?*

"Witness protection," I lied. "The men who killed my parents tried to kill me too. I had to make them believe I was dead so they would leave my siblings alone."

She wrote again. *Why did you come back?*

"They figured it out. I came back to protect you but...I didn't

THE RESURRECTION

come in time to save Jeff."

Evelyn started to cry and I sat there, just supporting her in silence. I couldn't imagine going through this. According to Jordan, Gallard had been a mess for the first few months after I died. I hoped that I would never experience that.

"I'm going to make this right," I said. "The man responsible won't get away with this. Jeff will have justice. I promise you that."

The doctor returned and gave her some medicine to help her sleep. I promised her that I would visit as soon as possible, though I wasn't sure when. I had a job to do and I wouldn't come back until Lucian was stopped. However, I hated the idea of leaving her here with no one. That's when I had an idea.

"Hello?" the person answered after the third dial.

"Hey, Curt."

"Lela, hey! I got your note. Is everything okay?"

"No." I bit my lip to keep from crying again. "Curt, my uncle Jeff died today. It was a car accident."

He grew quiet but I could feel him on the other line. Jeff hadn't been more than ten years older than him and had been somewhat like an older brother to Curtis and Aaron when he'd started dating Evelyn. Then he had a job opportunity in Texas and we hardly ever saw him except for on holidays. This was a huge hit for Curt as well as my family.

"How's Ev?"

"Grieving, but she is going to be okay. I actually wanted to ask a favor."

"Sure thing. What can I do?"

I paused for a while. "You know what, never mind. I have no right to ask you for anything. You've done enough for me."

"Lela, you know I don't keep track of that. Your dad saved my life and so did you. In return, I will do anything for your family. Now tell me what I can do."

"I have to take off with my brothers. It's…vampire related. I don't want her to be alone so I am thinking of having her transferred to a hospital in Tampa. That way you can check on her once in a while."

"I definitely can do that. Gabby was thinking of coming to town so I was taking time off anyway. Don't worry about Ev. She'll be in good hands."

"Thanks, Curt. You're a good man, you know that?"

I hung up then left the room so I could see my sister. I was in kind of a hurry and I wasn't paying attention to where I was going and ended up running right into someone. I was shocked that I didn't knock them down, and I looked at my victim. It was Gallard.

Chapter Eleven

Lucian wiped the excess blood from his mouth then rinsed his hands in the provided sink. He hadn't expected borrowing a lab coat to be so much effort. He'd found the locker room and taken it out but then someone walked in on him and threatened to call security. The scrawny, curly-haired orderly had tasted delicious but then he had a body to hide. The bottom of the laundry bin was the perfect spot.

Standing in front of the mirror, he finished buttoning the coat then stared at his reflection. Smiling to himself, he relished in the fact that he wasn't going to get caught. When he had strangled Evelyn, his hair was brown and his eyes were green. Now his hair was dirty blonde and his eyes were cornflower blue. The same shade as Robin's. Staring into her terror-filled eyes had inspired this look.

"Good afternoon, I am doctor Lu…Louis Crane and I am here to check your vitals," he practiced as he walked back into the hallway. He even stole a clipboard from the desk while no one was looking and pretended to write on it. It helped matters that he knew exactly where he was going so he wouldn't stand out.

He hadn't anticipated Evelyn surviving his attack. He had to admit, he did tend to be a little gentler when dealing with women. If she had been a man, he would have just torn her head from her shoulders but suffocation seemed less...messy. He got sloppy and now he had to finish the job. This time, he would make sure she was dead and then he would wait around so he could see the look on Solomon's face when he discovered her body. Yes, it would be a wonderful sight to see.

On his way, he realized he would be passing little Robin's room. He had planned to return her stuffed animal to rattle them up a bit and this felt like the perfect time. He approached the room, mentally practicing what he would say to the girl and started to go in when he heard voices inside of her room. He stopped in his tracks and pressed his back against the wall.

"I'll tell you what," a woman's voice said. "When we find this bad man who hurt your family, I am going to demand that he gives you back that teddy bear."

The voice sounded so familiar. He hadn't heard it in five hundred years and yet he could recognize it anywhere. It couldn't be. It was impossible. He had to be hearing things.

"What if he doesn't?" he heard Robin say.

"Then I'll punch him in the throat," another voice said.

His heart lurched in his chest and he struggled to remain upright. That voice he knew as well. This voice had laughed with him, screamed at him, and even cried to him for twenty-one years. He knew it by heart. He could hear it from anywhere in the house and know if she was in trouble or upset by something.

"Cherish, don't talk so violently in front of the little girl!" the first woman said. Hearing her name confirmed his suspicions and he was stunned speechless. He couldn't move or do anything but continue to listen.

"Why not? She's a Sharmentino and that means sooner or later someone is going to come after her. It's good to learn at a young age how to defend yourself. Especially us women."

"Self-defense is one thing and violence is another. But that's not the point. Robin, we're here to make sure that you will never have to defend yourself. We're going to take care of you, all right?"

"Okay. Melody?"

"Yes, hon?"

THE RESURRECTION

"Is that bad man sad?"

The women grew quiet then he heard Cherish speak. "Why do you ask that?"

"Because my mom said that sometimes when people are angry it means they're sad. I think he hurt my family because he's sad."

"Yes, Robin," Melody said. "I think my father is very sad. You know, *his* daddy hurt him when he was young and he never healed from that. Now he's mad at Solomon because my father trusted him more than anyone and then he did something to hurt him too. Solomon feels bad about it, but my father doesn't want to forgive him."

"Maybe he needs a hug. I know when Gallard hugs me I feel better."

"Oh he needs a hug all right," Cherish said. "Around the neck…with my bare hands."

"Enough!" Melody said. "I think you need some air. Go get us a couple of drinks."

He heard Cherish coming towards the door and he turned around just as she came out. He pretended to look at his papers while she stopped in front of the vending machine and he stared at her. She looked exactly as she had the day she died. Petite, but slightly endowed. Long, crimson hair, and a grim expression on her face.

How had Solomon tricked him into thinking his daughters were dead? Had he suffered from last minute guilt and turned them in order to save their lives? Why hadn't he told him they were alive when they'd spoken back in Italy?

He had to speak to her. Cherish. His favorite. She'd had the potential to be just like him and now he would get a second a chance. His wife, Florence, had been a less than adequate partner. He'd only married her because she'd seduced him and used him to turn her. He'd hated that she'd fooled him so easily with her beautiful long, light-brown hair and her almond-brown eyes.

As Melody grew older, it was apparent that she was going to be nearly an exact replica of how her mother had looked. This was probably the main reason why he'd paid less attention to her. She'd reminded him of the mistake he'd made in marrying Florence.

Cherish, on the other hand, was perfect. She had the tendency to bottle up her anger until it would explode at random, even when she was barely two-years-old. He had no idea so much rage could exist in such a tiny body, and he loved her for it.

Then Solomon came into the picture and ruined everything. He had taken away his Cherish; his protégé. And now, after five centuries, the news that his daughters were alive was creating a major rift in his plan. He had to find a way to get Cherish to be on his side. It wouldn't be easy since she and her sister were close. They had always been inseparable.

Walking down the hall, he dialed Kendell's number. It went to voicemail, but he didn't care. She would get his message eventually.

"Hello, my pet. Plans have changed. I no longer need you to watch the house so meet me at the hotel. I have something else in mind."

For a minute, we just stared at each other. I was still trying to process the fact that I was standing in front of Gallard, but he was probably ten times as stunned as I was. After all, to me it was like I'd just seen him a week ago, while to him had it had been a year.

He moved back a bit and it looked like he was about to buckle to the ground, so I grabbed onto his arms to try and steady him. He was hesitant to touch me at first and lifted a wary hand to my face, lightly pushing my hair away from it. Neither of us could speak. There were no words to express what either of us was feeling.

When he began to cry, I couldn't hold back my own tears, and I pulled him closer to me, wrapping my arms around his neck. Eventually, he put his own arms around me and I could feel him shake from his sobbing. The tears burned in my eyes and I squeezed him tighter, not wanting to let go.

He pulled back from the hug and stared at me again, this time with a smile on his face. He then leaned in and kissed my forehead, my eyelids, and both my cheeks; each kiss was like a validation that I was really there. Finally, when he'd kissed every inch of my face his lips met mine and he kissed me more passionately than he ever had before. He didn't hold back like he used to, and I returned it with the same intensity. Time stopped for us in that moment, and we were aware of nothing but each other.

When he stopped kissing me, he pressed his forehead against mine, closing his eyes.

"I'm sorry," he said speaking for the first time. "I'm so, so sorry."

"I'm not sorry that you kissed me," I said, smiling up at him.

He interlocked my fingers with his, bringing them up to his lips. "Are you really here? Am I dreaming?"

"Yes, I'm here. There's no getting rid of me, old man."

He chuckled then pulled me closer to him, and I buried my face into his chest. He smelled just as I remembered. And his touch was still the gentle touch I'd grown to love. He'd always been gentle towards me, which was one of the reasons I fell so hard for him.

"How are you here?" he asked. "Please tell me you weren't in that coffin all this time. Were you trapped in there? Were you—"

I interrupted him with another kiss. "It doesn't matter. I'm here now, and I love you."

"Oh, you're here!" I heard Solomon say. He came over to us and Gallard turned so that we could face Solomon.

"I came as soon as Jordan called me. Is everyone okay?"

"Evelyn is fine. Cherish and Melody are with Robin keeping an eye on her. Everyone is safe for now." Solomon smiled at me. "I see you've been reunited. I am happy for you two."

"As am I," Gallard said. He hugged me tighter and I let out a content sigh.

"Gallard, can I speak with you for a moment? It's about the police report. I figured I could fill you in."

"Sure, uh…Lela, why don't you go see Robin. I know you will make her day."

I nodded in agreement then smiled at him before walking down the hall. The anticipation of seeing my sister followed by the rush of reuniting Gallard had definitely helped ease the ache in my heart. I hated that my aunt had nearly died and that she'd lost her husband. I would make this right. No matter what it took, I would make Evelyn and my sister safe again.

I found her room and was going to go in when another woman

tried to enter as well. We bumped shoulders and I used my reflexes to catch the drink she'd dropped.

"Clumsy much?" She snapped.

"I'm sorry!" I said. "I'm not usually such a klutz."

The woman frowned. "Who are you anyway?"

"I'm Lela. My sister is in this room."

The woman stared at me in horror. I was getting used to this reaction from people.

"You're dead!"

"And you're British."

The woman blinked then started laughing and I laughed too. I hadn't laughed in a very long time and it felt good. My joke had been extremely cheesy but I was running out of responses for people who were asking how I was alive.

"I'm Cherish," she said. "Come in. Your brother and sister are in here."

I followed her in and when I saw my two siblings, I didn't know who I wanted to hug first. Robin was drawing on a notepad and Kevin was watching her. He must have sensed someone staring at him because he looked up and when we made eye contact he covered his mouth with his hands. He started crying and it broke my heart.

"Aw, Kev! Don't cry!" I said as I moved towards him. I gave him a tight embrace and held my baby brother as he cried. Robin finally looked at me and she smiled.

"Lela!"

"Hey, little Robin Bird!" I used one arm to hug her so I could have both of my siblings in my grasp. Robin climbed off the bed and I lifted her up and held her. it was convenient being strong. She was as light as I remembered, only taller. Kevin, on the other hand, had matured a lot in a year. He was about an inch taller than me and he was a very handsome man. He had our mother's facial features mostly.

"Lela, Gallard said that we weren't going to be sad anymore," Robin said. "Is that because he knew you were back?"

"I guess so, honey." I smiled at my little sister. "Look at you! You're getting so big!"

"I'm in kindergarten now and then I'll be in first grade."

I kissed her forehead, swaying her from side to side and Kevin hugged us both. I wished that Aaron could have been there with us. We would all be together soon. I basked in the reunion for a little longer and then acknowledged the other woman in the room.

"You must be...Melody? Solomon mentioned you were keeping an eye on my sister."

"Yes, I'm Melody Davis. You have quite the fan club here."

"I couldn't ask for a better entourage."

Solomon and Gallard came into the room at that moment. Gallard kept smiling at me with so much joy that I couldn't fight the smile forming on my lips. Robin noticed I was looking at him and she waved him over and he hugged me to his side.

"Everyone is safe for now," Solomon said. "We have police guarding Evelyn and Lela mentioned wanting to transfer her to Tampa. I think the best plan of action would be to find Lucian and confront him."

"I agree," Melody said. "He's doing all of this because he's angry about you for killing him and for the gypsies killing Cherish. If he knew that my sister was alive, he might relent."

"Mel, I'm sure he's upset about you too."

Melody forced a smile. "You're kind, Solomon, but I've accepted long ago that my father didn't give a damn about me. We all know it's Cherish's death he's angry about."

I wasn't completely sure what everyone was talking about, but I pretended to. The last thing they needed was to give me a recap. They had better use for their time like planning our next move and making sure everyone was safe. We were all in agreement that we should go back to the house and fill Aaron and Jordan in on everything that was going on.

We discharged Robin and dispersed ourselves between the two vehicles. Gallard drove the rental I came in and I saw in the front while Robin and Kevin were in the back. It was a very awkward ride because Gallard and I kept glancing at each other out of the corner of our eyes and then pretending we hadn't. He had a specific expression on this face and I recognized it as his nostalgic face.

"What are you thinking?" I asked.

"I can't believe I accused you of sleeping with Jordan."

I laughed. It was actually funny after the fact. I had been somewhat grouchy when we spoke. It also made me wonder if something like that had happened before. Did Jordan hook up with women often?

"So let me get this straight," I said. "Lucian's daughters have been alive this entire time?"

"That is correct. It appears that they are the same as you or vice versa. They came back after being dead a short time then went into hiding. They were the ones who were trying to keep him from returning."

We pulled into the driveway and we got out. I was about to walk up the porch when Gallard stopped me.

"Wait a second," he said pointing towards the door. "The door is cracked open. Something's wrong.

Everyone got out of the vehicles then Melody and Cherish crept inside. The two men followed while I remained outside. I wanted to watch in case I needed to warn them of anyone arriving and I wanted to look out for Robin.

Just then, Cherish went flying backward out the front door and there was a woman on top of her. They scuffled for a bit and the woman bit onto Cherish's neck. Cherish yelled then kicked the woman in the stomach sending her flying off to the side.

The woman quickly recuperated and lunged at Cherish again, tightening her fingers around her neck. Cherish struggled for a moment and I almost stepped in to intervene when Melody ran out of the house and sank her teeth into the woman's neck. The woman screamed as Melody drained her blood and then went silent.

Cherish pushed the dead woman off of her then stood up, examining her blood-stained clothes. I was still in shock over what I'd just seen. If I wasn't mistaken, Cherish and Melody were exactly like me; feeders of vampire blood. I thought I was some kind of freak and now I knew there were two women just like me. They could probably give me the answers I was looking for.

"I hope this washes out," Cherish said sarcastically.

"Where are my brother and Jordan, are they okay?"

"Yeah, they're fine. They didn't even know anyone had gotten in. Mel and I were searching the house when this one came out from one of the closets. I barely had time to react."

"Well, we better get this cleaned up before someone drives by," Melody said. She and Cherish picked up the corpse and carried it

THE RESURRECTION

into the house with me following not too far behind. Aaron, Kevin, and Jordan were standing in the foyer with Robin in Kevin's arms.

"Where should we put the stiff?" Melody asked.

"There's a bathtub downstairs and to the left," Aaron said, "We can leave it there and get rid of it later."

Melody nodded then she and Cherish carried the body down the stairs while Jordan held the door open for them. Not long after, Gallard and Solomon came from upstairs. The rest of the house was clear so the woman was the only one there as far as we knew.

When Mel, Cherish, and Jordan came back from upstairs, Solomon returned from the porch as well. He ushered us into the living room and we followed him, sitting in silence for a bit. The silence was the only thing we could give my uncle for now. It would be a while before we could have a funeral.

Solomon finally broke the silence with a bit of a lecture. I could tell that his cardinal side was coming out since he spoke like he was giving a sermon or some kind of eulogy. He was a very powerful speaker and very persuasive as well.

"Jeff is dead because we let our guard down," he said. "We got too comfortable with the lack of action on Lucian's part. Not only that, but he played us. He used the accident for a double motive, and if we hadn't gotten here in time, Aaron and Jordan would be dead right now."

"We could have taken her. It was two against one!" Aaron said.

Solomon glared and walked really close to him.

"I don't think you understand this situation very well. Lucian' isn't like you and your brother. He is stronger and more resilient. He has the sun on his side, and all it would take would be for him to throw you out of a window and you would be dead. If Gallard or I were to have a reason to kill you, you'd be dead before you even saw us coming. He's killed an almost an entire clan on his own, and not to mention he's the only one besides me that crossed Lucian and lived. Now take that and multiply it by two and that's what it would be like to fight Lucian. With that said, we need to find Lucian. He knows we're here, and now we need to know where he is. Gallard, do you still feel the pull?"

"I feel something. Lela and I noticed that the pull is weaker when day-walkers are closer together. It may not be as easy as if I were looking for him alone."

"That isn't an option. You're not going anywhere without backup. We need to clear out as soon as possible. We'll come up with a plan tomorrow then leave tomorrow night. Agreed?"

Everyone was in agreement, and Kevin handed Robin back to me before joining the men in the living room to discuss some plans for the future. I realized after they left that I was feeling hungry myself. I hadn't had blood since the night before, and I was starting to get cravings, especially with five vampires in close proximity. I decided to go upstairs and put Robin down for a nap. She had been through a lot that day, and I figured that she needed some time to recuperate.

After she was asleep, I found myself wondering into my old room. I must have packed it up when Aaron put the house on the market. There was nothing left, save for the green and brown paint on the walls. It was strange seeing it now.

I thought back to the night I had thrown myself out the window to test my abilities. I'd also leaped two stories to get back in. This had been the room where I'd taken the immortal drink of Lucian's blood and yet somehow it didn't feel like my room anymore. It represented my old life; how everything had been before.

"So, this was your room?" Gallard asked, walking in and looking around. "I never came in here when I was at this house last."

"Yeah. The colors just scream teenage girl don't they?"

He stopped in front of the window and turned around.

"I can't believe you were only fourteen when I met you," he said, laughing to himself.

"I know, you cradle-robber," I teased.

"Oh, really? If I'm a cradle-robber, what does that say about you?"

"Anna Nicole Smith in training I guess."

"Or I'm the Humbert Humbert to your Lolita."

"I wouldn't take it that far. I'm twenty, not twelve."

He leaned over and kissed my cheek. "I wanted to see if you were hungry. I know you haven't fed yet, and I'm sure you're really craving blood right now."

"Are you offering?" I said, joking around. He held his wrist out to me to show that he was serious and I took it in my hands. I looked at him again to make sure he was okay with it and he nodded, so I bit down. I didn't take too much since I wanted him to still have enough strength in case there was some reason for him to need it later on.

When I finished, I watched as his wrist quickly healed then held his hand in mine.

"Thank you. So, what's the plan, Stan?" I asked.

"I actually came up here because Cherish and Melody invited you to room with them for the night. Is that something you'd be interested in?"

"Only if you come too."

"Hey, Gallard!" Cherish called up the stairs. "You two coming?"

"Yes!" he shouted. "We'll be right down."

Chapter Twelve

I was so glad that I agreed to go to the hotel. It had been a long couple of days for me, waking up in Italy, flying across the ocean back to Florida. During that whole time, I'd only slept about seven hours, and I was beginning to feel it.

When I learned that the hotel they had booked a room in was the same one that I had stayed in the night my parents were killed, I was a little rattled. I could remember that night very clearly. Aaron had cut the bullets out when I fell unconscious and then woke up to learn he'd turned Kevin. The place brought back a lot of bad memories, but I didn't object since the two women had been so generous to share a room.

It helped that I didn't have any luggage with me, but it would have been nice to have another change of clothes. I figured that I would buy some the next day. Solomon had given me a new credit card and unfroze my bank account when he learned I was live. When Jordan told me I had about two million saved up I thought he was kidding until Solomon confirmed it. My family had been somewhat white collar but never that rich.

As we walked into the room, Melody placed her bag on the bed closest to the window.

THE RESURRECTION

"You guys can have the bed on the left. Just don't think about getting too friendly 'cause we're only two feet away."

"Mel!" Cherish exclaimed.

I knew my cheeks were growing extremely red.

"I'm just getting that out in the open," Melody said.

I sat on the bed and crossed my legs as I watched the two women unpack their stuff. I could feel myself winding down, and I could barely even make out what they were talking about. I was only brought back from my daze when Gallard spoke.

"I'm going to go run an errand. I shouldn't be too long. I'll try to be quiet when I come back."

"Okay, watch your back," Cherish said. "And stay away from any casinos."

"Will do. You mind if I take a key?"

Melody handed him the spare, and he kissed my forehead before going out the door. After that, Melody claimed the first shower and disappeared into the bathroom leaving Cherish and me alone.

The more I looked at her, the more I started seeing the resemblance between her and Lucian. They had the same, wine-colored hair and rare shade of blue eyes. Her expression wasn't as vindictive as his, but she looked tired, emotionally.

"So, how long have you known Gallard?" she asked.

How long had I known Gallard? I was still getting used to the fact that I'd missed a birthday, so I wasn't nineteen anymore. I'd turned fifteen the year we'd met, so that would mean in three months, I would have known him for six years.

"About six years. Believe it or not, but we met at a grocery store of all places. He defended me against this pervert who was trying to sell me condoms. I was only fourteen then."

Cherish chuckled and said, "Typical Gallard. Always trying to be the good guy." She scooted back against the pillows on the bed and crossed her ankles. "So that makes you…how old now?"

"Twenty."

"That's a year younger than when I died. I never had the five years of extra aging like normal vampires, so I remained stuck at that age."

"What is your technical age?"

"I was born in fifteen forty-two, so that makes me four hundred and seventy-three."

I gasped in shock at her old age. She was almost half a millennium, and she looked the same age as me.

"Wow, I'm just a baby compared to you," I said with a joking tone. I wondered if I would ever live that long. At this rate, I would be lucky to make it to twenty-one. People really needed to stop trying to kill me so I could actually live my life.

"How long have you and Gallard been together?"

"Um…we're…new. We've been friends for longer than we've been together."

I didn't really want to give too many details of our relationship, especially since I wasn't sure what theirs had been like. This was the first time that I had felt threatened when it came to other women. Even when Lydian had flirted with him, I knew it was just part of her nature, and it had always been harmless, though it was annoying. It was different this time. Cherish was an old friend of his, and I didn't want to think of the possibility that they had been more than that, especially now that she was here.

"You picked well. Gallard is a great guy and deserves to be happy after all these years."

I was starting to like Cherish. She was kind and very down to earth. More than anything, I wanted to ask her about her past and what had happened with her father and Solomon, but Melody came out of the bathroom before I could ask anything.

"Who's next?" she asked.

"Lela, do you want the next shower?" Cherish asked me.

"No, you go ahead. I showered earlier today."

Melody sat on the bed and tied her hair back into a ponytail. The more I looked at her, the more familiar she appeared to be. I was sure that I'd met her at some point, but I couldn't remember where. If she knew me, she hadn't shown any sign of it, unless she was a good liar.

I didn't want to bother them with more questions but I had so many. The two sisters were like me, sharing the same experience prior to waking up and the same diet. I figured that they must know something since they'd been around for so long.

"So…we feed on vampire blood, but what happens when they

THE RESURRECTION

feed on us?" I asked.

"Oh, they don't feed on us. We're too quick and strong for them. They don't stand a chance." Melody looked at me and smiled. "But to answer your question; nothing. I gave a vampire my blood once just out of curiosity, and he said that it tasted just like human blood."

Gallard and I were now each other's food. It was weird to think about and slightly creepy. There wasn't even a name for what we were. I was still trying to find out how I'd come back. I'd suffered from a broken neck and Melody and Cherish had had their throats slit; both injuries that were impossible to survive. If we had been dead, something had kept us from moving on, and I wanted to know what.

"And...periods. Do you still get them too?"

Melody laughed. "Oh, the joys of being female, right? But even though we are immortal, that does not mean we get supernatural eggs. I hit menopause at sixty-five, but my body looks like I'm still twenty-seven. I feel young, though. That's the upside."

"Does that mean I could have children then?" I asked this with a little too much enthusiasm. As I grew older, I dreamed of having children of my own. I loved babies and wanted a family. If that was possible now, I wouldn't mind the other side effects of coming back to life.

"No. I...tried to have children with the man I was involved with centuries ago, but I always miscarried within the first eight weeks. I don't think our bodies are compatible with a baby. If we don't drink blood, we get really weak and somewhat sickly. Could you imagine going nine months without blood? Unless the baby has similar characteristics as we do. But DNA is a funny thing. If the child had more of its mortal father's DNA, then it probably couldn't survive on blood, let alone vampire blood. You could risk turning the unborn child and it could get messy. That means we would have to live on food and..." she shuddered. "I love food, but no blood? That would be unpleasant. Think of the starving children in Africa and multiply it by ten. That's how bad it would be."

"Basically...children are out of the question?"

"After trying five times, I realized it wasn't going to happen. Just the same, if you ever decide to get close to any mortals, use protection. It will save you a lot of heartache, trust me. Better yet, stick with Gallard and you'll be fine."

By the time Melody's food arrived, I was exhausted and Cherish had curled up under the covers and fallen asleep. I got under mine as well and slowly drifted off to the sound of the TV. I learned a lot from Melody in that short time and felt fortunate that I'd run into her and her sister. Otherwise, I would have been in the dark as I had been when I first turned.

I had probably been asleep for an hour when the nightmares started. They didn't feel like memories, but my fears manifesting in my dreams. Only this time, the dreams were of Lucian killing my family while I watched, helpless and unable to stop him. I tried to wake myself up, but nothing worked. The darkness kept pulling me back in.

Gallard guzzled down the rest of his blood then set the glass on the counter. He hadn't planned to make a run up to Orlando, but he needed to talk to Bodoway. He needed his oldest friend's advice about how to handle the situation with Lucian as well as give him a personal update about Lela. Being here was better than dealing with his stress at the slot machines. He was determined to kick that habit for good.

When he'd seen her for the first time, his joy had been immeasurable. She appeared different; the odd black streaks in her hair and the mismatched eyes. But he knew it was her. He had fallen apart and as always, she'd supported him. He hadn't been able to resist kissing her and when she'd kissed him back, it was as if everything had gone back to the way things used to be.

"I can't believe the shark wrestler is back!" Bodoway said. "I wish I could have seen it. Given you something to look forward to."

"That's all right, B. I couldn't imagine our reunion being any better. Of course, it had to be right after she loses yet another person in her family. One life gained another lost."

Bodoway stopped drying the glasses and leaned against the counter in front of him. Gallard would never have thought three hundred and fifty years ago that he would be asking for advice from Bodoway. They met when he, Terrence, an old friend named Arnaud, and his younger brother Gaspard were caught spying on the Shawnee camp. Two native warriors dragged the three boys into a tent and kept them tied up for a night until Bodoway's father released them. Bodoway had cut off his hair as a way to get back at Gallard for walking into his sister's tent. They were friends ever since.

"Well, you know what I would do in your situation," Terrence said, butting in on the conversation as always. "You need to seduce her."

Gallard choked on a laugh. "Yeah, I'm sure that would fix everything."

"Nothing gives a person more morale like a long night of—"

"Okay, enough. You're not any help. But I do need advice on something you two really are experts on."

Terrence scoffed. "You doubt my expertise on women? This is me we're talking about."

"Yeah, and you haven't had a date in almost as long as I have. You're either here or trolling bars and talking to Vietnam vets." He nudged Terrence. "Anyway, it's about Lucian Christophe. He wants Lela's family dead and we need to find him before he kills someone else. Should we attempt a truce or just take him out?"

"Kill the bastard. You said he chased down her uncle's car and stole her sister's stuffed animal? He's crazy. A crazy vampire isn't something to let slide. Take Emiline for example."

Bodoway groaned. "I hated it when she stopped by here. She freaked out the customers with her borderline personality ways. I am so glad Lela finally exterminated that psycho."

Gallard nodded in agreement. When Lela told him that Emiline took compromising pictures then stabbed her, he had been livid. She never told him how they met, but he had ideas. Bodoway refused to own up to telling Lela their location and the bar was the only possible place Lela and Emiline could have run into each other.

"Whatever you decide, be careful," Bodoway said. "I would join you, but I have a bar to run."

"I could run it for you," Terrence said. "Tito could be bouncer."

"Yes!" Gallard said. "Please help us, B. We need you. *I* need you."

"It's not my fight. I told you my calling is to provide a way for vampires to feed without taking a life and here is where I belong."

Gallard understood. Bodoway had taken up a life free of violence years ago. Gallard and he were originally doing this cause together and he had the idea to open a blood bar. A real one, with no mortal wannabes. The business took off and now he had four bars. Bodoway was the corporate manager but he mostly stayed in Orlando. Gallard then left the business to him so he could continue his search for other day-walkers. He hadn't exactly lived the victim free life, but he drank from blood bags unless it was absolutely necessary to find a donor.

He checked the clock and saw that it was three in the morning. Lela would probably be asleep, but he didn't mind. He couldn't wait to sleep next to her after wanting to for so long. He never planned on letting go of her again. This time, he would be at her side and protect her the way he should have.

What made him happiest was that she hadn't changed. She was still the same brave, funny, and determined woman that he remembered. She had only been back for a couple of days and she had jumped right into the mission without a second thought. She was so accepting of the new members as well. But nothing made him happier than seeing her reunite with her sister.

"I should go," he said. "I'm supposed to be watching her and I'm failing at my job."

"See you around, Gal," Bodoway said. "Take care of your girl."

Gallard shook Bodoway's hand. He was going to let go when Bodoway jerked back really fast. His eyes had filled with terror. The same terror he'd seen in Dyani's eyes when she'd foreseen her death. That could only mean one thing.

"What did you see, B?"

"Nothing."

"Bodoway..."

"I saw...look, all I can say is that Lucian may not be the biggest threat to you. Keep an eye out, all right?"

Gallard wished he would have elaborated more, but didn't press it. Bodoway didn't like to always share what he saw because he didn't believe in changing fate. He felt that no matter what he told people, the outcome would always be the same. Gallard respected his wishes. That didn't mean he wasn't curious.

He took his check and tucked it into his pocket before transforming. Flying was a lot faster than driving and more relaxing. He focused on that instead of Bodoway's warning and the dread forming in his mind. He didn't let himself linger on what could be. He would rely only on the present.

The hotel came into view and he transformed just as he came to the door. Using the key card he went inside and took his time going to the third floor. He even used the stairs instead of the elevator. Why was he so nervous? He never used to be nervous around her. At least after they'd expressed having mutual feelings. Before that, it was hard to stand next to her without being overwhelmed with the desire to kiss her. She'd caught him off guard at the nightclub and he had tried to respond to her when Jordan became ill.

After that, he'd lost his nerve and even pushed her to go to Miami. He realized soon that fighting his feelings wasn't doing anyone any good.

What stopped him from being honest in the past was her reverse back to mortality. Back when they were both vampires, they were on equal ground; both cursed to wander the earth for eternity without ever really building a life together. He didn't have to worry about holding her back or robbing her of a normal life. Then she got her mortality back and everything changed. As much as he wanted to ignore all the setbacks, he couldn't. He would never be able to give her children and she would grow old when he wouldn't. He didn't have it in him to change her back just so they could be together so instead, he encouraged her to give Curtis a chance. That had failed too.

He realized that he had wasted so much time trying to be rational and selfless. If he had just given in to what he wanted, they would have had more than just a few days together as a couple. Her return had given him hope.

The hotel room was nearly silent when he went in. He heard deep breathing and the soft rumble of the air conditioner and nothing more. Despite his urgency to be next to her, he decided to take a shower. It wasn't like she was going anywhere. He shucked his clothes then waited for the water to be steaming hot and stepped inside. He liked to take hot showers because it was the only time he could ever be warm. His skin would absorb the heat and simulate that of a warm-blooded human. He missed that the most about mortality.

He stayed there until the water ran cold then got out and dressed. He saw that Jordan had texted him, but it wasn't anything important. He replied to it. No one at the house would be asleep except for Robin so he wouldn't be waking anyone. He started to send a message when he heard a voice.

"No." It was Lela. He could recognize her voice anywhere, with the exception of the angry phone call they'd shared when neither of them knew who the other was speaking to. She never used to talk in her sleep before. Not until Lucian had possessed her.

"Can you hear me?" she said. "I'm here! I'm not dead, I'm here! Gallard can you hear me?"

He hurried over to her and knelt down next to her. She was trembling and moving erratically. He took her hand and held it gently so she wouldn't wake up.

"I can hear you," he said softly. "I'll never leave you again."

Her breathing slowed and she stopped moving around. As he stared at her, he gave in to his instincts and leaned over, pressing a soft kiss on her lips. When he drew back he was surprised to find her eyes open. They gazed at each other for a few moments and without a word, she moved over on the bed. He didn't need her to explain and he slid in next to her. She turned so her back was to him and he put his arm around her and held her from behind.

There was no need to text Jordan. He was right where he belonged and he intended on being at her side. All of his fears left in an instant. He knew in his heart that everything would be okay. With that comforting thought in mind, he stayed with her for the rest of the night.

Chapter Thirteen

The scent of blood was powerful as Lucian walked towards the bar entrance. It wasn't fresh blood but still blood nonetheless. He had been curious about this bar that Gallard supposedly owned.

Following him had been easy. All he had to do was allow himself to feel the pull, and he could know exactly where Gallard was going. He was mostly there to spy and also to find more recruits. The few he'd chosen had proved inadequate and with Kendall dead, he would have to find his own lackeys.

Mimicking what Gallard had done, he knocked on the door. It appeared that the entrance was kept locked to avoid any drunk passerby's who were looking for another place to drink. It was actually a brilliant idea. It wouldn't be safe for the customer's identities if just anyone could walk in.

Someone opened the door, and he stared at the man in very tight pants. Lucian preferred fitted clothing, but this man had taken it to a different level. It was almost like the pants were part of his skin. He had to be the same man that Lela had an altercation with when she had come here the previous year.

"You're new," the man said in a Scottish accent. "I've never seen ye before."

"That is correct. I heard about this place through a friend and wanted to scope it out."

"All right. Since you're new, you're required to have a membership and that is achieved through an interview with my manager. Interview comes with a free glass of blood. You still interested?"

"How can I say no to free blood?"

"Not quite free. Five dollars a glass and twenty for a bag."

The man stepped out of the way and Lucian went inside. Before he arrived, he had changed his appearance so he could pass as a night-walker. He couldn't risk the notion that Gallard had warned them to keep an eye out for a man with his characteristics. His gaze passed over the room as he tried to single out anyone who looked like they needed something to do or a purpose in their life. So far, everyone seemed content. This wouldn't do.

"I'm Terrence by the way," the man said. "What name should I give my boss?"

"Cuthbert. Leonard Cuthbert."

"Got I.D.?"

He took out one of his many counterfeit drivers licenses and handed it to Terrence who scrutinized it for a few seconds then handed it back. He seemed convinced enough because he went through the swinging doors on the side of the counter and disappeared into the back room.

While Lucian waited, he continued looking around. Some people were staring at him, probably because he was a new face. A woman happened to share a glance with him, and he gave her a bow which caused her to get flustered and she looked away.

The doors opened again and this time a man of unknown descent came out. He wasn't very tall, but he looked strong. His skin tone undoubtedly allowed him to blend in better than any Caucasian. His eyes were slightly slanted and his dark hair was thick and pulled back in low ponytail. He had tribal tattoos on his forearms.

THE RESURRECTION

"You must be Leonard." He held out his hand to Lucian. "I'm Bodoway."

Lucian started to shake his hand when he remembered something. Lela had asked this man to glimpse into her future before, which meant he could easily be exposed if Bodoway were to touch him. He didn't want to come off as stuffy, so instead he gave another polite bow. Bodoway lowered his hand and did the same. No wonder Gallard was so polite. He was surrounded by polite people.

Lucian sat at the bar and Bodoway filled a glass for him. He took a sip and was amazed at the temperature. It wasn't cold as he'd expected. It was almost like drinking fresh blood.

"So, where are you from Mr. Cuthbert?" Bodoway asked.

"London. The life of a peer became such a bore so I came here to start fresh. I have always been an inconspicuous man and I wish to keep it that way. Switching to an all blood bag diet is my idea of maintaining that reputation."

"I see. Tell me; when was the last time you took a life."

The friendly smile left Lucian's face. He hadn't known it would be this kind of interview. It might ruin his chances if he were caught in a lie but he didn't want to be honest either. He chose take a risk and to tell the truth anyway.

"This morning."

"All right. And would you consider yourself a violent man? Do you often start fights or at least find yourself getting mixed up in them on a regular basis?"

"I have very few enemies. Petty arguments don't amuse me."

"Thank you for being honest. I am asking these questions because we have a no-violence policy here. You start a fight, you're out. We learn that you're killing indiscriminately, you're out."

He reached under the counter and handed Lucian a piece of paper. Lucian skimmed through it and saw it basically said everything Bodoway mentioned and then he signed the bottom. That was easy enough. Bodoway then filed away the paper then handed him a card. He used a special hole punch that looked like the sign of peace. He had seen it before in one of the books he read on popular culture.

"Cheesy but effective," Bodoway said.

"Was that Gallard's idea?"

The moment he said those words, he knew he'd messed up. Bodoway stood up straighter and glared at him.

"You're the man he's seeking," he said. "Lucian Christophe. What are you doing here?"

Lucian smiled and allowed for his features to change back to normal. The façade had been fun while it lasted but it had become apparent that no one there would be adequate to work alongside him. They were pacifistic anti-killing poor excuses of vampires.

"I wanted to see what Gallard did in his spare time. This is a wonderful facility he has here."

"Get out. Leave or I will have Terrence throw you out."

He felt someone come up behind him and in one swift move, he grabbed the person by the neck and shoved him against the counter.

"There is no need. I was just about to leave."

Bodoway ran around the side of the counter and shoved Lucian away from Terrence then held a long spear to his throat. By the looks of it, it was probably very old, but the tip was very sharp.

"I am only pacifistic ninety-five percent of the time. You're in that five percent where I make an exception. Get out of here or you'll leave with a spear in your throat."

Lucian nodded and Bodoway let him stand. He'd worn out his welcome here so now he would have to continue his search elsewhere. This set back his plans at least a couple of days and he wasn't too keen on that.

He was nearly to the door when someone touched his arm. He realized too late that it was Bodoway and he jerked his arm from his grasp. He could see in the man's eyes that he had been too late.

"No," Bodoway said. "That can't be right."

He reached for Lucian again but this time he was prepared and dodged.

"Do not touch me again, shaman!"

"Whatever it is you plan to do I won't allow it. You need to stay away from Lela."

Lucian held his breath. What the hell was he talking about? Lela was dead. He'd watched her die with his own eyes. Not once had his spies reported seeing a woman with her description. Had her family simply kept her well-hidden?

THE RESURRECTION

If she was alive, this changed everything. He had been so fascinated by her and her strength. He wanted Cherish and he wanted her. The three of them would accomplish so much together. He smiled as yet an even better plan began to form in his mind. He had a way to ensure they would be at his side.

"She is alive?" he asked.

"No thanks to you."

He smirked. "Oh, it is all thanks to me. If it were not for my persuasion, I would be here in *her* body right now instead of mine. Do not worry, shaman. I do not wish her harm. We had an agreement."

"It's not you harming her that I'm worried about."

Lucian ignored his last comment and hurried out the door. He didn't have time to ponder a mystic's mysterious warnings. He had a job to do.

He had almost left the alley when he realized someone was following him. Two people, exactly. He turned to see it was a man and a woman. Then three more people came out with them. He groaned, dreading the possibility that he might have to fight them. He usually liked a good fight but tonight he wasn't in the mood.

"What do you want?" he asked.

"We overheard you talking to Bodoway. You were spying on Gallard?"

He nodded. "I may have a score to settle with an acquaintance of his. I was here to recruit some followers."

"Why not choose us?" the woman said. "We're bored. We spend every night at the bar and our mornings shut up in a dark abandoned apartment. I want to kill something and I want it to be a challenge."

Lucian was impressed with this group. They weren't there for money or compensation. They wanted something to do. It would be convenient if he didn't have to promise pay in exchange for their services.

"Then you're hired. By chance, do you happen to know any more bored immortals? Say...fifteen?"

The man at her side nodded. "I'm sure I could make a few phone calls."

"Excellent. Let's get started."

Chapter Fourteen

I woke up to the sound of singing and rolled over to find Melody standing in front of the sink. She was putting makeup on and singing along to music with her ear buds in. It was very amusing, and I tried not to laugh.

Cherish groaned from underneath her covers and put a pillow over her head. I then looked at Gallard who was still lying next to me, and I saw that he had his eyes closed. I lightly kissed him, but he didn't respond.

"Are you asleep?" I whispered.

"Maybe," he replied, smiling.

I rolled over onto my other side and looked at the clock. It was only a hair past eight, but I was fully rested and ready to get up. The problem was that we didn't exactly have a plan, so I didn't have any reason to. Lucian hadn't shown up yet, my family was safe, and I'd reunited with almost everyone I cared about. Now all we had to do was wait.

Melody started singing even louder and then Cherish got out of her bed and threw a sock ball at her.

"For the love of God, stop singing!" she shouted.

"Why are you such a kill-joy? If you would be nicer, maybe you would have a boyfriend."

"I don't give a flying fu—"

"Whoa now, Cher. No need to start with the expletives."

Cherish rolled her eyes then flopped back on the bed. Gallard was chuckling at the whole argument.

"Déjà vu," he said.

"How so?" I asked.

"They are so much like how you and Lydian were that it's almost scary. You two were always going at it."

I found myself laughing as well. He was right. Cherish and Melody's relationship was exactly like mine and Lydian's.

When I finally stopped laughing, I grew a bit sad. Despite our differences, I really missed Lydian. Even though I hadn't been able to say goodbye, I was glad that I had been able to tell her that she was important in my life before she'd died.

"Who's Lydian?" Cherish asked, sitting up on her bed once more.

"She was friend of ours," Gallard replied. "She was one of the two donors that gave Lucian blood to bring him back."

"Who was the other?"

I lump formed in my throat as I remembered the answer to that question.

"My father, David Shepherd," I said.

"I knew David," Melody said, joining the conversation. "He was a cutie." She smiled then turned back to the mirror. "I also knew Lydian as well."

"How did you know about them?" Gallard asked.

"After Cherish and I came back, we found the gypsies behind the plan to murder our family. We made a truce with them in exchange for helping them escape from the coven they were trapped in. They told me the names of the people they had given the bottles of our fathers' blood to. David had not been a part of the plan since the original choice had stupidly given him the blood as a joke. He proved to be a better choice than I imagined.

"As for Lydian, her parents were friends with another gypsy acquaintance of mine. They told me that she was dying and asked if she could be one of the vessels and I agreed."

She set her makeup brush down then looked at me. "I have a

confession to make. I'm the one that picked you to drink the last bottle."

I sat up on the bed, interested to hear what she had to say.

"After I told David how to cure himself, I found out that he was involved with your mother. She was married to one of Solomon's descendants, and I jumped at the chance to find out what they were like. I never knew where his family was and once I found them, I watched from a distance. I still had one last bottle of blood, and I thought maybe one of the children in the house could benefit from it. I chose you. I sensed that you were a good person and wouldn't be a nuisance to mankind as an immortal. I left you the flier for the circus which then led you to Ajala."

I felt overwhelmed with all of this information. I didn't realize how many people were involved in the events that transpired in my life over the past five years. It was all so hard to believe. The three people I had cared so much about were all brought into my life because of seemingly random selections that were made by different generations of the same families.

I was also reeling from the realization that I'd only been turned because she'd felt I was a good choice. She hadn't known that I wasn't his descendant, and if it hadn't been me, Aaron could have been the one who'd turned that day.

"I remember you now," I said. "You were at the party. You told me to eat scrambled eggs to help my hangover."

Melody laughed. "Oh, yeah! I almost forgot about that. Well did it work?"

I nodded. By rights I should have been mad at her.

She'd used me as a ploy in her plan against her father and now I was sucked into this crazy immortal world. However, if it weren't for her, I would never have met the friends that I had; Gallard, Lydian, Jordan. Most importantly, I never would have met my real father. In a way I owed her a lot.

"What about me?" Gallard asked. "Did you choose me as well?"

"Yes, I did. I was working as a nurse during the French and Indian War. I treated you when you'd strained your bad leg. I heard that you'd helped an injured Native run to safety while you were injured yourself. I admired that. I also heard that you had a love of gambling. That was when I paid a man to put down the blood and do everything he could to make sure you won that game. The rest you know."

"That's amazing! I remember being in and out of consciousness back then, but I don't remember you. It's amazing that we've met again after all these years."

Gallard then got off the bed and went to the phone, probably to call Jordan. I decided to get in a quick shower before everyone decided what we would do for the day. I wanted to do nothing but be on guard duty for my siblings and aunt, but I knew that they were probably safe since they had Solomon with them. On the other hand, I was hoping to speak with him. I was interested to get to know this mysterious relative of my father's that had helped save my life.

I didn't waste any time in the bathroom, and was out and dressed in under fifteen minutes. When I came out, I looked around the room and saw that Gallard was gone, and Cherish explained that he had gone to meet with Solomon. I wished that I had been able to go with him, but I figured we would all meet up eventually, so I continued getting ready.

My hair was becoming a losing battle. Even when Cherish lent me her brush, I couldn't seem to get it to do what I wanted, and the fact that the black and blonde looked like a five-year-old had dyed my hair didn't help matters either.

"Do any of you have scissors?" I finally asked, giving up taming the beast on my head.

"You're not cutting your hair are you?" Melody asked, her eyes wide.

"Yes! I can't deal with it anymore."

She shook her head. "No way, Miss Lela, I *love* your hair. For some reason, my hair doesn't like to grow very fast and I envy people with long hair."

Cherish nodded. "I cut my hair really short about two-hundred years ago, and she cried for days. It's embarrassing how emotional she gets about hair."

I bit my lip and looked at the floor, unsure of what to do. I really wanted to cut it off, but I also remembered how much I'd hated it when I'd had short hair six years ago.

"What if I compromised and just cut off half of it? It would still be pretty long, about to the middle of my back," I said to Melody.

She pouted then dug in one of her bags and pulled out a pair of scissors.

"Fine. I guess I can make that compromise. But, you have to let me do it. I don't trust you. You might try to be sneaky and cut off more."

I nodded then pulled a chair next to the sink. I winced as she attempted to comb out more of the tangles, but I didn't complain because it would have been worse if it had been dry. I listened to the rhythmic cutting sounds of the scissors and felt as hair felt lighter and lighter with each snip. After she had finished, I started to get up from the seat, but she pushed me back down.

"Not so fast, missy, I still need to style it."

She sprayed some kind of sheen on my hair and began rubbing it through before taking a long-necked comb and parted my hair to the side. She fluffed it up over and over again, circled me to see every angle, and then sprayed more sheen.

"There, all done!" she said, obviously proud of her work. I got up from the chair and walked over to the mirror to see what magic she had performed. I had to admit that I was very impressed with her work. She had managed to turn my mop-of a mess into a style almost fit for a red carpet debut.

"Thanks, Melody. I love it," I said.

"Now the next order of business is getting you some new clothes. Sweat pants, really? Those are for sad single girls who sit around their house eating Rocky Road while watching *Gossip Girl* re-runs. Don't even get me started on that tacky souvenir t-shirt. You, my friend, are neither sad nor single, and you need to start dressing like it."

"I don't always dress like this. I was in a pinch," I said, defending myself. I didn't exactly have a fancy sense of style, but I didn't normally wear what I currently had on.

After everyone was finished getting dressed, Melody insisted that I borrow a few things of hers since she refused to leave the house with me in what I was wearing.

It was busy in the lobby since everyone was getting the continental breakfast, which smelled very good. Melody and I decided that we couldn't leave without at least grabbing a sausage and pancake to go. We ate them as Cherish tried to hail us a cab.

"So tell me, Lela, as a Miami native, you must know where all the best shopping places are," Melody said. "Where should we go?"

"I used to like going to the Dolphin Mall. Their stores have designer brands for lower prices, and it has a very laid back environment."

Melody raised an eyebrow, and I laughed.

"I sounded like an advertisement, didn't I?"

"Just a little bit," she said. "A darn good one, though. You have me sold."

A cab eventually stopped and we got in and I told the driver where to go.

It was so nice to be able to relax for once. All of my loved ones were accounted for, and for the first time, I wasn't worried. I had nearly forgotten what it felt like to actually live. Even with the threat of Lucian looming over us, I wasn't as afraid as I used to be. I was on the side of the people who had more backup than the enemy, and that was a good feeling.

Once we arrived at the mall, Melody went crazy and went into almost every single store, even the pharmacy. Cherish and I just watched in awe as she kept buying more and more things. I didn't want to buy that much and was content with three pairs of pants, four shirts, underwear, several socks, and two pairs of shoes.

I thought that after four hours Melody would be sick of the mall, but when we passed a Victoria's Secret, she begged us to go in with her. While she looked at the sweats and sweatshirts, I found myself in the lingerie section. I took random items off the racks and laughed at how revealing they were. I felt so immature doing it, but I couldn't help it since I had been raised with a negative view of that type of clothing.

When I was old enough to actually buy things from Victoria's Secret, Mark had strictly forbidden me from shopping there. He'd said that it was a sexist store that gave women the wrong idea about their bodies and men a place to develop lustful fantasies. He'd probably had a point, but I didn't see the harm in just buying something from there.

My thoughts were interrupted when Melody came up behind me and joined me in my browsing.

"Oh, Lela, you should get something."

"Why? I can't protect my family in a g-string."

Melody rolled her eyes at my sarcasm. "I'm not talking about that. I'm talking about for *Gallard*."

I immediately began to protest. I could see where this conversation was going, and I didn't like it. I started pleading and said, "No! No way, I'm not getting anything like this."

"Yes, you are. And I'm going to pick it out."

She started looking through all of the nightgowns and slips. I held my breath as she came across some that were pretty risqué and hoped that she wouldn't pick anything too revealing. I didn't plan on ever wearing it, but wanted her to enjoy the excitement of me actually using it.

"I found the perfect one," she said, pulling a navy satin slip with pink trim. It came with matching underwear. I gulped as I saw the six inch slit up the left leg. At least it wasn't see-through and didn't have a plunging neckline.

"Now go try it on," she continued. "From the look of you, you're a small right?"

"Try a medium. I'm five-eight, a small would barely come past my butt."

"Then small is perfect," she shoved the slip into my hand and pushed me towards the fitting room. I reluctantly went in and quickly undressed so I could get it over with.

I had been correct; the slip was barely long enough, and I felt completely self-conscious. I had worn swimsuits more appropriate than that slip. I didn't even want to imagine having Gallard seeing me in it. He had seen me in a two-piece several times when I went swimming in the pool at our apartment, but this was different. I would be wearing it *for* him. I started to take it off, but Cherish came in before I had the chance.

"You know, you don't have to do everything Mel tells you. She can be forceful at times, but she needs to be put in her place once in a while. Don't worry about hurting her feelings, she's tough."

"It's okay, Cherish. I don't mind. I'm actually having fun. I haven't been able to hang out with females in a very long time. Not ones that weren't trying to kill me anyway. I had Lydian, but we were so busy working and trying to lay low that we never actually did fun stuff together."

Cherish smiled then admired the slip I was wearing.

"Mel is right, though, Gallard is going love that on you. Trust me."

I raised an eyebrow. "And your confidence is based on what?"

She looked away. "We shared a lot of personal stuff when we were friends. It came up. He's a sucker for women in blue. Then again, he wasn't really dating anyone at the time. He was more of a...um..."

"I get it." I pressed my lips together. "He hooked up a lot?"

"Not...*a lot*. In his standards, I mean. He's a pretty old guy. Not as old as me, but old enough to have had his share of a few indiscretions. Don't worry, he wasn't like a man whore or anything."

I laughed and Cherish seemed confused. That was exactly what David had called him when the three of us first met. That memory had probably saved the moment from getting too awkward.

"Well, I guess I could trust that you're being honest about what he said. I'm sure he'd like it, but that's too bad, because he's not going to see it."

I took off the slip and started putting my clothes back on.

"Uh...why not?" she asked.

"Because this is not the best time for this. My family might be in danger, I'm still adjusting to missing a year of my life, and I have to decide what to do in regards to my aunt who doesn't know about vampires."

She chuckled. "Okay. Let's pretend that you aren't having these problems. If you weren't, would you be more up for it, or is there another reason?"

I hesitated before answering. I didn't really know her that well, aside from something about her that was vaguely familiar, so talking about this was strange. I usually only opened up about my worries with Gallard and because this one involved him, I didn't really want to. I decided to be honest and maybe grow closer to Cherish by opening up to her.

"We just started a relationship. It's too soon for sexy lingerie."

I finished dressing then started to leave the fitting room when she moved and blocked the entrance.

"Just hear me out for second. I know that you're in love with him. I could see that when you protected him last night and just by how you look at him. Considering the situation we're in, there's a chance that some of us aren't going to make it out alive. Not many who have crossed my father lived to tell about it. So with that said, you should live as though you might not have tomorrow. Buy this slip and try to make the most of the time that you have with your man."

    I had to admit that it was a convincing speech. I had spent the last five and a half years of my life worrying about the future and had forgotten what it was like to live in the moment. With that in mind, I bought the slip, and Melody seemed more excited about it than me.

Chapter Fifteen

When we finished shopping, Melody forced me to wear one of the new outfits I had purchased then we headed to the hospital. I wanted to check in on Evelyn and prepare everything for her to be transferred. Curtis agreed to be at the hospital for when she would be flown in, so that gave me peace of mind.

I spoke with the doctor who treated Evelyn, and they gave me some paperwork to fill out. Technically Aaron was supposed to be in charge of it, but that wasn't possible. It was a good thing that Evelyn wasn't in a coma or else she wouldn't have been able to give them consent for me to make these arrangements.

Once that was taken care of, I turned in the papers then went to visit her. They'd moved her out of recovery and she was now in one of the shared rooms. Solomon had made sure that she wasn't placed with someone who was weird or too talkative. Her roommate was a sweet older woman who had just had heart surgery.

Melody and Cherish waited outside so Evelyn and I could speak alone. I pushed the privacy curtain aside and started to speak to Evelyn when I noticed someone else was in the room. We made eye contact, and I immediately was flooded with rage. It was Simeon Atherton.

"Well, well," he said. "Look who is back from the dead."

"What are you doing here, Simeon?" I asked, keeping my voice down. I was very tempted to start screaming at him, considering out last encounter.

"I came to check on your aunt. I've known her since she was fifteen. Just like I've known you."

I laughed. "You say that like we're old friends. Tell me, did she invite you here?"

My gaze slid over to Evelyn, and I could see the discomfort in her eyes. She didn't want him there anymore than I did. Her grip was on her pencil and pad was firm. I hoped he hadn't been harassing her the entire time I was gone. He hadn't bothered to come around when my parents died, and he could stay away even longer for all I cared.

"I don't need an invitation," Simeon said. "I'm a friend of the family. But I don't think my presence should be the topic of discussion. How is it that you are here?"

I dragged Simeon into the hall. I didn't want to have this discussion in front of my aunt. She had enough to be upset about.

"I was in witness protection. That required making everyone close to me believe I was dead."

"And now you're back. Why?"

"Because my family needs me. Now if you don't mind, I must ask you to leave."

Now it was his turn to laugh. It sent chills through me, just like when Matthew would laugh. The two men had similar tendencies, and I didn't want to test Simeon's temper. I knew what he was capable of.

"Did that man of yours know where you were? If he did, he did a damn good job of pretending to miss you. I was so sure he cried real tears when he was at your funeral."

My nostrils flared, and the urge to hit him became almost overwhelming. I wanted nothing more than to pound on him like I did Andre. But I couldn't do that. Simeon was human, and it would be immoral to fight him when he had zero chance of winning. No matter how much of a scumbag he was.

"You're such an asshole," I said. "How did you even know I had a funeral?"

"Your brother told Sharon and Sharon told me. I showed up to

THE RESURRECTION

pay my condolences but…it seemed private. Plus, I couldn't risk getting seen by your man." He cocked his head to the side. "Tell me. What does he have that I don't? You had your chance to be with me. You would have been begging me for—"

Unable to control my anger any longer, I rushed up to him and shoved him against the wall. I wanted him to be afraid of me the way I had been afraid of him.

"You say another word and I will make you wish you'd never walked into my room that night. My aunt doesn't want you here, I don't want you here, and that is a damn good reason for you to crawl back into whatever maggot hole you came out of."

He chuckled. "You're so rough. Does your man like it this way?"

I punched him in the stomach, and he groaned, doubling over. I hadn't hit him as hard as I was capable, but I was sure I'd knocked the air out of his lungs.

"Is there a problem here?" Cherish asked.

"Not at all." I slowly let go of Simeon and stepped away. "Simeon was just leaving."

"Do I need to act as an escort?"

"No need," Simeon said while shooting her a smile. "I was just about to leave." He leaned close to my ear and whispered. "This isn't over."

Once he'd left, Cherish visibly relaxed. I was pretty sure she was ready to throw down with him if I asked.

"Who's the creep?" she asked.

"Family friend. Not someone you want to get mixed up with."

She looked off in the direction he'd gone. "Is he immortal?"

"No. Why?"

"I don't know. I got a whiff of him as he walked by. He smelled odd. Maybe I'm just hungry."

After I calmed down a bit, I went back into the room and sat in the chair next to Evelyn and tangled my fingers in my hair while resting my forehead on the bed. I hoped that he would wait a while to carry out whatever his threat was about. I didn't have time to deal with him and Lucian at the same time. I had a twisted wish that they would somehow team up so I could take them down both at once. Save me some dirty work.

I felt a hand reach over and take mine so I looked up and smiled at Evelyn. She used her free one to write on the pad and showed it to me.

Thank you for getting rid of him. It's hard to protest when you can't speak.

"I would do anything for you, aunt Evie. You know that right?"

She nodded then wrote once more.

Solomon told me about what he did...what he tried to do. Why didn't you tell your dad?

My eyes glistened with tears, and I squeezed her hand. "There was so much going on. Even when I came back, I didn't feel like I needed to. He was under the impression that Simeon had skipped town."

She scribbled a bit. *He came back because he wants Robin. Your dad put in his will that if anything were to happen to me, Simeon would get custody. He showed me two days ago.*

Anger pulsed through me once more. "That isn't going to happen. You'll be fine. Curtis is going to take care of you while I deal with this threat against our family. Once it's over, Robin will be in our care. Besides, if he has statutory rape on his rap sheet, there's no way he could get custody." I kissed her hand then stood up and kissed her forehead. "He won't get her. I swear that to you."

Evelyn needed rest, so I said goodbye and left her room. Cherish and Melody were waiting for me down the hall and the three of us headed back to the house. Solomon had texted Melody and said they had come up with a plan. I was anxious and eager at the same time. The sooner we could end this thing with Lucian, the better. Besides, I didn't want to be cooped up in the hotel anymore.

The group gathered in the living room and Solomon filled us in.

"We searched the hotel, but it appears we missed Lucian by a few hours. Where he's headed now is a mystery. Your brother suggested that we use your parents' timeshare up in Manhattan. We can stay there until Lucian is ready for a confrontation. We should be as far away from familiarity as possible. There's too much history here involving your family."

"It's to the Big Apple then? I have no problem with that. It will be nice to be somewhere different for a change."

"We haven't figured out how long we'll stay there since Aaron is still inquiring on the timeshare information, but I'm guessing it might be for a week or so."

We left that night as soon as the sun went down. All the guys but Kevin rode in my parents' car while the rest of us rode in the BMW. We stopped by the hotel so that Melody, Cherish, and I could retrieve the items that we'd left. I brought a suitcase from the house. That way I wouldn't have to haul everything in the shopping bags. I felt like luggage would just slow me down, but I didn't want to be stuck having to wear the same clothes all week long.

Heading north on interstate ninety-five, we began our long road trip. My group had traded Melody for Kevin since Solomon wanted the strength ratio to be equal. I rode in the passenger seat while Cherish was the one to drive. We left around eight-o'clock and planned to drive until three a.m. At that time, we would book a motel so that the night-walkers would have plenty of time to get out of the sun.

I turned on the radio so that it wasn't so quiet. Robin had fallen asleep again, and Kevin was listening to his iPod. I decided to talk with Cherish so that neither of us would be tempted to fall asleep.

"Have you ever been to New York?" I asked her.

"I lived there about thirty years ago. I originally went because there was an AC/DC concert in Madison Square Garden, and after that I fell in love with the city."

"*You* like AC/DC too? Gallard loves that band, I don't understand the appeal, though."

"As a matter of fact, Gallard and I met at that exact concert. It was eighty-three…wow. Feels like forever ago."

"What was he like back then?"

Cherish smiled before replying.

"He wasn't the nice, charming guy that he is now. In fact, he was a complete jerk. He put everyone around him in a horrible mood, and was not a fun person to be around. I just happened to see him feeding on some drunken girl, and I pointed out how sloppy he was being. He told me to go screw myself, only in a more colorful way. I called him a nasty name then I walked off and forgot all about the encounter.

"I was actually surprised when I ran into him again, only that time it was in a bar about a block away from the concert. I was having a few drinks by myself when I spotted him at a table playing cards with some shady people. I was feeling bold from the alcohol buzz and decided to walk over and see what game they were in the middle of. It was obvious that he was losing but he kept betting more and more money.

"Eventually, he lost and by his reaction, I guessed that it was a lot. He promised the guy he would pay him back as soon as he could, and then he walked off. I waited until he left the bar before I did something spontaneous. I wrote a check to pay off his debt. I didn't know why at the time. Maybe it was a subconscious need to help him since he'd been chosen against his will to drink my father's blood.

"The next day, I got a knock on my door, and when I opened it, he just walked into my apartment and started yelling at me about how I had no right to get involved in his problems, that he didn't want my money or my pity, blah, blah, blah; the usual guy stuff. I asked him how he found me, and he explained that the guy from the game gave him my address from the check I wrote. I then retaliated by yelling at *him* asking where he came off barging into my apartment and telling me off when he was obviously the one with the problem. He yelled something in French before walking out the door.

"I didn't see him for two weeks after that. I actually almost forgot about the whole thing until he knocked on my door at three in the morning. I got up to let him in, and when I did, he just walked in and sat on my couch like he lived there or something. He sat there for about five minutes before saying, 'You were right, I have a problem.'

"After that, we spent a lot of time together, and I made it my mission to slowly rehabilitate him from his addiction to gambling and break through the wall he had created around himself. It wasn't until we'd been hanging out regularly for two months before I actually saw him smile.

"Unfortunately, something came up. I was informed by an old friend that Samil was back in the states after nearly two-hundred years and that he was continuing his search for the blood. I had to leave town as soon as possible, and hired some people to pack up my apartment and send them to storage for me to pick up later. I didn't have time to say goodbye to him. All I could do was leave him a note encouraging him to continue on his road to recovery and to start living his life to the fullest; to fill his days with more joy than with anger, and to do what makes him happy."

When she was finished with her story, I noticed that she was a bit emotional. Her reminisce was visibly upsetting her, and I wondered if she'd cared about him more than just a friend. I wasn't sure if I wanted to know the answer, but I had to ask anyway.

"Were you in love with him?"

She smiled, but shook her head. "I've been in love once, and it didn't end well. I don't do relationships anymore."

It amazed me how alike we were. I'd said the same thing after what happened with Tyler, but Gallard managed to change my mind. I'd fought my attraction to him for so long until I couldn't deny it anymore. I was glad I gave love a second chance because I couldn't imagine being happier than I was with him.

"What happened?" I asked, feeling bold to ask such a personal question.

"I would rather not talk about it. I'm not into the whole share my feelings thing."

I could sense that her mood was changing. She wasn't as cheerful as before and her expression had hardened a little. Whatever place she had gone to in that moment, it couldn't have been pleasant. She had demons in her past. I knew because I did as well.

The rest of the drive was spent in silence with the exception of the radio. I even slept for about a half an hour and woke up as soon as the car came to a stop. I opened my eyes and found that we had pulled into the parking lot of a Motel 6. I rubbed my eyes and stretched before getting out of the car.

When I turned around I saw that Kevin was carrying the still-sleeping Robin.

"I can't believe she's still asleep, even after her nap this afternoon," he said.

"She's probably exhausted from the trauma she experienced, poor thing," I said, lightly stroking her hair. "Do you know where we are? I took a short nap before we got here."

"Solomon said we're in Summerville, South Carolina. You can

tell we're not in Florida anymore. No more palm trees. The weather is cooler too."

I watched Solomon go into the main office. He glanced over at Cherish for a second then quickly looked away. Whatever he'd felt for Cherish in the past, he obviously hadn't gotten over it. And she was ignoring him. I understood why she was mad at him, though Solomon hadn't let her die on purpose. If anything, she probably felt let down. He was supposed to protect her and he failed. I'd felt the same way when Lydian went behind my back and handed me over to Samil.

Kevin and Aaron were talking while Melody conversed with Jordan. They didn't look like they were flirting, but I was glad that Jordan was able to smile. I hadn't had much time to talk to him about what he was going through. We'd been thrust into chaos almost as soon as we'd arrived in Florida, and I wanted to ask how he was doing. He was right about being a good actor. He was either fine or excelling at appearing like he was.

Kevin set Robin down and she took Gallard's hand, leading him over to me. Her steps were slow and a bit sluggish from her drowsiness. Gallard must have noticed too because he lifted her up and she rested her head on his shoulder, falling asleep almost instantly.

"Have a nice drive?" he asked.

"For the most part, yes. Cherish told me all about your fun time in New York."

He raised an eyebrow. "Oh, really?"

"She said that you were a sourpuss and a jerk. Kind of hard to believe from the Gallard I know."

He laughed. "Well, she wasn't wrong there. She was being kind when she said that I was jerk. That was a major understatement. I was horrible to her. I'm surprised she stuck around as long as she did."

Solomon came back out at that moment and handed Gallard, Aaron, and Melody a key.

"We have three rooms, it doesn't matter who stays in which one, but I must warn you that all of them only have one bed. It was the best I could do at such an hour."

"One bed? That's a hook up waiting to happen," Cherish said.

"That's all right," Melody said, frowning at her sister. "Only four of us need to sleep anyway."

"Where should we put Robin?" Kevin asked.

"She can be with me," I said. I hadn't seen her in a while, and I would rest more comfortably if she remained in my sight.

"I'll carry her. You look exhausted," Gallard said to me.

I grabbed my luggage from the trunk and following him to the room. I sat my suitcase inside the closet near the bathroom and Gallard tucked Robin into the bed.

"You're really great with her, you know," I said in a soft voice. I didn't want to wake Robin.

"I'll admit she did grow on me. She's like a mini version of you." He took my hand and smiled. "She delivered your message, by the way. She said you loved me and that I shouldn't be sad."

"She did? I almost forgot I asked her to tell you that. She has a good memory."

My visit with Evelyn came to mind. Gallard would want to know about Simeon's visit, and I knew he would share in my disgust over the matter.

"I ran into Simeon today," I said. "He was at the hospital."

"You're kidding me? Solomon told me he stopped by and had dinner with them a few days ago. I didn't think he'd stay in town. What did the bastard want?"

"He was threatening to take Robin away. Then he made awful comments about you and me and…I lost it. I hit the guy and I don't regret it."

"Good! He deserves it. I'm surprised he isn't in jail. Men like that aren't one-time offenders."

Wanting to change the subject, I thought back to the conversation that I'd had with Cherish. I wondered if she'd opened up to Gallard about her reasoning behind not being in relationships, so I decided to ask him.

"When I talked with Cherish earlier, I kind of got the impression that something happened to her that turned her off of relationships. Do you know what it was?"

He didn't answer right away. He seemed undecided about what he wanted to tell me, and I suddenly regretted it. Secrets between friends weren't something to be revealed lightly, especially to someone who hadn't known one of the friends for long. I was surprised when he finally spoke.

"Don't tell her I told you because she would kill me, literally. When she was fifteen, she had an affair with an older man. He got her pregnant and promised to marry her, but instead he cut off all contact. Being the stubborn woman she is, she found the guy and learned he was already married. When she left, she was hit in the street by…a vehicle. I hadn't known who she was at the time, so I assume she meant a horse and carriage. Anyway, she lost the baby."

Gallard's story about Cherish made me want to cry. I felt bad about thinking that she had just been hung up on him, and the explanation had made her reaction to the engagement much more understandable.

"That's awful. I couldn't imagine going through something like that. The manipulation and betrayal, the loss. People can be so cruel."

Gallard put is arms around me and rested his chin on my head.

"I love you, Lela. And I can promise you now that I would never, *ever* hurt you like that."

"I believe you." As I leaned against him, I felt myself hit my breaking point in exhaustion and nearly fell asleep standing up. "I better go to bed before I pass out on the floor. Goodnight, Gallard."

"Goodnight." He lightly kissed my lips. "I'll just be outside the door if you need me."

I then walked over to the bed and took off my shoes before slowly getting under the covers as not to awaken Robin. She was breathing pretty hard, but she wasn't snoring. I was just glad that she wasn't tossing and turning from nightmares. I, on the other hand, was hoping that I wouldn't have any of my own.

Chapter Sixteen

Taking a drag of her cigarette, Cherish let it burn in her lungs for a bit before blowing it out. Talking with Lela about her past hadn't been easy and even though she was tempted to be completely honest, she didn't have the courage. She didn't want the woman's pity. She was there for one reason alone; help them stop her father. She wasn't there to make friends or bond with anyone. Especially not a woman who was a reminder of everything she could have been; everything she could have had.

Her issues had begun long before she was put in that coffin. She couldn't put her finger on the exact moment she became screwed up for life. Had it been when she realized her parents were blood-drinking monsters? Or when her own father took her out at night to watch him feed as a way to train her for the future? Or was it when he ignored her for months after losing her child? Then again, maybe it was the night she'd fought for her life and watched her sister be murdered while she could do nothing.

Therapy was pointless. Talking with Melody didn't help either. It seemed that opening up about her problems only led to more and more bitterness. So she did everything she could to stay numb. Drugs; alcohol; sex. Every now and then she would alternate when one would lose its effect. Years of self-destructing had all culminated to this. Her father was back, and she would finally have to face her past.

"Since when do you smoke?" she heard someone say. She turned to see Solomon standing on the deck behind her. She took another drag then blew it out right away.

"Don't pretend you know me, Solomon. I'm not the little girl you used to sneak candy to."

"And I am not the man who used to sneak candy to you."

Whatever he'd meant by that, she didn't care. She wasn't interested in anything he had to say. Melody may have forgiven him and was already back to calling him Uncle Solomon. Not her. Cherish hadn't forgotten the night she was murdered. The scream from her sister that woke her as the intruder came into their room. The ten long minutes she'd fought with the man, using a sword that was too heavy for her. The helplessness she felt as she watched a man slit her sister's throat and then the agony of choking on her own blood when another did the same to her.

It didn't matter how loud she screamed. No one came. She was alone. Once she'd accepted that she would always be alone, it became easier to keep going. To get from one century to another.

"I don't want an apology." She dropped the cigarette and put it out with the tip of her shoe. "Just kill my father so we can finally start living again."

"Do you really call what you are doing *living*?"

She whipped her head in his direction. "What has Melody been telling you?"

"Nothing. She only said that she is worried about you. She has been ever since you were a tiny girl. Cherish. you have witnessed things that no child ever should while growing up in that house. It's damaged you. I can see it in your eyes."

Her gaze returned to the darkness ahead of her. He had one thing right; she had seen things that she would have loved to unsee. Particularly when she was seven.

THE RESURRECTION

It was the middle of the night and she had woken up feeling feverish and her stomach hurt. She got out of bed and went to look for her father who always knew how to make her feel better. He wasn't in his room, so she went down the long staircase to find him somewhere in the house. She heard a familiar voice in the sitting room and went there first.

"Momma?" she'd said quietly. She stepped further into the room then froze. Her mother was on the floor and a man was on top of her. Both of them were naked and her mother was moaning. She was worried that the man was hurting her so she'd yelled, "Stop! Leave her alone!"

"Cherish?" Her mother looked at her but instead of having a grateful expression, she looked angry. "Your mother is busy. Go back to bed!"

"But he's hurting you!"

The man groaned. "Can you get rid of the brat?"

"I am working on it." Her mother looked at her again. "I won't tell you again; go back to bed!"

"But momma..."

"Go!"

Her lip began to quiver but then her stomach pain worsened. Her body convulsed as she threw up. She had forgotten why she had gotten up in the first place, and now she was feeling a little better.

"For God's sake!" Her mother had said. "Philippa!" She pushed the man off of her then wrapped herself in a robe. Philippa came into the room with a candle, and when she saw what had happened, she immediately got a rag and began cleaning it up. Cherish remained in the corner, crying and trying not to throw up again. Philippa then took her to the kitchen. She hadn't gotten any vomit on her nightgown, so she just had to wash her face.

The front door opened and she heard familiar footsteps. Her father was finally home. Her mood instantly lightened and before Philippa could stop her, she hopped down from the counter and ran back to the sitting room. She knew he would sing to her so she could go back to sleep. He always did if she asked. She stopped in the doorway, but the smile left her face when he started yelling.

"You disgusting whore! I told you never to bring them here!"

"What does it matter? You were out; the children were asleep. Klaus would have been gone before you even noticed he was here."

"And yet here I am, catching you whoring around with him in my house! We had an agreement, Florence!"

The man, who was now clothed stepped forward. "You need to calm yourself."

"Calm myself?" Her father's hair darkened until it turned black. "I will calm myself when I am bathed in your blood!"

In one swift move, he grabbed a sword from the wall, did a clean swing in a three-sixty angle, and the man sank to the floor in two pieces. Cherish couldn't stifle the scream that erupted from her lips. Her father turned around, his face covered in thick blood, and he dropped the sword. Afraid for her life, she ran up the stairs to her room and closed the door, shoving her chair under it. Melody had taught her that trick long ago. She'd never used it until then.

"Cherish!" her father shouted through the door. "Please, darling, let me in!"

"Please don't hurt me papa!"

"I would never hurt you! You are my Cherish and I love you!"

She sat with her back against the door and cried throughout the night. It wasn't until the morning that she had the courage to come out. Her father was just outside, leaning against the opposite wall. He was clean and he had changed his clothing. Her love for him was what kept her from shunning him forever. If only she had known his burst of rage was only the beginning.

The memory of that night still made her skin crawl. Oh, she had done worse than that. She wasn't oblivious to the fact that she had become just as much of a whore as her mother was. It was inevitable. She had betrayed her father's orders to get involved with men as a way to spite him. She would do whoever she wanted and he couldn't do a thing about it. Not while he was cold in his coffin.

"I believe things will turn around once he's gone for good," she said. "I'll even kill him myself this time around."

"Do you really mean that? He's your father."

"By blood, maybe. I don't have an ounce of affection for the man. Not anymore."

Giving in, she took out another cigarette and lit it up. Solomon brushed her cheek with the back of his hand and she pushed it away.

"Unless you're going to screw me, don't touch me."

His eyes widened in shock. "What?"

"Please. I know, Solomon. I know how you felt about me back then. You wanted me so badly, but you held back because you're a clergyman." She removed the cigarette from her lips then moved so she was standing three inches away from his face. "This is your last chance, Solomon. After all these years, you can finally have a taste of me. Enough to keep you satisfied, but not too much that you'll keep crawling back to me. Once this is all finished, I'm leaving and you won't see me again. It's your choice."

"Oh, *Accarezzare*." His eyes glistened with tears. "I pray that God gives your soul some peace. For only he can ease your suffering."

He walked away from her, and she was left feeling baffled. This was the first time in a while that a man had rejected her advances, or at least an offer. Mostly, she was the one doing the rejecting. He would be a tough one to crack. It didn't matter, though. What she truly wanted was to disappoint him like he had her. How she would do that, she didn't know.

Maximus glanced around the bar as he stood in the entrance. This was the last place he wanted to be and yet, he had no other choice. The pull had called him here, and it was too strong to ignore. Unfortunately, he didn't have a precise location for his target. He was forced to follow the trail of bodies and threaten the occasional immortal with violence. Didn't matter how long the vile creatures had been in existence. They still disgusted him to this very day.

His legacy had been passed down throughout their species for two thousand years. None of what they believed was accurate. Now and then, he would hear something incredibly drastic, but nothing surprised him anymore. Some believed he was the devil incarnate. Others thought he was the angel of death. None would believe that he had once been a student under the Apostle Paul.

Maximus had devoted his entire existence to reversing the deal he had made with Lucifer. He went against everything he believed and did things he never would have done in his previous life. Back when he was a holy man who could raise the dead.

The biggest struggle was keeping the voice at bay. The power he had obtained from Lucifer came with the unfortunate side effect of giving the devil a direct line to his mind. Unlike others who were tempted, he could hear Lucifer's voice as if he were standing next to him. Over two millennium and Maximus was tired.

That was why he was here now. If he could destroy Lucian, he would finally win his soul back. He could die an honorable death and be allowed into heaven.

He didn't have to follow up with his appointment one to know that Lucian had been resurrected. The moment it had happened, Maximus felt the overwhelming pull all the way from London. He had followed the two vessels, Gallard and Lydian, in hopes they would lead him right to Lucian. His appointed one learned of his presence and had the audacity to tell Maximus to back off. He was done letting someone else do the work. Maximus would end Lucian for good, and he would do it on his own terms.

The bar didn't have the usual vibe that Maximus was accustomed to. He expected to feel dirty or to see whorish women with men acting like pigs. Instead, he saw people laughing and doing innocent things like playing pool or watching a sports game on the television.

"Sir?" The goateed Scot said once again. Maximus had been let in by him. He was an old friend of Gallard's. He had followed the man there the same night Lucian had recruited his army.

"I apologize," Maximus said. "What did you say?"

"I was letting you know that we have a new policy. We've had issues with people trying to join under false pretenses. Any new members have to speak directly to my boss." Terrence looked towards the counter. "And here's the man you're looking for."

"Thank you for your help."

Maximus offered his hand and Terrence shook. Maximus hadn't touched the man until then, but he was pleasantly surprised that he wasn't flooded with memories of murder, death, and mayhem. Terrence was a model citizen. He fought in three American wars, spent several years traveling the country to find homeless veterans to care for, and had since been working for Gallard.

Terrence went back to guarding the door and Maximus sat

THE RESURRECTION

down on one of the stools, unwrapping his scarf. He never knew which type of weather to dress for since he changed locations more often than his undergarments. Sometimes, he would even be in animal form to make his life easier.

A tall, Native American man approached the counter. He was giving him a scrutinizing gaze. It was probably the eyes; Maximus' lime eyes often frightened others because of their tendency to glow. He could control that most of the time.

"You're not immortal," the man said. He looked over at the door. "Hey, T!" He spread his arms out. "What the hell? You call this upping security?"

"Get off my back, B!" Terrence laughed. "I figured we could use some excitement around here."

The man, B, shook his head and chuckled. "You're killing me, T." He sobered then returned his attention back to Maximus. "You're brave walking into a vampire bar. What's your story?"

"I come looking for a character you may have encountered. Goes by the name Lucian Christophe."

The smile left B's face and he rested his hands on the counter.

"Just tell me one thing; friend or foe?"

"Any foe of Lucian is a friend of mine."

"Good answer." B held his hand out. "Bodoway. My boy Gallard has beef with Lucian."

Maximus took his hand and the instant they touched, both men looked each other in the eye. In all his years, Maximus had never met a man with Bodoway's gifts. They were complete opposites. Maximus could see people's pasts while Bodoway saw their future.

"Who are you?" Bodoway asked.

"I'm just a man who made poor decisions in his youth. I only wish to undo them. Starting with ending Lucian Christophe and sending him to the depths of hell where he belongs."

Bodoway raised an eyebrow. "Wow. Sounds like you hate him more than Gal. I assume you want to know what happened when Mr. Christophe was here yesterday?"

Maximus gave a half smile. "Like you read my mind."

"He tried to trick me into giving away information on Gallard. He failed, but not before I saw a glimpse into his future."

"Did you see his death? If that is all the information you can give me, I would be indebted to you immensely."

Bodoway shrugged. "Sorry, man. I did not see his death. Not that far anyway. I'm afraid what I saw is personal."

Maximus frowned. "Personal?"

"It involved people I care about. For their sake, I have to keep it private."

This was not what he wanted to hear. Most of the time, Maximus prided himself on being civil. Concerning Lucian, he decided all bets were off.

He used his power to make Bodoway immobile. Bodoway realized what was happening and tried to move and failed. He couldn't speak or call out either. To ensure his safety, Maximus put a glamour over the two of them so the rest of the bar would only see two men talking.

"I apologize that it had to come to this," Maximus said. "But my patience has run out. You will tell me what you saw and you will not leave anything out."

"You will have to force it out of me."

Maximus' eyes turned black. He rarely lost his temper, but now was an exception.

"Tell me or I will pry into your mind and turn it to mush."

"Do it." Bodoway smirked. "I. Dare. You."

Maximus opened his mind and started searching through Bodoway's memories. He didn't need to go too far back since he'd only spoken with Lucian twenty-four hours ago.

Then he found it. The information that Bodoway had so desperately wanted to keep private. The man; a blonde man. It didn't make any sense. Why had he been so adamant about not sharing.

A pain shot through Maximus' cranium and he nearly cried out. The image changed, and he realized his and Bodoway's visions were meshing. What Maximus saw was more terrifying than anything he'd ever seen in his life. He let go of Bodoway, dropping the glamour, and backed away.

"What did you do to me?" he asked.

"Who's in that head of yours?"

"I won't ask you again; what did you do?"

THE RESURRECTION

"Two can play this game," Bodoway said. "You accessed private thoughts, so I invaded yours. I showed you your future. Or someone's future. It may be you or whoever is lurking in your brain."

Maximus trembled. "Who is he? The man?"

"That is unclear." Bodoway folded his arms once more, showing no fear whatsoever. "All I know is that Lela must be safe. You swear to me no harm will come to her?"

"What does she have to do with this?"

"I don't know that either. I just have this feeling. Gallard to." Bodoway held out his hand again. "Swear to me; mind-reader to mind-reader. Protect them at all cost."

Maximus shook his hand. He could feel that Bodoway was blocking him out this time and was doing a damn good job of it.

"You have my word."

"Gallard told me they were heading north. I assume Lucian won't be too far behind."

Maximus thanked him then left the bar. Terrence didn't look as welcoming as he had before. Not that it mattered. Maximus had the information he needed.

Did you hear that, Lucifer? Your future isn't looking too bright.

Your attempt at scaring me is comical. No one but the Almighty himself can be my undoing.

For the first time in centuries, Maximus let his guard down and allowed him access to his mind. He showed Lucifer what Bodoway and seen. Waiting for his reaction was making him tingle with anticipation.

It will never come to pass, Maximus.

You cannot change the future. How do you suppose you'll avoid this fate?

Watch me. You've seen me work before. Everything will work out for me.

Maximus doubted that. Lucifer may have been powerful, but he wasn't undefeatable. He'd been cast out once and it could happen again. With that in mind, Maximus was able to transport himself upstate.

Chapter Seventeen

I was the first one to get up the next day, even having slept until noon, but I didn't mind. I sat on a bench just outside of the room and ate a bag of chips. The salt helped with the cravings, and was a great distraction from how hungry I was. Unlike Melody and Cherish, I never filled up completely out of fear that I would hurt Gallard. This meant that my cravings were more frequent and I became hungry sooner.

A few of the other guests waved at me as they would leave to check out of their rooms. I even struck up a conversation with an old couple that had been celebrating their sixtieth anniversary. They told me all about how they'd met and all the kids and grandkids that they had. They were so cute that I couldn't stop talking with them.

Melody came out of her room not long after the couple left and sat next to me. She looked tired, though it was the middle of the afternoon. She must have had a hard time falling asleep. I would have too if I hadn't been so exhausted the night before. I slept like a baby and so had Robin.

"How long have you been up?" she asked. I didn't have a

phone or a watch, so I had to guess the time.

"About half an hour. I've spent too many hours cooped up in a motel room. I had to get some fresh air."

She took the bag of chips out of my hands and started eating some. She had the biggest case of the munchies that I had ever seen in a person. Almost every time I saw her, she was eating something. Food tasted good to me, but I didn't eat often since I didn't like the inconvenience of having to use the bathroom.

"Where's Gallard?" she asked as she snacked on my chips.

"He took Robin to town to get her some lunch. Why?"

She smiled as she put three more chips into her mouth. "When he gets back, you should put that slip on and attempt a seduction plot. Or better yet, leave him a note and ask him to wait for you in the shower."

I didn't answer that, and hoped that my silence wouldn't provoke anymore encouragement. Her and Cherish's constant suggestions for my love life were starting to be overwhelming.

"Um...Lela, that's when you say, 'Oh, Melody you're so brilliant!'"

"Thanks for the suggestions but I think I'll pass."

"Fine. I keep setting you up for all these opportunities and you just keep shutting them down. What's the hold up? Have you never done anything before?"

"It's not like I've done nothing! It's just that the nothing doesn't really technically count as something. So you could say I have done something but...not completely anything that would count as not being nothing."

Melody stopped chewing then looked at me with wide eyes.

"I was right, wasn't I? Lela, why didn't you say so?"

"I don't know, maybe because we were busy worrying about other things like all of us dying."

"Just answer me one thing, why? Is it because you want to wait until you're married? There is absolutely nothing wrong with that. Not everyone makes that choice, but I did."

"Wait, you're married?" I didn't know why this was so shocking to me. Maybe because she was so ancient. I'd never met an immortal who was married. I'd only assumed that she was single because I would have thought she would bring her significant other with us if she had one.

"It was a long, *long* time ago. About ten years after Cherish and I were killed. We'd parted ways because she was all bent on revenge and I only wanted to move on and be glad that we were released from our parents' authority.

"I was living in Northampton under the name Melody Clark. His name was Theodore Davis and he was a widow with a six-year-old son. We courted for a few months and then he asked me to marry him. I said yes. I loved him, and I adored his son. We were married in the fall, and I had never been happier.

"As the years passed, it became apparent to him that he was aging and I was not. His son had grown to a point where we looked the same age. When I told him my secret, he was surprisingly unafraid. He promised not to say a word and to keep my identity a secret.

"Eventually, as all mortals do, he grew old and died at the age of seventy. I stayed with him the entire time and didn't leave until he drew his last breath. I loved my Teddy, and I wouldn't give up those fifty-five years we spent together for anything."

She didn't look sad when she told her story. Talking about her husband made her eyes brighten and she came to life in a way she hadn't before. I was happy for her. It would have been heartbreaking if both sisters failed to find happiness. Cherish was ruined by her tragedy while Melody still found it in her to love.

"He was the one you were trying to have children with wasn't he?" I asked. She nodded then I asked, "Did you ever have any other relationships?"

"No. I never had the need to. Theodore was the one and I am content with the life I had with him. I don't need a man to be happy. The memories are enough."

I admired her way of thinking. Mark had said the same thing; that I didn't need a man to define me. It was one of the few important lessons that I'd learned from him. That was why he was so adamant that I pursue a higher education so I wouldn't need a man to support me. I'd taken it to heart, which was why when I lived with Gallard in Texas and Vegas I had jobs. I'd only relied on him for money up until I found a job. I didn't want him to feel like he needed to provide for me.

"To answer your question, it wasn't a choice," I said. "I was in a serious relationship but we broke up before anything happened. After that, I didn't date anyone until Gallard and we were separated after I died. We've only just now been reunited."

"Does he know?"

"Yeah, he knows. I want to be with him, but it's kind of hard to fit in time for romance when you're looking for someone who wants your family dead."

Melody had completely forgotten about the bag of chips at this point. She crossed her legs on the bench and faced my direction.

"Yeah, I can see how that would get in the way. But we're not going anywhere for a few hours. You could be spending time with him instead of sitting out here eating chips."

"That's all right. I am willing to wait for a better time. Besides, I'm too worried about Lucian showing up. At this point, I'd probably have to be drunk to relax."

"Of course!" she shouted. "Why didn't I think of it before?" She got off the bench and pulled me up as well by the arm and said, "I have to go get Cher! We are going to find us some liquor and we are going to loosen you up."

I quickly shook my head as she dragged me towards her room.

"Huh, uh; no way, I am *not* getting drunk! Can I even get drunk?"

"*We* can! We have a heartbeat and a functioning liver. We get wasted just like anybody else. The catch is that it that our livers are more resilient so it takes longer to get drunk and lasts for a shorter period of time."

She opened the door to her room and pulled me in.

Cherish was putting on a pair of shoes and was dressed equally as casual as Melody.

"Hurry and get your shoes on, baby sister, we're running an errand."

"I'd rather stay in," she said. She was still looking as depressed as she had the night before. I wondered if she was still upset about the discussion we'd had in the car. I hadn't meant to cause her to relive bad memories, and I felt bad.

"But we're going to get some alcohol. We're bored and, we want to get tanked."

"You want to get drunk? Right now?"

"Yes, right now! Lela needs our help so she can deal with her intimacy issues."

"Hey now," I said, somewhat offended. "I never said I had issues."

Cherish raised an eyebrow then got off the bed and grabbed her keys.

"I suppose we can go out. I need a drink myself, I'm feeling a bit pissy right now."

We let everyone know that we were going into town before Melody looked up the location of the closest liquor store on her phone then put the directions into the GPS. It was a nice place called George's Fine Wine, and when we went inside, I suddenly felt very un-fine, like I wasn't classy enough in my jeans and American Eagle tank top to be
there.

I hadn't the slightest idea what was considered 'good' liquor, so I let Melody do all the choosing. She chose a bottle of Silver and a bottle of strawberry flavored Smirnoff. She even bought three shot glasses for each of us to keep as souvenirs, though I wasn't sure if I was going to want to remember that whole experience.

When we got back to the motel, Melody could barely contain her excitement. We went into their room and she carelessly dumped the bottles and glasses onto the bed.

"Party time!" she said, eagerly twisting the lid off of the Silver.

"I wouldn't consider hard alcohol in a cheap motel room a party," Cherish said.

"Booo! Party pooper!" Melody said, already acting drunk before she even took a sip. She poured some tequila into one of the glasses then handed it to me.

"Bottoms up, Miss Lela!"

I put my nose to it and sniffed. I'd had tequila before and I didn't particularly care for it. But I decided that the party should only have one pooper, so I went ahead and downed it. It tasted bad, but I didn't protest when Melody refilled my glass and I downed that one as well.

After about six shots, I started to feel a bit light-headed. I looked around and the room started to spin. I could hear Melody laughing hysterically at something, but I didn't know what. Cherish turned the TV on to a music channel and cranked it up really loud, which made the whole experience even more disorienting.

I tried to pour myself another one but couldn't keep my focus enough to aim, so I just drank straight from the bottle. Melody cheered and clapped, still laughing, and I got off the bed and started dancing to the music. I didn't know why since I didn't know how to dance, but I felt out of control of what I was doing.

Cherish took a gulp of the Smirnoff before joining me, and then Melody turned the music up even louder. We danced for what felt like hours before I got dizzy and plopped down on the floor next to the wall.

"I like this! We should do this again sometime," I said.

"Seee," Melody said, slurring her words." I toold you that it was fuun!"

Cherish sat down next to me and handed me the bottle of Silver. I laughed before taking it from her and taking a drink. I then handed it back and started conversing with her.

"So what's this about your intimacy issues?" she asked.

I groaned. "I don't have issues. My only issue is that every time I want to be alone with him, there's an interruption or someone dies or *I* die. It's very annoying."

She nodded. "That would be very annoying." She took the tequila back. "I remember my first time. I was fifteen and it was at Melody's twenty-first birthday ball."

"Ugh, don't remind me," Melody said.

"Who was it?" I asked.

Cherish took another swig before answering. "I don't remember his name. I was interested in this other man; a Count. I told him I wanted to be with him, but he kept ignoring me. So to piss him off, I danced with this other man. He was tall and had a neatly trimmed beard. Long dark hair. He was actually very handsome. When no one was looking, I dragged him into one of the empty sitting rooms." She giggled. "I knew people would be looking for me, so I didn't want the inconvenience of having to undress. Back then clothes were a lot more complicated than just a zipper and a buttons. Anyway, we did it on a chair."

"Are you serious?"

"Dead serious. I mostly wanted to get it over with. I wouldn't give Byron the satisfaction of taking my virginity. So to spite him, I gave myself to a man I didn't even know. I think he might have been an Earl...I'm not sure."

I shuddered thinking about that. How could she just give herself to some guy? I had waited a year and a half of being with Tyler before considering going that far. And in a chair? I would either have to be very drunk or have lost my mind. Then again, everyone was different. Everyone viewed intimacy in different ways. Cherish was just more nonchalant about it like Lydian and Aaron.

"I don't think Gallard would allow us to...do that in that way. He seems like too much of a gentleman."

She snorted. "I don't know. That man...he sure can surprise you. We did it on the couch, on the floor, in the shower. I didn't think he had it in him."

"Cherish!" Melody shouted.

The realization of her words hit me, and I froze. My stomach turned, and I couldn't tell if it was the alcohol or Cherish's confession.

"I'm...I'm gonna be sick," I said, running to the bathroom. I got to the toilet just in time for the vomit to escape uncontrollably.

"Nice one, Cher, real nice," I heard Melody say.

The music was turned off then, but my ears were still ringing. It was almost as if the music were still playing. My head hurt so badly that I threw up again.

"What? Someone had to tell her eventually."

"But it wasn't your place. You were just being a bitch to her because you can't stand it when people are happier than you. I hate when you do that!"

"You think I'm jealous of her? Please! I'm just trying to be honest! She's a naïve little girl who's afraid of intimacy."

I came out of the bathroom at that moment. Her words cut right through me, and I didn't want to admit how much they hurt. I was a pretty tough person. It took a lot for someone to hurt my feelings. Hell, Emiline had said some pretty horrible things that got to me, but instead of crying about it, I set her on fire. Not that I would do that to Cherish. This was different. I had looked up to her. I had empathized with her because of our somewhat similar pasts and saw her as a mentor. This entire time, she thought I was a joke.

"Is that how you think of me?" I asked, feeling more sad than angry.

She shrugged. "I don't know. Do you want the truth or are you going to go cry?"

I clenched my teeth. "You know what; you're right. I am naïve. I was naïve enough to trust you after the last woman I ever got close to betrayed me as well."

Cherish chuckled. "Yeah, that was pretty stupid. What was even more stupid was believing that drink Ajala gave you was nothing more than just alcohol. Weren't you in for a big surprise? And you know what else I think? If you don't put out soon, Gallard is going to lose interest so you either need to get over your issues or let him be with someone who isn't turning him into a lap dog."

"At least I didn't seduce a married man and get pregnant!"

Cherish's eyes filled with fury, and she flew across the room towards me. I started to lunge at her too. I was ready for a fight. Hell, I was itching for one. Unfortunately for me, Melody stepped in and stopped Cherish before she had a chance to take a swing at me.

"Back off, Cherish!" Melody said. "You're crossing a line. You have no right to treat her that way!"

"Why? Am I not entitled to express my opinion once in a while?"

"*Entitled*? Listen to yourself, Cher! You're starting to sound like our father."

Cherish pushed an angry breath out of her nose then grabbed the keys and opened the door, slamming it afterwards. I hoped that she wouldn't do something stupid like get caught driving drunk or totaling the car. I would hate for her to get hurt even if I was pissed at her.

When I was sure that I was done vomiting, I went back into the bathroom and rinsed my mouth out. Melody had been right about the buzz not lasting very long. I could already feel the effects of the alcohol wearing off.

I came out of the bathroom and saw Melody crying on the bed. I sat next to her and sighed.

"This is my fault," Melody said. "I shouldn't have encouraged her to drink. What happened just now; that's why there's always a big gap in between our reunions. She gets mad about something stupid then she storms off and you don't see her for a decade or two."

"Is it because of what happened, her losing the baby?"

"That among other things. Our father really messed her up. He raised her with some sick plan of having her be his killing partner or something. He would purposefully get her angry and encouraged her to let out her rage. When she was just a baby, he would take away her toys just to see her cry and would only give them back if she threw a big enough fit to satisfy him.

"When she was about twelve, he started bringing her with him when he would feed every once in a while. I was always left with the nanny, and whenever she came back, she wouldn't talk for days. That's why we we've spent our entire lives trying to keep him from coming back. He's a monster." She stopped speaking for a second and wiped her eyes. "For the longest time I was so jealous of her. I loved her, but I wanted nothing more than for our father to pay just a little attention to me. When I saw how it was affecting her, I had to put a stop to it. I needed to get him to leave her alone."

"What did you do?"

"I…did something that I now regret. And even then, he didn't care. I often wonder which of us got the better deal. Cherish, for being favored and forced to do despicable things, or me, the ignored one who never got included in their sick games."

"I'm so sorry that you had to go through that. My father wasn't exactly pleasant, but he was nothing compared to what you described."

"I should feel lucky that he never bothered to give me the time of day, but at the same time, I wish that I had done more to protect her."

"What could you have done? Your parents were vampires, there was no way you could have stopped them."

Melody started sobbing harder and I wrapped her in a hug. I knew how she felt since I'd gone through the same thing with my own siblings. I had tried to keep my family away from the whole vampire world, and they'd still ended up involved. Even little Robin got caught up in all the craziness.

"You can go if you want," Melody said. "You probably want to talk with Gallard about Cherish's stupid, big-mouth revelation, and I think I need a nap."

THE RESURRECTION

I released her from the hug and gave her a half smile.

"If you need anything, I'm just three doors down," I said. "Hah! Three Doors Down, that's a band."

She chuckled then scooted backwards onto the bed and curled into the fetal position.

I walked out the door and softly closed it behind me before walking back to my room. I dreaded doing the walk of shame through the door and hoped that I didn't smell too much like alcohol or worse, vomit.

After I closed the door, I saw that Gallard was sitting with Robin on the floor against the front of the bed and she was eating a McDonalds Happy Meal. I was nervous about talking to him. I didn't know how to approach the conversation without sounding like a jealous twit. I hadn't questioned him about his and Cherish's past because I never felt the need to.

"Lela!" Robin said with the excited tone that she always used when saying my name, "Gallard got me McDonalds again."

"He did? I never would have guessed that you liked McDonalds."

"I *love* McDonalds," she said before turning her attention back to her food.

I kissed the top of her head then attempted to sit on the floor next to Gallard. I nearly sat in his lap in the process

"Are you okay?" he asked. "I heard yelling, but I tuned it out."

"I am A-okay! Really, I have better been never." I replied in a goofy voice. My mixed up words were an instant give-away. I felt so embarrassed that he had to see me that way, and I hoped that Robin wouldn't have a clue what was going on.

"Lela, are you drunk?"

I put a finger to my lips and looked at Robin to let him know to be careful with his choice of words.

"I may be a teensy, itty bitty, tiny bit on the wasted side. Melody said I needed to loosen up. But okay, I am. Hunky dory in time, I will be."

Gallard laughed, and I felt even more embarrassed.

"Miss Sharmentino, you are definitely hammered. And you're starting to sound like Yoda, what did you have to drink?"

"Tequila. Vodka. I went between them and sometimes had both

at the same time!" I said, suddenly getting the giggles like Melody. Gallard was still laughing too, and I was glad that he was amused instead of annoyed. If I were him, I would have been.

"Let's hope Jordan doesn't find out about this," he said. "He'll mock you relentlessly. I can't believe Cherish let Melody get you wasted. Then again, I kind of can."

"Why? Was she wasted when you two did it?" I asked, somewhat harshly.

I watched as his face went white, whiter than his usual color, and I suddenly felt bad for the tone of voice I'd used. It wasn't like he'd cheated on me. I just wished that I hadn't had to learn about his hook up with Cherish during a stupid drunken confession time.

"How did you...Cherish...she told you, didn't she? Was that what all the yelling was about?"

I didn't reply for a while and then I took Robin's hand and gently helped her off of the floor.

"Hey, Robin, why don't you hang out with Kevin for a while? He's in the room to the left of us," I said.

"Can I bring my food?"

"Yeah, honey. Gallard and I just need to talk. I'll come get you in a bit."

She happily obeyed and I watched her as she knocked on the door. Jordan opened it and he moved so Robin could go in. He then smiled at me and said, "Loooove youuu."

"Haha, you're hilarious."

"And you're drunk. Again. Your brothers and I were hoping for a cat fight, but you ladies are too civilized for that, aren't you?"

"Haven't you heard? I'm a stupid, naïve prude with intimacy issues. I'm too much of a pansy to fight."

Solomon came to the door, a sad expression on his face. I assumed that he'd heard the fight, which was awkward.

"Where is she?" he asked.

"She went to the BMW I think."

He then came out of the room and walked into the parking lot, and I headed back to mine to talk with Gallard. When I went in, Gallard had moved from the floor to the edge of the bed and he looked like he was about to be sick, almost worse than I did. I sat next to him and decided to let him do the talking.

"It was such a long time ago that I almost forgot about it. I'd

THE RESURRECTION

gone to her apartment because I was annoyed that she'd paid off my debt for the poker game I'd lost. I was yelling at her and she yelled back. Before we knew it, we were kissing and one thing led to another. After it happened, I left and didn't contact her for almost three weeks. I returned out of loneliness or boredom; maybe a combination of both. From that time on, we were just friends."

He turned to face me and looked into my eyes.

"I should have told you last night when you mentioned she talked about how we met. I guess it just slipped my mind, and I feel terrible that you didn't find out from me."

"Did you have feelings for her?" I asked, not sure if I wanted to know the answer.

"I cared about her, yes. But I wasn't in love with her. We only knew each other for a couple of months before she suddenly packed up and left town. It hurt that she hadn't said goodbye, but I eventually moved on. Her friendship had changed me, and I was a different man after that."

I felt a tear fall down my cheek, though I didn't know why I was crying. The leftover alcohol in my system was making me hyperemotional, and I was ready for it to wear off completely.

"Are you mad?" he asked when I didn't reply. I shook my head.

"I would understand if something happened between you two. She's a beautiful woman and you're only human. I just wish she hadn't rubbed it in my face the way she did." I looked at him. "On the floor? Really?"

"She told you that? What else did she say? No, I won't make you say anything you don't want to. It's bad enough that you know the details."

He bent over and rested his hands on the back of his neck. I could see that he felt really guilty about it and I didn't want him to. To ease his discomfort, I kissed his cheek.

"I'm not mad at you. You're so much older than me, and I never assumed you'd been some celibate monk before we met. You have people from your past, and it's just something we need to talk about."

"So, we're okay?" he asked, smiling.

"I wouldn't break up with you over something like this. That would be petty and immature. I love you, despite the fact that you're old and used."

"Used? Oh thanks. Now you're comparing me to a tissue?"

He chuckled and we embraced one another. I was glad that we had this talk but also dreading the discussion we obviously had to have.

Cherish had been pretty mad when she left, and I was mad at her too but I wasn't going to hold a grudge. A grudge was why we were all here in the first place. One way or another, I wanted to come to an understanding.

Chapter Eighteen

Cherish hurried out the door and hit the unlock button before getting into the car. She wasn't sure where she was going or if she really planned on leaving, but one thing was for certain; she was too drunk to drive.

She started the car anyway, and the radio came on playing a Coldplay song. She just sat in the seat and stared into space listening to the song, the anger slowly dissipating from her body.

Soon, all that was left was the same overwhelming regret she would have whenever she'd lash out for no reason. She felt bad about being so harsh toward Lela when all she'd done was be kind and welcoming. Her revealing her past with Gallard had been extremely cold and very inconsiderate, and she hoped that she hadn't caused problems between them.

Cherish beat her fists on the wheel then let a loud scream out of her lungs as she continued pounding on everything in reach. She didn't hit anything hard enough to break it, but she was pretty close.

"Are you happy, father? Are you proud of the creature you've created? Congratulations, I'm the monster to your Dr. Frankenstein!" she shouted out in the silence. She folded her arms against the steering wheel pressing, her head against them.

As she was trying to calm down, she was startled when someone opened the door on her side, and she looked up to see who it was.

"What do you want, Solomon?" she asked, pressing her back against the seat. She tried to put on a tough exterior so that he wouldn't know just how much seeing him made her angry.

"Move over, we're going for a drive," he said stepping out of her way. She frowned and slowly got out of the seat.

"Why should I go anywhere with you?"

"Because I'm tired of trying to tune out the TV while Aaron watches Skinemax. And because you're drunk, and I don't want you going off and crashing this car. We need it. I'd also like to talk to you."

"How do you know I'm drunk?"

"I've seen you when you've had too much to drink before. You're an angry drunk. Plus, I can hear everything that goes on in your room. I am right next door to you, after all."

Without knowing why, she decided to just go with it and walked around the front of the car to get into the passenger seat. She buckled herself in just as he did then he started the car and pulled out of the parking lot.

He didn't say a word as they drove through town, past parks and shopping centers. She didn't pay much attention to the scenery since her mind was on other things. She wasn't in the mood for an apology from Solomon and she hoped that that wasn't the reason for this random outing. She'd told him before the conditions of her forgiving him.

They drove for about thirty minutes before she noticed that she was starting to see the same things as she'd seen before, and then she realized that he'd been driving the same route the entire time.

Solomon pushed a button on the GPS and it said, "Turn left at next intersection."

"This truly is interesting. Remember when we had to use hand-drawn maps?" he asked, smiling. She rolled her eyes then looked back out of the window.

"We're not *that* old, Solomon," she replied flatly.

"Maybe not, but we are older than Shakespeare. Not too many

THE RESURRECTION

can say that, can they?"

She didn't reply to that. She was too stubborn to engage in any conversation with him. His jokes may have worked on her when she was little, but not anymore.

He continued to drive, taking different routes to the same location. The area was starting to become more and more familiar, and she had all the locations of all the stores memorized.

The car started making a dinging sound, which meant that it was on empty. Solomon pulled into a gas station and stopped next to a pump. He didn't say a word as he got out and went inside to pay for the gas.

Cherish rolled down her window and let the cool air brush across her face. She'd always preferred the cooler, spring season to summer time. She didn't like to sweat.
Solomon came back moments later and selected the fuel he wanted.

"Could you hit the button to open the gas cover?" he asked. She turned around to look for it and pushed the button. He began fueling, and she watched as he did it.

"A big step-up from a horse-driven carriage isn't it?" she asked, breaking the silence.

"There's the Cherish I remember. I used to love making you and your sister laugh. Your father would get so annoyed with me, but I didn't care."

She got out of the car and leaned against the door so that she could see him better. He looked like the same man that had visited her house when she was a child, minus the priest robes. He'd always brought the best gifts at Christmastime and had become Uncle Solomon to her and Melody. She'd always known that he was immortal, but he wasn't evil like her father.

When she was fifteen, after she'd lost the baby, he'd been the one to comfort her while her father had refused to speak with her. After a while, it became evident that Solomon had feelings for her. But he was a priest, and she didn't want to get hurt knowing that they couldn't be together. She was also still getting over the betrayal of the man she'd loved. Instead, she chose to distance herself from any romantic feelings towards anyone, even Solomon.

"Why the harsh words towards Lela?" he asked. "I heard what you said. Even for you that was pretty cold."

"A little honesty is good for the character. I felt like she needed a reality check."

"I see. And what about her makes you think she doesn't already grasp what's going on?"

"We're about to declare war on my father, Solomon. What is she doing? Worrying about her relationship. Don't get me wrong, it was hard telling her the truth. Hell, I had to get drunk to do it. I think I got my point across."

"You think she's wrapped up in her relationship? Cherish do you even know why she was killed in the first place?"

Cherish shook her head. Gallard hadn't really gone into detail. All he said was that Samil killed her and that Gallard had killed him in return. She could see that it hurt him to talk about it.

"She could communicate with your father." He pulled the hose out of the tank then hooked it up. "I don't know how or why it was possible but it was. Anyway, your father offered her a trade. If she helped resurrect him, he would kill Samil and rescue her sister. Her plan was that she and her father would do the bloodletting so Gallard would be free from Samil after all these years. In the end, her friend betrayed her and Samil tortured and killed her when she didn't provide the information he wanted. That was after he murdered her parents in front of her then forced her to drink her own brother's blood."

"Wow." She leaned against the car. "I had no idea. Well I officially feel like rubbish now. I don't understand. How is she so...happy?"

"She has a lot to be thankful for, I suppose. She got a second chance at life, just like you did, and she wants to use that second chance to protect her family. Look, *Accarezzare*, I'm not asking you to like her. I know more than anyone that you're not a people person. But I can ask that you respect her."

Cherish nodded. She would try harder to make nice. It wouldn't be easy, and she would definitely fail along the way, but for the sake of the cause, she couldn't afford to start fights within the group and destroy the dynamic. No doubt Gallard was not happy with her for revealing their past or for being so brutally honest to his girlfriend. Either way, she was glad Solomon hadn't asked her to become best friends with Lela. It wasn't going to happen.

Talking with him was getting easier, though. There were so

many things she had wanted to ask him for centuries but never had the chance to. She decided to take this opportunity to get everything out.

"Why did you let them kill me?" she asked.

"I didn't let them. The gypsies had secretly plotted your murders behind my back. They told me that you were demonstrating vampiric tendencies. One of them had seen you with your parents when they were feeding, and they assumed that you had inherited Lucian's traits. Instead of investigating their suspicions, they had you killed instead."

"So you watched as they slit my throat like it was nothing? Tell me something, did you even think about saving me, even after I'd begged them to spare me?"

"I didn't even know they were in your room. They were supposed to wait outside in case someone showed up. When I learned that you and Melody were dead, I was devastated. I killed the men responsible, but that never kept me from blaming myself for not protecting you."

"But I wasn't like my father. I was a mortal human being. I didn't crave blood, and I didn't want to take any lives. I just wanted to be a normal woman with normal parents."

He lightly touched her arm, and she contemplated pulling away, but she didn't. She was surprised when he pulled her into a gentle hug. He was breaking their agreement. There was only one condition under which she would allow him to touch her, and this wasn't it. Yet she couldn't bring herself to pull away.

"I can't ask you to forgive me. I don't deserve your forgiveness. But I want you do something for me."

"And what is that?"

"Don't be afraid to trust those around you, and you'll find that people actually aren't as bad as you think. And try to smile every once in a while. You have a beautiful smile."

She pulled back from the hug but still kept her arms around him and found herself looking into his eyes. They were filled with regret and a sadness that she knew all too well. She'd done things that she'd regretted as well. Things that were done because of the bitterness she'd had towards her father. She'd struggled to become her own person after he'd died because his teachings were all she'd known.

"I did care about you, Cherish," he said. "More than I should have. I still do. I wanted nothing but to save you from that monster, and I failed you. At least now I have a second chance to get it right."

She was puzzled by this. He'd cared about her? After all these years? He was a priest and forbidden from having any sort of romantic relationship. She may have felt something towards him years and years ago, but she'd all but forgotten that after what had happened to her and her sister. Yet his apology was somehow swaying her hardened anger towards him.

As she continued to stare at him, he formed an expression of uncertainty, which she didn't understand why at first until he suddenly kissed her. She was startled by it, but she returned it anyway. She had kissed many different types of men but never a priest. She'd always been curious about what that would be like.

He pushed her against the car and started kissing her more aggressively; his hands running up her back, and she wrapped her arms around his neck. They continued for another two minutes before he finally stopped and backed away from her.

"I apologize," he said. "I don't know why I did that. This was a mistake."

"Why, because you're a Cardinal? Don't worry, I won't tell the Pope."

She grabbed him by his belt loops and pulled him back towards her, kissed him again, and he didn't push her away. She'd been unexpectedly captivated by him and wanted more.

"I haven't kissed a woman in five hundred years," he confessed. "I could never bring myself to after you died." His kisses became softer and lighter until finally, he stopped it once more and took the keys, saying, "We should get back."

Cherish mentally pouted, not wanting their moment to be over, but obediently got into the car.

As they drove back to the motel, they didn't say a word. They avoided eye contact at all costs, and she began to wonder if the encounter had only been a daydream. One minute, she had hated his guts for what he'd done, and the next she found herself irresistibly attracted to him. Her emotions were all over the place, and she struggled to come to terms with what the kisses had meant to her. It was the first time she'd felt something with a man in nearly five-hundred years, and that scared her.

They were about five minutes away from the motel when Solomon turned onto a different street without warning and came to a stop. She looked at him then looked around to see what had caused him to change routes.

"What's going on?" she asked. He pointed off to the distance and she watched as a large group of people walked close together down the street. They were all pale and walked quickly, but not so fast as to draw attention to themselves.

"You don't think...?" she started to say, but he answered her question before she could finish.

"Oh, I think. We need to get back to the motel now, as in we should have already been there two minutes ago."
He put the car back into drive and accelerated to forty before pulling onto the correct road leading to their destination. She looked back as the group slowly disappeared behind the buildings, and she prayed that they would be prepared for what was about to hit them

Chapter Nineteen

I lay with my head against Gallard's chest and tried to quiet my brain. We had talked for over an hour about our relationship, or for lack of a better phrase, airing out our dirty laundry.

Not that I had any laundry to air. He'd insisted on being completely honest about everyone he could think of from his past. That way, there wouldn't be any more surprises, even if some of them were long dead. When he talked about the women, my stomach was constantly in knots, but I was grateful that he wasn't keeping anything from me.

We finished talking, and by that time the alcohol was almost out of my system completely. Gallard was disappointed, though, and claimed that he missed my Yoda talk. Melody had been wrong. The alcohol hadn't loosened me up, and it had just made me wacked out and a chatter box.

"That's everyone?" I asked.

"That I can remember. I'm sorry if I bored you with my endless talking. I wanted to be as honest as possible."

I smiled. "You aren't boring me. I like the sound of your voice.

THE RESURRECTION

It was what gave me hope while Lucian was in control of my body. Whenever I would hear you, I was at peace."

He softly pressed his lips to my temple. "I can't believe Cherish said those things to you. You know they're not true, right?"

In a way, I believed him. That didn't keep her words from echoing in my mind, making me paranoid. Could I blame her? I already had the lecture from Mark about how stupid it was to drink something from a stranger. And after I was freaking out about a stupid piece of lingerie that wasn't even that revealing, how could she not think I was a prude? In the end, the only person that mattered to was Gallard.

"I have to admit, the idea of being with you is scary. I've never let myself be that vulnerable with anyone." I looked up at him. "But I love you. And even though I am not as experienced as you, I want you to be my first and my last."

Gallard smiled. "I would be honored to be your first and last. As long as I can be everything in between as well."

I crooked my mouth. "Well, I suppose I can agree to that. Only if you're extra nice to me."

He captured my lips with a kiss, and I wrapped my arms around his neck. He rolled over so that he was on top of me, and the kiss deepened. His tongue swept gently over my bottom lip, and I welcomed it by parting my lips. His tongue found mine then he kissed me until I was dizzy. He interlocked our fingers, holding them to the sides, and I felt his ring. I had almost forgotten about it.

"What day is it?" I asked between kisses.

"April fifteenth. Why?" He moved down and lifted my shirt then began kissing my stomach and my ribs.

"It'll be your birthday next month. How old will that make you?"

He smiled. "Two hundred and seventy-six."

I laughed in surprise. He looked like he was barely older than me. It then hit me that I, too, would forever look young. Most people would probably love to be young for all eternity. I wasn't sure what I would prefer; youth or wrinkles.

"Wow. I'm dating an old man. What does that say about me? Are people going to start calling me a gold digger?"

He laughed. "That would only fit if I actually had gold to dig."

"So I'm dating a *poor* old man? Shows what taste I have."

"You are so feisty! Biting Jordan, punching Simeon, insulting me. I kind of like it."

Without another word, he kissed me again. It was very clear where this was headed, and I found that I was actually okay with it.

We sat up so that we were both resting on our knees and I let him tug my shirt off. I was slightly embarrassed, considering my choice in underwear. I was still limited to the Fruit of the Loom three pack of bras, and the one I'd chosen to wear had pineapples on it. I should have worn the slip that was going to waste in my luggage. He didn't even seem to care and that pushed away my insecurities.

I started unbuttoning his shirt and tried not to shake from nervousness. I undid the last button and he shrugged out of it and firmly presses his lips to mine, moving them gently to the corner of my mouth, over my jaw, and then the base of my neck. Somehow, I managed to take off my jeans then he reached behind me and fiddled with the clasp. After about ten seconds, a laugh escaped my lips.

"Sorry," he said. "I don't do this very often."

"It's okay. I think it's a good thing. If you were an expert, I would be worried."

I undid it then slipped the straps over my shoulders and l let it fall to the side of the bed. He stared at my body for a while then brought his gaze to mine and smiled. He then slowly lay me on my back and showered me in hot kisses, making sure to find every scar with his lips. Even though is body temperature was very low, my heated blood compensated for it and kept me from getting cold by association.

His right hand moved down to my hip, and I was so distracted that I didn't realize what was happening until I felt him touch me. A soft moan escaped my lips, and I couldn't believe how wonderful this was. I had heard stories from Gabby and from Aaron, but nothing could have prepared me for the real thing.

"Is this too much?" he asked softly as he continued pleasuring me. "If you're not comfortable, I can stop."

"Please don't stop." I let out a ragged breath. I was speechless and every time I tried to form a sentence, a wave of pleasure would

THE RESURRECTION

shut me right up. Finally, one phrase came to mind, and I couldn't stop it from coming out. "Marry me."

He stopped kissing me and stared at my face. I punched myself mentally. I couldn't believe that my big mouth had ruined the moment, yet again, and I started speaking for a second time, which only made things worse in my mind.

"No! I mean, I didn't mean that! I have no idea where that came from it just slipped out. I'm an idiot! Besides, it's tacky for the girl to ask the guy anyway. And where do I get off suggesting such a thing when we've only been seeing each other for literally a week, not counting the entire year that I'd been dead. I mean, yeah, we've known each other for six years, but that doesn't mean that would be any crazier. I seriously need to develop a filter and—"

"Yes."

I raised my eyebrows, confused at what he was saying yes to since I had said a ton of things he could easily have agreed with.

"Yes that it was tacky or yes that I need a filter?"

"Neither, I'm saying yes to the first thing you asked."

I didn't know what to say. I couldn't believe we were actually having this conversation. The entire moment was almost surreal, and I couldn't find any words to say and was glad that he spoke, clarifying his answer.

"Yes, I will marry you. And is it too soon? Maybe, but who cares? I'm done living a life where I worry about the future; about what will or will not happen. Who knows what's going to happen in the next few weeks? But if I have you, none of that will matter. All my relationships failed in the past because I was too afraid to say how I felt. What happened to Dyani hurt me, and I didn't want to go through that again. When you died, it nearly killed me, and it made me wish that I'd been honest with you sooner. We've already spent a year apart, and I want to begin my life with you as soon as possible. No more waiting, no more putting everything off. I love you, and I would be honored to spend the rest of my life with you."

I became so happy that I threw myself on top of him, wrapping him in a tight embrace. I almost forgot that I was practically nude, but at that moment I didn't care anymore.

"So, where were we?" he asked, kissing me again.

I started unbuttoning his jeans when someone knocked on the

door.

"Go away!" he shouted. I moved so that he could sit up and he sighed with exasperation. "I just talked to them ten minutes ago. This better be good."

"It's Aaron. Can I come in?"

"No!" We shouted at the same time. Since Gallard's shirt was closest, I threw it on then gathered my clothes so I could get dressed in the bathroom. The entire time, I kept smiling like an idiot as it registered what had just happened. Gallard and I were engaged. It didn't matter to me that we'd been interrupted because now we were going to get married. Nothing could ruin that.

When I came out, I handed Gallard his shirt. I hadn't wanted to wear mine anymore, so I had borrowed one of his t-shirts that was in the bathroom. Despite everything, I was glad we had gotten a little closer. I was more comfortable with him than ever and no longer afraid of going further with him. If only we could get away from everyone so we could finally consummate our love.

"This sucks," I said. "I want to be with you, but something stupid always gets in the way."

"I know. Death is pretty stupid, right?" He kissed my cheek and pulled me into a hug. "How about we set a goal? We'll wait until this whole Lucian thing is over."

"Are you going to make us be married too?"

"An even better idea!" He said with sarcasm.

"Seriously? Have you been talking to Melody? And isn't that kind of...archaic?"

"Completely. In fact, why don't we throw in a year of courting and Jordan can buy us a cow and some chickens for our wedding present."

We started laughing and I couldn't stop, even though it hurt my stomach. I knew that Gallard wasn't old fashioned in that sense. If he was, we wouldn't have done what we'd been doing for the past half hour.

A year ago, I probably wouldn't have gone as far as we did today, but I found myself getting more and more comfortable with him as we spent more time together.

"On a serious note, I think waiting for this to be over is a good idea," he said. "That way, we can plan ahead and get rid of any, uh...interruptions."

THE RESURRECTION

"All right, we'll wait." I shifted so that I could look at his face. "So how long are we talking, six months; a year until we tie the knot?"

"Oh, I'm planning on marrying you a lot sooner than that, Miss Sharmentino. I've waited a year to get you back and I don't want to spend any more time without calling you mine. I want to marry you so when people see you walking in the street, I can point to you and say, 'You see that woman over there. Not only is she a damn good plumber, she's my wife as well.'"

I laughed again then surprised him with a kiss. I pushed him onto the bed and he rolled over so that he was leaning over me, kissing me back with growing intensity. We were in grave danger of getting carried away again when Aaron suddenly burst into the room. When he saw us, he yelled in disgust and covered his eyes.

"Word of advice, if you two are going to be fooling around, you should lock the door!"

"Word of advice, knock on the door before coming in!" I said back.

Aaron slowly removed his hand from his eyes and walked further into the room. Gallard sat up and finished buttoning his shirt.

"What's so urgent that you had to bust in here like a cowboy in a saloon?" Gallard asked.

"Solomon and Cherish came back from a drive. They said that there's about fifteen to twenty vamps headed our way, and we need to prepare for a possible attack."

I got off the bed as well.

"Did you say twenty?" I asked. Aaron nodded.

"I wouldn't freak out just yet. There are eight of us after all. They only have twelve more than we do, and if Solomon's right about how he and Gallard are able to take out a bunch, then that's like we have twice as many as we really do. And we have our secret weapons."

I raised an eyebrow at his poorly done math. I got the feeling that he was using overly exaggerated statistics to cover up his fear.

"And what secret weapons are those?" I asked.

"Duh! You, Melody, and Cherish. You guys feed on vampire blood, they won't stand a chance!"

"But I'm not as strong as them. They drain the entire body while I just have small amounts at a time. I am not nearly as strong as they are, I'm dead weight!"

Kevin walked into the room at that moment holding Robin, and I felt an overwhelming pang of helplessness. I wanted so badly to protect my younger siblings, and the idea that I wouldn't be able to killed me inside.

"Take my blood," Kevin said, almost as-a-matter-of-factly.

"I can't, Kev. You're already one of the weaker ones. I couldn't take away your only means of defense."

He handed Robin to Aaron before walking towards me. I could tell that he hadn't shaved in days, and he looked so much older than the eighteen-year-old boy that he was. Even still, I couldn't see past the fact that he was my baby brother.

"If you drink my blood, I will be weak, but maybe we can use this to our advantage. I could take one of the cars and get Robin out of here while you guys hold the fort. I should still have enough energy to drive."

Gallard put a hand on my shoulder.

"I have to say that his idea isn't a bad one. Robin is the only one here who Lucian isn't bent on killing and as the youngest Kevin is our top priority right now. If he can manage to escape with her, then we can just focus on taking out the enemy."

"But what about the family blood thing?"

"Only applies to mortals."

Kevin stood next to me and turned his head, exposing his neck. The scent was intoxicating, but I held my ground.

"Do it Lela, we don't have much time!" Aaron said.

I bit down on Kevin's neck and began to drink. With Gallard, I would control how much I took by counting to ten. This time was different. I was going to drain Kevin almost to the point of death, and the thought that I wouldn't be able to stop scared me.

I kept drinking and drinking until I lost count of the seconds, and didn't come to my senses until someone pulled me away from him.

"I think that's enough, don't you?" Aaron asked. He put Robin's back pack on her back. The rest of the group made an appearance into our room a moment later, and we told Solomon our plan then began to give Kevin instructions.

THE RESURRECTION

The GPS was programmed to lead him as far as Fayetteville, North Carolina. It was a little over two and a half hours away, just far enough to get the vamps off his tale. He was to pull over at the first gas station he saw and wait for one of us to contact him.

Solomon gave strict instructions that in the event that none of us made it, Kevin was to leave the gas station before dawn and choose a place a hide at his discretion. Solomon gave him his cell phone and keys before telling him to be safe.

I buckled Robin into her booster seat and hugged her tightly. "I'll see you soon, okay my little Robin bird."

"Lela, are you gonna die again?"

My heart lurched in my chest and I fought to hold back the tears. She had experienced way too much death in her five years, and I hated that such a question came so natural to her.

"I don't know, honey. But I promise you one thing; *you* are going to live. You are going to get through this, and so is your big brother, all right."

I hugged her once more and kissed her nose before I closed the door. I then turned to Kevin and hugged him tighter than I ever had. "I'm going to see you again. This is just a temporary parting."

I heard Gallard speaking quietly to Jordan and soon after, Jordan walked over to the other side of the car and got in. Gallard explained that since Kevin was weak, he needed back up in case someone tried to follow them. I was grateful to Jordan for looking out for my siblings, but also worried that we may not have enough to fight.

I ran around to the other side to speak with him. I hated I that hadn't been able to say goodbye to everyone the last time I was in a dangerous situation that ended badly, so I made sure to do it this time.

"Take care of them, but also take care of yourself," I said. "I don't want anything happening to you either."

"Don't worry about me. I'm a D'Aubigne. We're survivors."

I gave him a hug and he enveloped me in his big arms.

"I love you," I said.

"Is this the alcohol talking?"

"No, I really do. You're just as important to me as Aaron, Kevin, and Robin. I just wanted you to know that."

I looked up and saw the silhouettes of the enemy coming closer, and I shoved Jordan a bit to get him going. He got into the car and Kevin did a back-up that belonged in a car-chase movie before speeding off down the road. I waited to see if any of the other vamps would try and follow him, but they didn't. They just kept getting closer and closer to the motel.

We created a sort of a flank, putting Solomon in front with Melody and Gallard on either side of him while Aaron was in the very back. Cherish and I were in the middle. We hadn't said a word to each other since the incident that afternoon, and to be honest, I was still mad at her. More so hurt.

The large group finally came to a stop about fifteen feet from us. They stood on the sidewalk while we remained in the parking lot, and I held my breath, waiting to see who was going to speak first. I then studied them to get an idea of who we were up against. Most of them were men while about four women were scattered throughout. The age range looked to be about twenty to thirty.

Finally, one in the back took off his hat, revealing his distinct red hair. It was Lucian. I hadn't expected him to make an appearance so soon, but here he was, hiding behind his army of vampires.

Melody and Cherish exchanged glances then Melody stepped back, taking her sister's hand. I couldn't imagine what they were going through, seeing their father again for the first time in so long.

"Good evening, ladies and gentleman. How do you fair?"

Solomon didn't reply right away, but by his body language, I could tell that he was itching to just tear his head off. At that moment, he reminded me of how Mark was whenever he was angry about something. He never had to say anything. I would just have to look at his face and know that he was irked.

"I am going to make an educated guess and say that the police are probably on their way as we speak," Lucian continued. "So, let us do this as quickly as we can."

Hearing his voice outside of my head was surreal. It was like a dream becoming reality. I'd heard it for so long and could recognize it anywhere. And he'd been somewhat of an ally up until he'd had my aunt murdered. After that, any sympathy I'd felt towards him disappeared.

He walked a little closer to us even though it was obvious that we could hear him from where he was standing. He had a cocky look on his face that made me instantly dislike him more.

"The police aren't a concern for us," Solomon said, speaking for the first time. "Just the same, we would like to finish this in a timely fashion."

"Agreed. But before we start with the violence, I must inform you that I want to make a deal."

"You lost the right to make demands when you threatened my family."

"That is rich, considering you turned my own family against me." He turned to Melody and Cherish then smiled "Cherish, Melody; how are my wonderful daughters?"

"Bloody fantastic, daddy," Melody said with extreme spite.

He smirked then fixed his eyes on Cherish, who refused to make eye contact with him. So far, he hadn't given me any attention, which was great. I didn't want him to. Our last few conversations were awkward and creepy. Hopefully he'd gotten over his weird obsession with me in the past year.

"So, about this deal," he continued, "Are you willing to negotiate, or will I send my army after you now?"

Solomon looked back at us as if to ask our opinion on the matter. Personally, I was wary of making any sort of deal. I'd made a deal with Lucian before and it didn't work out as planned, so I was against it.

But the choice would have to be based on the majority vote. I watched as Gallard and Melody nodded and then Cherish did as well. I turned around and saw Aaron nod and I knew that I was the only one who didn't agree. It didn't matter. I was outnumbered.

"We're listening," Solomon said. Lucian folded his arms and began pacing back and forth in front of us.

"I would like to make a trade, an exchange if you will. A life for a life."

"Go on," Solomon urged with a hint of annoyance.

"I want someone from your group to leave and join my side. In exchange, I will end this feud."

The group began talking amongst themselves and I stood in shock. Would he really change his mind about killing my family that easily? It would make complete sense. The whole reason for

this was to get back at Solomon for killing his family. Cherish and Melody were alive, which
destroyed the whole point of the revenge plot.

"Who do you want?" Solomon asked.

"My daughter, Cherish."

Chapter Twenty

We all turned our eyes to Cherish. She looked panicked at first, but then her expression changed from shock to anger, and her lips curled into a snarl.

"It will be a cold day in hell before I ever join your side!" she shouted.

Solomon waved us all together, and we broke our flank to discuss our options.

"My sister is not going with that maniac," Melody said.

"Even if it means that my family can be spared?" Aaron asked.

"We don't know if he'll really back out of the feud," Gallard said. "For all we know he was bluffing and ordered them to kill us all once Cherish is back in his custody."

I heard sirens off in the distance. It was only a matter of time before the parking lot would be swarming with cops. I didn't want us to make a rash decision based on urgency, but we needed to come up with one fast. Nothing would be worse than people getting caught in the crossfire of a vampire fight.

I hated the thought of handing Cherish over—despite our falling out—or anyone for that matter, but I didn't say a word as everyone else discussed it. Solomon and Melody were completely against it while Aaron was all for it. I sensed that Gallard was torn, which was understandable. I couldn't sacrifice one life for several. Everyone's lives were equally valuable, no matter whom I'd known the longest.

"Tick tock," Lucian said, "The police are not going to wait for you."

Cherish folded her hands and brought them up to her mouth, closing her eyes. Ultimately, the decision would come down to her. I hoped that she wouldn't comply; that she would convince the others to take back the deal and just get the fight over with.

She opened her eyes and looked at Solomon.

"Trade me for your family," she said.

"You would really do that for us?" I asked.

"It's too late for me to have a life, but not for you or Robin or your brothers. You still have a chance to live, and if that means I have to be forced to go back to my father, then so be it."

She looked around at the rest of the group and I waited to see if they would go along with it. Everyone nodded, and we exchanged glances one last time, and I mouthed *thank you* to which she replied with a curt nod.

"So, what is your decision?" Lucian asked.

"We'll make the trade." Solomon replied. "Cherish for a truce with me and my grandchildren."

The sound of that was very endearing to me. We were clearly further down his family line, but it was touching to hear him refer to us that way. It showed just how much he really cared.

Lucian gave a smirk and shook his head. A knot formed in my stomach and I wondered what he was finding so humorous.

"It appears that I've forgotten to give you the terms," he said. "Your family can go free...but not you, Solomon."

I grew extremely angry, and I could tell that the rest of the group was equally enraged by this wrench in our plan. It took everything in me not to go crazy and get violent.

Cherish began to plead, saying, "Father, please don't! You're alive, we're reunited again. Solomon's crimes have been reversed. Let him be!"

"I'm starting to lose my patience! Abide by the terms or the deal is off!" Lucian shouted. He then looked at me for the first time and

THE RESURRECTION

I held my breath. Gallard grabbed my hand, squeezing it tightly.

"Unless," Lucian continued. "You are willing to make one more trade. Lela for your life."

I hated that he'd suggested this trade. He knew that I wouldn't be able to resist making such a decision if it meant someone's life could be spared. Samil once told me that my compassion was my downfall, but I didn't care. If my compassion could save somebody, then I would gladly go with Lucian.

Before I could speak up, Solomon did before me.

"If she is the price, then I cannot pay it. Lela remains with us. I will not be exempt of the feud."

"Solomon, are you sure? I could help you. I could go with him and—"

"No, Lela. You've already given your life once. I should have been there to save you, and I wasn't. This is my chance to make up for it."

Cherish hugged Melody and told her not to worry and that she could handle herself. Melody began balling after Cherish left her side and I put an arm around her to comfort her.

The next thing Cherish did shocked me, and I bet the others felt the same way. She pulled Solomon to her by his jacket and kissed him, hard. What was even more shocking was that he embraced her and kissed her back. She finally ended it and as she walked passed Gallard, she touched his shoulder.

"I'm not okay with this," Gallard whispered. I wasn't sure if he was directing it to anyone in particular, but he stepped forward and grabbed Cherish's arm. "You don't have to do this. He's outnumbered. I'm not letting you go back to your father."

"If I don't go, he will only retaliate. I know him. He doesn't react well to defiance."

She began to leave again when he took her arm again, stopping her from following the other group, and the woman from Lucian's side stepped closer to them, drew a knife, and then stabbed Gallard in the eye, quickly pulling the knife out. Gallard yelled in pain holding his hands over his injured eye.

Cherish immediately fought back, and she attacked the woman first then Melody. I joined in only seconds behind. Cherish kicked her several times, throwing her around then I grabbed her arms from behind. The woman hissed at Cherish, then the sisters both took a hold of the woman and pulled as hard as they could until she tore in half, blood gushing everywhere. The three of us were covered in it at that point.

"No!" One of the men shouted. He glared at the three of us and then charged. As the rest of Lucian's army closed in on us, we each paired up so we could effectively take out each one with back up. Melody and Cherish worked as sort of a duo, with one holding a guy down while the other would rip him apart. Gallard and Solomon teamed up as well, and I assisted Aaron since I was stronger than two of him put together.

Twenty vampires seemed like a lot compared to the six of us, but we were holding our own quite well. Aaron and I made a good team. As he would fight one, and once he began to struggle, I would come up behind his attacker and rip his head off. My new strength was surreal to me. I had been pretty strong when I was a vampire, but whatever I was now, I was even stronger.

Aaron wasn't prepared for when two came up behind him, throwing him down onto the pavement. I was busy fighting one and couldn't get to him right away. He began to get up, but one of them, a woman, held his arms back while the other, a man, applied pressure to his neck with his foot.

I finally killed the vampire I was dealing with then pulled the two vampires away from him just as they were about to rip his head off. I did to the first one what they'd been about to do to Aaron then Gallard went after the other while I helped Aaron.

I lifted him up and dragged him off to the side, and little by little he showed signs that he was regaining his senses. I let out a sigh of relief as he kicked his leg.

"Are you all right?" I asked, "Are you healing?"

"Yeah, I'm fine," he replied, now able to move completely. "Just had a bout of temporary paralysis is all."

I looked around and saw that the fighting had all but stopped completely. There were only three remaining; Lucian and two men, one being the man who'd reacted to the woman's death. My group had gathered once more and, I helped Aaron stand so we could join them. I wondered what was to happen since we had obviously won. Would Cherish still go with him or would she back out of the deal we'd made?

THE RESURRECTION

"Bravo, I am impressed!" Lucian said. "Her actions were irrational, but they have been justly avenged. We will leave you now and no more violence will be done on my part as long as Cherish comes with me."

She looked back as us one last time before she took Lucian's hand and they ran off in a blur, leaving us bewildered and still in reeling from the fight.

The police were starting to show up, so we quickly gathered our things, piled into the BMW, and then left the area. I didn't have time to change, so I'd just quickly washed the blood out of my hair and off of my arms. The others were covered as well, but Melody was probably the worst. She had to have been extremely irked about having to stay dirty longer. The blood on her clothes had dried, and what was on her skin was dry and crusty.

Gallard stopped bleeding by then but still held his hand over his eye. I was beginning to get worried, especially when he asked Solomon if we could stop at a drug store before heading out of town. When we pulled into a Walgreens, he went in alone. I thought I could stand the secrecy, but I was too curious to know what he was hiding. I unbuckled myself and followed him in two minutes later.

I had no idea which aisle he would be in, so I had to look down each one until I spotted him in the section containing contact solution and eye drops. I walked over to him and when he saw me, he turned his head slightly to the right as if to avoid looking at me.

"Gallard, what's wrong? Why hasn't your eye healed yet?" I asked. He didn't answer me and continued looking on the shelf. I began to get annoyed with his silence, so I said, "Why are you shutting me out? What is it that you aren't telling me?"

He sighed and folded his arms before replying, "When that woman stabbed me, she didn't just injure my eye."

"Then what did she do?" I asked, my voice quavering. He stopped talking and I hardened my gaze to let him know that I wasn't going to leave him alone without answers.

"She cut it out," he uttered with hardly any emotion. I took his shoulders and turned him around to face me. I wanted to make sure that he wasn't just making a sick joke, but the reality hit me when I saw his sunken right eyelid.

"Oh, God. Gallard!"

"Hey, it's not all that bad," he said, wrapping his arms around me. "It doesn't even hurt anymore. It just feels...different."

"How can you be so nonchalant about it? Your eye is gone, and you can never get it back!"

"It's just an eye, Lela. I would give up any of my limbs if it meant that you or someone else would survive."

I looked into his eyes, or more accurately his one eye. He acted as if it weren't that big of a deal, but his voice said otherwise. After knowing him for so long, I was able to tell the difference between when he was concerned and when he was hiding his true feelings.

He kissed my forehead before grabbing an eye patch off of the shelf and said, "We should probably get going. Jordan and your younger siblings are waiting for us."

I held his hand as he went up to pay for the patch and then we left the store and got back into the car. While the two-hour drive was short in comparison to the trip we'd taken the day before, it felt longer. Perhaps it was the urgency I had to get to Jordan, Kevin, and Robin. The sooner they were back with the group, the more I would be able to relax.

I sat next to Aaron in the very back and had my arm crooked around his. I was thankful that he had survived the fight, and I was feeling very clingy due to all that had transpired that evening. I didn't want to let him out of my sight, which seemed silly since he was the older one. Our rocky relationship over the past few years became but a memory to me, and all that mattered was that he was still alive.

Melody texted Kevin as soon as we got into Fayetteville, and he informed us that he was at a gas station just off interstate ninety-five on Cedar Creek Road. We found the place easily, and Solomon pulled in and parked the BMW. I spotted the Toyota, and as I walked towards it, Kevin came out of the station holding Robin, who had a hotdog in her hand.

I ran over and hugged them both saying, "Thank God you're all right!" Robin all but forgot her hotdog and reached for me, wrapping her legs around my middle.

"Did you have any problems getting here?" Solomon asked. Kevin shook his head.

THE RESURRECTION

"Everything went smoothly. We got here around eight-fifteen and just chilled for a bit. Well, Robin did, but I was a nervous wreck."

Melody walked a view paces away while looked around the parking lot before asking, "Where's Jordan?"

"That's a good question," Kevin said. "I just saw him ten minutes ago."

"He probably went inside the service station," Gallard said. "I'll go in and check."

As he went inside, a feeling of dread crept up my spine. Jordan was all right. We were being silly worrying about him. He was probably inside as Gallard guessed.

When Gallard came back alone, I held my breath. Something was wrong, I knew it. His disappearance couldn't be good and I hated to think that Lucian had done something to him.

"He wasn't inside?" Solomon asked.

"No, I have no clue where he went. You didn't see him leave?"

"We just got here fifteen minutes ago," Kevin said. "How could someone have snatched him without me knowing it?"

Melody took out her phone and dialed then handed it to Gallard. We waited as he stood there listening to the phone ring. I wanted to shake the feeling that something was amiss, but I couldn't. No matter what reasonable explanations for his absence I came up with, they would always go back to the idea that Lucian had double crossed us and someone had been sent to kill him.

The phone stopped ringing and the voicemail greeting began to play. Gallard called again, and then a third time, and each try ended the same with the greeting.

"Where the hell is he?" I asked.

Chapter Twenty-One

Jordan drove the stolen Honda Civic into the parking lot of the Clay Pot Coffee Shop in Sanford, North Carolina. He took a contacts case out of his pocket and quickly but smoothly removed the grey ones from his eyes then put them into the little cups. He put the case back into his jacket and got out of the car. His eyes felt so much better without them, and he blinked few times, enjoying the comfort.

He walked into the restaurant and stood next to the "A Waiter Will Seat You" sign and waited for service. It was a bit busy since it was around dinner time, but he wasn't worried about getting a table since the person he was meeting had promised to save them one.

"Good evening," said a small blonde waitress. "Just one tonight?"

"Actually, I'm meeting someone. Max or Maximus?"

"Oh Max, he's here. I'll show you to his table."

He followed her towards the back by the window and sat down in front of Maximus. He didn't even acknowledge that Jordan was there, even after Jordan waved a hand in his face. He kept his eyes focused on the cup of tea in front of him and stirred it, changing directions every so often.

Maximus looked a lot different from when Jordan had last seen him. He'd cut his white hair extremely short on the sides leaving the top only slightly longer. He wore black pants with a bronze leather jacket and a black button-up underneath, which surprised Jordan since he'd told him years ago that he would never wear leather.

When he still hadn't looked up after three minutes passed, Jordan began to speak to him.

"All right, what's got you vexed this time, Maxy?"

Maximus stopped stirring and set the spoon on a napkin, folding his hands behind the cup.

"I hate when you refer to me by that nickname," he snapped.

Jordan gave a sly smile.

"What would you prefer, Gluteus Maximus? Perhaps Maxi-pad?"

"Enough with the jests! I know you failed to stop that monster from being resurrected. As my appointed one, are the only one strong enough to do so. Why is he still alive?"

The waitress came to the table before Jordan could answer. She took his order, and he requested a cup of organic green tea, vegetarian lasagna, and raspberry cheesecake. While he waited for his food to arrive, Max had returned to his tea stirring ritual and ignored Jordan once more.

Jordan's meal came about five minutes later and he instantly began devouring the lasagna.

"Mmm. This is fantastic! Don't get me wrong, blood is great, but nothing beats good lasagna."

"Answer my question, Jordanes. Why is he still alive?"

Jordan swallowed his bite of food then took a sip of his tea. He was still surprised to see Maximus, considering he'd been in the Middle East for the past two years living the life of a hermit. The last time he'd seen him, he was dressed in rags and had his hair and beard grown out. He'd said that he was trying to cleanse himself before God, but it must not have worked since he was back in civilization.

"It's not easy being my in shoes, Maxi-pad. They think I'm a night-walker, and I'm constantly surrounded by them. We are making progress, though. He showed up at our motel today and ended the feud in exchange for his daughter."

Maximus pushed his cup to the side with great exasperation, nearly knocking it off of the table. This made Jordan nervous, but he didn't let him see it. Maximus was always so uptight, which was why Jordan preferred to converse over the phone instead of in person.

"That abomination should have been killed the moment he was born. The only reason he lived past infancy is because I pitied his mother. And now he's stronger and more dangerous. Though he is not back to his full power. I saw to that when I told the gypsies only two were needed to bring him back. Could you imagine if all six of those he'd turned had done the bloodletting ritual? It would have been chaos!"

"Just figuring that out now, are we?" Jordan jabbed.

Maximus curled his fingers into two fists, pressing them hard against the table. Jordan watched as his eyes turned from green to black and everything began to shake. It was a slight tremble at first, starting with the glasses and forks then moving to the table.

Soon, every table in the restaurant was shaking and the customers began to panic and run to the nearest door frame. Jordan, however, knew what was going on and just watched in fear as the tremble grew stronger and stronger until his teacup burst into several pieces.

Almost as suddenly as it began, the trembling stopped. Maximus spread his hands on the table, closing his eyes as he breathed deeply then opened them once more. His eyes had returned to their normal color. Or...somewhat normal. glow-in-the-dark green wasn't exactly normal.

"What happened to being cleansed in the desert?" Jordan asked him. "Did God ignore you again?"

"One more snide remark and I'll kill you before doing the job myself, *Lucian*."

Jordan stopped chewing for a moment then continued, setting his fork on the plate. He brought his eyes up and glared at Maximus. "Don't call me that," he said angrily.

"Why not? It is your real name after all."

THE RESURRECTION

"Maybe in another life, but now I am Jordan D'Aubigne. I don't want to be associated with that man."

"That's a shame because after he's dead, I will give you something in return. Something that I know you will be unable to refuse."

"And why should I listen to you anymore? It's not like you're helping me kill him. You turned me and that is all. Why don't you just take care of it yourself?"

This was a pointless argument. Jordan already knew why Maximus couldn't kill Lucian. It had been explained to him in the beginning. After Maximus had dappled for too long with the Devil, he'd begged God to release him from his grasp. God, in response, said that he would as long as he chose someone to take his place. Maximus then, by saving Lucian's life as an infant, passed on the demonic power he'd felt had separated him from God, only to become greedy in the end and save some for himself.

Of course, this all seemed like a bunch of B.S. to Jordan. He thought it was just some romanticized version of the truth. Maximus claimed to be the creator of vampires even though no one knew who the first vampire was.

Whatever Maximus had gotten himself into, it was very dark. The trembling tables were just a snippet of what he was capable of, and Jordan didn't want to know what he'd been like before he'd supposedly given Lucian some of his power.

"I led you to Gallard," Maximus pointed out. "Without him, you wouldn't have gotten to Lucian. I sensed that Samil was getting closer to finding a way to bring him back, and I pointed you in Gallard's direction to speed things up. And what did you do? You bonded with him, and you let Lucian get away when he was right in front of you! Let's not mention your falling for that woman friend of his."

Jordan stopped eating, suddenly losing his appetite. He hated being conflicted with what his main agenda should be. He hadn't expected to bond with Gallard. He'd left his family behind years ago when Maximus had recruited him to kill Lucian. But the more time he'd spent with Gallard, the more he'd wished that he'd taken the time to be involved with his descendants. He hadn't felt so welcomed by anyone since he'd been taken in by the D'Aubigne family many centuries ago when he was eighteen. He had spent so much of his life wanting revenge that he'd forgotten how to live.

And Lydian. He hadn't been ready for his feelings to hit him so hard. He hadn't felt more alive than when he was with her. Her eccentric ways and loud personality had him hooked from the second he'd laid eyes on her. He could never get tired of her presence, and when she'd died, that small light that was bringing him back to who he used to be had gone out. The only thing that kept him going was his relationship with Gallard. That and hatred for Lucian. He wanted to see him burn.

"I have a question," Jordan said. "His daughters; they're different. They appear to have mortal bodies, but they are immortal and feed on vampire blood. What are they?"

Maximus closed his eyes in the dramatic way he always did.

"Maybe they are God's retribution. The opposite of everything evil, created to destroy the immortals that inhabit the earth," he opened his eyes again and his expression turned angry once more. "Or they're just proof that abomination begets abomination."

Having had enough of Maximus' biblical ramblings, Jordan stood up and tossed a few bills on the table.

"I need to get going. I left without telling anybody, and they're probably wondering where I am."

"You haven't even heard my offer yet, Jordanes. Don't you want to know what I will reward you with?"

Jordan sighed, folding his arms. He couldn't think of anything that Maximus could give him that would inspire motivation. He'd made promises of riches, which he would inherit upon Lucian's death, a climb in social status; none of which he truly wanted.

"All right, Maxi-pad; what are you going to give me?"

"I can help you get Lydian back."

Jordan looked up and unfolded his arms, resting them on the table. "You're lying. She's dead; she's been dead for a year. Unless she's like Lela, she can't come back."

"You forget how powerful I am. I can bring her back, Jordanes, if you do as I ask."

Jordan couldn't believe what he was hearing. Getting Lydian back would bring him more joy than anything in the world. This would change everything. If Maximus wasn't lying, and he could have the love of his life back, there was nothing he wouldn't do to make it so.

"Fine. I will make sure that Lucian is destroyed, and in return, I expect you to follow through."

"And I expect you to follow through as well, Jordanes. Because if you don't, I will take matters into my own hands. You know how much damage I can cause when I'm angry."

Jordan then he got up and left the restaurant. Maximus' warning had somewhat rattled him, and he was trying to come up with a strategy. He had no idea how he was going to stop Lucian, and he didn't want to wait around to see what Maximus would do if he failed.

Back when they were still trying to find Solomon, Maximus had actually threatened to kill Gallard, Lela, and Lydian if Samil wasn't stopped by the end of February. He didn't take Maximus seriously until he heard that he spied on Lela in Florida and then helped Gallard's crazy charity case sneak into her hotel and drug her. After that, he never underestimated the threats again.

Once he'd gotten back to his car, he turned his phone back on. There were four voicemails from Melody and five texts from Solomon. He sighed before hitting the call-back button for Solomon's number and waited for an answer.

"Hey, Solomon, it's Jordan. No, everything is all right. I just needed to take care of something. Yeah, I'll be there in about an hour. Bye."

He hung up and tossed the phone onto the passenger seat. He then flipped the visor down and looked at his eyes in the mirror. He was tired of wearing contacts and couldn't wait for the day when he could just have his regular brown eyes. He was grateful, though that he had naturally black hair so that he didn't have to dye it. He'd had to dye it brown when he'd first made contact with Gallard so that he would appear more human, but it had grown out by then. He reluctantly put the contacts in each eye before pulling out of the restaurant and heading towards I-95.

Lucian waited expectantly for his messengers to bring Cherish to the restaurant. He wanted to celebrate their reunion with a nice dinner. For the occasion, he had gotten himself a new suit that was black with silver cufflinks and a matching vest. Underneath, he wore a white-button up with a grey tie decorated in silver and white calligraphic swirls. On his feet, he wore black Shortwing Bluchers that were brand new and without a scratch. He'd been warned before-hand that the restaurant was that of the semi-formal nature, but he didn't care. He wanted to look his best.

One of his sycophants made a reservation at the 21 Main at North Beach in South Carolina. He wanted to surprise her with a nice meal, assuming that she could eat. He had a feeling that she could. She was just like him, his Cherish. She'd always been like him in looks, temperament, and intelligence. As an immortal, she had to be everything that he was.

He looked up just as she'd walked into the restaurant and he got out of his chair. She wore a deep-purple evening gown with the sweetheart neck-line and a bodice fashioned to look like butterfly wings. The exact dress he'd specifically picked out for her. Purple was her favorite color.

She took her time getting to the table, but he didn't mind. He wanted to look her over before giving her a proper greeting.

"Cherish, daughter. You look lovely," he said, wrapping his arms around her. He was surprised and a bit disappointed when she didn't hug him back. She just stood there. He finally let go and pulled a chair out for her, motioning that she should sit, and she obeyed. He scooted her in before taking a seat in his own chair.

"Why are you sad?" he asked. "Solomon is alive, just as you wanted. Your friends have been spared."

She looked everywhere but at his face. Before he could speak again, the waiter arrived and began taking their orders. He realized that he hadn't even looked at the menu and quickly browsed before saying what he wanted.

"I will have the braised lamb shank," he replied, "What about you?"

Cherish sighed as she looked at her menu. He thought back to when she was a little girl and had refused to eat any vegetable besides potatoes. He wondered if she was still as picky.

"I'll have the New York strip, medium well," she finally said,

THE RESURRECTION

handing her menu to the waiter. When he asked what they wanted to drink, Cherish spoke before Lucian could.

"What the most expensive stuff you got?"

"That would be Ace of Spades. It's champagne," replied the waiter.

"We'll take it."

Lucian was shocked by her bold move. Ordering the most expensive drink in the restaurant was spontaneous and rash, none of which fit her character. He felt that perhaps he'd been wrong about her being the same girl.

"I did not know that you had a taste for alcohol," he said. She folded her arms and leaned back in her chair.

"Champagne is all right, but I prefer hard alcohol. Takes the edge off when I'm feeding. The more buzzed I am, the less I feel bad about it."

Lucian wasn't sure how to respond to that. Her new personality was throwing him for a loop, and it was taking some getting used to. He decided to change the subject.

"Your sister seems well. I'm sure she is as plucky and bossy as ever."

"What do you want from me, Lucian? I hope you didn't threaten my friends to get me here just so we could have a nice dinner and chit chat."

The waiter returned with their food and Lucian forced a polite smile as he gave them their plates then poured the champagne into their glasses. Cherish grabbed her glass and guzzled half of hers before starting with her meal. He had never seen a lady drink that much alcohol at once in his life. He'd always kept company with stuffy women who would daintily sip their wine, as if everyone else around them were a bunch of drunkards. Still, he thought a woman getting drunk was uncouth behavior.

"I asked for you because I missed you. You are my daughter, and I love you."

She burst out laughing, and he flinched at her sudden outburst. He didn't understand what was humorous about what he'd said. He'd only spoken the truth.

"You love me? You *love* me?"

"Yes, that is what I said."

"You don't know how to love! You call dragging me out in the middle of the night to watch you murder innocent people *love*? You call stealing my chance at a normal life *love*? I don't care that we're biologically related, you were dead to me...to *us* before Solomon put you in that coffin. And you know what? Thanks to you, I don't know how to love either."

He just sat and took her berating while she yelled. He couldn't understand what had changed. She had been a nearly perfect child.

"What happened to us, Cherish? We were so close when you were a little girl. Why can we not go back to those times?"

"Because I'm not a little girl anymore, Lucian. I grew up, and you kept treating me like I was still a child. I wanted to go out; attend tea parties with Melody; have a coming out party when I was of age and not when I'd reached the age of a spinster. Find a husband who would love me. But you wanted me all to yourself. And as always, you got mad because you didn't get your way."

Lucian did his best not to lose his temper. This wasn't the place to unleash his growing rage, so he decided to try and stay as calm as possible. He had to admit that she was very right. He had wanted her to himself, and he did get mad when she rebelled and began an affair.

"I would not have had to grow strict with you if it were not for your behavior. You brought it on yourself, Cherish."

"You see? This is why! Instead of being a father and comforting me, you ignored me for months before you even looked at me without being angry. Melody was there for me and so was Solomon, but all I wanted was for my father to hold me and tell me that I was going to be okay. You had your chance to fix our relationship, and you let it pass by. It's too late now. Melody and I are done with you."

"If you only knew what your sister was really like, you wouldn't say such things." He threw his knife on the table and glared at her. She looked down at the table and began poking her

steak with her fork. He felt her attention slipping away again, and he wasn't about to let that happen. "She isn't as innocent as you think she is. What she did was far more barbaric than anything I've ever done."

"You think I don't know her secret? Because I do. What

separates the two of you is that she actually felt remorse for what she did all those years ago. Unlike you."

A laugh escaped his lips. "Does not matter anyway. What was done was done. You want to be done with me? Then you shall get your wish." He took a sip of the champagne. "My daughter, I need you do take care of something for me."

He watched as she began to tremble, and he smiled at the fact that he'd managed to finally shake her up a bit.

"What will you have me do?" she asked, nearly whispering. He picked up his knife once more and cut a small bite of his lamb before putting it into his mouth. Since he was paying so much for it, he didn't want it to go to waste.

"I want you to get Lela. Since you have made it clear that you want me out of your life, I am willing to compromise."

She poured more champagne then drank the whole glass in one gulp then took a big bite of her steak. He knew she was trying to distract herself from the conversation. She never used to have an appetite like this.

"If, hypothetically, I could get her to join you, how would I do this?"

He took a bite of his lamb as well before replying.

"By seducing Gallard."

She started laughing, but he didn't see what was funny. He'd been absolutely serious, yet she found it comical.

"You want me to seduce Gallard? How the hell am I supposed to do that? He's in love with Lela. He doesn't care about me in that way."

"Cherish, you and I both know that a man doesn't have to care about you to sleep with you."

The smile on her face turned into a painful grimace, and he almost felt bad for making that comment. What her lover had done to her was cruel, and though Lucian resented her for getting pregnant, he did pity her situation.

"You're a bastard, you know that? I pour my heart out to you for the first time in centuries and you still mock me. I'm not doing anything for you."

"I am sorry, darling. Forgive me. I should not have insulted you that way. It is in the past and cannot be undone." He set his fork down and folded his hands. "But I was serious about Gallard. Make her think he does not love her and she will come to me. I am sure of it."

"And if I decide not to?"

"Then I will change my mind and kill Solomon."

"I thought you were going to kill him anyway."

"I was not. But this is not the first time I have threatened to take his life. If he crosses me again, I may not be so lenient."

She smirked, pouring more champagne. "Well, he let me die, so he can rot for all I care."

He studied her as she spoke and he detected that she was lying. She'd kissed Solomon before they left and he saw true emotion behind it. She hadn't done it to spite him; she felt something for Solomon and Lucian knew it.

"I know you care about him, but you are wasting your time. He lusts after you just like he did all the other women. Once he gets what he wants, he will leave you. Remember, I am your father, and I love you unconditionally. I am the only one you can trust to stay by your side."

Cherish fell silent and he continued eating while he waited for her answer. He loved the tension that he'd created and the adrenaline rush that came with his influence. He knew that she would resent him no matter what her decision was, but he didn't care. If he pushed her to her breaking point, she would have no choice but to retaliate in anger, and that would mean that he'd finally won.

"And if I succeed?" she asked.

"I will let you go then you and your sister can forget you ever knew me."

"How generous of you." She set her wine glass down once more. "All right, I'll do it. I'll try to seduce Gallard."

Chapter Twenty-Two

As we waited for Jordan to arrive at the gas station, I watched as Solomon leaned against the BMW, praying quietly to himself. I had almost forgotten that he was a Cardinal, especially since there had been some serious lip action going on between him and Cherish before she'd left. I had a feeling that that wasn't the first time something like that had happened, and I was curious to know how it started.

Gallard, Aaron, and Kevin had taken off to get blood bags at one of his bars that was about a mile out of town. Melody was reading a book to Robin. I smiled as I listened to my sister laugh at Melody's horrible voices. I was glad that Robin was still able to laugh despite the horrific circumstances. She was handling everything better than I was.

My worry over Jordan was overwhelming me after a while, so I decided to talk to Solomon. I hadn't really had a chance to get to know him since we'd been so busy traveling, and I wanted to get a better sense of who he was. I quietly walked over to him so that I

wouldn't interrupt and stood next to the car. He stopped praying, did the sign
of the cross then looked up at me.

"Why did you stay in the church for so long?" I asked. "Wouldn't it be boring living with a bunch of religious old men all of the time?"

He laughed and stepped closer. When I studied his face, I saw a lot of Mark in him. It was scary how much he resembled him, as well as Aaron.

"I stayed because I loved God. I still do. But lately, it's getting harder and harder to commit to my responsibilities what with Lucian being back and everything. I love the church, but my family is more important right now."

"Will you go back when all of this is over?"

He shook his head half-heartedly then sighed.

"As much as I want to continue serving, I think that it is time that I move on and find other ways to serve God. I have given almost five-hundred years' worth of service, attempting to do penance for my part in the deaths of Cherish and Melody. Upon learning that they came back to life, I have finally forgiven myself. I can move on now and work on finding myself."

I liked listening to him talk. He sounded very intelligent, and his accent was extremely interesting since he tended to go back and forth between English and Italian. Gallard had a slight French accent, but it was barely noticeable after knowing him quite a while. He'd told me that it used to be very strong until he lost it from being in the states for so long. I would often forget he was French until he would get mad and yell or when he was being affectionate.

"Is that why you're really thinking about leaving, or is it because of Cherish?" I asked, suddenly feeling bold.

"I've always loved Cherish. I was around the Christophes quite often after Lucian turned me. I grew attached to both of his daughters since I never had the chance to be a proper father to my son."

"What happened to him?"

"His mother married and had children with her husband, but my son was always treated differently than they. He finally left the family to make a name for himself. I visited him once in a while, but I had to stop when it was apparent that he was growing older and I was not. I wanted to help him in some way without hurting his pride. When I had to appear dead to the world, I left him nearly everything I had, saving only a small fortune for myself that I eventually rebuilt. As a bastard, he couldn't legitimately inherit my title and the Sharmentino line was no longer that of peers. Just very wealthy men.

"While I was searching for another church to establish myself in, I left England for about six years then returned to see how Lucian's family was fairing. Cherish was all grown up by then, and I had to pretend that I didn't notice. I had already broken all of my vows, and I didn't want to be that man anymore.

"After seeing her again after so long, I found that I still had those feelings. So to answer your question, yes; she is part of the reason I want to leave the church. And I hate that her father manipulated her into going back to him. But we'll get her back. And when I do, I'll make sure he doesn't go near her again."

I put a hand on his shoulder and he lightly touched it, saying, "It doesn't matter to me that you aren't biologically my descendent. You love your family, and that makes you just as much of a Sharmentino as your brothers and sister. I will be as quick to protect you as I would them."

"Thank you, Solomon. That means a lot to me, really."

I turned my head and saw a blue Honda Civic pull into the station and park next to the 4Runner. Jordan was finally back, and I let out a sigh of relief as I jogged to the car. When he got out, I slapped him upside the head, startling him.

"How could you do that to us? You had us all freaking out! We thought someone killed you!" I shouted.

He rubbed his head and said, "I'm sorry, I didn't realize that my phone was off."

I hugged him and he returned it. Whatever he was doing, I didn't really care. All that mattered was that he was back with us. I couldn't bear it if I lost another person I cared about. And Gallard would have been devastated if his only living family member was gone.

Gallard and my brothers arrived as well and when Gallard saw Jordan, he walked up to him and hit his head as well.

"Is everyone going to hit me?" Jordan asked sarcastically.

"Why did you take off? Do you know how worried I was?"

"Again, I apologize, *dad*." He looked at Gallard's face and his eyes grew wide. "What happened to your eye?"

"Lost it in 'Nam," Gallard joked halfheartedly. He folded his arms and said, "I can't lose you, Jordan. You kept me going while I went through hell this past year, and I can't go through that again. You're my only blood relative left, and I'm not going to let you die over something as stupid as going off on your own and not telling anyone where you're at."

Jordan nodded and promised that it wouldn't happen again. He never explained where he was, but I trusted that his errand was important.

We then got back into the Toyota and the BMW, leaving the Honda behind, and left the gas station. We didn't plan on traveling too far since we'd lost about an hour.

Gallard found my old driver's license in his luggage, so I was able to drive the BMW. Melody was still too shaken up about being separated from her sister, and I offered to drive for a while. Melody, Jordan, and Robin rode in the back of my car with Gallard in the passenger seat while Solomon and my brothers rode in the other. At that point, we weren't concerned about spreading out the strengths. Lucian ended the feud, and we were safe.

Our next stop was Blacksburg, Virginia. Aaron had suggested it but didn't say why, and Solomon agreed that stopping there for the time being was a good idea so we would have time to plan a rescue mission for Cherish.

I wanted to turn on the air conditioning to keep me awake, but I didn't want Robin to get cold. Jordan and Melody took turns reading to her until she fell asleep, and the ride was silent for a long time after that.

I drummed my fingers to the beat of the low-playing music on the radio until I twitched and realized that I couldn't remember the past five miles. I rolled down my window a bit to let the cold air wake me up and Gallard took my hand in his then kissed it.

"You look beat; do you want me to drive for a while?"

"I think I'm all right. Why don't you talk to me and keep me awake? Tell me something funny."

He massaged my hand with his thumb as he thought.

"Before I convinced the manager to give me my job

THE RESURRECTION

back, I had to resort to stripping. They let me have Lydian's old job." he said, maintaining a straight face. He sounded so serious that I almost fell for his joke. I rolled my eyes and nudged him with my elbow.

"Liar!" Jordan said from the back seat. "They wouldn't hire him because he's an old man and they didn't want him to sue if he broke a hip."

"At least it was because I'm old and not because I'm ugly," Gallard replied.

"Easy for you to say, Cyclops. You'd have better luck joining a freak show than being a stripper."

"Ouch, want some water for that burn?" Melody said, joining the conversation.

I was laughing so hard that I woke myself up. The drowsiness had drifted away for the time being, and I was able to keep my eyes open for the rest of the drive.

Around one-thirty, I followed Solomon into the parking lot of the Gigi's Inn and I was a tad disappointed that the drive was over. I would rather stay on the road then spend another day in a motel. But my brothers and Jordan couldn't travel during the day, so stopping was our only option. I slowly exited the vehicle and yawned as I stretched my legs.

We went through the usual routine of checking in to our rooms and deciding who would stay where. I ended up with Robin and Melody while the men piled in to the other room. I put Robin to bed before Melody and I showered then changed out of our bloody clothes and into some clean ones. I was still wearing Gallard's shirt, but it was now dirty. Melody and I decided we would find a Laundromat the next day so that we could do some much needed washing of everyone's clothes.

"How are you doing?" I asked Melody. She was sitting on her bed while I was on the other, braiding Robin's hair.

"Disappointed in myself. I should have done more to stop him from taking her. But I was too afraid to stand up to him."

"What's so scary about him anyway? He didn't seem all that terrifying. He mostly pissed me off." I paused and looked at Robin. "I mean...he made me very angry."

Melody chuckled and scooted to the edge of her bed.

"My father terrifies everyone. He has a short temper and he tends to yell. He always made Cherish cry when she got in trouble, and I did my best to be the angel child. It paid off since he never yelled at nor scolded me."

"I didn't let him boss me around. He was always trying to tell me—"

"Wait, when did you meet him? I thought he'd only just gotten back a year ago. Weren't you dead?"

I suddenly realized I'd never told her or Cherish the entire story. All they knew was that David and Lydian gave their blood to resurrect him. The rest of the details didn't seem important to our mission.

"This is going to sound crazy but...ever since I was a baby...I heard Lucian in my head."

"What? That's incredible! You mean he talked to you? What kinds of things did he say?"

"Well...he trashed my father mostly. I know now that it was because he has a grudge against Sharmentinos. Other than that, he just told me not to kiss anyone or sleep with anyone because, quote, 'once they get what they want they'll leave you.'"

Melody laughed even harder and Robin looked confused but didn't say anything.

"Speaking of sleeping...I noticed you were wearing Gallard's shirt earlier tonight. Did you get a little closer to that boyfriend of yours?"

I bit my lip and glanced down at Robin with my eyes to try and hint that this wasn't the best time for this conversation.

"How about we speak in code words?" she suggested. "Did you and Gallard...go to the park?"

"The park? That's the best you could come up with?"

"Yes or no?"

"No. How about...we went to the park...but we didn't go on the jungle gym. We just went on the swings."

She groaned and lay on her back. "These code words aren't working."

"Okay, I'll try to clarify." I thought for a moment then smiled. "Let's just say it's not just backs that he's good at massaging, if you know what I mean."

THE RESURRECTION

Melody giggled then sat up again. "You naughty little thing. I knew you weren't a prude like Cherish accused you of being. I am so jealous."

"You should be. That man has magic hands."

Robin turned around and looked at me.

"Gallard can do magic? Can he make a bunny come out of a hat?"

Melody and I started laughing so hard I was afraid we wouldn't be able to stop. I was glad that she was able to laugh. I'd wanted to cheer her up and in the end, Robin ended up doing that instead.

"There's something else," I said. "We're waiting until this is over to tell everyone but…I have to tell someone. While we were fooling around, I…kind of asked him to marry me."

"What! Lela are you serious? Well…what did he say?"

"He said yes!"

"You're getting married?" Robin shouted.

"We are," I said, my smile growing by the second. "Gallard and I are engaged."

She started bouncing excitedly in her seat, and it was painfully adorable. I hugged her and kissed the top of her head.

"Does that mean he's going to be my dad now?"

I laughed. "I don't know, honey. I do know that he loves you. He'll always be there for you and me."

The next morning, I awoke feeling groggy and a bit cranky. I sat up, stretching and looked at the clock. It was only a little after ten. I thought about going back to sleep for a few more hours but became restless after lying down for fifteen minutes more. I got up and went to the bathroom to brush my teeth.

As I finished getting ready, I realized that Melody and Robin had been gone the entire time and I hadn't even noticed. I quickly tied my hair back and pulled my shoes on before walking out the door to investigate their absences. I jogged down the stairs to the second floor where the others were and knocked. Aaron answered the door, only slightly cracking it open.

"Hey, Lela. What's up?" he asked.

"Is Robin with you?" I asked, trying not to sound freaked out.

"Yeah, she's here."

I stepped forward to walk into the room, but he blocked the way so I couldn't enter. I folded my arms and raised an eyebrow.

"What are you doing? Why won't you let me in?"

"Because...uh...we're all naked in here."

"Right. I'm sure you would all be having a nude party with our baby sister in there."

I tried to force the door open, but Solomon pushed past him, closing the door behind him. I became even more confused by everyone's weird behavior and hoped that he would give me an explanation.

"Are you up for a little trip?" he asked.

I shrugged. "Depends...where are we going?"

"You'll see. I think you'll find this outing enjoyable. Your brothers would have taken you but they can't exactly go outside, so I offered."

He clicked the unlock button on the BMW and I followed after him. I got into the passenger seat and buckled myself in then he pulled onto the road. He took a piece of paper out of his pocket and began hitting buttons on the GPS. After struggling for a while, he handed me the paper and asked if I would mind putting the address into the machine. I nodded, smiling since I found it funny that he still had trouble figuring out modern technology.

He drove through town and into a cute little neighborhood with houses of the same design but painted different colors like brown, green, and off-white. He took a left, a right, and then another left before pulling into the driveway of a small, one-story cottage with a white picket fence and an amazingly green lawn. The siding was olive, and the windows had black shutters. The trim was white as well, and the front door was painted a stunning apple-red.

I kept staring at the house even as Solomon got out and opened the door for me. I slowly stepped out, admiring the décor of the porch.

"You're probably extremely confused right now, aren't you?" Solomon asked. I gave a half nod and began following him up steps and onto the porch.

"Whose house is this?" I asked.

He smiled and said, "You'll find out in a minute. They said that someone would be home, so if you ring the doorbell, someone should answer." He walked back down the steps and I followed him.

"Where are you going? Are you leaving me here?" I questioned.

He opened the back seat and pulled out a small bag saying, "Melody packed a few of your things while you were asleep. You're going to stay here for a few days."

"Should I really be left here all alone and defenseless?"

"We both know that you aren't defenseless. Anyway, you've been through a lot this past year, what with you dying and coming back to life. And you've been busy worrying about your family and it's time that you focus on yourself for a bit. Besides, there are some people that want to meet you."

He handed me the bag and lightly touched my cheek before getting into the driver's seat.

"I'll be back in a couple of days."

He started the car and drove off, leaving me alone at some random stranger's house. Though the situation was a little weird, I decided to trust Solomon. He wouldn't do anything to put me in danger. I would have to learn how to stop seeing the unknown as something negative.

Chapter Twenty-Three

I stood awkwardly in the driveway for a few minutes before walking back onto the porch and staring at the door. I had no idea who would be on the other side and hoped that Solomon was right about me enjoying this mysterious visit.

My finger stroked the doorbell a few times before I built up the courage to push it. I listened to the generic tune it played and shortly after, I heard footsteps. They were faint, but I discerned that it was because the person was further inside the house.

The footsteps got louder and louder until the person stopped at the door and opened it. I stopped breathing as I stared at the guy who had answered the door. He was tall, about six-three, with light brown skin and short, curly black hair. He had light blue eyes and a lean figure. But his physical appearance wasn't what had my attention; all he was wearing was a bath towel around his waist.

"Well, well. To whom do I owe the pleasure?" he asked, smiling flirtatiously. It took me a second to find my voice, but I spoke with a slight stutter.

"Um…my name is Lela…Sharmentino. And you are?"

"Noel Shepherd. My dad said that I was to look out for a young blonde woman. You're Uncle David's daughter, right? Robin's

THE RESURRECTION

sister?"

My heart lurched when he mentioned David. I couldn't believe that I was standing face to face with his relative, and it was almost like a part of him was there with me.

"Yeah, how do you know Robin?" I asked.

"She stayed with us about a year ago. Uncle David had gotten himself into some trouble and needed us to take care of her. I was surprised when my dad told me you were coming. We were led to believe that you were both dead."

"I was, but now I'm not."

He stepped aside, and I walked into the house. The inside was even lovelier than the outside. The wood floors were stained a dark mahogany color and a lot of the furniture matched. The whole house smelled like roses.

"Make yourself at home," Noel said. "I'm going to throw some clothes on. I'll be back down in a minute."

I wandered over to the loveseat then sat down. The pillow covers looked like they were hand-sewn. There was a photo album on the coffee table, which I picked up and began looking through. The first part was filled with black and white pictures of people dressed as if they were from the twenties. I turned a few pages until I came to one that was taken up by a single photo of a large family. The mother and father were sitting in the front with three young women to their left and four young men to the right. I studied all of their faces until I came to one in particular; David's.

"Pretty crazy, isn't it?" Noel asked, entering the living room. He was now wearing a long-sleeve maroon Abercrombie shirt and jeans with a dark wash. He sat next to me on the couch, and I turned my attention back to the album.

"You keep referring to him as Uncle David. Was he around a lot?" I asked.

"He was here every Thanksgiving up until five years ago. I didn't realize something was off about him, but when I found the pictures, my father thought I was old enough to handle his secret. I was freaked at first, but the whole thing sort of became cool."

I flipped through more of the pages trying to spot David in some of them. He appeared in very few, but I was still happy to see his face.

"How old are you?" I asked.

"Twenty-two. I've been away at college but moved back home after graduating in June. I have a degree in English but not a clue what I'm going to do with it. I'm thinking of maybe going back and getting my masters so I can teach history. I don't care what grade level. I really like history. It's kind of a passion of mine."

"At least you went to college. I didn't finish high school but received a GED. I never really had the drive to pursue a higher education. After I turned, my life was kind of put on hold."

"Well, you are immortal. You have all the time in the world to go to college." He leaned back on the couch and stretched his long arms over the back. "Let's not talk about school, that's boring," he said. "Tell me about yourself. Do you have a boyfriend? A girlfriend? Both?"

I lightly laughed before answering, "A fiancé actually." I hadn't said it out loud before, and it felt good to.

"That's great. Congratulations!"

"Thanks. What about you? Boyfriend? Girlfriend? Both?"

He laughed. "I think I'm going to like you. To answer the question, I am seeing someone. We met our sophomore year of college, and we've been together ever since. She's currently working in a different city, but the long distance thing is actually going well. I visit a lot."

The front door opened, and we both stood up. A middle-aged man with greying hair and blue eyes that matched Noel's walked in with his arm around a petite woman. She was darker than Noel and had brown eyes. Her hair was cut extremely short, and her makeup was done very subtly.

"You must be Lela," said the man. He came over to me and gave me a light hug, which I politely returned. "I'm Declan Shepherd. My grandfather was your father's brother. It's wonderful to finally meet you."

I was then formerly introduced to his wife Paula and the four of us talked as if we were old friends. They told me stories about David from years before I'd met him and even showed me his Medal of Honor that he'd received for saving the surrounded U.S. soldiers in World War Two.

The most endearing information that they gave me was of how he'd told them about me even before I was born. He'd shown them

THE RESURRECTION

pictures that my mother sent from each of my birthdays, which they showed me copies of. They'd kept every picture from my first birthday until my fourteenth.

Before we knew it, it was dinner time, and I continued talking with Noel and Declan while Paula worked hard to prepare a meal. I offered to help, but she insisted that I just relax and let her do everything.

"Do you even eat?" Noel asked.

"I can, but I don't very often. It's not that I don't like it. I just can't sustain myself on it."

"Well, I'm glad that you can eat," Paula said, "Because I can't wait for you to taste your grandma's homemade chicken-pot pie recipe."

"My grandma? As in David's mother?" I asked.

"Her recipe has been handed down for many generations. Hasn't changed at all since the day she wrote it down."

Paula was right; the chicken-pot pie was amazing. I hadn't had homemade food that delicious in a very longtime. I didn't speak much while we ate but listened to the family have their own conversations, learning more about them as they talked. It was evident that they were all close and got a long very well.

I never had nice dinners with my family. My parents were almost completely silent the entire time while my brothers and I talked amongst ourselves. My mother never looked at Mark in the loving way Paula looked at Declan. Or the way Gallard looked at me for that matter.

The joy in the Shepherd house was contagious, and I instantly felt like part of the family. Other than Mark's grandmother Vera, there weren't any other relatives we spent time with. My mother lost her parents at a young age and never really had a family. She spent her childhood in foster care then immediately after she aged out, she went to college where she met Mark. They bonded over similar losses; his parents having died when he was a junior in high school. His grandmother took care of him and Evelyn until both graduated and then she'd died of a heart attack just before Aaron was born. Death was a common thing in my family, yet I still wasn't numbed when I lost someone.

I went to bed feeling more relaxed than I had in a while. For once, I wasn't anxious or in a constant state of worry. I put on the night clothes that Melody had packed for me then crawled into the guest bed.

It was nice not having to sleep on a hotel bed after so long and the flannel sheets were extremely soft. The brown comforter was warm and I buried myself underneath it with only my head exposed. I was asleep within minutes, my dreams void of anything horrifying.

Chapter Twenty-Four

The taxi pulled up to Gigi's Inn, and Cherish watched for any signs of life. It was well past midnight and her people were bound to go out. They had spent a lot of time in hotels and probably had cabin fever. She saw that the BMW was parked in the front, but she wasn't sure which rooms the group was staying in.

Cherish got out, paid the driver, and then stood in the parking lot, dreading what she would have to do. She hated that her father still had such a powerful influence over her. She'd told herself the entire way to the restaurant that she would not give in to his manipulation but failed the moment he'd offered her a chance of freedom.

Gallard was one of her dearest friends, and splitting him and Lela up would break her heart. She had come to terms with the fact that Lela would hate her even more, if she pulled it off, but it also meant that she and her sister would finally be free of their father. That was what kept her going.

It was more than just wanting a way out. She was afraid that if she continued to defy Lucian, he back out of the agreements then kill Solomon and the rest of the Sharmentino family after all. She couldn't let that happen, and if hurting her friends was the way to keep them safe, she would do whatever it took.

Her father had given her a deadline, which she couldn't decide was a good or bad thing. She had two weeks; fourteen days, three hundred and thirty-six hours. She'd calculated the time as she'd driven from Myrtle Beach to Blacksburg. She'd taken the long way, having gotten off the freeway in Greensboro instead of merging onto highway fifty-two.

Cherish had a feeling she'd been followed. Her father never trusted her after she'd gotten pregnant, so she doubted he would let her do this without spies watching from the distance. If she didn't carry it out, word would surely get back to him, and the consequences would be massive.

A door on the bottom floor opened, and she watched Aaron and Kevin come out and then Jordan and Solomon. It was Solomon's face that sparked the courage for her to go to them. She wanted to be with him for some of the time before she would become his enemy. She wished that she had more time to sort out what she was feeling for him.

When he'd kissed her, she felt electricity. She hadn't felt electricity with a guy in many centuries. Her pull towards him frightened her and she was confused as to what she should do about it. But she also had to prepare for the fact that she may never get it all figured out and she would carry the memory of those three kisses with her to the grave.

Cherish walked towards the four men, but they took off before she could speak. She was surprised they didn't see her. It could be a blessing in disguise. This way, Gallard was left somewhat alone. He was the only one who hadn't come out of the hotel besides Lela and Melody.

She stopped in front of the door and took a moment to calm her nerves before knocking on the door. She wouldn't try anything tonight. That would be too strange. The first couple of days would be filled with subtle hints that she cared about him more than a friend and lots and lots of flirting whenever they were alone. The third day, she would initiate touching; a hand over his, shoulder rubbing; anything that was obvious and then she would make a move on the fourth day.

THE RESURRECTION

Who was she kidding? Two weeks was not an adequate amount of time to pull of something like this. Her father put way too much confidence in her, which was insulting. He'd basically said that she was easy and that any guy would jump at the chance to be with her. This was partly true, but she didn't want to admit it.

Gallard opened the door, and she forced a smile. He didn't say anything at first but then smiled back and gave her a hug. She'd forgotten that he gave really good hugs.

"Cherry Pop! How did you get here?" he asked.

"My father let me go. He was under the delusional impression that I was the same as I was four hundred years ago, but that isn't so. He didn't like the new me and sent me away."

She went into the room, closing the door behind her. She wouldn't stay long since it was too soon for Lela to catch them in a compromising position, but she wanted to make some progress before going to see her sister.

"Where's Lela and Melody?" she asked. "Melody is probably upstairs with Robin in room twenty-five, and Lela has been at a relative's. She hasn't had a chance to breathe since she got back, so she's taking some time to relax. We've been trying to come up with a plan to get you back as well."

It touched her that they hadn't just let her go. She knew Melody would try to help her, but knowing the others wanted to as well made her feel even guiltier for sneaking behind their backs.

"You would come for me? Even if it meant you would risk your life?"

"Yes, of course I would! It's what I do. What *we* do. We would all risk our lives for anyone in this group."

Cherish was beginning to lose her nerve. He was such a good man. He always had been, despite his initial defensiveness. Once they'd gotten to know each other, she'd seen him for what he really was; a kind, gentle, and caring individual. No wonder Lela fell in love with him.

"Have I missed anything?"

"Not really. Solomon has been praying a lot, and I've been keeping Robin busy. Oh! Lela and I are engaged."

That put a damper on her plans. If they were getting married, then their bond would be even harder to break. She was up for the challenge. Her freedom and Melody's was depending on it.

"Can I ask why so soon?"

"Why wait? We know each other extremely well, and we've already been apart for a year. We were going to get married sometime anyway. As they say, there's no time like the present."

He was starting to get suspicious. She could see it in his eyes. If she didn't give him the punch line to all of these questions, he was going to figure out something was wrong.

"I have to ask. Why did you tell Lela about us?" He asked.

"I was drunk, I was angry. You know me. Plus, seeing you again brought back memories." She smiled. "That was a pretty wild night, wasn't it?"

She could tell he wasn't amused by her comment.

"I'm not like that anymore." He went over and sat on the bed. "I will admit that it's different with her. I've never been in a relationship with…"

"A virgin?"

He slightly nodded. "Dyani had been with other men before. It wasn't uncommon for women of her race. I was in the process of getting comfortable with Lela. It really didn't help matters that you gave a detailed description of what happened between us."

"It wasn't detailed! God, you people are so sensitive."

"*You* people? Last I checked, we were *your* people." His shoulders sank. "What's going on with you, Cherry Pop? You never used to be this…angry all the time. Yeah, you've lost your temper before, but this is different."

This wasn't going as well as she'd hoped. She walked over and sat next to him on the bed. Gallard was always easy to talk to and she never had a problem opening up to him. But she had a job to do. No matter how much she'd missed her friend and asking for his advice, she couldn't. Instead, she had to try and seduce him.

"I guess I'm feeling a little uptight. I think a good roll in the sack might help." She sighed. "When was the last time you got any?"

"What does that have to do with anything?"

"Just tell me. You and Lela obviously aren't doing anything, so it has to have been a long time."

Ten seconds passed before he answered. "I'm only telling you this because we're friends. You were the last person I've been with."

She hadn't seen that one coming. "Really? Wow. Nothing at all? Not even a good hand job?"

Gallard chuckled. "Not even. I haven't spent much time with women. I helped Bodoway run the bar for a few years and then I went searching for others like me. I always went home alone. I haven't had the desire to be intimate with anyone until...well, until I fell in love with Lela. Believe me, it hasn't been easy. But now I have this amazing woman who wants to marry me, and I can't wait to be with her." He put an arm around her. "I want you to be there when I get married. I know you and Lela don't get along, but could you make an exception?"

"I suppose. So what is it about Lela Sharmentino that has you so eager to tie the knot other than the fact that she's a typical tall, hot blonde with legs for days? I thought you said blondes weren't your type."

"No, I said that I don't like box blondes. Lela is natural. And there's nothing typical about her." He turned towards her. "What is it about her that has you so eager to bash her every time her name comes up?"

"You really want to know?"

She couldn't hold in her anger anymore. It had been building and building ever since she got the phone call from Melody that their father was alive. Everyone kept telling her what had happened ever since she and her sister gave away his blood to four people and it seemed that all of it was a waste.

"I just don't like her. Do I need a reason?"

"No, but I would like to know how I can balance my friendship with you and my relationship with her when you don't like each other. I guess...I just have to spend time with you separately. Lela loves your sister though. I think she sees her as sort of a mother figure."

Cherish rolled her eyes. "Please. My mother was one of the worst out there. She did everything but physically beat me. Mothers are overrated."

"What are you talking about? I had a great mother. And Cherish, you would have been a great mother too. If you had the chance."

He reached to hug her, and she let him. When she

released him, she looked where his right eye should have been then lightly touched the patch with her finger. She hated that her father's lackey had done this to Gallard. And she was glad that the woman paid for it.

This was enough initiative for now. She was tired and needed more time to plan ahead for future flirting techniques. She also wanted to see her sister, so she said one last thing before leaving.

"Lela's a lucky woman. As for your request, I promise I will support you at your wedding."

She started to leave when Gallard stopped her.

"Wait, before you go I need a favor."

"Does it involve stealing something? You know I'm good at that," she said, giving a mischievous smile.

"No, though it would be funny. What I need to get would take more than just a day of planning to steal anyway. But I do need your help with something."

The noise level of the bar was so deafening that Maximus was surprised anyone could think. Unlike Gallard's place, the entire facility reeked of alcohol, gluttony, and greed.

As he watched the men swallow shot after shot and the women who clung to them, clad in suggestive clothing, he nearly set the place on fire. It was not nearly as bad as some of the things he'd seen in Las Vegas. That place was a modern day Sodom and Gomorrah. Here, it was just irritatingly bad.

His heart lurched a bit at the same time that the door opened and two men stepped in. He knew they were the ones he was looking for. He could sense an immortal from a mile away. The pull wasn't as strong as the one he felt towards Lucian or Jordan, but it was noticeable nonetheless. He pretended to be interested in his drink while they approached the bar and looked at the menu. They were standing right next to him. If he could just lightly brush by, their minds would be an open door to him.

THE RESURRECTION

Ever so slightly, he reached for the tray of nuts that he knew were most likely littered with germs and in the process, accidently nudged the man closest to him. The man glared but didn't address the incident. Maximus smiled apologetically then closed his eyes as the memories flooded his mind.

This man's name was Kenneth Manning. He was born in nineteen seventy-two and turned in ninety-one. He had a girlfriend, whom he later turned as well, and both had recently been recruited by Lucian. During a recent battle, his girlfriend injured Gallard and Lucian's daughters killed her. Kenneth wasn't too happy about that.

"God!" Kenneth said after downing a shot. "I hate this! My girlfriend's dead and I can't even get drunk!"

"I here ya," the second man said. "I would suggest you pick some chick up and have her for dinner, but I doubt you feel up to that."

"Damn right I don't. What I want is to kill something...someone. Instead, we're stuck here in Virginia of all places making sure some broad seduces some guy. What is he paying us again?"

"Ten grand up front. I would take the money and run, but you saw what he did to the last guy who tried to bolt with the money. Daniel was it? Lucian found him on a bus to Reno, and he made it crash."

Kenneth nodded. "That sister of hers should pay. She can't just take Jamie away from me and expect to go on without punishment. I want her dead, and I want her blood all over me."

Maximus cringed at the hatred in his voice. He didn't require blood to survive, so he never had the need to kill for survival or other reasons. The only lives he'd taken were that of immortals. As long as Lucian was alive, he was trapped on this earth. If only the

bastard hadn't called off the feud, then those who were after him would want him dead.

What they needed was a reason to kill him; a little push. If he could manage to pin something on Lucian that would make them angry enough to want revenge, it would have to be a terrible crime.

Maximus didn't have it in him to do something cruel but…an angry man who just lost his girlfriend might.

"I think I know how to help," he said. The two men looked at him.

"I'm sorry, were we speaking to you?" Kenneth asked.

He smiled. "It seems to me that you are in need of assistance. You want to escape Lucian, and you want revenge for your girlfriend. I can help you obtain both goals at the same time."

The men exchanged a glance then the second man said, "We're listening."

"I say you go ahead with your revenge plan. Nothing enrages those people more than when you kill one of their own. They know you work for Lucian so they will think he is behind it. And while they're off killing him, you have a
chance to escape."

Kenneth smiled and a throaty laugh escaped his lips. "That is genius. And who are you exactly?"

"If you have a moment, I will tell you everything. Now, here's exactly what you must do."

Chapter Twenty-Five

I slept longer than I'd intended and crawled out of bed around nine forty-five. I quickly got dressed and headed into the living room just as Declan and Noel had returned from a jog. Their love of running explained why I liked to run. It must have been a Shepherd thing.

"Good morning!" Declan said. He wiped his face with a towel then hung it around his neck. "I hope that your bed was comfortable enough."

"You have no idea. When you've slept in a coffin for a year, a regular bed is heaven."

The two guys stared at me as if they were trying to figure out if I was joking or not. Noel then laughed really hard and so did Declan.

"Oh I get it," Declan said. "It's a joke against the stereotype right?"

"Yeah," I said, sensing that being honest would darken the mood. "Gotta love those stereotypes right?"

"Can you turn into a bat like David could?"

"Not anymore. It's probably a good thing since I looked like a drunken bird when I flew."

After the guys were both showered, the four of us had a wonderful brunch that Paula prepared. I was beginning to get cravings since I wasn't getting my required nourishment, but I did my best to hide it. I did talk more, though. I was quickly getting as comfortable around them as I was my friends.

"Did your parents ever figure out what you were?" Paula asked me once we were all seated at the table.

"My mom knew because of David. And I think Mark figured it out when...when the men came to our house and held us hostage."

Paula touched my hand sympathetically and I forced a smile. It was getting easier thinking about that night without falling apart, but it still hurt. I hated picturing the look in my mother's eyes as they murdered Mark then snatched Robin out of her arms.

"Can I ask you guys a serious question?" I asked.

"Of course, dear," Paula replied.

"I know that I'm David's daughter and everything and that you spent a lot of time with him...but...were you nervous when I showed up? I mean, I would be if a vampire I'd never met before came to my house."

Declan chuckled as he continued eating.

"You're wondering why we welcomed you so easily. Well, Lela, that's a good question. Most people probably wouldn't have been so nonchalant about inviting a vampire to stay, but we've become somewhat desensitized to vampires. It's probably not a good thing because if I met one on the street, I would most likely wave and say hello. I guess I kind of feel sorry for them. Not all chose to be what they are. Take you and David for example. Both of you were turned under false pretenses. I know that not all of them are as safe and under control as you and your brothers, but I can't judge them all because of what a few do, right?"

I liked that way of thinking. I used to believe that only those of my kind could be trusted, but the more time I spent with the Shepherds, the more I started having hope that maybe not all mortals were like Tyler; afraid of what they didn't understand. After what happened with him, I lost all trust in the mortal world, but now I was slowly changing my mind.

Around noon, we drove into town so that I could have a tour. I'd heard of the school shooting that had taken place there, but other than that, I knew nothing about Blacksburg. They showed me the site of the Draper's Meadow Massacre and the memorial that was built.

The best part of the trip was when they took me to the house that David had grown up in. We couldn't go in since someone had recently moved there, but I enjoyed admiring it from inside the car. Declan told me that after the youngest child had moved out, his great aunt Ruth, David's parents moved out and lived in a smaller house just a few miles outside of Roanoke. They showed me that house as well, but it was a forty-minute drive, so we didn't get back to their house until evening.

We were all tired from the long day, so we ordered pizza for dinner. By then, my cravings were practically unbearable and I developed habits like tapping my foot and fiddling with a small section of my hair. Noel noticed and started asking me about it.

"Are you okay? You're acting like a junkie that needs a fix."

"I like that. From now on, when I'm hungry, I'll say I need a fix. Anyway, It's just been a while since I've...fed. It's like human hunger, the longer you go without eating, the hungrier you get."

"Oh, I see. So, you said you drink vampire blood. Do you have a regular donor or do you constantly have to go out and find one?"

"Gallard lets me drink his blood. I don't like to, but he always insists, so I let him help me out."

"Wow, kinky," Noel said, raising his eyebrows suggestively.

"No...ew!" I replied, lightly pushing him. He laughed and I couldn't help but smile.

"So how old is this fiancé of yours? I'm assuming he's a vampire as well?"

"Yes he is, only of the more normal sense. He survives on human blood. To answer your question, he'll be two hundred and seventy-six next month."

"What? Are you kidding me, he's older than America!"

"Yeah, we joke about our age difference all the time. But age is just a number, baby."

The pizza arrived and we ate while watching a movie. Noel had picked *Runaway Bride* as a joke in light of my impending nuptials. I felt lame having never seen it since it was such a popular movie, and the further we got into the movie, the more I wished I'd taken the time.

"So, after you get married and all that, you should bring your husband here," Noel said. "You could keep up David's tradition of coming on Thanksgiving and when you have kids you can bring
them too."

"I think we'll do that. But as for the kids, we won't be bringing any. Vampires are dead, they can't reproduce."

"You never know. I'm sure your dad thought the same
thing and here you are. That's why they say 'you can't go wrong if you shield your dong.'"

"That's not a real saying, you just made that up!" I said, laughing hysterically.

I then finished eating then headed off to bed, but not before saying goodnight to everyone. I was running on about six hours of sleep.

I'd had a great two days with my newfound relatives, but I was ready to rejoin my group. I needed to feed before I went crazy, and I wanted to help them come up with a plan to get Cherish back.

It made me sick that she'd been coerced into leaving us and I hoped that she was all right. Melody had mentioned that Cherish's relationship with Lucian was disturbing and sadistic, which made me wonder how he was treating her now that she was older and had been free of his control for so long.

I stayed with the Shepherds for two more days before Aaron called. He asked to have them pass on the message that Melody would be picking me up the afternoon of my fourth day there.

Packing up my things was a bittersweet affair. A part of me wanted to stay with Declan and his family forever and just forget about my chaotic life, but another longed to be reunited with my other family and friends. So I decided to spend as much time with the Shepherds as I could before she arrived.

"Our home will always be welcome to you," Paula said. "We would love to see you again. And that adorable little sister of yours as well."

I hugged Paula, trying my hardest not to cry. She'd been so good to me over the past few days, and parting with her was like parting with my mother. When I finished hugging her, I turned and hugged Declan, saving Noel for last. Noel almost instantly pulled back from the embrace and shook his head.

THE RESURRECTION

"Is that all you got? I know you're stronger than that. Hug me like you mean it!"

I went in for another hug, this time squeezing him hard, but not hard enough to break his ribs. I could tell that he was feeling smothered, but he acted more amused than anything else.

"Was that better?" I asked, playfully punching his arm. He nodded.

"I'll see you later, Lela. You're the first female relative in my family not to drive me up the wall."

"Thanks, I guess," I replied. "You're not too bad yourself. And about going back to school. I say go for it. You'd make an awesome teacher."

A car pulled into the driveway and I lifted my bag off the ground, slinging it over my shoulder. I hugged each of them once more, thanking them for everything then walked out the door.

I walked to the car feeling a bit glum when I looked up and saw that Melody was standing by the car, but she wasn't alone; Cherish was standing next to her.

"What? How are you...when did—" I kept stuttering until I was at a loss for words and she hugged me, to my surprise.

"It's good to see you too, Lela." She pulled back and stuffed her hands into her pockets. "Look, I know we're not exactly on friendly terms, but I am willing to put our differences aside for Gallard's sake. He's my friend, and I don't want to put him in an awkward place. Truce?"

"Sure, yeah. I can live with that."

Melody drove us out of the neighborhood and Cherish went on to explain why Lucian had let her go. She said that he didn't like the person she had become; that she wasn't as easily influenced by him as she used to be, so he'd disowned her, making her as much of his enemy as the rest of us.

She also assured me that he was going to keep his promise about my family having immunity, which was comforting. But even as she told me about her reunion with Lucian, I couldn't shake the feeling that she wasn't telling the truth. She seemed more detached than usual; more solemn.

I was so immersed into the conversation that I didn't even notice when we'd taken a different route than Solomon had. I wasn't even sure we were headed to the motel at all.

"Mel, where are we going?" I asked. She and Cherish exchanged glances before looking at me.

"We thought we'd have some more girl time, you know like get our hair and makeup done; something like that," Melody said.

"Can we really afford to spend another day just chilling out? We've been here for over four days."

"Why not? We have nothing to run from. My father called off the feud, so the only thing left to do is head back to Chicago and Miami. We're taking time to celebrate!"

She pulled into a Paul Mitchell salon, and I decided to just go with the flow. Cherish had told me before that once Melody put her mind to something, there was no turning back. We walked in, and the lady at the desk greeted us before checking us in. Apparently, this wasn't a spontaneous trip since the salon was by appointment only. Melody had called in earlier that day.

I sat and read a magazine while I waited for my turn. I was finally called five minutes later, and the stylist took me to the back to wash my hair. I hadn't had my hair washed by another person since I was very young, and I felt extremely pampered.

As she conditioned it, she complimented my complexion and said she was jealous of my eyebrows. I had never paid much attention to my eyebrows or thought about whether or not they were nice or not because to me they were just eyebrows, but I thanked her just the same.

After my hair was dried, she smoothed it with a flat iron then began curling it. I continued reading my magazine while conversing with her at the same time.

"Who did your highlights?" she asked.

"No one, actually; they're natural."

She turned my seat around to face her and asked, "Really? You're blonde and you have *natural* black highlights? I have never heard of that before, that's amazing! You kind of a Christina Aguilera look goin' on."

Cherish came over and sat in the seat next to me. I looked at her for a moment then laughed. She was wearing a blonde wig, about the same shade as my hair.

"Trying for a new look?"

"No. Your aunt said that we looked alike, and I wanted

THE RESURRECTION

to see if it was true." She cocked her head to the side. "Damn. I could be your twin. Your shorter and curvier twin, that is."

I glanced back and forth between our reflections. She was right; we did look a lot alike. That was when I recalled the several dreams I used to have when I was younger. She was often in them and until now, I hadn't known they were Lucian's memories.

"*Accarezzare,*" I said.

"What did you just say?"

"That was your nickname, wasn't it? I remember now."

"Where did you hear that?"

"Simeon. That creep from the hospital. When I was fourteen, he called me that. Said I used to be a better liar. I got the feeling he thought I was someone else."

Cherish shifted her eyes in thought. "I've never met him before in my life. I don't see how he could have known me or hat nickname. Only one person knew me by it."

"Who called you that?"

Her eyes turned away. "Solomon. It's Cherish in Italian."

The woman finished curling my hair then started pinning it back into a really fancy up-do. I wanted to tell her that I would have been content with just the curl, but Melody gave me a look before I could say anything.

Once the three of us had our hair done, Melody drove us to the New River Valley Mall. I thought she wanted to do some shopping, but she led us straight the makeup section at JC Penny. To my surprise, Melody had set up appointments there as well. I was then forced into a chair as a man with extremely tight pants and crazy thin drawn-on eyebrows began applying eye shadow and blush. I was still suspicious that Melody and Cherish were up to something, but I didn't question them. I grinned and bore everything they forced me to go through.

The makeup artist turned me around when he was done and I admired his work. He'd put a pretty Gold eye shadow on the top of my eyes with a hint of brown on the corners, and on the bottom was a light blue, and my eyelashes were covered in thick mascara, which made them seem twice as full as they really were.

"Miss Lela, you look stunning," Melody said, admiring the man's work. "I think it's time that we get back to the motel, don't you, Cherish?"

Cherish looked down at her phone, texted someone, and then looked up at us.

"Yeah, let's head out."

Neither of them uttered a word as we drove back, and it was starting to get creepy. We all had our hair done and were dolled up like we were about to go to prom, and they still hadn't given me a reason for why that was so. It was one thing to get your hair and makeup done, but it was another to be all decked out. I finally decided I couldn't take the secrecy anymore.

"All right guys, I've done everything you've dragged me into, now you have to tell me what this is for."

"You'll see in a little bit. You'll like what's coming next, I promise," Cherish said.

"Yeah, Solomon said that before he dropped me off at my relatives' house. Is there another family I don't know about that you want me to meet?"

"No, this is even better," Melody promised.

We finally arrived at the motel around three thirty and parked next to the Honda. I grabbed my bag before getting out, but Cherish took it from me and Melody put her hands in front of my eyes, but not touching them as not to ruin my makeup.

"O...kay this is interesting," I said. Cherish took my hand and began guiding me forward. She warned me when we got to the stairs and told me each time when I needed to step up until we got to the top. Melody then told me to walk to the left and I listened as Cherish opened the door to Melody's and my room. I slowly walked in, being careful not to trip and then we finally stopped and Melody took her hands away from my eyes.

I opened them and found myself staring at the bed. But it wasn't the bed that I was mesmerized by; it was the beautiful white dress that was lying on it. It was long and strapless with a Queen Anne neckline. The bodice was creased and there was a small belt on the waist covered in diamonds. The skirt had a very slight poof. I then realized what the entire day had been about.

"You guys," I said, trying to not to cry in fear of ruining my makeup. "Did you plan a wedding while I was away?"

"Surprise!" Melody said. "It was Gallard's idea. When Aaron suggested that you stay with your relatives for a few days, we were going to try and get Cherish back. But then she returned on her own. We thought this was a good way to celebrate."

"Yeah, I even had to go to the Department of Health with him and pretend to be you to obtain a marriage license. It took a few days to finalize, but it was done in time," Cherish said.

"The ceremony goes down in an hour and a half, which is when the sun is due to set," Melody said. "Do your best to stay occupied in here because you're not allowed to see the downstairs room yet."

She and Cherish hurried out the room leaving me alone and I wondered what I was supposed to do for an hour and a half by myself.

I turned on the TV and watched *Friends* for a bit. I was too excited to focus on the show, but then my cravings resurfaced and I finally found something to distract me. I texted Melody about it and three minutes later, she arrived with two Styrofoam cups full of blood along with a note from Gallard. It said, 'drink up, can't wait to see you.' I smiled before finishing the drinks. It was extremely refreshing, and I was then able to focus on being excited once more.

I used my brain for the first time in few days and decided to call Curtis. I wanted to know how my aunt was doing. No doubt we would be traveling back home soon and Tampa was the first place I intended to go. Evelyn would need me and my brothers during this hard time. We were all she had left since she had no children of her own.

"Curtis' phone, Gaaaabriella speaking."

"Gabby? It's Lela!"

"What! Lela Sharmentino, what the hell are you doing calling me from beyond the grave?" She laughed. "Curt told me you were back, and I had to fly down here."

I held my breath. "He told you, did he? What exactly did he tell you?"

Gabby didn't answer right away, but then she said. "I know, Lela. I know that...you're a vampire. Don't worry, Curt didn't blab or anything. Aaron and I hooked up last July and he bit me. He thought it would be sexy or something but it just freaked me out. Anyway, he kind of told me everything."

"I'm sorry, did you say you hooked up with Aaron? What about Edison?"

"Lela, you and I both know that Edison and I aren't in love. I know for a fact he's banging one of the art dealers he works with. Oh, by the way, I have been visiting your aunt. She loves my baby girls. We've been playing Pictionary."

I smiled, glad that my aunt was being taken care of. I felt bad that I'd left her behind, but Gabby seemed to be keeping her in high spirits. I wouldn't know for myself until I saw her again.

"Thank you so much, Gabs. By the way, I have some big news…"

"What's bigger news than being a vampire?"

"Well…I'm kind of getting married tonight."

"Shut up!" her voice grew quieter. "To whom? How did you manage to meet someone while you were dead? Did you bring someone back with you from the afterlife?"

Someone was coming up the steps. "I'll text you pictures. But I have to go. Tell Evie I love her and Curtis too."

I hung up just as Melody came into the room. She'd changed into a tiffany blue, knee-length chiffon. She looked very pretty and it was a wonderful color on her.

I quickly got undressed so she could help me into the gown. Once she'd zipped me up, she sprayed some of her expensive Elie Saab perfume on my neck and arms then applied a nude-colored lipstick finished off with some clear lip gloss. The last thing she did was pin an elbow-length veil underneath my up-do, fluffing it until it came around and hung around my shoulders.

"You look amazing. I am so jealous right now," she said, admiring my final look. "Are you ready?"

"Am I ever."

Melody began to walk with me out of the room but looked down and shrieked.

"Lela, your shoes! I can't believe I almost let you get married in Nikes!" She knelt down onto the floor and pulled a small box from under the bed. She opened it and handed me a pair of white heels with a silk toe and a small, diamond-studded flower on top. I slipped off my tennis shoes and socks before replacing them with the heels.

"Melody, how did you pay for all of this?" I asked.

THE RESURRECTION

She smiled and replied, "I didn't. Aaron told me that Solomon had put a butt-load of money into your account so I jacked your card. I figured you wouldn't mind. I only used it to pay for the dress and the shoes. The rest is on me. Oh, and Gallard paid for the rings, his tux and the marriage license."

I hugged her before continuing out the door. I hadn't walked in heels in a very long time, so I had to walk slowly as I descended down the stairs. I couldn't believe this. I was on my way to my own wedding.

Chapter Twenty-Six

When I rounded the corner, I was surprised to see my brothers, Jordan, and Cherish lined up on either side of the door, all dressed in formal attire. Robin was in the middle wearing an adorable knee-length dark green dress with a shiny pearl colored belt. She had a little basket with petals and her hair was up in a cute bun.

"Surprise!" she said, throwing some of the petals in the air. Everyone laughed. Aaron pulled his hands from behind his back revealing a small but gorgeous bouquet of white roses, which he then handed to me. I mouthed *thank you* to you him and he smiled.

"Um, Jordan. That's your queue," Melody said.

"Oh right, the music!" he said, taking his iPhone out of his pocket. He pushed a few buttons and then turned up his volume as Pachelbel's Canon began to play. Kevin then crooked his arm, and I put mine through it.

"As your favorite brother, I reserved the right to be the one to give you away," he said, winking at Aaron who rolled his eyes. I squeezed his arm affectionately as we walked to the rhythm of the music into the room with Robin walking in front of us, dropping petals to her left and her right.

The room had been transformed from that of a cheap motel to a lovely, little wedding venue. The beds and furniture were gone, and there were green and white flowers everywhere with white netting strung along the walls. Further into the room was an arch with a white curtain draped over it.

When I saw Gallard, my heart skipped a beat. He was wearing a black tux, a matching vest, a white button-up, and dark-green tie that matched Robin's dress. I had never seen him so dressed up, and I liked it, a lot. He was smiling, which caused me to start grinning like an idiot. I didn't even notice the eye patch. All I saw was him and how happy he looked. Solomon was standing next to him, adorned in his bright red Cardinal robes. I tried not to laugh at how flamboyant it was, but at least he wasn't wearing a huge hat.

Kevin and I stopped in front of Solomon, and he unhooked his arm from mine before joining the rest of the group behind me. Gallard then took my arm and turned to face Solomon as well.

"We are gathered here today to celebrate the joining in marriage of Gallard Warren D'Aubigne and Lela Charlotte Sharmentino. Or, if we are going by the names on the marriage license; Gallard Evergard and Charlotte Hainsworth."

Everyone chuckled before he continued with the ceremony. He promised that he would keep it short unlike the traditional Catholic weddings. He gave a small speech on marriage and the importance of love, trust, and how God always leads people to the one he wants them to be with. It was very touching and I could tell that Melody was trying not to cry.

It was time for the vows, which Solomon said that Gallard had chosen to prepare on his own, and I began to panic since I hadn't thought to prepare anything during the hour I'd had to myself. I would have to improvise, and that meant I would probably end up babbling. I turned and looked at Melody who smacked her forehead and mouthed *sorry*, obviously just remembering that she'd forgotten to give me that bit of information.

"Lela," Gallard began, "*Mon ange de ténèbres*. If someone told me six years ago that I was going to fall in love with you, I would have told them they were crazy. I was trapped in a cage, forced to stay in my animal form, wondering if I was ever going to get a chance to escape. Then there you were; you released me from my prison and just let me perch in your hands like you dealt with bats every day. From then on, I wanted nothing more than to protect you and make sure that you were taken care of. You were like the little sister that I never had, and I enjoyed getting to know you and watching you grow up.

"That was what started it all; you grew up. You weren't the fourteen-year-old girl that I first met anymore. Instead, before me was this beautiful, kind, and loyal woman. I wasn't prepared for that, and you threw me for a loop.

"That entire year that I spent without you was torture. I was as lost as I was thirty years ago, and I prepared myself for a life that was void of your presence. And when you came back and I held you for the first time in over ten months, I never wanted to be a part from you again. I love you, and I promise to love you until the very day we become ashes unto the sun and the stars in the night sky."

When he was finished, I was rendered speechless. I'd thought it was impossible to love him more, but he'd proved me wrong. Now it was my turn to follow up to his wonderful vows, and I had squat.

"Gallard...you never told me your middle name was Warren," I said, chuckling. The others did as well. "Anyway, um...wow. When I first met you, I was touched by your gesture. Defending my honor against that creep at the grocery store. Then the second time I saw you, I must say that you scared the hell out of me. You body-slammed me, and I thought you were going to kill me. But after I got to know you, I knew that you would never hurt me.

"When I first turned, I was alone. I thought that I was going crazy, and after I'd figured out what I was, I felt even more alone. I had no one else around me who knew what I was going through. Then you came along. You taught me how to survive and how to live my life as a vampire without losing who I was as a person. But most of all, you taught me that I can be loved. That just because I am a vampire doesn't mean I don't deserve to be loved, and I am forever grateful for that.

"As I grew older, I realized that everything about you was what I wanted in a partner. You were wise, gentle, loving, and you never broke your promises. You listened wholeheartedly whenever I talked to you, and you made me feel comfortable telling you everything. When you looked at me, your gaze made me feel warm, even though I didn't have a heartbeat. Your smile froze me in my

THE RESURRECTION

steps, and your touch rendered me speechless.

"When I asked you to marry me, I was afraid that you would think I was being presumptuous about the status of our relationship or that I was being extremely tacky for breaking the tradition of the man asking the woman. But you said yes, and that was the happiest moment of my life. And here we are in fancy get up with a priest—Cardinal, I'm sorry—and the whole shebang! I am beyond happy right now, and I couldn't imagine wanting to share my life with anyone else. *Je vais vous aimer toujours et toujours;* I will love you always and forever."

When I was finished, Solomon said, "Let us now exchange the rings."

Jordan came forward with a small box, and I wondered what Gallard had picked out. I wasn't picky when it came to jewelry. I was confident that I would love it, no matter what. Jordan opened the box and handed me a gold ring with a tiny diamond imbedded in the center.

I held it in my right hand as Gallard slipped a ring similar to his, only with a smaller band and a raised diamond, onto my forefinger and repeated after Solomon saying, "With this ring, I thee wed, and with it, I bestow upon thee all the treasures of my mind, heart, and hands." I then put the other ring onto Gallard's finger and repeated the same words.

"By the power vested in me by the Holy Catholic Church—not by Virginia, though we won't tell anyone—I now pronounce you husband and wife. You may kiss your bride."

Gallard pulled me close to him and softly kissed me, but I got more into it and threw my arms around his neck while everybody clapped. We ended the kiss then Gallard and I made our way through the group, hugging and thanking them before the two of us left the room. I'd noticed Cherish was missing but then she reappeared and hugged us before going inside.

Once we were outside, he kissed me again and said, "I love you, Mrs. D'Aubigne."

"And I love you, Mr. D'Aubigne. Wow, I can't believe we just did that. We're married, like, for real!"

"Not quite; we still have to sign the paper."

"Oh, right. Well let's sign it and make it official."

I dragged him back into the room and located the paper then we both signed it. Solomon did as well then Jordan signed it as a witness. Afterwards, we went back outside and he took my hand, leading me upstairs to the other room.

We went inside and found the whole room filled with lit candles, and I figured that that was what Cherish had been doing when she'd quietly slipped away. I stood in the middle of the room with Gallard's arms around me, basking in my happiness.

I turned around and my lips found his. He kissed me tenderly while holding on to me and I slowly loosened his tie, casting it aside then he took off his jacket. I then unbuttoned his shirt and he slid the zipper down on my dress. I slid out of it, gently dropping it to the floor so I wouldn't ruin it and he removed his shirt completely.

Then suddenly he stopped kissing me and stared at my face, an uncertain look suddenly forming in his eyes. I wondered what was going through his mind so I spoke up.

"What's wrong?"

"It's...I'm sorry. I know I said we would go through with this once the whole Lucian threat was over but..."

"It's okay, you can tell me."

He sighed then held me as we continued standing in the middle of the room.

"I don't want our first time together to be in some cheap motel. Call me sentimental. I want to be somewhere special. You and I have spent more than an adequate amount of time in rundown places, and I want to break that habit." He looked at my face. "Would you be mad if we waited just a little longer?"

"Yes. In fact, I am furious. You are such a tease!"

He laughed, knowing that I wasn't being serious, and I laughed too. I had to admit that I agreed. I was tired of being in cheap motels and I definitely didn't want our big night to be here. It felt kind of trashy, like it was a hook up and not the time I would finally be with him.

"Okay, let's hold it off then," I said. "We'll go somewhere nice and make sure that night will be memorable."

"Agreed. Now the problem is figuring out what we'll do instead."

"Well, we could always go back downstairs and help them take down the decorations. They did so much and I'd like to pitch in somehow."

He smiled and kissed my cheek.

"Good idea."

I picked my dress up from the floor as Gallard put his shirt back on. I put on the first thing I could find in my suitcase then we headed back out the door, hand in hand. I didn't mind that we were putting everything on hold. We had plenty of time to be together. All that mattered to me was that we were married, and I was blissfully happy.

When we got to the bottom of the stairs, we caught Jordan and Kevin as they were loading the rented arch into the back of the BMW. They looked confused when they saw us and I wondered why.

"What are you two doing down here?" Jordan asked. Melody came out and she looked almost mad that we were there.

"I'm wondering the same thing!" she said with appall.

"We wanted to help," I explained. "You guys set all of this up for us. The least I can do is help clean."

"But...it's your wedding night!" Melody protested. "You were only gone for five minutes."

Jordan smirked then said, "He's a D'Aubigne. We only need five minutes."

Gallard and I groaned at the same time. I'd thought that us finally being in a relationship, let alone getting married, would stop our friends from making dirty jokes about Gallard and me, but I was wrong. It only made them worse.

"Says the one who passed out after hooking up with Lydian," I shot back. Gallard laughed, and even Melody couldn't hold back a giggle. Kevin was laughing the hardest, though.

"You passed out?" Kevin asked. "Like... lost consciousness?"

"It wasn't because of...it was my illness okay! I had kidney failure for crying out loud!"

"More like heart failure," Gallard mumbled, though it was clear that everyone heard it.

We continued laughing, despite Jordan's annoyed look, then went into the hotel room to finish tearing everything down. It didn't take long since there were eight of us, plus Robin, though she spent most of the cleanup time riding on Gallard's shoulders while he put stuff in the car.

Once everything was packed up, Solomon and Kevin left to return everything that was rented. Melody kept hinting at me that I should go upstairs with Gallard, but after that failed, she tried to make hints to him. He made eye contact with me and smiled. Cherish finally had to pull Melody away from us and convinced her to go get some dinner. I was glad, because the pressure was too much. It felt like Melody was more eager for Gallard and me to do the deed than we were.

The two guys got back a half an hour later then we regrouped to discuss future plans. Solomon wanted to get all the business stuff out of the way so we could relax for the duration of our stay. I didn't mind businessy talk, though. Solomon always made it sound interesting.

"Check out is at ten, so we'll head out around that time," he said. "Who wants to ride with whom?"

"Mel and I are going back to Chicago," Cherish said. "You could come with us and fly out to Italy from there."

"I think I'll do that." Solomon smiled at Cherish, probably longer than he meant to and I nudged Gallard who noticed as well. "What about you boys?" Solomon asked Aaron and Kevin.

"We're leaving tonight," Aaron said. "Since we can't travel in the day and all. We're going to Tampa to check on our aunt."

"Lela, Jordan, and I will fly back to Tampa as well," Gallard said. "Are you taking Robin with you, Aaron?"

"No! I want to stay with you guys!" Robin said, grabbing my hand.

"Then you'll leave with us," I said.

We all said goodnight to one another and then Gallard, Robin, and I went upstairs to the other room. I could tell that my sister was close to passing out and I wanted to get her to bed. Melody tried one last time to give us alone time by hinting to Robin that she should sleep downstairs, but I insisted that it was fine.

I put Robin to bed, and she was fast asleep within ten minutes. I kissed her forehead before curling up next to Gallard on the other bed. I was still feeling giddy from our wedding and kept replaying every moment over in my head. His vows had been perfect and though mine had kind of droned on, I'd gotten in everything that

THE RESURRECTION

I'd wanted to say.

I heard Robin stir in her sleep and I glanced over at her for a second. I'd forgotten until that moment that Evelyn was her legal guardian. My aunt and uncle had gotten custody of her after my parents died, and with Jeff gone, I couldn't ask her to continue with that responsibility. I most certainly was not letting Simeon Atherton become her guardian. If all possible, I wanted to be the one to take care of her.

"What are you thinking about?" Gallard whispered to me.

"My sister. I'm sure that Evelyn won't want to move back to Texas, and she'll have a lot to deal with adjusting to being on her own. I want to talk about it with her first, but I think it would be best if she transferred guardianship of Robin to me."

"Then that's what we'll do. I don't know the process or what steps we'd need to take, but I'll make sure it happens."

I sat up and looked at him.

"You would do that? I know it's a lot to ask of you since you've already spent four years taking care of me. And we've barely just gotten married. Would you really—"

"Lela, I don't see the past four years as time of sacrifice. I wanted to look out for you and I would do it again in a heartbeat. If raising Robin would make you happy, then it would make me happy." He put his arms around me, resting his head against mine. "Bodoway was right all those years ago. I was lonely, and I didn't want to admit it. Now that I have you, I know I won't feel that way anymore. Besides, Robin is a sweetheart. We can't have our own children, and Robin is just as good as any child we could have if we were able." He looked up as if to check to see if Robin was still asleep then looked back at me. "There's something you should know. Before David died he revealed something to me."

I sat up, suddenly more awake.

"What did he tell you?"

"He told me that Robin...was his daughter as well."

I stared at Gallard, trying to let this information register. It was such a huge hit that I couldn't reply right away. Robin was my full sister? I'd thought all of my mother's secrets had been revealed the night I'd gone home. Apparently, I'd been wrong.

"I can't believe he didn't tell me this. It makes perfect sense, though. Why she's more like me than our brothers; why she's a smarty pants like David."

"You mentioned that your parents' marriage was toxic, yet they had two more children after you. It would make sense if your mother went back to David at one point, right?"

"Yes. I could see that. Kevin was an accident, or so I've been told. I doubt Kevin is David's though. He has Mark's hair and build." I lay with my head on the pillow. "I'm so glad we're not like that."

He kissed me then held me in his arms and I closed my eyes.

"*Je t'aime*," I said to him. "Goodnight."

Chapter Twenty-Seven

Gallard waited until Lela had fallen asleep then quietly slipped out of the room. It wasn't that he didn't want to be next to her. Cherish had mentioned wanting to talk to him and this was probably his last chance before they would go their separate ways again. Melody and she promised to keep in touch but he preferred face to face conversation.

Closing the door behind him, he took in the crisp, cool air of Virginia. He hadn't been to this state since the pull had drawn him to David, and he'd forgotten the parts of this place that he loved. He could see why David's family had never left. The state had so much history and made him nostalgic for his childhood days when he was innocent and hadn't suffered devastating losses.

He wished there was a place for Lela and him to settle down. If they were mortal, he would give her as many children as she wanted and they would grow old together and spoil their grandchildren. They would live in a house big enough to fit ten people and invite their relatives over for holidays. That may be a fool's dream, but he couldn't help but wish he could give Lela a better life. They could still have part of that life with Robin. He would treat her like his own daughter and do everything he could to keep her safe. Maybe down the road they could consider adoption too.

The door to the other hotel room opened, and he smiled when Cherish came out. He'd loved spending the past few days with her while they planned the wedding. Without her, he wouldn't have been able to pick adequate wedding rings. He knew Lela wasn't materialistic, so he wasn't so worried about not getting a big enough diamond. He wanted something simple but beautiful at the same time.

"You're crazy, you know that right?" she said.

"I don't know what you mean."

"Please! You're finally married and yet you two aren't sealing the deal? You're Gallard D'Aubigne. You could get a woman to sleep with you just by smiling at her."

He laughed. That statement wasn't entirely true. He'd spent a lot of his life brooding and bringing other people down. Women would hit on him all the time, but they would quickly move on once they found out what a jerk he was.

Occasionally there was a time when he would meet someone who didn't care that he was nasty, but he never really let himself get close to anyone until after he met Cherish. She helped him break down his wall and from then on, he focused on staying positive and using every opportunity to use his abilities for good. One of those instances had been when he'd overheard the scumbag in the grocery store making inappropriate remarks to Lela. The rest was history.

"I told you, that's not me anymore, Cherry Pop. Lela is precious to me, and I want to give her the honeymoon she deserves."

"Fine by me. So what did you want to talk to me about? If you're reconsidering that bachelor party idea, it's too late. I already put my stripper costume away."

He laughed again and draped an arm around her shoulder then suggested they go for a walk. It wasn't cloud for the first time in days and the moon was beautiful.

For a while, they reminisced on all the crazy things they did back in the eighties. Cherish used to dress like she'd stepped out of a John Hughes movie and he just let himself go and forgot how to use scissors and a razor. A lot of the antics they pulled off were definitely illegal and both had spent a night in jail. He missed those carefree days and he wanted to be that way with Lela.

They stopped at the bridge on Virginia Smart Road and watched traffic go by. There was a small pond just underneath and the area was surrounded by beautiful trees. He preferred this growth to the palm trees of Florida. They seemed more real.

If this had been thirty years ago, he would have dared her to jump in. But he wasn't here to get crazy. He wanted to find out why she was acting so strangely. Ever since she came back, claiming to have been let go she had been distant and quiet. She was also making an effort to be around him as much as possible. At times, he could have sworn she was flirting with him. Sometimes it was a simple touch or the way she was looking at him from beneath her eyelashes.

"What really happened between you and your father?" he asked.

"Nothing too exciting. He claimed that he wasn't really going to kill Solomon or his family, which I believed. I can't tell you how many times we've done this dance. When I was eight, I remember Solomon did something to make my father angry. I heard yelling and then he yelled, *Get off my property! If you come within fifty feet of my gate, I will kill you!* I was concerned until I saw Solomon in our living room literally two days later. They were talking as if nothing ever happened."

"Okay...so the feud really is over. That's comforting. But really; did he just let you leave? I may not know him that well but I do enough to know that he doesn't do something without expecting payment."

She looked away and never gave an answer to that question, worrying him further. He had to be right. He wanted to know whatever had her so terrified that she wouldn't even tell *him*. Cherish was the most fearless woman he'd ever met, other than Lela. It had been hard getting her to admit why she felt animosity towards Lela and he doubted he could get another confession out of her tonight.

"Gallard...I'm sorry I left without saying goodbye," she said. She took his hand. "I guess...we had the same problem for different reasons. Whenever I get close to someone, I'm afraid that they'll let me down so I try to do it first. I had the time to explain my departure and yet I left a letter anyway."

"It's all right, Cherish. It did hurt but I'm glad that I have you back in my life. It's a time of restoration for all of us. You and your sister can stop hiding and Lela and her siblings can stop running. I have a feeling that everything is going to be okay."

He hugged her and she held onto him tightly. He could feel her slightly trembling and it broke his heart. The part of him that always rushed in to help people wished that he had been alive back before all of this happened so he could save her all the pain she'd been through.

When she pulled back she then stared into his eyes. She'd leaned in about two inches away from his face before he realized what was going on. He moved at the last second and put distance between them.

"What are you doing?" he asked.

"Gallard, I'm sorry that this is so sudden. I fell for you the moment you opened my door and yelled at me. I've thought about you every day since then."

He stared at her, baffled by her sudden confession. While it was very heartfelt, it sounded completely phony. It had to be phony. When she'd started to leave with Lucian it had been Solomon she kissed, not him.

"What's really going on, Cher? You and I both know that if you feel that way about someone, it's not me."

A pained expression crossed her face and she created even more distance between them.

"Forgive me," she said. "I had no choice."

He started to press on the situation, but she took off down the street in a blur, leaving him alone on the bridge. Her last words rang in her mind and he tried to make sense of them. What had some brought him out here for? There had to be a reason for her sudden profession of love and it wasn't because she actually did. The whole way back to the hotel, he tried to come up with theories but none of them
seemed plausible.

THE RESURRECTION

I was jolted awake by the sensation that I was falling. It took me a second to become aware of my surroundings. Gallard had his arms around me, and I turned around and saw that his left eye was closed while the other was still hidden under the patch. I kissed him then he looked at me.

"Hello, husband," I said, smiling. "What time is it?"

"About nine o'clock. You've been out since midnight." He paused then said, "Why does Robin keep asking me to do magic tricks? She told me that you said I can do magic."

I felt my cheeks flush and I looked away.

"No reason. I just think you're magical is all."

"You liar. I know there's more to this story."

"So, how much more time do we have?" I asked, sliding on top of him and kissing his neck. I suddenly remembered that Robin had stayed in our room and quickly looked over at the other bed. She was gone and I assumed she was downstairs with our brothers.

"Solomon said that he and the sisters are going to ride in the BMW. They're leaving the Toyota for us."

I rested my head on this chest. It felt so good to not have anywhere to be or any danger to run from. We could just enjoy each other without a care in the world.

"Well, I'm going to shower really fast." I thought for a moment. We'd decided to put our romantic night on hold, but that didn't mean we couldn't have a sneak preview. Feeling bold, I asked, "Want to join me?"

He gave me a smile. "You know, that actually sounds like a wonderful idea."

We both got up, and I took his hand, leading him over to the bathroom. He closed the door behind him, and I turned the water on so it would be nice and hot by the time we got in.

I kept my back to him while I undressed, still feeling a little self-conscious. We'd never seen each other naked before and it made me nervous. The last naked man I'd seen was Simeon and that hadn't been a pleasant experience. I was sure Gallard wouldn't give me the same reaction. I loved him, and I knew I would love every part of him.

When I turned around, I was met by his same handsome smile. I allowed myself to take a look at him and was relieved when there were no feelings of revulsion. Just love and appreciation. He was mine now and no one could take him away from me.

"You're perfect, Mrs. D'Aubigne," he said, as if he could read my mind. He cupped my chin in his hand and planted a soft kiss on my lips. "After you."

Grinning like a crazy person, I pushed the shower curtain back and got in. Not long after, he got in behind me, and I picked up the shampoo that came with the hotel and started to squeeze some into my hand when Gallard took it from me.

"I believe that's my job."

I trembled slightly as he began to wash my hair. Not only was he great at back massages, but he was a master of washing hair as well. His fingertips made my scalp tingle, and I nearly fell asleep while standing up. When he finished rinsing the conditioner out, he even combed the tangles out with his fingers.

"How are you so good at this?" I asked.

"You really don't know?"

I shook my head. "What's your secret?"

"I learned from you."

Quickly, I turned around to face him. "Really? How?"

"You cut my hair on several occasions while we lived in Vegas. You always insisted on washing it first so it would be easier to cut. It was something I looked forward to and I couldn't wait to get off work on hair cut day."

I laughed, hugging him around his waist. I liked this; learning about his secrets that he'd kept in before we got involved. Now we didn't have to hide our feelings or desires anymore. We could be open about them and share them with each other.

My lips found his and he began kissing me. I wasn't feeling nervous anymore, and now all I wanted was him. Showering together had probably been a bad idea temptation wise, but I didn't care. I could tell he was losing the battle as well by the way he was touching me. His hands explored my body and I welcomed it. I began doing the same to him, feeling his firm back, his strong arms, his tight backside. Then my fingers found an abrasion and I pulled my hand back.

"What is that from?" I asked.

"Huh?" He reached back and touched it. "Oh that." He chuckled. "It happened when I was fifteen. My brother and I were fighting, and he pushed me to the ground. To my luck, there were a few nails on the ground that were perfectly aligned with my bony ass. I bled all the way to the house and couldn't sit for two weeks."

"You poor thing," I said, trying hard not to laugh. It reminded me of all the scrapes my brothers were always getting in when we were young.

He kissed me one last time then backed away. "I should go. I promised I would help gas up the cars while everyone got all packed."

I pouted. "Can't you do that later? We were just getting started."

"That's exactly why I need to go." He reached out a grabbed a towel, wrapping it around his middle. "If I don't leave, I'll start something I'll intend to finish, and I would never forgive myself if we lost control in here."

He got out, and I sighed in defeat. He was right, though. We were clearly headed down a road we wouldn't be able to turn back from. We'd promised each other to save our moment for a different environment, and I wanted that to happen. Still, our alone time in the shower had been wonderful.

I got my suitcase out of the closet and pulled on some black jeans, a blue long-sleeve shirt, and a light jacket. The weather was getting colder and colder as we traveled further north, and I no longer could get away with just capris and a t-shirt.

After I packed all of my things, I grabbed the dress and zipped it into the large black bag that hung in the closet and then exited the room. I wanted to say goodbye to everyone before they left and thank Melody and Cherish for everything they'd done. Hopefully they would keep in
touch too.

Melody was outside leaning against the railing as Robin skipped back and forth across the deck.

"So, Mrs. D'Aubigne, how does it feel to be a married woman?" Melody asked.

"There are no words to describe how happy I am right now."

"Marriage can do that to ya. By the way, do you know a...Gabriella? She keeps texting me and saying your husband is hot. When I told her who I was, she asked if I was single because her brother Riley needs a girlfriend."

I laughed. As promised, I had texted wedding pictures from Melody's phone. I had no idea she would continue to text back. That was hours ago.

"She's a childhood friend. I told her about the wedding and promised pictures."

"Speaking of marriage, where's the hubby? You know, I suggested he leave Robin with me before he went back to your room for a reason. I thought it would be a lot harder to get him away from you."

"We've decided to go on a honeymoon. He wants to go somewhere nice, so we're holding off for a little longer."

She sighed. "You two have more self-control than anyone I've ever met. If it were me, I would have been all over him the second I walked out of the chapel."

I laughed. "To answer your question, he's with your sister."

"She did tell me she was leaving with him to gas up the cars. Maybe she wanted to say goodbye to him."

"Hmm. Is it just me, or is she a lot quieter than usual?"

"You're not the only one to notice that. Cherish isn't the most articulate person, but it's been like pulling teeth to get her to say anything lately. I'm worried about her, and I think her encounter with our father shook her up more than she's letting on."

Robin came skipping back towards us, and I playfully swept her off the ground and twirled her around. She giggled as I came to a stop and set her back down. I kissed the top of her head before she skipped off once more.

"Thanks a lot, Mel; for everything. You are awesome, and I couldn't ask for a better friend."

Melody shrugged off my comment like it was no big deal, but I could tell she was touched. I then went down the stairs to say goodbye to my brothers while Melody stayed with Robin as she continued playing on the deck.

Solomon had just finished bringing out all the luggage as I got to the bottom.

"Are you almost ready to head out?" I asked. He nodded.

"We're all packed. We're just waiting for your husband and Cherish to get back from gassing the cars. Jordan thought about tagging along so you could be alone with Gallard, but since Robin wants to be near you guys, he's sticking with his original plan."

"Speaking of Jordan, could you let him know I want to talk to him?" I asked.

He nodded then went back inside. While I waited, I saw two hooded men come out of the room at the end of the deck. I thought they were just guests, but the way they were looking at Melody made my stomach turn.

I took one step forward, and the first thing I saw was the long, silver blade that one of the men slipped out of a sheath strapped to his back. Robin stopped skipping and moved closer to Melody. I knew she was as leery of the men as I was.

Before I could react, the man who wasn't holding the sword grabbed Robin then when Melody tried to help her, the other man held the tip of the sword to her throat.

"Call for help and they're both dead!" The one with the sword shouted. I started breathing hard and glancing towards the door. Solomon had probably told Jordan I wanted to speak with him but because he couldn't come outside, both men most likely assumed I would be going in. I had at least five minutes before they would either come looking for me or Gallard and Cherish would show up.

"Okay, I'm listening." I looked at my terrified sister, memories from two Decembers ago flooding my mind. "What do you want?"

"I want my girlfriend. Thanks to you and this bitch, that isn't going to happen. So I'm giving you a choice."

The man holding Robin lifted her up and dangled her over the side of the deck. I moved forward but then the other man pressed harder in the sword, cutting Melody's neck. I quickly understood what was going on; they wanted me to choose between Melody and Robin. They were too far apart for me to save both of them. I was fast, but I wasn't Superman.

"Please," I said, keeping my eyes on my sister. "She's only five years old. Is there any way I can change your mind?"

"Oh, I'm sorry. I forgot the part where I said you get to make the negotiations."

He shifted her and she screamed as he dangled her by her left leg so that she was hanging upside down. She was failing her arms and crying. It infuriated me that I couldn't rush over and save her. Not without condemning Melody to death. I hoped that Solomon and Jordan had heard that. They had to.

Other people were starting to come out of their rooms. The man holding Robin used his free hand to take a gun out of his pocket, commanding them to go back inside and they quickly obeyed. One of them was bound to call the police.

"I want you to pay for what you did to Jamie," he said. "So make a choice. Is it this freak of nature here? Or your baby sister." He said *baby* with a mocking tone. "Choose quickly because the moment one of your friends comes out here, I'm making the choice for you."

"Lela, don't pick me," Melody said quietly. I looked into her eyes and didn't even see a hint of fear. She even smiled at me. "It's okay."

How could I make this choice? Yes, I loved my sister; she was actually more like a daughter to me because of our age difference. I had given my life for her and would easily do it again. But I hated the idea of trading a life. Melody was an amazing woman, and I had bonded with her in a very short time. On the other hand, I didn't want her to have to live with the idea that she had lived in the place of a helpless little girl. So I made my decision.

The door opened just as I was about to speak. Solomon came out, and I looked at him then back at the two men. I had missed my chance. The man holding the sword removed it from Melody's throat but then made a swing so fast I could barely see it. He separated her head from her body and finally the yell building in my throat came out, echoing throughout the parking lot.

I ran across the lot and halfway up the stairs when the second man dropped Robin. She hit the ground with a sickening thud, and I screamed before jumping over the rail and going to her.

Solomon had taken action and started fighting the men, but I knew he would get killed if I didn't help. I left Robin's side to try and save Solomon, and since I'd fed not a few hours ago, I was feeling very strong.

I lunged at the man who'd decapitated Melody, but he ran the sword through me. Thankfully, Solomon had wrenched from the other man's grip. As he tried to attack, both men shoved him backwards so that he collided with me and we fell. Before we could get back up, the men took off down the stairs.

The two of us didn't even take a minute to recover, but ran

THE RESURRECTION

down to check on Robin. I knelt beside her, unsure if I should move her in case she had a back injury. Her head was bleeding and she was unconscious. Solomon took his phone out and called 911.

"Hello? Yes, we need an ambulance. There's been an accident; my niece was dropped from the top of the stairs and my friend was killed. No, she's not conscious, but she's bleeding. We're at the Gigi's Inn on 545 Cedar Street. Hurry!"

Jordan had come out at that moment. It had become very overcast so it was safe for him to be outside. He looked from Robin to Melody and then back to Robin.

"What happened?" he asked, shouting in disbelief.

I tried to speak, but I was still mute from the shock. My voice was raspy and harsh, but I managed to get a few words out saying, "There were two men. They came out of nowhere. Then...Melody...and then Robin he...he dropped her."

"She feels cold," Jordan, touching Robin's cheek. "I don't think she'll make it to a hospital."

"Don't say that, she's fine!" I shouted.

Jordan got out his phone and dialed a number, which I assumed was Cherish's and explained to the person on the other line what was going on.

The BMW came back first and then the Toyota, both stopping in the middle of the lot. By then a crowd had formed on the balcony and a woman screamed when she saw Melody's body.

Gallard and Cherish got out and ran toward us. He opened his mouth as if to speak, but when he saw Melody's body at the top of the stairs, he stopped himself. Cherish saw too, and the look on her face was so devastating that I couldn't keep my eyes on her anymore.

"Melody!" she shouted. She started to run up the stairs but Gallard held on to her. "Melody! No!" She sobbed uncontrollably and Gallard did his best to console her.

"This is unbelievable," Solomon said. He'd picked up Robin from the ground and was gently holding her, supporting her head. "I had a feeling that Lucian let us off too easily, but I had no idea that he was up to something this...oh, poor Melody." He couldn't even finish.

"He...he wasn't behind this," I said. "At least I don't think so.

The man was angry about his girlfriend."

"Like hell he wasn't behind this!" Cherish shouted.

I heard the sirens in the distance and held on to Robin's hand, hopeful that it would arrive in time. There was a horrible gash on the back of her head and it hadn't stopped bleeding.

Cherish, who had stopped crying at this point removed herself from Gallard's embrace and stepped forward.

"This is my fault. I brought this upon us," Cherish said. We all turned our gaze to her and waited for her to explain and she continued, "Lucian wanted Lela. He wanted to trade her for me." She paused, trying not to cry again so that she could finish. "He knew she wouldn't leave unless she had a reason to be angry with Gallard, and he wanted me to get him to cheat on her. I should have known he would lose his patience. He gave me two weeks, but I couldn't do it. I defied him and now she's dead!"

"You tried to sleep with Gallard?" I asked, finally finding my voice again.

"It didn't work. He wouldn't fall for it, and I gave up."

"So it wasn't that you couldn't do it but that he wasn't interested."

My anger building, I slapped her as hard as I could across the face. I had never done that before and I couldn't believe I did. It was one thing to not like me; I could get over that. But she had gone behind my back just like Lydian had, and she was willing to manipulate me into joining Lucian by trying to get my husband to betray me. She must have really hated me if she could have done it so easily.

"Lela...," Gallard cautioned.

"No! I am done with her. I am so done that you can't even know."

Losing my temper wasn't going to help this tragic situation any. I was surprised that Cherish hadn't even retaliated. I expected a punch or even a slap back. Instead, she just stood there, stunned and frozen.

When the ambulance arrived, we threw our luggage into the back of the two cars. I rode in the back with Robin while the others drove behind.

I held Robin's hand as the EMT's pressed gauze to her wound and hooked her up to an IV. All I could think about was how I'd

THE RESURRECTION

failed her. I'd promised her that she was going to live; that she was going to grow up and have children of her own and die surrounded by her children and grandchildren. More than anything, I had promised myself. My parents were dead as well as my uncle. Now Robin could be headed down that same path.

Chapter Twenty-Eight

Jordan waited until no one was looking then ducked outside of the police station. After the events of that day, he couldn't ignore the nagging feeling in the back of his mind that Maximus and not Lucian had something to do with this chaos. It was too much of a coincidence that not a week ago Maximus threatened to take things into his own hands.

Centuries ago, Jordan had made Lucian's life his obsession. He learned everything he could about the man; who he spent time with, what his wife did when he wasn't around; how he entertained his daughters.

He grew to know Lucian better than he knew himself. He was a rash man who acted impulsively and constantly changed his mind. His mood swings were unpredictable; calm and pleasant one moment then psychotic and violent the next. But one thing was certain; Lucian wouldn't harm a child.

The fact that Solomon killed him for murdering two children had always baffled Jordan. Years of spying on him and not once had Lucian ever fed on or harmed anyone younger than the age of eighteen. He would stalk the alleyways where orphans would scavenge for food in the garbage and young teens would offer to shine shoes for money. Every single time, he would look past them and go for the old drunk or the crazy rambler.

When Jordan learned that two children's bodies were found on his property, a red flag went up. Jordan suspected Florence, but her M.O. was lower class men she would seduce then kill.

So why would he have his lackeys kill Robin? Especially after he'd promised Lela she was exempt. Or Melody for that matter. He may not have paid attention to her as a child but he would never kill his own daughter. Not after what his father had done to him. Filicide wasn't in his nature. It was the one thing that Jordan admired about this fiend who had stolen his life.

Against Maximus' wishes to never call him, Jordan dialed his number. He thought about approaching this calmly, but as he thought of little Robin and how bloody she had been, he threw that out the window.

"What is it, Jordanes?"

"You disgusting piece of —" he realized he was shouting so he lowered his voice. "A woman is dead and a child's life is at stake here. I know you're behind this."

"I told you before. You act or I act for you. I will not apologize for following through with my warning."

"She's a child!" Jordan was shouting again. "Five years old, Maximus. She's barely had a chance to live! What the hell?"

Maximus sighed. "I never told them to include the child in their plan. That was their doing. You cannot blame me for something I had no control over."

"And Melody? Was that something you had no control over? She was the purest soul I've ever met. She wasn't even religious, but I am sure God would accept her into heaven over a hypocritical bastard like you. This is your fault. You need to fix this."

He chuckled. "Fix this? How?"

"Save the little girl. I know you can do it; don't pretend that you can't."

"My patience is running thin, Jordanes. I have one goal in this life and one alone; kill Lucian and earn my soul back. Now I promised you that I would resurrect Lydian if you followed through. It's either one or the other. Who is it going to be? Lydian? Or Lela's sister?'

This was completely unfair. Maximus new his weaknesses and now he was using them to prove a point. When Lela had come back, he truly was happy. He would rather see Gallard's suffering lifted than to get the woman he loved back. Now he had a chance to be with Lydian again and Maximus was making him choose between her and a child.

"Forget I asked," he said. "I'll handle this on my own. Goodbye."

He hung up then left the room to speak with the others. He hadn't exactly made a choice, but he had a backup plan. He wasn't going to let Lela lose her sister. He would save her one way or another and he would do it without Maximus' gift.

"Jordan?" Gallard called from the doorway.

"Yeah?"

"The police want to get your statement now. You ready?

He nodded. "Sure. I'm coming."

When we had gotten to the hospital, I was forced to let go of Robin's hand as they wheeled her to the emergency room. The others found me not long after and we went to the waiting room.

Solomon paced the room, praying quietly to himself and I held onto Kevin's hand while Aaron stood close to the hall, wanting to be ready for any new information. They'd had to fly all the way back from Florida to be here and I was grateful.

The elevator dinged and I saw Cherish come in with Gallard and Jordan. They'd been speaking with the police about what had happened and were late coming to the hospital. I let go of Kevin's hand and walked over to them.

"Any news?" Gallard asked. I shook my head and he put his arms around me. While we stood there, I thought about Cherish's confession; that she'd attempted to get Gallard to cheat on me so I would leave him and go to Lucian. Did he really think that would work? For being in my head for so long, he didn't know me at all.

"I need to talk to Cherish for a minute," I told him.

"Sure, I'll come get you if we hear anything." He gave me a soft kiss before releasing me from the hug and taking my spot next to Kevin.

Cherish and I went down the hallway so we could talk in private. She'd already explained why she did what she did, but that wasn't what I wanted to discuss. Melody's death was tragic and none of us were prepared for it. Even though Lucian had made a truce with my family, something needed to be done.

"Lela, I don't even know where to begin. I'm so—"

"I'm not here to yell at you or demand an apology."

She gave me a puzzled look. "Why not? I deserve it. I plotted behind your back and tried to get Gallard to be unfaithful. You should hate me."

"I don't think I'm the one who is full of hate here. I just want to know why you dislike me so much that you would do something like this."

Her eyes met mine and the despair in them made it hard to be angry with her. She'd lost her sister today. The one person left in the world, and possibly the only person, that she truly loved. No one deserved that.

"Because I'm jealous of you," she finally admitted. "When I look at you, I see me. Trying on that wig yesterday kind of freaked me out. If I were blonde, we could pass as sisters. We've both suffered. We've both been betrayed by people we care about, and we've both experienced loss and a life of always hiding what we are. But we turned out differently. I self-destruct and you're all rainbows and sunshine. And you laugh. Do you know how long it's been since I've genuinely laughed?"

Tears formed in her eyes. "I haven't even cried until today. Five hundred years and I haven't shed a single tear. It shows how broken I am. I resented you because you were able to feel, and I wanted that so badly. I would have given anything to feel something other than hate. I guess I got my wish, didn't I?"

I felt moved to hug her. I couldn't stay mad at her. I knew all too well what it was like to pay the price for defiance. And unlike when Lydian betrayed me, she didn't follow through. Even if she'd tried, Gallard wouldn't hurt me like that. I trusted him. I didn't want to fight with Cherish anymore. She would need us now more than ever because she was alone.

I released her from the hug and went to look for some tissues. I went back into the waiting room but noticed my brothers weren't there. Solomon was speaking quietly with Gallard so I approached them.

"What's going on?"

Solomon looked at Gallard before walking away, and my stomach turned. Whatever I was about to hear couldn't be good.

"Lela, Robin is in a coma. She's on life support and she can't breathe on her own."

"Oh God, no. Not her too. Not my baby sister, I just got her back! I can't lose anyone else, I can't!" I began to ramble and he took my face in his hands just like the night I panicked when my mother was having complications. His gaze calmed me a bit and I took a deep breath.

"Where is he?" Solomon said. The three of us looked at him because we didn't know what he was talking about. "Accarezzare, where is your father?" He clarified.

"He was in Myrtle Beach when I left. The Hampton Inn. He said he'd be there until I sent Lela to him."

Without another word, Solomon walked out of the hospital. I wondered what he was going to do. He didn't seem like the kind of man who was bent on vengeance, but he did kill Lucian once. Would he try to kill him again?

"Your brothers are with Robin now if you want to see her," Gallard said.

I nodded then took his hand as we walked down the hall. It seemed like a long way to her room. I couldn't get there fast enough, my pace quickening by the second.

The possibility that she would never wake up was too hard to think about. She was tall for her age but she was so fragile. Aaron told me that she'd been born prematurely because of my mother having so many complications and had been in and out of the hospital for the first two years of her life. How could she survive this?

When we got to the door, Gallard let go of my hand so I could be alone with my siblings. Jordan had been standing outside to watch in case Lucian decided to send anyone else after us. He gave me a hug before I went inside.

There were so many tubes attached to Robin that I couldn't even

THE RESURRECTION

count. A machine next to her kept going up and down, making a hissing noise, and I assumed it was what helped her breathe. Her entire little head was covered in a large bandage. She looked so still; her eyes weren't even fluttering.

"What did the doctors say?" I asked Aaron.

"There's a twenty percent chance that she'll wake up," he said. He sighed then took her hand. "But...there's even less chance that she'll wake up normal. She could have severe brain damage. She might not even be able to walk."

Kevin started to cry, and I stood behind him, holding onto him. I still hadn't shed a single tear. I didn't know why. I wanted to cry so badly, but I couldn't.

"This isn't going to happen," Aaron continued. "I'm not letting her die like this, she's just a baby. She should never have been part of this!"

I looked at him then at Kevin. They didn't have to spell it out with words. I knew exactly what they were suggesting.

"What? No!" I shouted. "You're not doing this! I can't believe you guys are even thinking about...that would be cruel and barbaric; she's five years old!"

"She'll be ten when she's fully transformed," Aaron argued, "She wouldn't be five forever."

"And being ten forever is better? Trapping her in a child's body would be worse than killing her!"

I kept looking at each of their faces for any sign of relenting, but I found none. Jordan came into the room at that moment, probably because he heard the commotion.

"Sorry, Lela, but it's already been done," Aaron said. He stood up, revealing that he had a needle in his hands, and I realized what had happened. He must have injected his blood into her.

"How could you?" I shouted, lunging for him. I was so angry that I'd lost my self-control, but Jordan and Kevin held me back. I normally would have been stronger than them, but Jordan's grip was unusually strong for some reason. I pushed Kevin away, but Jordan was determined to keep me from intervening.

What stopped me from going after him was Robin waking up. I stopped struggling since it was too late for me to do anything.

Jordan let go of me and I fell to my knees. I felt nauseous, lightheaded, and the feeling grew worse as I listened to Robin yell in agony from the pain of the transformation. The machines were beeping like crazy, so Aaron quickly unhooked her from everything before lifting the crying Robin off the bed.

"Come on, we need to get out of here before the doctors show," Aaron said. I tried to but I couldn't move. These past couple of hours felt like a horrible nightmare that I couldn't wake up from.

Jordan ended up having to pick me up and practically carry me out of the room. We went out into the hall just as Gallard was coming towards us.

"What happened, what's going on?" he asked.

"We'll explain in the car," Jordan said.

I finally found my legs and hurried along with the others. We didn't even bother with the elevator, but ran down the stairs instead. I could hear doctors coming behind us but we were too fast for them.

Cherish, and Gallard got into the BMW and Aaron handed Robin to me before I got in as well. I quickly strapped her into her booster seat as we took off then I turned away. I couldn't bring myself to look at her. I wish I'd done more to stop them; that I'd done more to protect her.

Around one o'clock, we were close to making it past city limits when Gallard turned the BMW into the parking lot of some gas station. I'd thought we were going to go further, but he probably wanted to discuss our next plan of action as well as the mystery of Robin's sudden recovery. Solomon had left and was probably long gone.

As we got out of the car, we stood in silence, reeling from the craziness of everything that was happening that night. One thing kept happening after another, and I didn't think I could handle any more chaos. Gallard looked livid. I'd never seen him so angry and I felt exactly the same way.

"Will someone care to explain how Robin is suddenly not in a coma?" he asked.

I looked at Aaron, who was looking at the ground. I was hoping he wouldn't be a coward and own up to his horrible deed. But he didn't give an answer, so I decided to speak for him.

"I'll tell you what happened," I said in a condescending voice, which was directed towards my brothers and Jordan. "After Aaron told us Robin's prognosis, he irrationally suggested that we turn her in order to save her. I told him it was a stupid decision, but it was too late." I felt the overdue tears welling up in my eyes. "He injected her with his blood while we were out of the room and now she's a vampire."

"You did *what?*" Gallard asked Aaron. "You reckless, stupid boy! Are you mad? She's only a child, how could you be so…Gah! I can't even look at you, you disgust me!"

He let go of Aaron, allowing him to stand up. Aaron then began to try and defend himself.

"She was dying! I didn't have another choice. I *saved* her! You should be thanking me right now!"

Now it was my turn to wail on him. I threw him down and began hitting him as hard as I could, using more and more force with each strike. I wouldn't have been able to stop if Cherish and Jordan hadn't pulled me off of him. By then, he was pretty banged up, but his injuries were healing.

"I hate you, Aaron! You've done terrible things in the past, but you've crossed the line! You turned Kevin against your better judgment, and you then you turned Robin. I will *never* forgive you for this!"

"Why do you hate me? You hate me for saving our sister; for giving her a chance to be able to defend herself? It was inevitable that she was going to die!"

"Tell her that in fifty years when she's still a child and wonders why she doesn't grow up! You made a permanent decision for a temporary situation! She was still alive; she still had a chance to recover! If you had just waited —"

"Wait? *Wait?* That's all we've done is wait and look where that's gotten us. Well, unlike the rest of you, I'm not going to wait around for Lucian to come kill us all. I'm done being a coward running around wondering if and when he's going to strike next. I'm out of here!"

Gallard grabbed his arm before he could leave and said, "Aaron hold on, you're not thinking clearly right now. None of us are. Just wait until tomorrow to make a decision."

"No, this is bull! I'm done. I'm leaving and don't try to stop me."

He took off down the road and no one went after him. There were now six of us, which meant we were more vulnerable than ever. Everything seemed so hopeless at that moment. What had started out as a good day had turned into a nightmare in less than four hours.

Kevin, who was now holding Robin, came up to me, keeping his head down so that we couldn't make eye contact. He had taken off her bandages and I could see that the wound on her head was healed. She was still in her hospital gown.

"You were right about making a permanent decision for a temporary situation. It was wrong to let him do that to her, and I see that now. I don't know what came over me. I guess I was just so afraid of losing another person in my family that I panicked."

"You were supposed to be the level head among the three of us. I trusted you to make the right decisions and you failed. You failed our sister, and you failed me."

Kevin looked down and shifted his feet then said, "Maybe it would be best if I left too."

Gallard joined the conversation at that moment saying, "No, absolutely not! Don't you see? This is exactly what Lucian wants! He wants us to quarrel so that we would separate and become even easier targets than before. Solomon is gone and so is Aaron, so there are only five of us left. Some unforgivable things were done tonight, I won't deny that. And I understand if some people won't be quick to forgive as well. But one thing is certain; we have to stick together. If we lose any more people, then Lucian will have won. And I will be damned if I were to let that happen!"

We all nodded in agreement. Gallard was right; if we split up, we were all as good as dead. Melody had been one of our strongest and she'd been caught off guard and paid for it with her life. We weren't about to let that happen again.

There was another matter that I couldn't ignore; something that had been weighing on my mind for the past few hours. What had happened to Robin was a tragedy. She'd been robbed of any chance for a normal life, and in my eyes, she was dead even if she was still moving and talking.

I pulled Gallard aside and led him far away from the group so that no one would hear. What I had to say to him was of a dark

THE RESURRECTION

nature, and I didn't want to risk anyone trying to get involved. We stood in silence as I came up with a way to say what I needed to say.

"Gallard, I love my sister. I loved her from the moment I met her, and I would easily give up my life for hers."

"I know you would, Lela. I would do the same for you and your brothers. Even Aaron, though I could kill him right now."

I couldn't look him in the eye. I was too overcome with sickness over what I was about to ask him.

"She can't have this life. She'll only grow up to be ten years old. I don't want that for her, it's not living."

Gallard gave a concerned look and folded his arms. "Lela, what are you saying?"

I couldn't say the words out loud. If I said it, I probably wouldn't be able to do it. Once it was done, nothing would ever be the same again. I wouldn't be the same. I'd done some horrible things in my lifetime, but this would probably be the worst. The only difference was that I was doing it out of love and not as some senseless act.

"I would be the one to do it. She trusts me more than anyone in this group, except maybe you or Kevin, but I couldn't ask him to live with that, even if he did have a hand in what happened to her."

"Lela, you're talking about euthanizing your own sister!" He paused for a moment then lightly touched my shoulder. "Are you sure you could handle that? It would probably be the hardest thing you ever do."

"I know. I can't worry about how it will affect me. I'm doing this for her. It's better this way."

Gallard nodded then pulled me into his embrace then replied, "I'm leaving this decision up to you. Whatever you decide, I will support you."

I began the long walk back to the group. I didn't want to take my time in fear that I would use it to talk myself out of it. I knew it was the right thing to do.

Once I got back, I smiled at Robin before taking her out of the car. The clouds had gotten darker so I wasn't worried about her being outside. I also grabbed one of the blankets out of the trunk. Kevin gave me a questioning look as I walked by him.

"She...she needs blood," I lied. It was the only thing I could think of that would get him to let me leave with her, without any suspicion.

I then walked off with just her away from the group once more. There was a small forest nearby that would guarantee I would be alone with her.

"Where are we going?" she asked.

"Just a little walk. I need to talk to you about something," I replied. I finally stopped in a small clearing and found a large boulder to sit her on. She gave me a toothy grin, which revealed that her fangs had come out. The scent of my blood had probably caused this since Melody said it was just like human blood. I stayed calm, trying not to show how upset I was. The less stressed I appeared, the less she would feel anxious.

"Robin, do you remember when you fell earlier tonight?" I asked.

"Yeah, I hurt my head. But I feel better now."

"Well, you may feel better, but when you hit your head, you got sick."

"Is that why I was in the hospital?"

"Yes. But you don't have to be sick anymore; I can make you better." I touched her cheek. "You know I love you, right baby?"

She smiled. "I love you too, Lela. You always take care of me."

I pulled her close to me, hugging her and she squeezed my neck. I closed my eyes, preparing myself for what I was about to do. I kissed her forehead and told her that in order to get better, I would have to bite her and that it would hurt a little bit, but then she would be cured. She said okay and I tilted her head to the left.

When I bit her, she let out a little whimper, but I ignored it. Nothing could stop me at that point. I kept drinking and drinking until I felt her body go limp, but I continued still. I didn't stop until the blood stopped flowing.

I then lifted her body off of the rock and lay her gently on the ground while I spread the blanket out. I lay her on it then carefully swaddled her inside, covering her entire body. She needed to be with my parents; with family where she belonged.

Gallard was in the middle of speaking to Jordan in French, probably discussing what they were going to do next. My brother was on the phone, and from what he was saying, I guessed he was calling Aaron and trying to convince him to come back. Cherish was sitting on the ground, crying and hugging her knees to her chest. No one even noticed that I'd returned, so I sat on the curb next to Cherish. She wiped her eyes and looked at me.

"Lela...what did you do?" she asked. I didn't answer her, but kept staring into space. "Lela?" she questioned when I maintained my silence.

"She's gone, Cher. Just like your sister. I did what I thought was best."

She gasped in horror, and then Kevin and Jordan's attention was brought to us. Kevin dropped his phone and ran over to me, pulling Robin out of my arms.

"What did you do?" He unwrapped it around her head and when he saw her face he began to cry. "No! Oh God, Robin! Lela what did you do?"

He hugged her little body to him and sobbed while Gallard put a hand on his shoulder. I couldn't bring myself to cry over this. Not anymore. Everything around me felt surreal and my vision became a little hazy like I was on the verge of passing out.

"They're not going to get away with this," I said. "I'm not waiting for another person I love to be slaughtered. Cherish, call those men who were spying."

She frowned and looked at me. "Why?"

"Just do it."

Cherish hesitantly took her phone out of her pocket and dialed the number. Once I heard it ringing, I took the phone from her and waited for someone to answer. I didn't know what possessed me to do this, but I was angry.

I'd never felt this kind of rage before in my life and I needed to let it out. I couldn't kill Lucian, not yet; it wasn't the right time. But someone needed to answer for Melody and Robin's deaths.

"Hello," someone said. I recognized the man's voice as the one who'd dropped my sister. He was exactly the one I wanted.

"This is Lela," I said to him. "I know that Lucian wants me. I will go to him, but you have to take me there yourself."

I heard him exhale hard on the other end, like he was having difficulty deciding what to do. I didn't see what was hard about this decision. No doubt they would be rewarded for retrieving me.

What was there to think about?

"How do we know this isn't a trap?" he asked.

"You don't. You're just going to have to trust me. I'm five miles outside of Blacksburg. There's a diner just off of interstate eight-one. Meet me there in two hours."

"And what of his daughter?"

I looked at Cherish and she shook her head, letting me know that she wasn't coming with me. I understood why. She didn't want to risk having to go back to Lucian. What she didn't know was that my plan involved the opposite.

"I will be alone. And you better be too, or I will change my mind."

I then hung up and started making my way up the hill towards the freeway. The others were still distracted, so Cherish was the only one who knew of my plan.

"Lela, wait. What are you doing?" Gallard asked as he hurried after me.

"You know what I'm doing. They're going to pay for what they did to our sisters."

"Are you crazy?" Cherish asked. "What if my father sends ten men after you? If you go alone, you won't stand a chance!"

"Then come with me."

She opened her mouth to speak then closed it. I knew her answer from that. She would not come. It didn't matter to me anyway. Alone, assisted; either way I was going to kill them.

I tried to leave again when Gallard grabbed my arm. My rage overtook my sense and I actually turned around and growled at him. When I saw the concern in his eyes, I calmed down a bit. But not enough to change my mind.

"I'm leaving," I said, shrugging him off. "You can't stop me."

Without another word, I ran up the hill, leaving them behind. Gallard called after me and I tuned out his voice. I knew they would come after me but by then I would already be halfway to the diner.

Chapter Twenty-Nine

Lucian turned around when he heard commotion in the hall. He hadn't heard from the two men he'd sent to spy on Cherish yet, and was hoping it was them returning with news that she was making progress. She'd said that she was going through with the plan, but he had his doubts. She wasn't the daughter he remembered, so he wasn't able to take her word for anything.

This had been a test. A test to see if she truly was able to be controlled. For a while, he had wondered if it would be best to try and reconcile with both her and Melody so he wouldn't completely be out of their lives. They were his only family left, after all.

Lucian didn't have the time or patience to find out, though. He had an agenda and was determined to go through with it.

Someone yelled and then he heard a loud thud before someone kicked in the door. He froze when he saw who it was; Solomon. He was the last person he thought would come seeking him out. Lucian knew by his arrival that Cherish hadn't succeeded. But he didn't know why Solomon was here.

"Sharmentino. To what do I owe the pleasure of having your company?"

Solomon rushed up to Lucian and threw him across the room.

Lucian hadn't expected that and didn't have a chance of eluding the maneuver.

"You should not have done that," Lucian said through clenched teeth.

"I thought the crime you committed all those years ago was cruel, but this is beyond barbaric!"

"What crime, my dear Solomon? You call a little deceit a crime? You are such a—"

"Melody is dead. One of your men killed her and Robin was injured in the process. She's dying the hospital as we speak."

Lucian opened his mouth then closed it. Solomon wasn't one to make things up. If he was telling the truth, then his men had gone against everything they'd been commanded to do.

"My...my daughter is dead?"

"Don't pretend to be surprised. Admit it; you never cared about Melody. After you came back, all you could do was berate me about Cherish and how you lost your favorite daughter. Did you even care that she'd been killed as well that night?"

"She...she wasn't part of this. She wasn't to be touched; not even...I only told them to watch."

"Oh yeah? Well that watching turned into an attack. Their blood is on your hands, Lucian!"

Solomon turned away while Lucian remained on the floor. He was too stunned to get up, still reeling from this information. Melody never deserved to die; not in the past and not now. Though he'd never been a proper father to her, he still felt horrible about it.

"Why did you come here?" Lucian finally asked. "Was it to kill me? You really think you would succeed a second time?"

"Yes I do. But if you stay away from my family and from Cherish; especially Lela, I will spare you. So much as set foot on any of their doorsteps and I will not hesitate to rip you apart."

"How generous of you."

"Be quiet, Lucian. Five hundred years and you still haven't learned your lesson. You keep hurting those around you and making everyone miserable to hide the fact that you're miserable, yourself. You hate being alone and you think the only way to get people to stay is by threatening them."

"Well it worked because you stayed. Or have you forgotten?"

"I didn't stay because I was afraid of you. I stayed

THE RESURRECTION

because...believe it or not, Lucian, you were my friend. For years, I tried to get through to you because I missed the man you once were. Now you're just out of control and after tonight, I am done with you."

Solomon then left the room and Lucian finally stood up. He didn't know what to do with himself or what he would do in general. What had started as a plot for revenge, turned into a compromise, and then instead of walking away, he'd had to have the last say, as always. Now Melody was dead and a little girl was dying. This was a nightmare.

One of his followers opened the door about twenty minutes later and two men came in, dragging someone in with them. Lucian stared at the third person but couldn't distinguish who he was.

The man was charred beyond recognition and he could still smell the smoke on him. He'd smelled this before. It was the smell of a night-walker who had been caught in the sun. He'd been saved just in time, and a little blood would heal his burns in no time, but he looked like he was in extreme agony.

"Who is this?" Lucian asked them. They tossed the man on the bed and he groaned in pain. His clothes had been burned onto his skin, and Lucian couldn't tell where his clothes ended and his skin started. Nearly everything was black save for the man's right ear and part of his left hand.

"He came looking for us shortly after Solomon left," Damien said. "Got himself caught after sun up, and we had to douse him in water before he was fully consumed. He didn't tell us his name."

"And the Kenneth and Evan? Did you know about their attack against the group?"

Damien hesitated before replying. "Kenneth wanted revenge for Melody killing his girlfriend," said one of the men. "He knew it was against your orders. Evan helped him."

Lucian almost killed the man, but remembered he wasn't the one in charge of the mission. They hadn't messed everything up, and he would deal with the others later.

The truth was, the news of Melody's unplanned death hit him harder than he'd expected. He wouldn't have been as angry if they'd gone through with killing Solomon. He was still angry with him, but Melody didn't deserve to die. Cherish would surely blame him, and he knew he'd lost her forever.

"Where are they now?" he asked.

"Apparently Lela called them and said she wanted them to bring her to you."

Lucian smiled then began to laugh. He couldn't believe his spies had fallen for that trick. At the same time, he could. They didn't know her like he did. She'd called to meet them all right, but it wasn't to surrender. Melody and Robin would be avenged and he had no problem with that.

"Well. It appears we will now be short two men. Tis inevitable that she will slaughter them. I have seen her wrath. Tis not something to be taken lightly. She is angry, and they are dead men."

Lucian then turned his attention to the charred man and grabbed his man's face, turning it towards him and the live piece of charcoal winced. The prostitute he kept around was huddled in the corner of the room, so he called her over. She stood up reluctantly and started walking towards him. She was too slow for him so he grabbed her arm and pulled her towards the bed and she yelped. He bit down on her wrist, creating a descent cut and held it to the man's mouth.

The stranger didn't have the strength to sit up and drink, so Lucian helped him out. Lucian wasn't particularly concerned about the man. He was just curious to know who he was. He had some ideas, but it wouldn't be determined until his skin was healed.

"Cut his clothes off and give him something else to wear," he ordered his followers. "And do it quickly. It would be a shame if his clothes healed into his skin permanently."

One follower, an ex-cop who Lucian had found living in squalor, pulled a knife out from his pocket and began cutting the clothes away from the skin. The man's yells echoed throughout the room, and one of the other men had to put a gag in his mouth to silence him.

Once they'd done as they were told, he then ordered them to leave and check on the two spies. He wanted a report to see what exactly Lela planned to do to them. And he wanted to speak with the injured man alone.

Lucian studied the man some more and waited to see if the blood would heal him. So far, he could see some improvement. By rights, this man should have been ash and Lucian contemplated putting him out of his misery.

Eventually the wounds completely healed and there was no sign that he'd ever been burned. And Lucian finally knew his identity.

"Well, well; Aaron Sharmentino. I am impressed that you have brought yourself to me."

Aaron chuckled, coughing as he did. Looking at this boy caused Lucian to put things in perspective. Technically Aaron was older than he was when he'd stopped aging; twenty-three. Lucian had been twenty; a year younger than his daughter Cherish had been when she'd died and six years younger than Melody. Melody who was now dead, for good this time.

Aaron's fast healing gave him the strength to stand and put on the borrowed clothes he'd been given. "If you want to kill me so badly, why did you save me?"

"Curiosity I suppose. I did not recognize you at first. Why are you here? Did you come with Solomon?"

"No. I came on my own accord. I'm tired of running, and I thought maybe I could make a deal, since you like to make them so much."

Lucian laughed. His enemies in the twenty-first century were a lot bolder than they had been back in his time. Lela had proved that several times by talking back to him. Aaron was a different kind of bold. His eyes looked to Lucian as if he cared about nothing and had nothing to lose. If he had been a day-walker, Lucian would have been afraid of him.

"What sort of deal, Sharmentino? This better be an adequate request or I might be tempted to toss you back outside."

"I'll get Lela to come to you."

Lucian raised an eyebrow. This boy was so willing to give up his sister and he wanted to know why. What had changed? Only a week ago, Aaron had been fighting at her side. But this was an offer that was going to be hard to refuse.

"What do you want in return?" he asked Aaron.

"I want you to let Kevin, Robin, and me disappear. We won't be in your way when you go to kill the others. Frankly, I'm tired of this stupid war between you and Solomon. I want out."

"The war *is* over, Sharmentino. Solomon showed up and told me what happened to Melody and Robin. Why are you so quick to give up your sister?"

Aaron shrugged. "I'm dead to her. I turned Robin into a vampire to save her life and Lela didn't take it too well. None of them did. I've been listening to vampires tell me what to do for too long and I'm done. I don't care what happens to the rest of them. I just want my two siblings; my full siblings to be left alone. Lela's on their side now."

Lucian mulled over everything Aaron had said. Aaron had made his younger sister immortal. Not the smartest decision on his part. He was surprised that he was willing to give up his other sister so easily. The same sister that had lost her life to save her family. The sister that had loved him so dearly. He knew this because of all the times she'd confided in him as a child when she would take the fall for something her brother had done. Then again, Lucian knew all too well that family bonds could break. He'd killed his parents, or the ones that had raised him anyway. Whatever had caused Aaron to leave the group, it had to be a good reason.

Lucian went over to the small cabinet next to the microwave and took out the tiny bottles of hard alcohol that came with the room. He didn't feel like plotting anymore. In fact, he had no idea what he would do now. The feud was over, Cherish hated him, and now he had no purpose. All he wanted to do was forget these past few weeks even happened.

He chugged the first bottle and then the second, the alcohol burning as it went down his throat. He hadn't gotten drunk since the night he'd returned to London after partying with Solomon for weeks on end. After that, he'd sobered up to be an adequate father to Cherish.

"I don't want Lela," he said to Aaron. "I don't want anything. All I want is to drink."

"Okay...then where does that leave me?"

Lucian chugged a third bottle before answering. "I learned from Lela that you know how to have a good time. I do not know how to do that in this century. I want you to teach me."

Aaron let out an amused laugh then folded his arms.

"I'm not against that. But I really think we should go somewhere else. I know a place where you can really lose yourself."

THE RESURRECTION

Lucian finished off the last bottle then tossed them into the trash. "And where is that?"

"New York. And I have a place we can stay as well. You game?"

Maximus stepped into Selena's Diner then looked around. When Jordan had told them that a child had been harmed during the secret plot, it had sickened him. He'd pretended that he wasn't concerned by it but inside, he regretted ever helping the men responsible.

They were supposed to motivate Jordanes' group to kill Lucian, not form their own vendetta and kill innocent people. He wanted to speak with them and deal with them on his own. Men like them were the reason he started following God in the first place.

He spotted them sitting in a booth by the window and he sat across from them. They had these pleased looks on their faces as if they were proud of the destruction they were responsible for. If this were a different setting, he would set them on fire and burn them to ash. He couldn't do that here. He had already risked exposure by demonstrating his power in the other restaurant.

A waitress approached him and he ordered a hot raspberry tea. The two men had barely addressed him but kept glancing at the door as if they were expecting someone. Maximus finally snapped his fingers in front of Kenneth.

"Care to explain?" he asked.

"Explain what?"

"I heard about what you've done. You hurt a child?"

The other man, Evan, smirked. "She was probably slowing them down anyway. Think about how much more they'll want to kill Lucian now."

Maximus glared at him, his power radiating throughout his body. The smile left Evan's face and then his nose began to bleed. He grabbed a napkin and wiped it away just as Maximus stopped what he was doing. Bleeding him out sounded like a wonderful idea. It was less conspicuous than setting him on fire.

"Do not test me," he said. "My wrath is not something to trifle with. You did not follow my instructions and now…" both Evan and Kenneth had glanced towards the door again. Frustrated, Maximus took two forks and stabbed it into their hands, causing them to yell. "Look at me when I am talking to you!"

"Okay! We're listening!" Kenneth said. He yanked out the fork, tossing it onto the table.

"Good. Now you called me here for a reason and I suspect that it was to give me a progress report?"

"No," Evan said. "It's about the girl's sister. Lela? She contacted us and asked that we meet her here. She's going to hand herself over to Lucian."

This was the last thing Maximus needed; Lucian to have a strong person on his side. Lela was loved by everyone in her group and if she sided with him, they wouldn't bring themselves to kill her. They would sooner let Lucian go free and his plan would be ruined.

Then again, she could be bluffing. If she thought Lucian responsible for her sister's accident, then she might be bent on revenge. More so even towards the two men involved. She might very well be on her way to kill them. He couldn't have that and he needed them to act as his insiders.

"Do you have backup?" he asked.

"Yes. There are more guys in here. Lucian sent them in case the group figured out that Cherish was deceiving them and killed us before we could report. They know nothing of our extracurricular activities."

"Good. Gentleman, as you know, I am a very powerful man. Though you deserve to rot in hell for what you did to that little girl, I will keep you alive. You just need to trust me."

The bell rang as someone came into the door and he turned to see a tall blonde woman. It was definitely Lela, and she was on the prowl. Her eyes were emotionless as they scanned the diner for her targets. Closing his eyes, he focused on her and altered her mind. If this were to work correctly, she would be seeing what he wanted her to see.

Then her eyes locked on the two vampires that were sitting a few booths in front of him. He smiled, knowing that it had worked. In her eyes, she was seeing them as the men who had killed Melody while in fact they were sitting across from him. She stalked towards them then stopped by their table.

"Can I help you?" the young man asked.

"No, but I can kill you."

Without another word, she dragged him out of the booth. People gasped in shock and Maximus was also surprised by her actions. She picked up one of the chairs and began beating him with it over and over. The other man tried to stop her but she shoved him about ten feet away with one push of her hand. One of the diners tried to intervene but it only took one growl from her to cause them to back off.

Lela beat the man until the chair was broken and then picked him up and sank her teeth into his throat. She tore violently at it, causing the blood to get all over the floor and table. Once the man was still, she threw him onto the ground. The other man went for her and she dodged him and pinned him to the ground. She ripped open his shirt the grabbed a steak knife from the bussing cart and drove it into his chest, slicing him open. By then, the customers were in a panic and began running out of the restaurant.

Once she'd created a massive hole in his chest, she reached in and grabbed onto his heart. In one jerk, she ripped it out and he yelled in agony. His would bleed out quickly then he shriveled into nothing but skin and bones.

At that moment, three more immortals came inside. They saw the damage and Lela whipped her head in their direction. They took one look at her and went bolting out the door. She dropped the heart and the knife, chasing after them. Just like that, the horrific act was over.

Maximus turned to the men across the table and saw their fear. They had witnessed what would have happened to them if he had not protected them. Now they owed him their lives.

"How…how did she not see us?" Kenneth asked.

"I told you. I am a very powerful man."

Sirens began to pierce the air, so Maximus finished his tea and stood up. This act of violence wasn't particularly shocking. He had grown up in the time of the Romans. They had inflicted worse damage on their prisoners than this. He had become desensitized to mindless murder two millennia ago.

"We must go before the police show up," he said. "I am not entirely sure what we should do next, but I will come up with a plan. For now, continue to spy on Lucian and pass on his activities to me. When it is time, I will let you know."

Stepping around the bloody mess, he left the restaurant. He transformed into an eagle just as the police flooded the parking lot. He had the ability to change into any animal form that he wanted, except for a dove; God's anointed bird. Maximus could have allowed his creations to do the same, but chose to let them change into bats instead. They were the vilest of creatures, and because they fed on blood just like the immortals, he figured it was poetic that they share the form.

He perched on the roof of the gas station across the street and watched the scene unfold. It had been difficult watching her kill those men. Because she was immortal, he could feel a pull towards her and he felt her pain. Empathy was another gift he had been cursed with. He learned long ago that ignoring it would keep him from losing his mind.

One day, he would be at peace again. One day, he would earn his soul and stand before God. He was well aware that he would be judged, but in the end his Lord would take him back. He had to. If not then, he would rather be damned to hell then continue living like this.

Chapter Thirty

"Why did you let her take off by herself?" Kevin asked Cherish. They'd been driving for several hours trying to find the diner Lela had mentioned and they still hadn't found it. The sun was already beginning to rise, but the trees along the road blocked out the sunlight.

"I didn't *let* her go. There was no reasoning with her. Didn't you see her eyes? She was beyond pissed off."

Cherish felt horrible for not trying harder to stop Lela. On the other hand, she understood Lela's drive for revenge. She'd had the same rage when she'd lost her child. Though she'd lost the baby as the result of a freak accident, she still wanted someone to blame.

"This isn't like her," Gallard said. "She doesn't just leave. She knows it isn't safe."

"Maybe she's picking up habits from your relative here," Kevin said in regards to Jordan. Cherish had no idea what they were talking about but didn't ask. There were more important things to worry about. She didn't want Lela to end up outnumbered and forced to go to Lucian.

But he would love Lela the way she was now; furious; pushed beyond her limit. Cherish hadn't seen anyone that angry since her father killed her mother's lover. He'd frightened Cherish so badly that she couldn't go near him for days without being afraid. He kept promising he would never hurt her, but he ended up hurting her in ways he never comprehended.

The clouds in the sky began to part, and though it was nearly sunset, the two night-walkers could possibly be in danger of exposure. Cherish took off her jacket so Kevin could hide. It was because of her that Robin was hurt, so she wanted to make up for it by taking care of Lela's younger brother. He quickly transformed and she hugged his tiny form closer to her, keeping him completely covered from exposure. Gallard did the same for Jordan, though it was harder since he was driving, so now it was up to the two of them to find Lela.

The traffic became more frequent, so they turned off the first exit into town. They were back in Blacksburg. She recognized the few shops and truck stops from when she'd driven there from her father's hotel room. The diner had to be somewhere near there. It was the only area with restaurants within fifty miles.

"There's Selena's Diner!" Gallard pointed out.

Cherish looked ahead and the neon sign came into view. Gallard parked the car then they left Kevin and Jordan in the car before jogging across the street at a somewhat normal speed because of the amount of people walking around. There were several police cars parked in front of the diner and caution tape was stretched out all around.

Gallard was the first to move then she followed him to go inquire about the crime scene. Nobody would say it out loud, but Cherish knew that Lela had to be responsible for whatever happened there. It would be too much of a coincidence if someone else had caused this much commotion.

"What happened here?" Gallard asked a woman. A small crowd of people had formed nearby and they were bound to know something.

"I don't know all the details, but two men were murdered here last night. I guess it was pretty bad. I heard that they were torn apart."

"Do they have the culprit in custody?"

"No. Apparently she ran off after they were dead. Left a set of bloody footprints behind, but they lost the trail in the woods. They

THE RESURRECTION

have dogs searching for her right now. Can you believe a woman was responsible for this?"

Gallard thanked the woman for her help then Cherish and he ran off to search for these footprints the woman had spoken of. They would have a better chance of following the trail than the dogs. Her ability to track vampire blood was stronger than Gallard's so she stayed ahead of him.

The tracks started close to the window on the left side of the diner and she followed them until more police came into sight. There was a K9 Unit van parked near the entrance of the forest, so she went further ahead to avoid running into anyone.

The scent became more and more faint the further she got into the forest and Cherish was worried that the blood had dried too much for her to be able to find Lela. What helped was that the scent seemed to stay in a general direction instead of appearing all over the place. Cherish was sure they were going in the right direction, but had no idea how far Lela had run. Had she tried to head back to where they were earlier that night?

Abruptly, the scent changed. It was less subtle, like it was inside of a person instead of on the path. This only meant one thing; a vampire was nearby. She knew it wasn't Gallard. She had his scent engrained in her memory so she could differentiate him from the enemy.

Cherish stopped moving then held up her hand, commanding Gallard to do the same. She closed her eyes, inhaling deeply through her nose. It took five seconds to trace the location of the scent and she opened her eyes, running off in its direction without warning Gallard.

She collided with the unsuspecting immortal, shoving him to the ground and grabbed him by the throat. Gallard caught up with her and she began questioning the man.

"You. Are you working for my father?" She demanded. He whimpered in fear and she tightened her grip. "Answer me! Do you work for Lucian?"

"Yes, I used to. But he is no longer in Myrtle Beach. He left after his army was killed."

She looked back at Gallard then slightly loosened her grip on his throat.

"What do you mean his army was killed?" she asked.

"Lucian found out that Lela had called his spies that he sent after you. He knew they didn't stand a chance against her, so he sent the rest of us to watch. I stayed behind in case it wasn't safe, but she got to them. I heard yelling and I cleared out of there before could find out what was going on."

"She killed them all," Gallard said, nearly whispering.

They needed to find Lela before she tried to do something irrational. Killing these night-walkers was one thing, but her father was twice as strong as they were. Though he was obsessed with Lela, he wouldn't take an attack from her lightly. He'd been attacked several times in the past and wouldn't let her get away with it. He cared more about his own life than he did having Lela at his side.

"Get out of here," Cherish said to the man. "If you tell Lucian where we are, I will do worse to you than she did to the others."

She let go of him and he ran off without another word. He hadn't exactly been helpful, but now she knew the extent of damage Lela had done. In a way, she'd helped them out by ridding Lucian of back up, but she feared for Lela's state of mind. If she was capable of a massacre that brutal, would they be able to reason with her? Cherish wouldn't know until they found her and it needed to be soon.

"Let's keep looking," Gallard said. "With him wandering around out there, she's bound to go for the kill."

"Unless she smells you first," Cherish said.

She continued following the trail again and the scent became strong once more. The blood was beginning to be more and more visible along the path, showing up on leaves and splattering all over the rocks and trees. She wouldn't be surprised if they stumbled across the bodies Lela left behind. If Lela had done to them what she did to the men at the diner, Cherish was hoping she wouldn't find herself tripping on a limb or stepping in any guts.

A loud cry echoed from up ahead and the three of them stopped walking. Cherish was right; Lela had been waiting for that man to make an appearance and now he was meeting the same fate as the rest of Lucian's men. She'd probably waited all day for him to come out of hiding.

THE RESURRECTION

The two of them ran in the direction of the yelling. Gallard got there first and she wondered why he'd stopped so suddenly when she saw what he was looking at. Someone was definitely feeding on the man they'd just spoken with, but the woman was unrecognizable. She dropped the body then stared down at it, breathing hard and standing completely still.

"Lela?" Gallard said. She looked up at him, her expression blank and emotionless. Cherish couldn't believe what she was seeing. Lela was covered in so much blood that her blonde hair was completely red, just like hers. Her skin was nearly black from the dried blood and so were her clothes. The only part of Lela that was clear and visible was her eyes.

Gallard took a step forward and Lela moved back. Her movements were almost animal like; feral. Who knew how long she'd been in hunting mode. Both vampires and hybrids alike, Cherish knew that if one stayed this way for too long, it was easy to lose human instinct and completely surrender to the monster.

"Lela, do you recognize me?" Gallard continued. She cautiously began walking towards him and Cherish held her breath, preparing herself in case she would need to step in and save him. Lela was unpredictable and Cherish wasn't even sure if either of them were safe. She needed to protect Gallard for Lela's sake. She knew Lela wouldn't forgive herself if she hurt him.

Lela stood in front of Gallard and neither of them said a word. The only sounds that could be heard were Cherish's heartbeat, Lela's, and the slight breeze rustling the trees. Time seemed to slow, as they waited for her next move. Would she attack him, or would she snap out of her animalistic state?

This question was answered when Lela put her arms around Gallard's waist, resting her head against his chest and he hugged her back. Cherish could see that he was trying hard not to cry, but she couldn't tell if it was from relief or sadness. Lela might be with them physically, but only time could tell how far gone she really was.

Gallard unlocked the door to the hotel room then opened it, stepping aside to let Lela in. He was tired of staying in hotels, but he and Jordan agreed that Lela and Cherish shouldn't travel yet. Not after what they'd been through. The tragedies they had just experienced still hadn't hit him.

Jordan and Kevin were in the room next door and Cherish was two doors down, claiming to want some time alone. Gallard had been shocked by Jordan's actions. He'd confessed to being the one to find Aaron a syringe as well as guarding the door in case any doctors showed up.

Jordan wasn't usually one to make such irrational decisions. Then again, he had been acting different lately, first with the mysterious disappearance for several hours then helping Aaron do something incredibly cruel. Something was off, and Gallard hoped that whatever was going through his mind would be resolved before anything worse happened.

Lela sat on the edge of the bed and stared off into space. When Lela talked with him about what she wanted to do in regards to Robin's immortality, Gallard hadn't been sure how to react.

Her decision to euthanize her sister had baffled him at first, but then as he thought about it, it made more sense to him. The truth was he'd almost done the same thing with Jordan. He didn't like to watch him slowly die from cancer, and he'd often contemplated just ending it for him. But Gallard hadn't wanted to lose him, so after consulting his friends, he'd turned him.

Of course Robin's situation was different, but the choice had been the same; let her live a life of an immortal or save her from the pain that came with it and give her an escape. Lela had chosen the latter. He was amazed by this; by her strength. He hadn't had the strength to kill Jordan. Just the same he was afraid of what it would do to her.

What worried him more was how her actions against Lucian's army would affect her. He remembered when he'd done the same to Samil's men after Dyani was murdered and it had taken him a long time to recover; to find himself again. The guilt was almost too much, though he felt that he'd done what Dyani's family could not. Her death was avenged but not without almost losing his humanity. Lela had preserved hers for so long. Robin's death probably broke her.

THE RESURRECTION

He sat next to her on the bed and took her hand. She didn't acknowledge him, but he held it anyway. He could feel her slipping away from him as each moment passed. She wasn't the same happy, funny, and determined woman that she used to be. She'd been through losses before and he'd been there to comfort her each time. She was frozen. She wasn't even crying.

"Do you need anything," he asked, stroking the back of her hand with his thumb. Usually, he would always know just what to say to make her feel better. He was at a loss for words. Nothing he could say felt good enough. For now, he would just do the best he could.

As her husband, her problems were now his problems. Her pain was his pain. It had always been like this, long before they were married, but to him, their marriage made this even more important.

"I want to take a shower," she said in a voice void of emotion. He couldn't tell what she was feeling by her tone. It was empty. He wanted to ask her how she was feeling, but such a question seemed too dense to ask. If she wanted to tell him how she was feeling, he was going to let her speak on her own time when she was ready.

So he just nodded and let go of her hand as she stood up, taking slow and ghost-like steps into the bathroom. It was almost as if she'd floated there. Cherish had helped her wash most of the blood off in a nearby creek, but she was still covered in it.

He listened as the water turned on then took off his shoes before lying on the bed. He was tired, mentally as well as physically and feeling a little weak from not having fed in days. He wanted to try and wrap his mind around everything that occurred the night before.

When Cherish had revealed why she was acting so strangely, he didn't ask any questions. He'd ordered her to drive them back to make sure the others were all right. Then they'd gotten a phone call about Robin. He hadn't been prepared for what had happened to her, but Melody; she hadn't deserved to die, especially since she'd died protecting someone she cared about. She'd spent her entire life trying to keep her father from rising again and for what? So she could die by his hand? It was a tragedy and he hated that she'd perished that way.

Gallard also wished that he'd been able to convince Aaron to stay. What he'd done was undeniably unforgivable but he was still Lela's family. He was still in danger, and it would be horrible if he'd been caught by Lucian and killed. Wherever he was, he wasn't safe.

An hour went by and Lela still hadn't come out of the shower. He was worried about her and her state of mind. She had a history of using harmful ways to cope whenever she felt her life was out of control and there was no telling what she would do; what she was capable of doing to herself. This wasn't just a loss; it was a loss by her hand as well as many deaths in result of her retaliation.

He lightly knocked on the door, but there was no response. It was unlocked, so he walked in and shut the door behind him in case she hadn't heard him knock. There was no steam in the bathroom even though the fan wasn't on. It wasn't even humid. He saw her clothes on the floor then picked them up, stuffing them in the sack and replacing them with some clean clothes.

Gallard pulled back the curtain and let out a sigh of relief when he saw that she was fine. She was better than fine; she was just standing there under the water, her long hair plastered to her skin. The blood had completely washed off and he could see her clearly again. He stuck his fingers under the water and found that it was on the coldest setting. That was when he noticed she was shivering. He touched her arm and it was ice cold.

"Lela, you're freezing," he said, shutting off the water. He looked around and found the bathrobe that came with the room and pulled it off the hook. He wrapped it around her, but she didn't give him any indication that she was getting out so he took initiative and lifted her out. He carried her into the bedroom and laid her on the bed then went to turn on the heater. Afterwards, he went back into the bathroom to find a towel and grab her clothes. Sitting next to her, he attempted to dab the water out of her hair. He figured if her hair was dry, she would warm up sooner.

He tossed the towel on the floor when he was finished drying her off completely then started to put her clothes back on. He was surprised when she helped him, making the task a lot easier. But still she didn't say a word, even after she was fully dressed. She continued to stare ahead, the light nearly gone from her eyes. She wasn't shivering anymore, but he still felt like he wasn't doing enough.

Gallard was startled when she suddenly flinched and her body became less taut. Her shoulders were relaxed and she began looking around.

"Where's Robin?" she asked. He didn't think he heard her right. He was more startled that she'd spoken for the first time in an hour than her question. Then a feeling of dread came over him. Was she really in denial, or had it been a philosophical question?

"What do you mean?"

"I must have fallen asleep in the car. I don't even remember getting here." She rubbed her face with her hands then looked at him. "Is she with Kevin?"

He folded his hands and hung his head. It was just as he'd been afraid of; she was in so much grief that she'd blocked out what had happened. He remembered she told him she used to do this back when she was a child. When things got too hard to handle, she would make herself black out. Afterwards, she wouldn't remember what she did or how long she'd been walking like a zombie.

"No, she's not with Kevin," he said.

"Did we leave her with the Shepherds? They took care of her before. It would make sense for her to stay there. It's not safe with us."

He reached up and took her chin in his hand, turning her face to his. Her eyes were not as blank as before. Her mood switch was almost eerie.

"Lela. Babe, she's...she's not with Kevin or the Shepherds. She's gone," he said, struggling to say the words. He was afraid of how she would respond. If she truly had blocked it, she wouldn't take it well the second time around.

"Gone where? Don't tell me Lucian got to her! I was holding her in my arms. She was with me in the parking lot. Where—" she stopped speaking for a moment then she looked down. "The woods...oh God, I...took her to the woods."

Lela started shaking and he lightly massaged her back. She was still sitting, but suddenly got up and paced the room.

"I killed her!" she said. "I killed my own sister; sweet innocent little Robin. She was helpless, and I took her life!"

By then she was completely distraught and hyperventilating. He stood up, set on trying to comfort her, but she backed away from him as she continued rambling on.

"What have I done? We have to get her back! We have to. Please! Please help me get her back!" She wrapped her arms around her middle, trembling as she sobbed. "I can't breathe! It hurts too much! I feel like I'm dying, I can't handle this. It hurts!"

Gallard finally got her to stop avoiding him, and he pulled her close as she was about to crumble to the floor. She was sobbing uncontrollably and he was now crying himself. Crying for her and the overwhelming pain she must have been experiencing. He sat on the floor against the wall, easing her into his lap and rocked her as she wept. He wanted to take away everything she was feeling. He wanted to take the agony upon himself to give her some relief.

"It's going to be okay," he said. "I promise you that you're going to be okay."

She probably cried for a solid half an hour. Eventually, her sobs grew quieter and quieter until she stopped altogether and grew extremely silent. He stood up with her still in his arms and carried her to the bed again. She wasn't asleep, but motionless.

He pulled back the covers, laid her down with her head against the pillow then slid into the bed next to her, tugging the covers around the two of them. He kissed her cheek as he held her close to him and said, "I love you." For he had nothing else to say that could comfort her.

Chapter Thirty-One

Sitting in the room all alone was making Cherish crazy, so instead of curling up in a ball and crying her eyes out, she went downstairs and wailed on the punching bag in the gym. She was surprised that the hotel had such nice equipment. She would rather hit something than run or work on the elliptical.

As she threw punch after punch, she tried to get the images of her sister out of her mind. She couldn't even remember the last thing she'd said to her. It probably wasn't something meaningful. Melody and she didn't always get along, but Cherish had adored her. When she was little, she wanted to grow up to be her; beautiful, confident, ambitious. Lucian had thwarted any chance of that happening. Instead, she became a cold, angry person with trust issues.

Thinking about her father made her even angrier, and she punched the bag so hard that her fist tore through it to the other side. Thankfully no one else was there because of how late it was. It was a sign that she needed to go back to the room before she would damage any more equipment.

Draping her towel around her neck, she guzzled her water as she walked down the hall. Two young men dressed in swim trunks were coming towards her and gave her the eye. She thought about ignoring them but then stopped. This was the perfect opportunity to self-medicate. She had the hotel room all to herself, so she wouldn't have to worry about interruption.

"Hey," she called after them. They stopped and turned around. "You two busy?"

They exchanged a glance. "Not really. We were thinking of sitting in the hot tub."

Cherish put on her best sexy smile. "Well, my room is getting kind of lonely."

"What did you have in mind?" the dirty blonde asked. Hoping they would take the hint, she continued down the hall. Sure enough, they followed her to the elevator.

While they rode up, the men introduced themselves. Apparently they were in town for spring break. She didn't really care about their names or back story. She just cared that they would make her forget for a few hours that her sister was dead.

Opening her door, she let them into the room. She tossed her key onto the sink counter then took her hair down. They had both sat on the bed and she approached them, trying to decide who to go for first. She chose the brunette with the perfect eyebrows. She got on top of him and began kissing him while undoing the laces on the front of his swim trunks. She was about to go down on him with someone knocked on the door.

"Cherish?"

She swore. It was Solomon. She hadn't expected him to show up so soon. She thought he would have gone off to kill her father, spend time atoning for his crime and then find his way back to the group. This was the worst time for him to show up.

"You have to go," she said to the two men. They groaned in disappointment as they got dressed. Once they were decent, she opened the door and let them out. Solomon gave both of them a hostile glance, which encouraged them to move faster.

"What are you doing?" Solomon asked once they were alone.

"Don't judge me. I needed to vent, and they were helping. Or at least they were about to."

He opened his mouth to comment but then didn't. "Where are

the others?"

"Jordan and Kevin are next door. Gallard and Lela are two rooms down."

Solomon sat on the bed, and she sat next to him, resting her head on his shoulder. She was glad that he'd come back. He always came at the right time and made her forget her problems. At least he had before the whole tragedy four hundred years ago.

"Kevin told me about Robin," he said. "I can't believe Aaron turned her. What was he thinking?"

"He wanted to save her. That poor little girl. Her life was cut short at five years old. And Lela...she's devastated. I don't think she'll recover from this."

"She will. We will all recover from this in time."

Cherish burst into tears and he hugged her once more. She could easily cry with him. Fooling around with those men would have numbed her for a while but with Solomon, she could be as emotional as she wanted.

"Oh, my *Accarezzare*," he whispered. "I miss her too."

She slightly pulled back from the hug and looked into his eyes, just as she had that day at the gas station. And just as he had then, he kissed her. It was restrained at first, but soon it was so intense that she could barely handle it.

He dragged her onto the bed and they began to remove each other's clothes. She wanted him. She wanted solace in his embrace; to forget all her pain and her grief she had because of her loss. She wanted him like he was a drug. Compared to those other men, he was like heroin compared to cannabis.

They were close to going further when Solomon suddenly pushed her away. He was gentle about it, but she was still unprepared for it.

"Cherish...we can't do this," he said, his tone apologetic.

"Why? Are you afraid of taking advantage of me? I'm not—"

"No. *Accarezzare*...I can't...I don't want do this with you."

She didn't even try to change his mind. Instead she got up and began to get dressed. She sat on the edge of the bed, pulling her shirt back on. As she did, she tried to comprehend what had just happened. She was confused by the whole encounter. Confused by how she felt about his rejecting her.

"I can't believe we almost...I almost—" Solomon said, not finishing his sentence. She turned around to face him. He was still under the covers and staring at the ceiling, the look in his eyes a combination of guilt and wonder. She almost felt bad, even though both were participating parties. He would have been just as responsible as she was.

"You almost what? Made the mistake of sleeping with me?" she asked. "It's okay if you don't want me. I'm used to rejection."

She tugged on her workout pants then walked around the bed to go to the bathroom, but he grabbed her arm to stop her. She gazed into his eyes and her heart sank when she saw how hurt he looked. She hadn't meant for her comment to sound so cruel. She'd only responded to protect herself. Part of her wall that she'd spent so many years putting up had been shaken by him, and yet she was still having a hard time trusting him.

"I didn't mean it like that," he explained. "I meant that... Cherish, I'm a Cardinal. And even though I'm planning to leave the church, I still need to honor my vows until the day I turn in my robes. There was a time when I didn't honor them at all, but I've changed since then. It would have been a huge mistake. Not to mention, you had probably done this with those two strangers not ten minutes ago."

Cherish scoffed. She'd heard all about Solomon's wild days before he'd had a life-changing encounter while he was off on a sabbatical. He'd stolen, lied, killed several people, and fathered a child with some woman he'd only known for one night. Melody had told her upon eavesdropping on a conversation between him and their father. Cherish admired him for staying in the church despite his many sins. And now she was the one who had tempted him into breaking his vows after so many years of following the narrow path.

She was no different from him. She may have had different reasons for living precariously, but she'd committed the same sins. When she'd met Count Byron, she'd only involved herself with him because she'd longed for a normal life. She'd wanted to be like her sister; not a worry in the world and free to be a woman of society.

For years, her father had raised her to be a fighter, waking her up at the crack of dawn to spar and get her into shape. He'd used the same training that was required of the Royal Army. While

THE RESURRECTION

Melody was out buying fabrics for new clothes and having brunch with other young women their age, Cherish was home pushing her body to limits no woman should ever have to.

Then Byron came along. She'd made his acquaintance at Melody's twenty-first birthday celebration. Cherish had only been fifteen, and she was captivated by him from the moment she laid eyes on him. She hadn't known he was married at the time. He was the first man to give her any special attention and in return she'd given him everything; her heart, body and soul. And when he'd betrayed her, she swore she would never let any man treat her that way again. She didn't trust men anymore, and she was determined to not let Solomon hurt her as Byron had.

"I know exactly how you meant it, Solomon. I tempted you, and now you feel guilty. It's okay, I understand. I'll leave you alone so your celibacy won't be in danger."

Cherish started to walk off again, but he stopped her once more.

"Don't do this. Don't say things you don't mean just to protect yourself from getting hurt. This wasn't just an indiscretion to me. It actually meant something."

She looked away, unable to face him. It had meant something to her too. She was just too scared to admit it out loud.

Cherish wanted her sister. Melody, though her lectures were infuriating, had always given her the best advice. Cherish didn't always want to hear it and instead of admitting that Melody was right, she would lash out and disappear for years on end. Now that she was gone, she wished that she'd spent more time with her. She would never forgive her father for taking her away.

"I may have let you down in the past, but I promise you that I'm not that man anymore," Solomon continued. "I've had five hundred years to change. And now I'm going to protect you from your father just as I should have in the first place. You can trust me, Cherish. I will show you that not every man is out to ruin you. You've been wronged in the past, and now it's time that you heal from it."

She fought hard to hold back her tears. He was right. He'd only said the same thing that her sister had been telling her for years, only it was just hitting her now that Melody was dead. She owed it to her sister to see their father destroyed. They'd spent a life time trying to keep him from returning and had failed. Cherish was done with him. He needed to be ripped to pieces and all of his blood disposed of so that he could never come back.

Overcome with emotion, she lay back down next to him and cried for the hundredth time that day. He embraced her, continuing to stroke her hair. She was so tired of crying, yet the tears would somehow sneak up on her. After being angry for so long, all that was left was her raw emotions.

She started kissing him again, one each one had meaning to her. She could tell he was conflicted by them, but he returned them just the same. As she began to kiss his neck and then his chest, he suddenly pushed her away.

"We can't," he said firmly, but apologetically. "I'm sorry, I don't want this on my conscience."

He was not making it easy for her. She had been raised Catholic by her father, but they were never practicing Catholics. She knew all of the basic rules and regulations that came with the faith. She just didn't follow them.

She went into the bathroom, closing the door behind her and tried to tell herself not to be upset. She didn't know exactly what Solomon wanted. Did he want her to wait for him? Or did he only kiss her and nearly sleep with her because they'd been caught up in the moment? Either way, she wanted to find out where he stood or else she wasn't going to bother.

Jordan flipped through the news channels to see if Melody's murder as well as the murders at the diner was being broadcasted in the area. So far, only one of them had mentioned Melody's death and the rest were about the two men as well as the several bodies discovered in the forest. He was afraid Melody's death would be linked to the others, which would make sense because of how horrible the crimes were. It wasn't every day that a woman was beheaded and left on the balcony of a motel. He still shuddered every time he pictured the bloody scene. It was not a pleasant way to die but at least it had been quick.

THE RESURRECTION

What had followed wasn't originally in his plan, but it had been a blessing in disguise. He'd been trying to devise a way to motive the group to pursue Lucian and Robin's death had done just that. No one had said it openly, but he was confident that they were all leaning in that direction. He wasn't completely comfortable with how everything was going, but he couldn't afford to waste any more time. Maximus had been right; he was stalling, and only because he cared too much about the people he was with. If he could just stop caring, he could do what was necessary.

Kevin was sitting by the window, struggling to come to terms with the death of his sister. Even though Lela had been the one to kill her, Jordan still felt responsible since he'd allowed her brother to change her. Jordan wasn't initially going to help him, and he was glad he'd stopped Lela from hurting Aaron. Kevin wouldn't have been able to hold Lela back without his help. He was stronger than the group was led to believe. He was just as strong as Lucian was. It had been hard for him to feign weakness. Soon, his true identity would be made known to the group and he couldn't wait for that day. He was tired of hiding. Tired of lying about whom he was.

They would be furious. Especially Gallard; his blood descendant. He was the only one he dreaded telling the truth to. He'd spun many lies to him over the past year and a half. Lies about families and bloodlines that didn't even exist. He'd hoped that maybe creating stories of Gallard's brother Gaspard and how happy his life had been would give him some comfort. In the end, they would be false memories. Gallard's parents died of old age and Gaspard had died of at the age of sixty, leaving no children to follow after him. After their deaths, Jordan and Gallard were the only ones left of the D'Aubigne bloodline.

But they weren't really D'Aubignes at all; they were Christophes. After centuries of trying to accept this reality, Jordan still wasn't all right with it. Lucian may not have been a member of the family, but he had still caused the name to be associated with pain, suffering, and madness. Jordan didn't want any part of it; he just wanted to avenge the death of his parents.

Jordan starting growing restless, so he shut the TV off. The others were most likely occupied with other things. He would be able to slip out into the daylight without anyone noticing. The only problem was convincing Kevin to not let the others know about his secret outing.

"Hey, Kevin. I'm going for a walk," he said. He grabbed the hotel key and headed for the door.

"All right, see ya," was all Kevin said. Jordan was relieved that it had been that easy; no questions asked. He left the room and went downstairs to the lobby. As he saw the daylight though the glass doors, he nearly sprinted towards it. He hadn't been in the sun in so long that he was feeling starved for its warmth.

Jordan burst through the doors and closed his eyes, turning his face towards the sky. He probably looked strange to those who saw him, but he didn't care. The sun seemed to energize him. He couldn't get enough of it. He took off his jacket exposing his bare arms and shoulders. His black tank top absorbed the heat and he was aware of nearly every ray of sun that touched him.

He relaxed his muscles then opened his eyes before heading through the parking lot and onto the sidewalk. It was only eight in the morning, but the sun was high in the sky. They had only made it to Harrisonburg, Virginia and then the group checked into a Best Western for a rest.

Until Solomon returned, Gallard didn't want to go anywhere else so he could meet up with the group. Jordan hoped that once they were reunited, the real action would start. Not some petty fight in a parking lot against a few of Lucian's new creations, but an actual battle. He wanted to get his hands on Lucian and kill him. Maximus was counting on him. And he'd been promised something in return.

Lydian. How he longed to see her again. To listen to her rambling on and on about something non important, but he would pay close attention anyway. He loved how she'd always had his hand in hers and how she always sat in his lap no matter where they were. If Maximus could bring her back, all of his problems would be forgotten; all of his regrets and mistakes.

No doubt, he was in line. There were plenty in the group that had a reason to want to kill Lucian themselves. Lela wanted him dead for Robin's sake; Cherish would want him dead for killing Melody, and Solomon wanted him dead because he was a threat to his family. But Jordan was the only one who stood a chance against Lucian. He was the only other person who had been turned by

THE RESURRECTION

Maximus, so he had the upper hand compared to the others.

Jordan looked at his phone and calculated that he'd been gone for about twenty minutes. He didn't want to risk being looked for in case Gallard had decided to drop in and check on Kevin and him. So he rounded the corner and doubled his way back to the hotel. He wasn't ready to get out of the sun, but he was putting his secret in jeopardy, all for a few moments of exposure.

He opened the door at the side with his card key. It was further away from the stairs, but he was trying to be stealthy. Most likely he would run into someone if he went through the lobby.

As he went towards the elevator, he looked down the hall and saw Kevin standing in front of it. He looked pleased with himself, as if he were proving a point.

"I knew something was off about you," Kevin said as he leaned against the wall. "When I found your contact case in your jacket, I began to have some suspicion. But now that I've seen you come in from outside in the morning, my suspicion was proven correct."

Jordan pulled his jacket off of his shoulder where it had been hanging during his walk and dug in the pockets.

"Looking for this?" Kevin asked, holding the contact case up for him to see. "I took it the night before last. I wanted to see how long it would be before you noticed it was gone."

Jordan reached for the case but Kevin jerked it out of the way before he could take it. Jordan glared at him, frustrated by his uncooperativeness.

"Give it back, Kevin. You don't know how important it is that no one knows about me," he pleaded, trying not to sound desperate.

"Show me first. What color are your eyes, really?"

"Brown, and no I'm not going to show you. What do you want in return for your silence?"

Outwardly, he was coming off as though he weren't bothered by his being found out, but inside he was panicking. It wasn't time for the group to know him yet. Somehow, he would have to convince Kevin to keep his secret for a while longer.

"You know what I want?" Kevin began. "My parents, my uncle, Robin; they're all dead. Aaron left the group and is probably dead as well, so Lela and Evelyn are all I have left. I want to know if you are on our side or not. Because if you're a threat to my sister—"

"I'm not a threat!" Jordan nearly shouted. "I *am* on your side. I have secrets. Everyone does. You're just going to have to trust me."

Kevin let out a humorless laugh. "Yeah? Well, I trusted that girlfriend of yours, and thanks to her, my sister was kidnapped by Samil and then killed. She's back now, but it could have saved a lot of trouble if that whole ordeal had been avoided."

As much as he wanted to, Jordan could not try to justify Lydian's choices. She'd been afraid, and her fear had led her to betraying someone she'd been close to. He'd turned her away at first, but was able to forgive her after she'd sacrificed herself. It was then; the moment that she'd died that he knew he would never love anyone else like he'd loved her.

"I would never hurt Lela, Kevin. I love her like my own sister, she's family to me. Always has been."

"And I see you as family as well. We're in-laws now. I know that you wouldn't do anything to harm Gallard, and he's married to my sister. They're a package deal. You hurt her and you hurt him. Are you getting my drift?"

Jordan nodded. This was the first time he'd seen Kevin display any authority. He was usually quiet; quieter than he was. And of everyone in the group, he was probably the least corrupted. As the youngest person, he had the most innocence. Jordan would hate to see that taken away from him.

"I swear to you I have no intention of harming anyone in this group. There are some things that I cannot say. Not yet. If you trust me, I assure you that Lucian will die, and we will win."

Kevin reluctantly held the contact case within arm's reach and Jordan took it from him, quickly shoving it into his pocket.

"I'll keep your secret, Jordan. I hate lying, especially to my sister, so don't make me regret it."

"You won't. I guarantee that."

I wanted so badly to sleep, but I couldn't. I just lay there, waiting for my thoughts to quiet down. I'd been so overwhelmed with grief and guilt that I'd somehow managed to block out time between Robin's death and when Gallard had dressed me after apparently finding me close to hypothermia in a cold shower.

When I'd snapped out of my daze, everything I was feeling hit me at once, and it was too much to handle. I freaked out and turned into a crazy, rambling mess. The only thing that had kept me from losing my mind completely was Gallard's presence. If it weren't for him, I probably would have remained in my catatonic state for much longer.

I thought back to the first time I saw Robin. She was tall for her age, like I had been my whole life. Her long, curly hair framing her round and rosy face. She'd been smart for someone so young. A trait she'd picked up from David, no doubt. She would have grown up to be an amazing person. And now she was dead because of someone's need for revenge. It set in motion a chain of events that would lead to her demise. Choices were made, and just like that; she was gone. I almost wished the fall had killed her instead.

I rolled over onto my back, folding my hands across my stomach, and I became aware that there was something on my finger. I lifted my hand into the air and admired my wedding ring. I couldn't believe that I had gotten married not twenty-four hours ago. We'd barely been able to call ourselves boyfriend and girlfriend and now we were husband and wife. I liked those titles better. Gallard always seemed more like a husband than a boyfriend.

He wasn't lying next to me anymore. I'd pretended to be asleep while he'd gotten up to take a shower. I wanted to go to him, but I didn't yet have the will to get myself out of bed. I finally understood what my mother had gone through. I figured it was inevitable that I would end up like her. She'd been depressed for the majority of my life. And she'd claimed that having Robin had helped her to not need pills anymore. I could believe it. Robin brought joy to everyone who was around her.

My eyes darted over to the bathroom as Gallard came out. He had his eye patch on and it didn't look so bad. I was starting to get used to it. One eye or two, he was still very attractive. I thought the patch was a little sexy.

He was wearing the jeans I loved and a black shirt. We'd taken our luggage with us, and I was glad we hadn't left it behind in the midst of chaos. I'd had my credit card in my pocket, so I wasn't without money. But money wasn't important to me. I never really cared for money. It could never replace those that I lost.

Gallard sat on the bed and took my hand, lightly kissing it. I tried to smile, but it was as if my muscles didn't work; like I'd forgotten how to.

"Are you hungry?" he asked. I shook my head. I wasn't hungry; I wasn't tired; I wasn't anything.

He then lay next to me. I wondered how Cherish was holding up since she was all alone in her room. If she was anywhere as messed up as I was, it was going to be hard for us to continue on our journey. I didn't even have the desire to kill Lucian anymore. I should have wanted him dead, yet I didn't. I couldn't possibly hate him as much as I hated myself. I loathed myself for what I'd done.

"How many vampires did I kill?" I asked him. My memory from before hadn't come back completely, but I did remember being covered in blood. I told myself that I didn't want to know what happened, though I needed to.

"I'm not sure. Maybe ten? We didn't stick around to count the bodies."

I turned away from him, fixing my gaze on the ceiling. It finally happened; I lost all control and became no better than Lucian or Samil. I'd killed men who had nothing to do with Robin's murder, but only because of their association to Lucian. I should have stopped at the two spies at the diner. The other deaths were unjustified, committed by the monster I'd become.

Gallard sat up and stared at me. "Talk to me. You'll feel better if you get everything out."

"I slaughtered those men. It may have been because of Robin and Melody, but it doesn't matter. What I did was inexcusable and I don't see how that makes me any different from him...from Lucian."

"I think the fact that you're worried about it answers your questions. If you were evil like Lucian, you wouldn't be conflicted about what you did."

I closed my eyes, squeezing them tightly in an attempt to see if I could cry. I wanted to cry more than anything, but I was unable.

"You once said that you admired how I could go through so

much and still not lose myself. Well, I think that I did...lose myself." I turned back around to face him. "I've been to hell and back, but I've never done anything this horrible. I've crossed a line that I promised myself I never would and I can't take it back."

Gallard leaned his head against the backboard of the bed. I wanted to know what was going through his mind. Had I scared him? No doubt my being covered in blood and acting like a crazy person had concerned him. I wouldn't blame him if he was afraid of me.

I had times when I lost control when feeding, but I had never gone this far. That was before I was bombarded with more and more death. I had been able to handle my parents' passing. I had been shaken by it, but I'd had the strength to carry on.

After David died, then Lydian, Jeff, Melody, and then Robin, I was tired. I had buried too many people in only a year's worth of time. Maybe other immortals had lost people in their lifetime, but I'd barely been able to experience life. I was only twenty years old. And I was exhausted, body and soul.

"When I first met you at the store, I couldn't forget our chance encounter," he said. He leaned forward and took my face in his hands. "For some reason, I found myself caring about what happened to you, even though I'd just spoken to you for a minute. And when I saw you again three days later and realized that you'd been turned, it broke my heart. I hated what had happened to you because I knew what lay ahead. I had to pretend that I was conflicted about letting you come with me on my journey west, but in truth, I couldn't bear to leave you. I wanted to protect you; to somehow shield you from the pain and suffering that came with being immortal because I cared about you so much. I may not have always been *in* love with you, but I've always loved you. I realize now that it's not enough. I have to learn that there are some things that are out of my hands that only you can do for yourself. I can't relieve you of the guilt you have, but I can love you. Just know that I'll never stop loving you and I'll be there to support you while you work out everything you're going though."

I pressed my forehead against his. Everything he'd said made sense to me. I had been hoping that he could make me feel better when in reality, only I could find the will to forgive myself. I didn't expect to feel better right away; it would take time and healing. Someday, I might forgive myself for killing Robin and those men, but that wouldn't happen overnight.

I could start by forgiving Kevin. His part in the tragedy had been miniscule compared to what I'd done, and he was also the only one left in my family that I could count on, besides Solomon. Kevin had been handling everything so well. Not once had he expressed feeling in over his head. He was younger than me, yet he was more resilient and uncorrupted.

Unlike Aaron, he hadn't let his immortality change who he was. He may have made mistakes, but so had I. He wasn't perfect, but he wasn't letting his mistakes get the best of him. Robin's circumstances could have been handled differently. We'd acted based on desperation. I couldn't blame him for wanting to save her life. He was losing his family little by little. I didn't want to lose him too, in the figurative sense. We were all each other had.

I wasn't completely recovered from my breakdown, but our talk was helping me feel better. I was bound to cry again sometime in the near future, but at least I was past the point where I was in denial. Gallard had given me good advice and now it was time to take baby steps.

"I love you too, Gallard," I said. "But I still wish we could just forget Lucian and run away to Russia or Tibet; anywhere but here. I'm sick of him. I'm sick of his name, I'm sick of his stupid red hair. I'm sick of his sexy eyes—"

"You think he has sexy eyes?"

"No, I meant…well, one time when I spoke with him during my near-death experience, he looked at me with sexy eyes, like he thought he was irresistible, and he's not!"

"Well, I know why he wants *you* so badly." He slid his hands down my sides, resting them on my hips. "He thinks *you're* sexy, and he wants your body. I know I do."

I raised an eyebrow. "Oh, really?"

"Mhm. But he can't have you." He then laced the fingers of his left hand through mine so that our rings were touching. "You're mine, Mrs. D'Aubigne."

Suddenly, I started getting other things on my mind. Our shower had been a wonderful preview to our impending honeymoon, and I wanted another one. He was looking extra sexy with his wet hair, and I was in desperate need of a distraction.

"Do you want to fool around a little?" I asked. "I don't know about you, but I'm kind of in the mood."

His eyes met mine. "Is that a good idea? You're grieving right now."

"I am. But you're helping me feel better. I think it might be the perfect thing for the both of us to get our mind off of everything."

I leaned forward until my lips met his, and he kissed me back. We started out slow and then he got more into it, tangling his fingers in my hair. I tugged off his shirt and moved onto his lap so I was straddling him.

He nipped at my bottom lip with his teeth and gave me a sexy grin. I was surprised by his playfulness and intrigued at the same time. Two could play this game. I pushed him back so that he was lying flat on his back and started nibbling on his earlobe. Lydian once told me that some men liked that, but I was too chicken to try it with Gallard. Until now.

My hands found the button on his jeans, and I slowly undid them then pulled the zipper down. Third base was still a step in our relationship we hadn't crossed yet, which made me want to all the more. We were slowly experiencing all the firsts, one step at a time.

Gallard looked into my eyes, probably realizing where I was going with this.

"Are you sure you're okay with this?" He asked. I could sense him going into protective mode.

"Yes. If you are. What you did to me in that hotel in South Carolina…it was nice. I want to do something for you now."

"I don't expect anything from you, Lela. I love making you feel good and that's good enough for me."

I gave him an exasperated look then leaned forward so our faces were two inches apart.

"Let me make myself clear. I want all of you. I want to do this. *Comprendre?*"

By the way his pupils dilated, I knew he was surrendering to me. I took his silence as an okay to continue then finished undressing him. His skin was so soft and smelled good from the soap he'd used. He'd used the same soap for years and I always knew when he'd taken a shower because the scent would fill the entire house in Texas. Fresh rain and peppermint.

Going down on Gallard was a very interesting experience. His hips bucked, and I had to gently hold onto him to keep him steady. He kept saying something over and over in French in a voice so sexy it was turning me on. I would have suggested we go further, but I could feel my mood going sour again. Intimacy could only distract me from my pain for so long.

His body shuddered as he had his release, and I moved so that I was laying on top of him with my head on his chest. He had grown quiet and did nothing but rub circles between my shoulder blades with his other hand resting on the small of my back.

After a while, I couldn't take the silence.

"Was that okay?" I asked.

"More than okay." He rolled over so that we'd switched place. "I don't think I can wait to be with you much longer. I want you too much."

I looked away from him. I was afraid to be honest and admit that the entire time we'd fooled around all I could think about was my sister and what I'd done to her. It had been my idea to do this and he was right; it wasn't the right time for intimacy.

"As much as I want your body as well, what I would like more right now is a nap," I said. "I hope you don't mind."

He gave me an understanding smile. "I don't mind at all. Get all the rest you need. I'm feeling tired as well."

He lay down and I shifted so that my arm was around him and my head was on shoulder. He began to stroke my arm and the sensation was soothing. I closed my eyes, and tried to get my mind on more pleasant things.

I thought back to the wedding. How I'd been surrounded with everyone I loved and felt completely happy for the first time in a while. I remembered how beautiful Melody looked in her dress and how adorable Robin was when she'd tossed the petals everywhere. Those memories were all I had left of them.

The afternoon came and went in a blur. It was already eight o'clock, and I'd slept the entire time. Gallard had forgotten to turn off the heater, so the room was scorching hot. I was hoping that I could find some relief by lying close to him, but it wasn't helping.

I crawled out of the bed, hobbling across the room to turn on the air conditioning. The room was so hot that I was starting to get light headed. After I successfully switched the settings, I went into the bathroom and splashed cold water on my face. I instantly felt better.

I shut the light off in the bathroom as I headed back to the bed. Gallard hadn't said a word, so I lay back down next to him and stared at his face. His eyes were closed, but I doubted he was asleep.

"Hey, I'm gonna to go check on Cherish," I told him.

"Want me to come with you?" he mumbled.

"No, that's okay. I just want to see how she's doing. It might be a good idea for you to get dressed though. They might not like your cute butt as much as I do."

He chuckled and opened his eyes. "Will do. I haven't perfected my stripper routine anyway."

I gave him a quick kiss on his forehead before getting up and leaving the room. I hadn't been able to really speak with Cherish since the night before in the woods, and I could imagine she was still shaken up.

I knocked on the door and she answered a few seconds later. She looked sad, but better than before. We didn't say a word and just hugged each other for a while. She seemed relieved, probably because I had snapped out of my catatonic state. I was glad that we were friends now. I would need her since she understood what I was going through. We'd come to an understanding and all was forgiven.

Solomon got out of the shower a few moments later and surprised me. I hadn't known he was back. He gave me a hug as well then said it would be a good idea to have a group meeting. I liked that he was organized and thorough, which probably helped us more than anything on this mission. He carefully planned out all of our stops, making sure we didn't waste too much time in one area and was basically the leader we all needed.

Cherish and I went into my room and the three of us waited for Solomon to find Kevin and Jordan, who were for some reason not in their room. I wasn't too worried, though. Kevin had promised he wouldn't run off like Aaron had, but Jordan on the other hand proved he had a tendency to disappear without saying anything. I doubted he would pull that off now. Not after everything we'd been through.

Someone knocked at the door and Cherish opened it, letting Jordan, Kevin, and Solomon in. Cherish gave Solomon a strange glance and I wondered what that was all about. It didn't help that things were still tense between Gallard and Jordan.

"I talked to Lucian," Solomon said. "Actually, I kind of threatened him. However, that was before…still, I think it's over."

"My father would be a fool to try and come after us in light of what Lela did, so I think the best thing we can do is go back to our lives," Cherish said.

"Are you sure?" Jordan asked. "For all we know, Lucian is cooking up a retaliation plot this second. He killed your sister, shouldn't we do something?"

"He told me his men went against his instructions," Solomon said. "It doesn't excuse his actions, though."

"I think we've done enough," Gallard said. "I'm tired of this whole 'will he or will he not kill us' tug-of-war. Personally, I want to get out of Virginia and help my wife her with funeral arrangements. I'm sure the rest of you have better things to do than drive all over the east coast."

No one said a word and I hoped that they would agree. I wanted to enjoy my new marriage as well and do some personal healing. There were still some things that needed to be cleared up in Florida, like Jeff's funeral and maybe Robin's. I was sure Cherish wanted to grieve her sister's death and finally live her life, void of worrying about her father and anything to do with him.

"All right. I suppose we can do that," Solomon said. "All in favor of giving up on chasing Lucian, say aye."

"Aye? What are we, Parliament?" Cherish said. "Let's get the hell out of here. I miss my bed and I'm sure you miss the Pope."

Chapter Thirty-Two

Loud music boomed from the connecting room of vacation suite. It jolted Lucian awake and he moaned as he sat up on the bed. His head pounded from all the alcohol he'd consumed the night before. Aaron had taken him to some night club and he'd downed every shot that Aaron gave him. He'd lost count after six.

He looked over to his left and found a sleeping woman was lying next to him. It took him a moment to remember before he recalled who she was. He'd talked to her about all of his problems and for some reason, she'd listened. At some point in the night, they'd ended up kissing and then they took a cab back to the hotel. The rest he clearly remembered.

Reluctantly, he got up, tugging on his pants as he walked across the room. He opened the door, causing the music to grow even louder without a barrier to insulate it and he walked in to find a very shocking sight. There were about four women, all dead, lying on the floor and Aaron was feeding on another in the Jacuzzi. The stereo was blasting an obscene song that made Lucian cringe. He shut it off then turned to Aaron and folded his arms, giving him a condescending glare.

"Tis irresponsible behaviors like this that nearly got Solomon and me exposed back in our day. People are going to start asking questions when all these women come in here and none of them come out."

Aaron stopped feeding, then let go of the girl's body as it fell over, slightly bobbing in the water. He slicked back his wet hair and stared at Lucian while resting his arms against the side of the hot tub.

"Relax, Chris. Can I call you Chris? It's better than Lou, right?"

Lucian sighed out of exasperation. He wasn't sure why he'd kept Aaron alive. He was starting to regret it. He was proving to be more trouble than he'd bargained for. Going with him to New York was a mistake, even if he'd needed him to show him around. Not only was he causing trouble, he was annoying Lucian because of how much he was like Solomon.

A woman screamed and he found the woman from his bed had gotten up and saw the bodies. Lucian swiftly moved towards the door, stopping her before she could leave. She screamed again, and he covered her mouth before breaking her neck then dropped her to the floor.

"Take care of this, Sharmentino. I refuse to clean up your mess."

"You are so uptight, Chris. I thought you were supposed to be enjoying yourself. You know, taking a break from murder plots and letting loose?" Aaron got out of the tub and dried himself off with a towel. Draping it around his neck then started going through Lucian's clothes that were hung up in the closet.

"What's with all the suits?" Aaron asked.

"What about them? I like them. They are comfortable and business-like."

"You know, Chris. For being technically younger than me, you sure dress like you're a nineteen twenties gangster. If you want to be approachable, you need to dress more…modern."

"How does a suit make me unapproachable?"

"Twenty year olds don't wear three-hundred dollar suits. When I was twenty, I wore jeans and college sweatshirts. Lela didn't fall in love with Gallard because he wore Armani. If you want her to like you, you need to dress in a way that attracts her."

"I told you, I am done with her. No doubt she hates me for what happened with Robin. I am done with that lot."

Lucian sat at the table in the middle of the room and rested his head on his fist. It was a rather beautiful room. There were cream-colored walls and carpet that matched. On the ceiling were two, small chandeliers with real crystal. Two beds were against the wall towards the far left, both queen-sized.

Along with the hot tub was a descent sized dining table made of oak and big enough to fit five. Mark must have paid a descent amount for such a nice place. The timeshare had the room available for ten days, with free breakfast and lunch.

It had been surprisingly easy for him to adapt. With the help of a few unwilling teachers, he'd spent the past year catching up on American as well as European history. He'd done quite a bit of reading to learn about pop culture, technological advances, and even obtained a driver's license, though he never drove. All that learning was exhausting to him, and now he was being told that he wasn't dressing the part.

"*You* do something about it then, since you know so much. Go out and buy me clothes you think are fitting for this century." He dug in his coat pocket and pulled out three, hundred dollar bills. "Go…uh…what do they say these days…knock yourself out? That phrase makes no
sense, why would you render yourself unconscious?"

"You trust me to leave on my own?"

"No, take Antonio with you."

Aaron went into the bathroom to change then took the money from him upon leaving the room.

Lucian hadn't a clue how he was going to do. Eventually, the partying would have to stop. Though he was young on the outside, he felt too old for this kind of behavior.

What annoyed him more that his plan to get Lela to join him had failed. He kept saying he didn't care, but he was lying. He hadn't been able to get her out of his mind since he'd seen her lying dead in Gallard's arms.

Why had she gotten married? And so soon? She hadn't to have been with Gallard for very long. It may have been normal to do so at one point in time, but this was a different culture. Marrying someone so early in a relationship was looked down upon.

What bothered him most was that he cared so much. He shouldn't care what she did or didn't do. He shouldn't care what anyone did. He'd stopped caring about people. He'd been willing to try and salvage what he had left of a relationship with his daughter, but she'd been very clear about not wanting him in her life. It was false hope anyway. She'd been influenced too much by the world around her and had forgotten everything he'd taught her.

But Lela was different. She was the first person, or woman, he hadn't been able to frighten into doing something they didn't want to do. Many times before she'd died, he'd forced Florence to change her careless ways.

And Solomon. He'd frightened him to the point where he'd been driven to kill him when he was in his most vulnerable state; while he'd been asleep. Cherish was afraid of him as well, which was why she'd done nearly everything he'd ever asked her to do. Then there was Lela. She'd been so feisty whenever they would have a heated discussion. She had no idea who she was up against, yet she didn't hesitate to challenge him.

Lucian had a few of his followers get rid of the bodies. He hadn't the patience to do so himself. He'd done enough cleaning up of other people's messes. Once the room was back to normal, he pulled on a shirt then lay on the bed. His hangover hadn't dissipated yet and his head was throbbing.

"Old habits die hard, don't they Lucian?" someone said.

Lucian sat up to see who was speaking. He was growing tired of unexpected visitors and wanted some peace. It was a man, short in stature with white hair and green eyes. He didn't look particularly intimidating, but something about him made Lucian nervous. There was an evil presence surrounding the stranger.

"Who are you?" Lucian asked.

The man held up his hand and Lucian's body became filled with an uncomfortable sensation. He fell off the bed, clutching his head and yelling as the pain grew more intense. It felt like he was being bled out all over again, his nerves and blood vessels bursting and tearing. He begged for the man to stop and finally the pain came to an end.

"That is a shame," the man said. "That move usually kills any other immortal. You are still too strong for me to kill. Does not matter to me. There is still one who can." The man sat at the table and Lucian remained on the floor, still recovering. "My name is

Maximus. I created you."

"You are the one the legends are about," Lucian said. "The one who started it all. You had not created a vampire in over three millennia, why create me?"

"Your mother was a whore and deserved her fate. However, I took pity on her. When I saved your mother from dying, my plan was to empty my power into her stillborn child and bury it, but I became greedy. By then, I was addicted to my power and wanted to keep some for myself and didn't finish the process. And when you came back to life, I knew that I'd failed. Now the only way to cleanse myself of all evil is to finish what I started."

"Finish what you started. How, by killing me?" Lucian asked.

"No. By giving you the rest of my power. Then I can die in peace and join my brothers and sisters in paradise. And you will be nearly invincible."

"Thanks for the offer, but I am going to have to decline. I do not want power, or to be bothered. All I want is to be left alone."

"Ah. See, here's the thing. You seemed to have missed the part where I didn't give you a choice. I never said you had an option."

Maximus rushed over to Lucian and put his hands on either side of Lucians head before Lucian could even react. He tried to pull away, but whatever Maximus was doing was weakening him.

A surge of energy coursed through Lucians body, making him feel stronger and more powerful than he ever thought possible. It was all so exhilarating that he lost himself in the glory.

Then everything changed. He no longer felt good, but his high was replaced by evil. He could feel the malevolence, and it overwhelmed him until he felt sick. He didn't care for this. It was almost as if his very soul were being burned alive. He tried to pull away to put an end to this misery, but Maximus wouldn't let him.

When Maximus finally released his hold on Lucian, he hurried away and ran out the door, slamming it behind him. Lucian didn't go after him. He was still trying to recover from what had just happened. It was like recovering from being electrocuted.

He heard a knock at the door, and it sounded so loud that he groaned. He had given the guards instructions to not let anyone in without his clearance and figured that it was Aaron having returned from the store. He slid off the bed and took his time answering the knock.

"Who is it?" he called.

"Nash," the person said. Lucian opened the door and the man walked in.

"What?"

"Solomon and his group have decided not to have a confrontation. They are heading back to their homes. Should we take action?"

"Did I not tell you that it is over? Leave me be! Trouble me not with useless information. Go!"

Nash shut the door then Lucian found his way back to the bed. His mind was beginning to get clouded and it became hard for him to form a coherent thought. He heard voices; whispers and angry threats. They overwhelmed him until it was nearly unbearable and he begged for them to stop. And suddenly, it was completely silent and he fell into a deep sleep.

Jordan hooked the gas nozzle back in its place before grabbing the receipt. He couldn't allow the others to see it, but he was not happy about their decision to stop going after Lucian. This thwarted his entire plan. He couldn't do it alone; he needed them. Without their help, Lucian would not be killed and he would never get Lydian back.

Everyone was headed in different directions. Cherish planned to return to her apartment in Chicago and Solomon wanted to go back to the Vatican and resign from his position. Gallard and Lela decided to take care of her family's funeral by going to Florida. Kevin was leaning towards crashing at their friend Curtis' place until he got a job. Jordan had no plans.

Gallard finished gassing up the Toyota at the same time Jordan finished with the BMW then the group gathered next to Solomon. This was a weird goodbye. It felt unearned, like nothing had really been accomplished. Their parting was supposed to be happier than this, and Jordan knew why. Deep down, everyone had to feel what he was feeling. They may not want to fight Lucian now, but eventually they wouldn't be able to sit back and let him walk the earth. He was too much of a danger. To them and to humanity.

"Do you know where you'll go yet?" Gallard asked him. Jordan was surprised he was even speaking to him. He'd been furious when he learned of his part in Robin's transformation. He didn't really have a good reason for why he did it. Pity, perhaps. He remembered what it was like to have a daughter and to want to do anything to protect her. The fact was, a lot of pain could have been saved if they'd let her die by taking her off of life support instead. If only.

"No, but I still have the money I saved. Maybe I'll get back in the agriculture business. I miss farming."

This wasn't really a lie. He did miss working on the farm where life was simple and the biggest worry was getting the pigs fattened in time for selling. He would have been content dying all those years ago. Maximus interrupted his peaceful existence and ruined his life. Jordan had given and given his services for years and never received anything in return. His parents were still dead, he had no inheritance, and Lucian was still living with his birth name.

But one thing was for certain. His brother-like relationship to Gallard somehow made all of this suffering worth it. If he wasn't going to fight alongside him, Jordan at least wanted to reconcile with him.

He gave Gallard a firm hug. Something he normally didn't do, but it was his way of saying he was sorry. This would be the first time since he'd moved into their apartment two and a half years ago that they would not live together. He would miss the brotherly banter and Gallard's dry humor that matched Lela's. He would miss both of them.

"Take care, Jordan," Gallard said. "And if you can't find someplace to go, don't hesitate to contact us."

"Thanks, Cyclops. You take care of that wife of yours."

He turned to see Lela standing behind him and he hugged her as well. He wanted to apologize properly to her, but he couldn't find the words. He could only embrace her and hope that she knew he was truly sorry for what he'd done. She was always quick to forgive. He'd seen this in her relationship to Lydian, who was always messing with her and making inappropriate comments.

Once everyone had said their goodbyes they formed somewhat of a circle and stood in silence. Everyone was reluctant to leave. He could see it in their eyes. He silently hoped that they would change their minds at the last minute. It was false hope, though.

"Who's driving what?" Lela asked.

"I am driving Cherish back in the Toyota to Illinois before flying to Italy then I'll have the car sent back to you." Solomon said. "You and Gallard get the BMW so you can return it to the rental place. Jordan, are you sure you want to take a bus? I would be happy to drop you off somewhere along the way."

Jordan shook his head. "I'm all right. Thanks for the offer though."

"Kevin are you coming with us?" Lela asked her brother.

"No, I'm tired of driving. I think I'll just fly down to Tampa."

Everyone got into their designated vehicles then Jordan and Kevin waved as they drove in different directions. Just like that, everyone was gone. Now he would really have to step up his game if he was going to take on Lucian alone. Lela may have killed his army, but that didn't mean Lucian wouldn't make more.

Jordan started to go inside and purchase a bus ticket when he noticed Kevin was following him. The airport wasn't too far from there, so Jordan was confused why he hadn't headed that way.

"What's our next move, partner?" Kevin asked.

"*Our* next move? Since when are you coming with me?"

"Since now. You know you need me and I know that you aren't going to go work on a farm."

Jordan hadn't expected Kevin to be on board with the Lucian attack. He'd never said anything about supporting it or being against giving up. Had he latched on to Jordan because his brother was gone? He didn't have time for this. Kevin would easily be killed in a second if he tried to cross Lucian and Jordan didn't want to be responsible for another one of Lela's siblings dying.

"What exactly would you do to help me? Act as bait?"

"I am an expert at being the getaway driver. Remember in Italy when I ran off with Lela? And a few days ago in South Carolina? I got us out of there in twenty-seconds flat. If you needed a fast escape, I'm your guy."

All this time, Jordan had internally whined about not having a partner on this mission when he never even considered Kevin. He would be helpful since he already knew of Jordan's secret day-walking ability. He was also very lucky. Kevin never once had been close to dying or in danger. He had a knack for being in the right place at the right time. Jordan needed that reliability.

"Besides that, what else are you good for?"

"I never told Lela this, but I was on the track team in high school. She inspired me to run, and I was actually pretty fast. I'm even faster now that I'm immortal. I'm pretty sure I could beat Lucian. He's slow, I've seen him run."

Jordan laughed at Kevin's claim. He didn't sound cocky about it, but confident. Kevin was an all right kid and unlike his brother, he wasn't unpredictable or sketchy. Jordan could never trust where Aaron's loyalties lay while Kevin showed unfaltering devotion to both his sisters as well as the group.

"Okay. I suppose you can join me. But I'm not lying when I say you could be killed."

"I won't. Nobody messes with the Sharmentinos. My dad taught me that and I'm not going to let some stupid ancient immortal mess with my family anymore. Lela has tried to save our family several times and now it's my turn."

Cherish stuck her key in the door then turned the knob, opening the door to her apartment. Her mail had piled up on the floor and she quickly kicked it to the side so the pathway would be clear. Solomon came in behind her and shut the door as he admired her living space. Though she'd cleaned it the night before meeting

Melody in Miami, it had gotten dusty again from her being away for a week and a half.

She went into the kitchen and checked her messages. She had ten of them, half from her boss and half from her coworker. She never called anyone when she'd left so she'd been fired for failing to show up to work without notice and Penelope kept calling and threatening to call the police if Cherish didn't call her back.

"Great, now I bet there's police out there looking for me," Cherish said.

"Why did she have reason to worry?" Solomon asked.

"I had a...blind date the last time we spoke. She joked about my getting tossed in a dumpster. She probably thought the worst when I stopped answering my phone."

Cherish erased all of the messages then turned around to face him. He never said when he was planning to go back to Italy, but she was too scared to ask him if he would stay longer. After being mostly alone for several centuries, she didn't want to be alone now. And she wanted to know if he was serious about how he felt or if their near tryst had only been a result of confused emotions and getting caught up in the moment.

"You should go to bed," he said. "You've had a long week and need some rest."

"What about you?"

"Don't worry about me. I'll be in the living room."

He lightly touched her cheek then walked to the couch before she went to her bathroom to take a shower.

It was so good to be home and use her bathroom. She stood for several minutes, letting the warm water pour over her face, taking her time getting out. She put her robe on then stared in the mirror as she brushed her hair. It was getting long; too long. But she couldn't bring herself to cut it. Melody would have hated that.

As she thought of her sister, she began to cry. Never again would she look forward to her random phone calls or hear her lectures on life. What hurt most was that she'd been killed by those sent by her own father. She'd always been a good person and her death wasn't supposed to happen.

Cherish finally composed herself then took out her contact lenses, letting it rest on the tip of her finger. The day they'd been invented, she purchased them to hide her different eyes. Melody never cared about what people thought and Cherish decided that from now on, she wouldn't either. Without a second thought, she tossed it in the trash along with the case and half-bottle of solution.

She threw on some night clothes then went into the kitchen to get something to eat. She was half hungry and half curious to see what Solomon was doing. It had to be boring sitting in the living room all night. The TV was on low and she peaked around the corner. He was watching some old show on the Hallmark channel. She smiled as she returned to the kitchen and began making some spaghetti.

The TV turned off and Solomon joined her in the kitchen just as she'd finished cooking the meat. She felt bad that he didn't have the ability to enjoy food like she did. The cook at the Christophe mansion always made the most elaborate meals for her, Melody and her father, but Cherish rarely ever ate any of it. She didn't acquire a taste for food until she was older. She'd been picky as a child.

"If you were hungry, I could have picked something up for you," Solomon said.

"That's all right. I've been craving homemade food anyway."

After she mixed up the sauce, she dumped the noodles into a colander before returning them to the pot. She was about to get a plate when Solomon handed one to her and she smiled at him.

"Your father used to get so mad when you wouldn't eat your dinner," he said.

"I remember. And you bribed me with gifts to get me to eat. You said you would ask Philippa if I tried anything new and then gave me candy. Florence always told them to stop babying me and that I would eat eventually."

He laughed then leaned against the counter while she filled her plate with food. She eased herself onto the counter next to him before grabbing her plate again and took a bite of food. Spaghetti never tasted so good. She'd mostly sustained herself on blood for the past week and food was a nice change.

"Was your mother as horrible as Lucian or did she ignore you like she did the rest of us?" he asked.

"I couldn't stand that woman. She didn't believe that Byron was the father of my child. She said that no man would even think about touching me and accused me of having an affair with my own father. She was warped, so I just stopped caring after a while."

Solomon's expression grew sympathetic. This conversation was supposed to be nostalgic, not reminisce on her screwed up childhood. She was only being honest. She never hated her mother, she just didn't care about her the way a daughter should. Her mother made disgusting claims about Cherish and her father, which proved how strange of a person she was.

Cherish never even cried when she learned her mother had been killed. If anything, she felt relieved and so did Melody. They would never have been free to live their lives if their parents hadn't died. But somehow, their parents influenced them from beyond the grave. It took years before either of them recovered from everything they experienced.

She finished eating then rinsed off her plate and put it in the dishwasher. She didn't want to think about her mother or her father anymore. Florence was dead and Lucian was off doing his own thing. He was no longer a part of her life and Cherish hoped he would stay away from her for the rest of eternity.

"I think I'll go to bed now," she said.

"Goodnight, Cherish. I'll see you in the morning."

She started to leave when she stopped and turned around. Solomon hadn't kissed her since they were in South Carolina almost three days before, and she desperately wanted him to right now. She wasn't sure if he'd sworn off all physical contact between them or if he was still open to some things.

He hadn't changed at all since he'd last been at her house over four hundred years ago. He once told her he'd stopped aging at thirty-eight, but he didn't look close to forty. More like thirty-five, though he did look older than her father. It didn't matter to her. Solomon would be attractive to her if he was fifty or sixty.

"You know, you don't have to stay on the couch," she said. "You could stay in my room if you want."

"Oh, *Accarezzare*. Why do you tempt me so?"

"Because I want you. And I know you want me."

Cherish traced her bottom lip with her tongue and he laughed, moving a few inches away from her.

"What? So you can't kiss me anymore either?" she asked.

"As much as I want to, I can't." He kissed her forehead then smiled. "I will let you go to bed now."

She pouted then reluctantly walked to her room. She hated that he'd left her hanging. But she couldn't imagine how difficult it was for Solomon to stay away when she could barely control herself around him. He'd hinted that he wanted to be in a relationship with her after he left the church and she still couldn't decide if she wanted to just continue having her fun with him or actually devote

THE RESURRECTION

herself to him. She had offered him a chance to hit it and quit it, but she knew he wouldn't be up for that. And for the first time, she worried that she would be the one to break his heart instead of the other way around if opportunity presented itself.

Chapter Thirty-Three

Gallard looked over at Lela, who was sitting in the driver's seat. They'd been driving for almost eight hours, taking turns at the wheel so Lela could rest. She wanted to get back and see her aunt and give her uncle a funeral before they decided where to spend their time recuperating.

Lela leaned over, kissing his cheek then stretched. He wanted to ask her to trade even though it had only been a half an hour since they'd switched. But he knew she was exhausted.

"We should stop in Orlando," he suggested. "I'd like to talk to Bodoway, and I think you need to sleep."

"Okay, we can stop. But we don't have to stay there. I'm fine."

She cracked her neck and rolled her shoulders, trying to wake herself up. The temperature was warmer now that they were further south so she had the air conditioning on. It helped, somewhat, but he could tell sleep was winning.

"I'll drive the rest of the way if you want," he said.

"I can make it for a few more hours."

"Yeah, the last thing I need is for you to crash and fly through the windshield. Pull over."

She slowed the car down, coming to a stop on the side of the

THE RESURRECTION

road then got out after checking for traffic. He got out as well and as they passed by each other, she spanked him. He grabbed her arm, tugging her towards him and kissed her hard. He hadn't forgotten their moment in the hotel. Lela surprised him every day with her passionate side, and he wanted to experience more of that.

It had been his idea to hold off on their honeymoon, but it had been a tough decision. He wanted her so badly and it was getting harder for him to control himself with her.

When he finally pulled back, she was out of breath. She chuckled while smiling at him.

"Wow. If I wasn't awake before, I definitely am now."

"Good. But I'm still not letting you drive."

Gallard spanked her back as she walked away and she wiggled her eyebrows suggestively before getting in on the passenger side.

He found Bodoway's bar about twenty minutes later and parked on the street in front. He didn't usually come here by vehicle and hoped that none of the guests would try and steal the car. They followed the bar's rules, but anything outside of the bar was fair game.

Lela held his hand as they walked down the alley, and a wave of nostalgia hit him. The last time they'd walked down this same alley, they'd barely known each other and now they were married. The past few years, minus the one where she'd been dead, were the best of his life, and he was glad he'd decided to bring her along on his search.

He knocked on the door and within seconds, Terrence opened it. He gave Gallard a polite nod then shot Lela an annoyed look.

"Oh no. It's you again," Terrence said.

"Don't worry, I come in peace," she replied.

Terrence stepped out of the way and the two of them went into the bar. Once they sat down on the stools, Gallard waited for Bodoway to make an appearance.

"What was that between you and Tight Pants?" he asked her.

"He doesn't like me, and I don't like him. It's a long story."

"She broke the no violence rule!" Terrence said, sitting next to them. "She attacked me for no reason."

Lela scoffed. "No reason? Whatever, I politely asked you to let me in and you tried to bribe me by requesting a sample."

"Don't listen to your girlfriend. She was breaking the no violence rule, and I was only heavily enforcing it."

"She's not my girlfriend," Gallard said, grinning at her. "She's my wife."

"You married the shark wrestler?" a familiar voice said. Gallard and Lela turned around and found Bodoway standing next to them. Gallard stood up and gave him a firm hug before Bodoway did the same to Lela.

After Bodoway got Gallard a glass of B positive, he sat on the stool. He kept aiming a happy smile back and forth between Gallard and Lela for a few moments and had suddenly gotten this look like he knew something they didn't.

"What brings you back so soon?" Bodoway finally asked. "You usually wait at least two months before making another visit."

"We have a few things to take care of in Tampa," Lela explained.
"After that, we're not sure what we're going to do."

"And Lucian; is he defeated?"

Gallard shook his head regretfully. He wished that something had been done for Lela and Cherish's sakes. Until he was gone, he would always be haunting the two women, plotting to try and make them his protégés. Gallard hoped that he and Lela could stay on the down-low to keep that from happening.

"We're hoping he'll take the hint from something that we did so he'll leave us alone," Lela said.

"It will work out. It always does. Just a year ago, everything seemed hopeless and now look at you. You're together again and you're married. That's nothing short of a miracle, am I right?"

Gallard took Lela's hand and caressed it with his thumb. Bodoway was right; everything did work out in the end. If only he could have the same faith in the Lucian situation. Then the two of them would finally be free.

He could see that Lela was growing tired once more, probably because she'd used her last bit of energy talking with everyone, so after talking for an hour with Bodoway, Gallard suggested that they head out.

Gallard bought a small supply of blood bags and was about to leave when Bodoway stopped him. Lela saw that he wished to talk alone, so she took the sack of blood and said she'd wait for him outside.

"What's up, B?"

"I wanted to tell you something that I couldn't ignore."

Gallard folded his arms to let him know he had his attention. Occasionally, Bodoway would tell him of these predictions or messages he claimed to receive and because many of them came true, Gallard took them seriously. Dyani had been able to do the same thing as well as other members of their family.

"When I hugged Lela tonight, I saw the same thing that I did the first and second time," Bodoway continued. "It was the man. The one with blonde hair and blue eyes."

"Are you saying that I should watch out for competition?" Gallard asked, trying to make a joke of it.

"I don't know, Gal." He paused. "I saw two men this time. The second, I couldn't see as clearly as the first. She cares for them."

Gallard's shoulders sank. "You see two men with my wife? You mean I have to worry about two men trying to take her from me?"

Bodoway closed his eyes for a bit. He sometimes would do this to try and analyze his visions. Not only could he see them by touching people, but he could retain them as vividly as if he'd just seen them.

Bodoway looked so serious and it was starting to worry Gallard. Two men that Lela would care about? This was his worst nightmare.

"I'm afraid there's more," Bodoway said. "After you were here last, Lucian showed up and recruited some customers into doing his bidding. Before he left I touched him."

"Okay. And what did you see?"

Five seconds ticked by before he answered. "I saw him with Lela. They were...happy and Lucian was holding a child. I could feel that he loved that child."

Gallard's stomach turned. "B, what are you saying?"

"I'm not sure what it means, Gallard. It would be horrible of me to keep something this big from you. But I can tell you this; if you don't kill him, there's a chance that this may come true."

"Hold on." Bodoway's words were starting to register. "You're telling me that Lucian...fathers a child with Lela?"

"Like I said; I don't know what it means. I see the man in her future, but I also see Lucian and her together. None of it is connecting. I can't magically put the pieces together. I can just tell you what I see."

Gallard thanked him for the heads up then left to find Lela. Though he wanted to play off this warning as nothing, he couldn't shake the feeling that it was something important. Two men were going to change their lives? And what about the whole thing with Lucian and some mysterious child? Lela wasn't going to leave him for Lucian, was she? He couldn't bear to think of that ever happening. The only way to know for sure was to wait and see what exactly this premonition meant.

They arrived in Tampa a little after three o'clock. She'd dozed off for a while and opened her eyes just as he pulled up to Curtis' house. She'd expressed that she was tired of hotels and Curtis said they were welcome to stay.

Gallard parked the car on the street then they grabbed their luggage and walked up the steps and to the door. She lifted a pot, retrieving the spare key, then they went inside. The house was dark and there were baby bottles and baby clothes everywhere.

"Where do you want to crash?" he asked.

"How about the floor? Anything that doesn't involve standing sounds wonderful."

He lifted her into his arms and carried her as he walked down the hall.

"Curt said we could use my old room," she said. "But don't try to get frisky. I don't think I'm up for it tonight."

"How dare you deny me my husbandly rights?"

She laughed quietly, which made him smile. It was good to hear her laugh and know she was still capable. He opened the door and gently laid her on the bed. Instead of having him walk around to the other side, she moved over until there was enough space for him to lie next to her and he practically fell onto it. He lay on his back with her arm around his waist and they didn't even bother to get under the covers.

He kept his eyes closed the entire night until he felt Lela stirring. It was close to seven, giving them time to relax. He saw that she was still asleep, so he decided to get up and stretch for a little bit. He took a long shower, trying to forget all his worries and concerns. It was peaceful in there. Bodoway's words kept haunting him and he kept trying to decipher what his vision meant. He felt in his bones that Lela loved him and that she would never feel that way about any other man, especially Lucian. On the other hand, Bodoway's visions were never wrong.

As he stood in front of the mirror, he suddenly heard faint voices. He'd tuned out all noise when he'd been in the shower, so he hadn't heard Lela leave the room. The voices didn't sound distressful, so it must have been someone she knew.

When he was finished getting dressed, he headed into the living room to see who Lela was talking to. The voice sounded familiar and when he saw who it was, he figured out why.

"Oh hey!" Lela said. "Morning, babe."

Curtis stood up and Gallard shook his hand. The look Curtis was giving him was of confusion, and he wondered what was wrong.

"Okay, I'm confused," Curtis said. "I remember you having two eyes."

Gallard laughed and so did Lela. At first, losing an eye had been unfortunate, but Jordan's nicknames and jokes helped him look at it in a positive way. And Lela said she liked the patch, so he wore it often.

"I am sure Lela explained some of it to you, but basically, I'm not just a vampire. I'm also a Cyclops."

Lela laughed again as she got out of her seat. Gallard liked that something as simple as a joke about his eye had made her smile. The more she smiled, the more he would be comforted, knowing she was going to be okay.

Someone else came into the room, and he smiled at the woman. She resembled Curtis a lot, and he figured they were siblings. Lela mentioned that he had a younger sister. She was holding a baby and slightly bobbing her.

"Gabby, hey!" Lela said. "Oh my goodness, it's your baby!"

"One of them. Wouldn't you know, I had twins."

"Curt told me! Where's this little one's sister?"

"Nat is asleep. Dude, why are you excited about my babies when you're back from the dead?"

Gabby handed Gallard the tiny infant then threw her arms around Lela, hugging her for a long time. He hadn't realized they were so close, and he was glad she had a mortal friend. The less vampires she was associated with, the better.

While the two women sat on the couch, he continued to hold the baby, unsure of what to do. It was one thing to spend time with Robin, but she had been five. This child couldn't have been more than five months old. She had honey brown eyes and auburn hair like her mother, only it was a little darker. The baby stared and stared at him. He relaxed a little and started rocking her from side to side while smiling at her. She smiled back then giggled.

"Oh wow, I can't believe how rude I'm being," Lela said. "Gallard, this is Gabriella Edison. Gabby, this is my husband Gallard D'Aubigne."

"Damn, Lela! He's even hotter in person!"

If Gallard could turn red, he would have. He was always self-conscious when people complimented him. It was why he preferred to bring Jordan along as much as possible. Though they looked very similar, Jordan was always deemed the more attractive of the two because of his outgoing personality. Gallard preferred to be on the sidelines.

"H...husband?" Curtis asked with a shocked expression on his face. Lela lightly shoved Gabby.

"You didn't tell him?"

"Sorry! Hey Curt, guess what! Lela got married."

Lela rolled her eyes and laughed. None of them seemed to notice that he was still holding the baby, so he decided to speak up.

"So what's your little girl's name?"

"Oh! I'm so sorry," Gabby said. She took the baby back and Gallard slightly felt disappointed. He'd liked holding her. "This precious girl is Nicola. Her sister, Natasha, sleeps enough for both of them. They have their mother's looks and I pray to God not their father's mental instability."

Gallard raised an eyebrow but didn't comment. Lela had mentioned that Gabby married to somewhat legitimize her children. Whether she was referring to her husband or the babies' birth father was up in the air.

The four of them decided to have brunch in town, and Curtis drove. They chose IHOP since it was close to the house and Lela raved about their breakfast. Growing up, Gallard mostly ate hot cereal and bread for breakfast and wished he could experience what modern food was like. Apparently, pancakes and hash browns were on her list of must-haves. Despite her love of breakfast, she ordered a small meal and barely touched it.

"You not hungry?" he asked.

"A little bit, but I intend to steal some from Curtis."

"What are you two going to do now?" Gabby asked.

"Not sure yet," Lela said. "Go and see Evelyn, obviously. We're going to give it more thought after the funeral."

This was what Gallard had looked forward to; planning their future. Ever since they'd gotten together, he'd wanted to settle down with her, get a place of their own and enjoy life for the first time. He would get a job and she could too if she wanted. He didn't care what she did as long as she was happy.

"We could go house hunting," Gallard suggested. Lela stopped eating and looked at him.

"Really? Like for an actual house? By ourselves?"

"By ourselves. No roommates, no extras. That would be weird, wouldn't it?"

Lela only ordered French toast so she stole a bite of Curtis' eggs, just how she used to steal a sip of Gallard's blood bag when they lived in Texas. This got him thinking. She'd once said that Arlington felt like home and he had liked the house that they'd rented. He wouldn't mind going back there again.

He would bring up the idea later. For now, he wanted to spend time with her and focus on the present. There was plenty of time for them to decide what they would do.

"When did you two get married exactly?" Curtis asked.

"Three days ago, actually. It was a small, spur of the moment thing. Gallard planned it and surprised me."

"Well…it was my idea, but I didn't plan it. Melody and Cherish did all the big stuff."

"Melody the single British woman?" Gabby asked. "I told you about her, Curt. I wanted Lela to set her up with Ry. God knows he needs a woman to help him get his life together."

"Yeah um…Melody died the day after we were married," Lela said. "She was killed by one of the same men who killed Jeff." She paused. "Robin is gone as well too. She—"

"She was injured that same day," Gallard interrupted. "She hit her head during the struggle and there wasn't anything they could do."

Lela smiled at him in appreciation. He didn't want to force her into talking about it just yet. She still could use some time to heal and maybe one day she would be able to tell her friends the truth. By how they interacted with each other and how they were handling the reality of her immortality, he had a feeling they would understand.

"Oh no...Lela, I'm so sorry," Gabby said. Tears filled her eyes and she wiped them away. "I liked that little girl. I used to baby sit her for your mom way back when. She was a good kid."

Curtis set his fork down and sighed, his expression empathetic. Gallard could see why Lela cared about him so much. Curtis was there for her when she was dealing with her parents' deaths and Robin's disappearance, and he'd been the one she'd called when she'd come back to life and needed someone to help her. In a way, Curtis reminded Gallard of Tyler, the way he was so generous and understanding. What separated the two was Curtis' reaction to the vampire world. He didn't freak out and cut Lela out of his life as Tyler had.

"When are you going to get away from these dangerous people?" Curtis asked.

"Lucian...the man responsible, he made a truce with my family," Lela said. "We should be safe for now."

"Yeah, until another psycho vampire shows up and drugs you or attacks you at a bar."

"A vampire attacked you at a bar?" Gallard asked. He didn't remember Lela mentioning this. Maybe she'd had her mind on other things. He wasn't too worried, though. She'd been attacked several times and survived. She'd even come back from the dead.

"Don't worry, I won the rematch," she said.

"You're *fighting* vampires now?" Gabby asked. "Did you kick his ass?"

"Gabs!" Curtis said. "Don't encourage her. I don't want her fighting anyone." He shuddered. "I still have nightmares about what happened in the hotel last year."

Gabby nodded. "Such a badass, L! You fought off a vampire while you were mortal *and* had a stab wound to the gut. Remind me to call you if I ever need a body guard. God knows I might need one with Spence coming to town."

Lela frowned. "Spencer Hendrickson? The douche that…"

"Humped me and dumped me, yeah that guy."

Gallard nearly burst out laughing, though it would be completely inappropriate to do so. He was starting to like Gabriella. She was straight forward and able to joke about serious things. He wondered how things would have turned out had Lela told them years ago what she was. They could have been an amazing support system for her.

"Why is he here in town?" Lela asked.

Gabby pressed her lips together. "He owes me a favor. He said he wants to see the girls too, but I said hell no. He wants to act like father of the year and I told him Curt would play the violin."

"Please yes," Curtis said. "I haven't played since I was twelve, but I'd love to make him go deaf with my screeching."

Gabby and Lela laughed.

"Hey, L," Gabby said. "Would you mind watching the girls tomorrow? It would be just for a few hours."

"We'd love to," Gallard said before he could stop himself. Gabby smiled.

"Cute, polite, and good with kids. Lela, what island did you find him on and where can I get one?"

The three of them finished eating then Curtis drove them to the hospital. Apparently, Evelyn was improving and was off the respirator. There was a chance she would be able to leave by the end of the week. He could see that Lela was partially happy to see her aunt again and partially nervous. She would have to give her the news of Robin's death and was concerned about how it would affect Evelyn.

Curtis and Gabby remained in the lobby while he accompanied Lela up to the second floor. She was gripping his hand tightly, so he brought her hand up to his lips and kissed it. The anxious expression on her face softened and she smiled. He couldn't find the words that would bring her comfort and the only way he knew how to make her feel better was in small gestures. They seemed to be working.

She stopped in front of the door and waited a moment before going in. He followed her. He was ready for this to be over with;

not the visit itself but the news of Robin's death. To their Evelyn was awake and standing up. She was packing her suitcase. When she saw Lela, she smiled.

"Hey you," she said in a soft, raspy voice. "I was worried about you."

Lela went over and hugged her aunt then they both sat in the chairs next to the bed. He remained standing behind Lela.

"Evie, you remember Gallard, right?"

"Of course. Robin adores you. Your visits were always the highlight of her week."

"Same as mine, Evelyn," he said. "How are you feeling?"

She bit her lip and shrugged. "I'm on medication so I'm not in pain. But hydrocodone doesn't take away the hole left by Jeff."

Lela squeezed her aunt's hand, and Gallard hung his head. He wished he had done more to protect her and her husband. Maybe if they had been honest about what was really going on, they wouldn't have taken off and the accident wouldn't have happened. If he could change that day, he would.

"Evie...I'm afraid I have some good news and some bad news," Lela said quietly. "We had a confrontation with the man who caused the accident. Things got out of control and in the end he made a truce. He's never going to bother our family again."

Evelyn started crying but they were happy tears. It made Gallard sick because he knew they would soon turn to tears of sorrow. Lela was doing very well at remaining composed. Her eyes weren't even showing hints of tears.

"I've prayed for this day from the moment I learned my brother was dead." Evelyn's smile softened. "But you said there was bad news?"

Lela turned to Gallard and they had a silent conversation. They were going to stick with the accident story. As far as Lela was concerned, Robin was dead from the moment she fell into a coma. The rest was irrelevant because keeping Robin alive would have been worse than euthanizing her.

"The reason he called a truce was because someone was killed during the confrontation." Lela swallowed. "They took Robin...she fell—"

"Oh God no!" Evelyn began to sob even harder "No! Not the baby. Not the little girl! Why? She was just a baby! Why did this happen?"

Gallard sensed this was a private moment for the family, so he left the room and allowed them to grieve together. Thinking about Robin's last moments was making him emotional as well. He loved her like a daughter, and she was supposed to fill the space for the child he and Lela could never have. Now she was gone and it was almost like his own flesh and blood was gone.

The elevator opened down the hall and when Gallard saw who stepped out, it felt like a wire went loose in his head. He nearly comprised his identity by rushing up to the man and pounding on him.

"What the hell are you doing here?" Gallard asked.

Simeon laughed and folded his arms. "I was wondering when I would run into you again. Where Lela is, you are not far off."

"I thought from your last conversation that you would stay the hell away. Clearly you have trouble taking a hint."

Simeon took cautious steps towards him and Gallard contemplated whether or not he should get physical. There was no way he was letting this pervert anywhere near Lela or her aunt. Not unless he was in a body bag.

Raised voices came from inside the room and not long after, the door opened. Evelyn and Lela came out and Evelyn had her suitcase in her hands. When they saw Simeon, they stopped talking and stared at him.

"Evie?" Simeon said. "Are you all right?"

"No." She looked at Lela. "No, I'm not all right. Everyone in my family keeps dying. I'm alone."

Lela shook her head. "You're not alone. I'm here. Kevin is coming home soon, and Aaron...he's still alive."

"For how long? How long before you leave again? Or someone else tries to kill you? I don't want to live my life worrying about whether my family will live or die."

Simeon reached his hand out. "Then come with me. I will keep you safe."

"Don't go!" Lela said. "Please...Evelyn, just give me a chance. I swear to you that our enemies are no longer targeting our family. We're finally safe." She pressed her lips together. "Remember what he did to me?"

Evelyn kept looking back and forth between her niece and Simeon. Gallard wanted to speak up and attest to what Simeon did, but doing so would put him at the scene. Evelyn might see him as an accomplice or think he was somehow involved with those who killed her brother. He couldn't lose her trust if he wanted her to get away from Simeon.

"She's lying," Simeon said. "I would never hurt her. Your niece has been keeping things from you. Starting with that man of hers."

"Simeon, stop," Lela said.

"He was there the night she went missing," Simeon continued. "I caught him trying to leave with Lela. That's when he nearly beat me to death to keep me from calling the police."

"You bastard! He did that because of what you were doing to me!"

"I've been watching for years," Simeon said. "Don't you think it odd that Lela happened to disappear after Aaron called and told us he'd found her in Texas? Then nine months later, Mark was dead. Killed the same night Lela came back to town."

Evelyn's mouth opened in shock. Gallard's stomach turned, and he knew this situation was headed south very quickly. Simeon knew too much. He'd been paying attention to everything and secretly watching from the sidelines.

"Is this true?" Evelyn asked. Her eyes filled with tears. "Lela...please tell me he's lying."

Lela cast her gaze to the floor. "It's true." She slowly raised her head to look at her aunt. "I was there. The man he...he followed me. He forced his way into the house. And he made Kevin and me watch while he killed our parents and then took Robin."

"Oh God." Evelyn dropped her bag and sat in one of the chairs in the hallway. "You were there. Why did they spare you?"

"They left me for dead." She swallowed. "Aaron he...saved my life. I was shot and he cut the bullets out. He saved Kevin and me and we lied to the police so we could handle the investigation ourselves."

"How can I believe you? Everything I know is a lie! You weren't really dead, you weren't kidnapped, you were there when your parents were slaughtered." Evelyn suddenly became angry. "Where were you went Robin was killed?"

"I...I was—"

THE RESURRECTION

"Where were you! You're conveniently everywhere else, but you're not there when you're needed! You didn't warn Mark that he was in danger! You didn't come back before someone crashed our car and killed Jeff! And you weren't there when that poor baby was murdered!"

The conversation had caused everyone in the vicinity to become silent. The hallway was eerily quiet and Gallard waited to see what would happen. He wanted so badly to step in and defend Lela, but didn't know if it was appropriate or not. He was leaving it up to her whether or not Evelyn should know about the existence of vampires.

"I'm going now," Evelyn said in a quiet voice. He could tell she'd strained her injury by how softly she spoke. "Simeon...is that invitation still on the table?"

"Absolutely." He went over and picked up her bag. "I'm staying in the Westin. We'll drive up to Orlando tomorrow."

Evelyn nodded then stood up and followed Simeon towards the elevator. Gallard remained silent until they'd disappeared then Lela grabbed his hand, hurrying down the hall to the elevator. It wasn't until they were alone that she hugged him and began to cry. He held her and gently massaged her back to soothe her.

"She's right," Lela said. "It is my fault. All of this is my fault."

"You know that's not true." He hugged her tighter. "You didn't kill your family. You didn't cause all of this pain."

"Didn't I? Samil came for me because I was a day-walker. He targeted my family because he wanted my blood. If I hadn't been such an idiot and drunk that bottle from the gypsy, none of this would have happened!" She took a deep breath. "The only good thing that has come out of this is you. If I hadn't turned, I wouldn't have met you again. At least I have you, right?"

He couldn't stand seeing her so depressed. If she sad, so was he and it had been that way almost from the moment he met her. Though this probably wasn't the best time for spontaneity he had to do something. She needed a break from all of this grief.

"Let's do something crazy," he said. Keeping her arms around him, she looked up at his face.

"Like what? We already got married. What's crazier than that?"

"We've always lived a life of saving money and spending the

bare minimum. How about for once we don't care and just blow a bunch of it on a nice vacation? We'll go away somewhere and stay for a weekend, or a week. However long we want."

She still had tears in her eyes, but she was smiling. It has been too long since he'd been spontaneous, and she inspired him to reawaken that part of him. He'd only shown her the reserved side of him because their circumstances called for it. Now that they were living worry free, he wanted to show her the part of him that wasn't a worrier; the way he was when he lived threat free.

"Okay," she said. "Where are we going Mr. D'Aubigne?"

Chapter Thirty-Four

At Curtis' place, Gallard and I sat in front of the computer and looked up different vacation spots in Florida. I knew of a few, but they were mostly attractions for families with children and not romantic getaways. Curtis was at work and Gabby was at her meeting with her baby daddy, so it was just the two of us and the babies. We'd put them down for a nap before doing our research.

Gallard wanted me to pick the place, and I had no problem with that. I sat in his lap while he reclined and read up on a few that stood out to me. Like a good husband, he would nod and smile whenever I would read an online brochure. The only time he voiced his opinion was when I read about one that had organized activities that required all the couples there to participate.

"Oh, listen to this one! It's called the Gladiator Hotel. The outside is plated in gold and it's the largest hotel in the east coast. There's a Jacuzzi in every room and they have a balcony with a view of the beach."

"Beach view, Jacuzzi. I don't think we'll find anything better than that."

I turned around and smiled at him. Despite the horrible day I'd had before, I was feeling a little better. I'd had a nightmare about

Robin the previous night and Gallard had held me all night while I cried. Now we were laughing and talking pleasantly. I really wanted to start our lives together. His idea of house hunting had gotten me excited for marriage and normalcy.

"Okay so now that we have our honeymoon planned, we can discuss houses," I said. "Did you have something in mind? Big, small; two story, one story?"

"I'm thinking two story. I want to be able to have company. Unlike last time, we won't be loners." He wrapped his arms around my waist. "I think we should have a big yard too. And put a dog in it."

I laughed. "You make a dog sound like it's a tree or a swimming pool. But yeah, I'm down for a dog. Preferably a big one."

"Big, but friendly. Good with kids. You know, in case Gabby brings the girls over or…I don't know."

That caught my attention. Of all the topics to discuss, I didn't think he would bring up kids. We were both aware that having children together wasn't possible, so I figured it just wouldn't be part of our plan. Then again, I never asked him about it.

"Gallard…do you want kids?"

He grew quiet and got his serious face. It was the same expression he got when he accepted my proposal and way back when he told me to guard my heart when I was dating Tyler. Part of me was also afraid of what he would say.

"I don't mean to bring the past into our relationship but…I don't know how to get my point across without doing so."

He cleared his throat, signifying he was nervous.

"When I left for the war, what kept me going was that I had someone back home waiting for me. Dyani and I wanted to build a home and start a family. When I lost her, I lost all desire for the future. Fast forward to now, I've found that same happiness with you, and I also find myself wanting those things again. Including children. And it wouldn't matter to me if the child or children were not blood related to me. I would love them because I would be raising them with you."

Gallard studied my face and I tried my best not to look too freaked out. The truth was, I didn't want children anymore. Robin's death was still too fresh, and I probably wouldn't even be open to considering it for a long time. I was all about being Aunt Lela to

Gabby's adorable little girls, but I couldn't see myself as a mother.

"Oh Gallard." I touched his cheek. "I wish I could say I feel the same way. But I don't."

I could see the light in his eyes darken a bit and it broke my heart. We were bound to disagree on a few things. We were best friends but we were also human...sort of. I just wished this wasn't on our list of differences.

"You're still hurting," he said. "How inconsiderate of me. I shouldn't have brought it up."

"No! Gallard, don't be sorry. These are just some things we will have to discuss sooner or later. I only want to be honest with you. I...I don't want children."

The sound of a baby crying echoed through the house. The timing was so perfect I almost thought it was comical. I got out of his lap, but he beat me to the room. Gabby said that the girls usually had a bottle after their naps, and I went into the kitchen to heat up some water in a sauce pan. Nicola had the bigger appetite so for her I opened a jar of Gerber sweet potatoes.

Everything was ready to go by the time Gallard came into the kitchen. He had one baby in each arm and when I saw him, I was speechless. Having those babies in his arms looked so natural and I could see in his eyes he was enjoying holding them. This whole picture was like a slap in the face. My own depression might rob him of this.

"Um...I'll take Natty," I said. "Since she wants the bottle."

"Sure thing." He gently handed her to me. "I can feed Nic. You have a spoon?"

I nodded then pointed towards where the food was. He put Nicola in her high chair then pulled up a chair in front of her and proceeded to feed her. I kept one eye on Natasha and watched him from a side glance. Nicola really liked him. Whenever he would spoon food into her mouth, she would giggle, which made him laugh as well.

When Nicola was finished, Gallard wiped her chin then picked her then stood by me while Natasha drank the last of her milk. I lay her over my shoulder and patted her back.

"Do you think Gabby will let us borrow them sometimes?" he asked.

"Not likely. Not with her living in New York." I reached over and stroked Nicola's cheek. "I hate that she lives so far away. I've already missed out on five years of her friendship."

"Then we'll just have to visit as often as we can. I don't want you missing another...oh!"

At that moment, Nicola grabbed onto his eye patch and pulled it off. We both laughed as she began examining it then put it on her head. Natasha took interest in the commotion and opened her eyes to see what was going on. Gabby hadn't been kidding when she said Natasha was a sleepy baby. She'd nearly fallen asleep on my shoulder before her sister woke her up.

The front door opened, and I figured it was Gabby. Curtis wasn't due back for another three hours and promised to be home in time to send us off. We would most likely come back after our honeymoon and visit some more since we still didn't technically have a place to live. Gallard's idea was that we would crash at my parent's house until either Aaron showed up and made a decision about it or Evelyn signed it over so we could sell it. I doubted either of those possibilities would happen.

"Hey, love birds," Gabby said when she came into the kitchen. She reached for Nicola, but the little one turned away from her, burying her face into Gallard's shoulder. "Wow. It seems I've been quickly replaced."

Natasha, on the other hand, reached for her mother right away, and Gabby took her from me. I put the bottle in the sink and handed Gabby the burp rag.

"You two have fun with my little monsters?" Gabby asked.

"They were far from monsters," Gallard said. He made a seat with his arms so that Nicola was facing us. "I think I made a new friend."

"Did she take your patch? Oh, that girl! She's always getting into things."

Nicola blew raspberries at Gabby then laughed. That little girl sure had personality. Her sister and she were complete opposites. Natasha hadn't laughed once since we'd been there and she was more attached to her mother than Nicola.

"Did you find a place to go?" Gabby asked.

"We did," I said. "The Gladiator Hotel."

She stared at me with wide eyes. "The Gladiator Hotel? Lela

THE RESURRECTION

that's the nicest place in all of Florida!"

"We're spoiling ourselves." I reached over and took Gallard's hand. "By the way, did you still want to go shopping?"

"Hell yeah! Just let me call my mom real quick and give you two a chance to pack."

Gallard followed Gabby into her room so he could help her put the twins in their crib, and I went to my room to start putting things in my suitcase. We'd been there for three days and would probably return after our getaway. I didn't want to go back to Miami just yet. I was dreading having to live in my parents' house, but we didn't have much else choice.

Trying to think like Melody, I decided to change into some jeans. I even picked out one of my nicer shirts too. I could just hear her voice in my head saying my sweats and t-shirt were sad, single girl clothes.

I was in the middle of changing when Gallard came into the room. He looked surprised when he saw me.

"I'm sorry, I should have knocked."

I laughed. "Gallard, you don't have to knock. We're married, remember?"

He chuckled. "Right. I'm still getting used to that."

I went over and kissed his cheek. That's when I noticed there were four big splotches of food on his shirt.

"Looks like your knew friend decided to use your shirt as a canvas."

"Yeah, I noticed. Must be an artist in the making like her mother."

"I can wash that if you want. I was planning to do a load before we took off. Nothing worse than not having enough clothes."

He tugged off his shirt and handed it to me then I put it in the makeshift laundry bag I'd made from an extra pillow case. I turned around to look at him and suddenly became very aware that we were both half dressed. I could see in his eyes he was thinking the same thing. Without a word, he rushed up to me, taking me in his arms and kissed me.

Before I knew it, we were on the bed in the middle of a really hot make-out session. My shirt somehow ended up on the floor and his jeans were as well. I wrapped my legs around him, trying to get as close to him as possible. He kissed my neck, find the exact spot that he knew was my weakness. He kissed me harder and that prompted me to remember something.

"You better not give me another hickey, Mr. D'Aubigne," I said.

He stopped kissing me. "Another? I don't know what you mean."

"New Year's Eve, two years ago. When we fooled around. You gave me a hickey and Lydian saw it."

His mouth opened in shock. "Oh wow. I had no idea!" He then started laughing. "No wonder Jordan kept making jokes. He must have seen it too."

I brought his lips back to mine. He kissed me for a bit then moved away from me.

"Hey! Where are you going?" I asked, pulling him back into my arms.

"This isn't happening here. Just a few more hours. We'll be alone, and I'll be all yours, Mrs. D'Aubigne."

I smiled, remembering how I'd said that to him when we went swimming in India. He was right, though. We needed to control ourselves until that night. I was amazed at how much self-control he had since I was always the one getting us into these compromising situations.

He got up and started getting dressed, so I did the same. I gathered our dirty clothes and started to leave for the laundry room when he stopped me.

"I hate to talk about this now, but…I need you to know that I'm driving down to Miami while you and Gabby go shopping."

"Oh? What for?"

He took my hands in his and kissed them. "I need to burry Robin. I won't be able to have some peace until it's done."

I nodded in agreement. I wanted nothing more than to give her a small service and put her to rest, but I couldn't. I knew if I saw her go into the ground I would lose it. I wanted to keep everything together for a few more days so I could enjoy my husband. Then maybe after that I could allow myself to grieve her properly.

"Are you sure you want to do that?" I asked. "I couldn't ask that of you. When Kevin gets home, we could do it together."

"Of course I want to do this. She meant a lot to me, and I loved her." He kissed my forehead. "I'll be back in time for us to head out

THE RESURRECTION

for Fort Lauderdale."

"Thank you. I love you."

He then stepped out the door. I was so grateful to him for doing this. I couldn't ask Kevin to bury his baby sister. He'd already had to go through the pain of burying me and our parents. One day, I would take him to visit her grave but not anytime soon.

Chapter Thirty-Five

When Gabby and I talked while I packed, she started criticizing my wardrobe or rather lack of indecent lingerie. All I had was the blue slip that Melody forced me to buy and the rest was a few things from my closet in Las Vegas. She liked the new clothes I'd gotten recently, but she said the secret to a successful marriage was slutty lingerie and cooking skills.

I held Nicola in one arm and Natasha in the other while Gabby tried something on, and I swung them from side to side. Nicola kept smiling while I did it. Her cooing was adorable while Natasha had fallen asleep, again.

When Gabby and I were kids, she used to go on and on about how when we got married and had kids, our children would be best friends. It was impossible to live up to that dream now, but I wanted to be in Gabby's life somehow. I had enough money to visit her in New York as much as I wanted.

She stepped out in a green dress that had a neckline so scandalous that I barely covered her. The hem stopped at least a foot above her knees and still there was a tiny slit on the side. She turned around to model it for me, making a
point to stick out her butt.

"What do you think?"

"It's definitely...sexy."

"Good." She looked at herself in the mirror and fluffed her air. "Sexy enough to get lucky?"

I laughed. "Oh yeah. What's the dress for anyway? Please don't say Spencer."

"I wouldn't touch Spencer again, even if I was wearing a hazmat suit. No, this dress is for Edison." She looked back at me and her expression became serious. "I need him to get me pregnant."

I gave her a sympathetic look. "Does he not want another baby?"

"No, that's not it. I want to have a child with him so he won't leave me. I feel him pulling away from me, and it's more than just the cheating. I think he's resenting marrying me to save me from Spencer."

I looked down and gently pressed my cheek to the top of Nicola's head. She cooed again and Gabby kissed her nose. I knew my conversation with Gallard about children wasn't over. He wanted a family in the sense of children while I just wanted surround myself with people I loved.

One thing was certain. I wouldn't trade the wonderful man in my life for anything. I would rather be childless than be trapped in a loveless marriage.

"I don't think you should do that, Gabbs. I was so afraid of this happening, and it's my fault for not being honest with you back before you got married."

"Honest about what?"

I sighed. "When I look at you, I see my mother. She married Mark because she cared about him and she hoped she would grow to love him. They had a child together but then she cheated, and to make up for it, she gave him another son in hopes that it would fix everything. Obviously it didn't. I would hate to see you follow that same path. I'm not saying you shouldn't have a baby with Edison, but do it because you want another child and not because you want him to stick around. Because you might grow to resent the child if it doesn't work."

Gabby gave a half smile. "When did you get all wise?

Remember when I used to be the one teaching you everything? I bought you your first box of tampons for crying out loud."

We both laughed. It was true that Gabby acted as my mentor even though she was only two years older. The four of us were inseparable for years. All that changed when I turned and had to leave home.

She strapped the twins into the double stroller then moved on. While looking in another section of the store, Gabby suddenly pulled something off of an underwear display and tossed it at me. I unfolded the garment and admired the pretty white slip. It wasn't as scandalous as the blue one but still subtly sexy nonetheless. I actually liked it and wasn't against the idea of wearing it either. Marriage had given me new confidence.

"This is great, Gabby," I said. "I was actually wondering what I would wear tonight."

"Well, I was going to suggest nothing but…"

I lightly shoved her. "Seriously. I wanted to wear something nice for him."

"Well, I think he'll love it." She squealed. "I'm so happy for you, Lela. All your tragedies aside. You found a man who is the complete package; attractive, sweet, and protective. Unlike me, you did things right. Promise me you won't mess it up."

I laughed. "I promise."

We pulled up to the honeymoon place and stared in awe at how tall the building was. I'd found it online, but had no idea it was so massive. The price was insane as well, though Gallard said we weren't going to take price into account.

The hotel was located a few miles outside of Fort Lauderdale. I hadn't been there in years, so it was a nice change. I held his hand as we walked up the several steps to the entrance. At the top, we were greeted by two men in navy blue uniforms and they opened the glass doors for us. We thanked them then continued inside.

When we entered the lobby, we stopped to admire the interior. The carpet was burgundy and the ceiling seemed to soar up into the air. In each corner of the room were spiral staircases with a shiny finish and the furniture was all beige leather.

"Maybe we should have just stuck with a Red Lion or something," Gallard said.

"No way. We are done with sub-par hotels. We may not look like we can afford this place, but we paid for it, so we're going to act like we're rich."

"And how are we going to do that?"

"Watch and learn, old man."

The people checking in at the desk walked away so we went up for our turn. The woman working there had a suit similar to the men at the door and had horn-rimmed glasses. I couldn't tell if she was in a bad mood or if she was just focused.

"Hello, welcome to the Gladiator Hotel. Do you have a reservation?"

"Yes, we have a room under the name of D'Aubigne," I said in my best French accent. Gallard looked at me funny and I tried to hint at him to just go with it.

"Under…Gallard?"

"*Oui.*"

I was trying to hard not to laugh, but I couldn't keep a straight face. The woman didn't even acknowledge my weirdness and just clicked a few buttons before handing us two keys.

"Your room is four-twenty on the eighth floor. You can take the staircase on the east end of the lobby or you can take the elevator. Both routes will get you to your room. Enjoy your stay, Mr. and Mrs. D'Aubigne."

Gallard and I were feeling equally lazy so we chose to ride the elevator. I had to admit that hearing someone call me Mrs. D'Aubigne made me giddy. I loved the sound of that and I loved that I was his wife. He was the one that brought me back after I'd had an emotional break down and he was helping me get over my recent tragedies.

The one thing that was a blessing was that I still didn't remember what I'd done after leaving them in the parking lot. Robin's death was all I remembered and everything after that was a hole in my memory. I felt guilty, knowing that I had done horrible things in a violent rage, and I dreaded when it would all come back to me.

But with Gallard at my side, I could get through it, just like I'd gotten through everything else. He was my own personal counselor as well as my friend and husband. The perfect partner that came into my life at the right time. And now we were going to begin our lives together, starting with a romantic weekend at a fancy honeymoon place.

The elevator stopped at our floor and we got off, taking a left to go towards our room. The hallway was so long that it seemed the more we walked, the further away our destination was. We ended up walking too far and had to turn around.

"I'm starting to understand why we had roommates," Gallard said. "We would be so lost without a third party."

"We seriously need to get out more."

"Or…we could stay in and save ourselves from public embarrassment."

He slid the key into the lock then opened the door, holding it for me. I walked in, but before I got a chance to look around he grabbed my arm and pulled me back out.

"What's wrong?" I asked.

"I forgot to carry you over the threshold. Isn't that a tradition?"

I laughed. "You're too late, old man. You were supposed to do that on our wedding night. Don't worry, I forgot too. Tradition isn't really our style, though is it?"

He gave me a loving smile then picked me up and carried me through the door. He set me down once we were in the middle of the room, and I leaned against him while I took in the décor. The room was dimly lit with fireless candles lined up along the wall leading to the bathroom. There was a queen-sized bed against the left wall and the comforter was covered in red rose petals.

I moved away from him to check out the rest of the space and found glass doors that led to a balcony overlooking the city. It was big enough to fit a small table and two chairs, which had a bottle of champagne and two glasses on top.

Moving further inside, I headed for the bathroom, and I gaped at how beautiful it was. There was a bathtub as big as a Jacuzzi with flowers floating on the surface and candles along the edge. We'd definitely gotten our money's worth.

"What do you think?" I asked. He turned me around to face

him.

"I think I love you."

I put my arms around his waist and kissed him. His kisses pushed away every sorrow I had. All that existed was me and him.

Suddenly becoming extremely nervous, I stopped kissing him for a moment. After all the waiting we'd done, I was slightly freaking out that this moment had finally come. I needed a second to get rid of my nerves.

"Do you mind if I go to the bathroom for a second?" I asked him.

"I don't mind at all." He kissed the side of my head and smiled. "Take your time."

I closed the door behind me and slipped out of my clothes before stuffing them into my suitcase. That was when I remembered that I'd packed the new slip Gabby had picked out and wondered if I should put it on. It was kind of funny that I'd gone through with the trouble of buying it when I'd probably only wear it for a total of maybe five minutes at the most.

I quickly put it on before I could change my mind then took my hair down, running my fingers through it until it looked decent. I took a deep breath to calm my nerves. I shouldn't have been nervous. It was just Gallard. Nothing to be afraid of. Still, I needed a second to prepare myself, and when I was sure I was ready, I opened the door.

I found Gallard slowly pacing around the room. He was still dressed and he was twirling his car keys. If I wasn't mistaken, he seemed to be more nervous than I was. He wouldn't even make eye contact with me. I approached him and he finally stopped moving.

"What's wrong?" I asked.

"Nothing." He looked into my eyes and knew that he'd been caught. He let out a sigh and took my hands. "I want to enjoy this weekend so much. I want to spend time with you and forget everything we've been through these past few weeks, but...I'm afraid. I'm terrified that all of it is going to be ripped away at any second."

I brought his hands to my lips, just as he had to me when we reunited at the hospital. Something had to put these worries into his head. They hadn't come out of nowhere. I noticed he had been acting strangely ever since we spoke to Bodoway. It had to be related.

"What did he see?" I asked.

"What?"

"Bodoway saw something, didn't he?" I looked into his eyes. "Ever since you spoke with him, you've gotten even more sentimental than usual. Talking about wanting kids, carrying out old wedding traditions. Something spooked you. What was it?"

"It wouldn't matter if I told you. He's never wrong." A humorless laugh escaped his lips. "I can never win. Whenever I have a glimpse of happiness, it's taken away from me."

He walked over to the glass doors, staring out the window. It was breaking my heart seeing him like this. He had always been so strong. Over the past few weeks, he and Solomon fought to get us through every adversity and even though we didn't all escape unscathed, we had succeeded in ending the feud. Gallard was finally able to let his guard down instead of being forced to boost the morale for the sake of the group.

I walked up behind him and hugged him tightly. I agreed that trouble always seemed to find us. Our happy moments were very few and I cherished those moments. This getaway was supposed to be a distraction from everything before we went back to the real world to deal with the aftermath of our war with Lucian. I wanted to somehow cheer him up.

"You don't have to tell me what he saw, but I can say this. We're not going to let fear ruin what we have." I forced him to turn around and look at me. "No matter what happens in the future; what loss we suffer or what enemy we're fighting, we have tonight. Nothing can touch us tonight because we love each other and we always will."

Gallard smiled at me, and I saw him become more visibly relaxed. He looked down at what I was wearing then brought his gaze to mine.

"*Vous êtes belle*," he said. "But, I am afraid it will go to waste."

"How so?"

He took the hem of the slip and slowly pulled it off over my head. He then picked me up and carried me to the bed, gently laying me on my back and removed his jacket. I helped him pull off his shirt then undid his belt. He got completely undressed, and for a while, I just beheld this beautiful man. I couldn't believe that I was finally here with him or that he was truly mine. My best friend, my husband, and now my lover. I could see in his eyes that he was still a little nervous but also excited. I was feeling the same thing.

I finished undressing as well then moved the covers so he could lay next to me. We lay on our sides, gazing into each other's eyes. I hoped that he didn't hear my heart beat because it had picked up significantly.

I decided to make the first move and pressed my lips to his, softly at first then he rolled so that he was on top of me. I let my hands roam over the span of his back then rested them on his hips. His own hands traveled down my sides and over the sides of my legs. It felt amazing and I chuckled to myself.

"What is it?" he asked.

"Oh, nothing. Personal joke."

He raised an eyebrow. "Does this have to do with the magic hands thing? You never told me about that."

I looked away for a moment then brought my eyes back to his. "Why don't I show you instead?"

I shifted us so our places were reversed then began to touch him. His eyes widened in surprised but then he closed them. I wasn't exactly sure how all this worked; all of it was new to me, so I just continued doing that. I could feel his body reacting to my touch. It was a mesmerizing experience, and I was slowly coming out of my shell.

After a few moments he reached for my hand and took in in his, interlocking our fingers then sat up. By then, we were both ready to be together. The leading up to it had been amazing, but it all culminated to this.

We switched places once more and he gave me one last kiss before finally joining us as husband and wife. My body tensed up as I waited for the discomfort to pass. It wasn't anything I didn't expect, but it was also astonishing.

"I'm sorry," he said, kissing my cheek.

"No, don't apologize."

"Am I hurting you? I know this is your first time."

I turned his face to mine and smiled at him. "Don't worry about me. I don't want you to hold back on me either."

He kissed me once more then began moving slowly and gently until all I felt was pure bliss, and I was finally able to love him back.

I felt numb yet so sensitive to every movement we made. I felt shy, yet open and alive. When I thought it was too much, I wanted more and my body waited on his very touch. This was the greatest act of love I could show him. This was the night I fully became his; the night he loved me and I loved him.

I couldn't imagine doing this with any other person but him, and I was glad that I never had. It was just me and him for the rest of our lives. However long that would be. I grew closer to him in those next several moments than I thought possible, opening up to him in more ways than one; a kiss, a thought, a touch. Every second was filled with so much love and I couldn't get enough of it.

When Lela told him not to hold back, Gallard was finally able to be with her completely and without abandon. He kissed every inch of her, finding every scar, every blemish, and every part of her that told her story; their story. He had waited for this night for so long, and now that they were finally here, he could barely contain his joy. Instead, he showed the best way he knew how; through actions.

Just when he was sure she couldn't surprise him anymore, she would blow his mind. She knew exactly when to move and where to touch him that would jumble his thoughts and send him into a state of pure euphoria. He used to think they were in sync before, but as the night went on, he was even more convinced that this woman was made for him. He wouldn't even have to say anything and she would know what he wanted her to do and vice versa.

It had been years since he experienced this. After losing Dyani, he thought it wasn't possible to feel this way again. He had slept with many women, but tonight was the first time in nearly three hundred years that he was truly making love to someone. He couldn't have chosen a better person to be with.

"Are you tired yet?" He asked her as she planted soft kisses on his chest.

"No." She eyed him seductively. "Why? Are you?"

"I'll be honest and say I am a little thirsty. Not tired, though."

"I got this."

Lela put his shirt on then slid out of the bed, and he watched as she went over to his suitcase to get a blood bag. It reminded him of the time back in Texas when he'd held her as she cried herself to sleep. That was the first time she had slept next to him and from that moment, he knew he wanted her at his side for eternity, be it as friends or lovers. His desires had been exceeded and now she was his wife.

Holding the bag in her hand, she slowly came back over to his side of the bed. She kept staring at it with her eyebrows furrowed. He sat up, resting his hands on his knees.

"Something the matter?"

"I was just wondering." She looked at him. "Why don't you drink my blood?"

He raised his eyebrows. He never thought about that before. The thought of feeding from her always bothered him, even if he let her do the same with him. Then again, she had said she wanted him to be more comfortable with her.

"You mean now or for the duration?" he asked.

"Well, it would be convenient. You wouldn't have to rely on blood bags anymore. I need you for blood and you need me. What's mine is yours, and I want to give you all of me. Including my blood."

Setting the bag down, she held her wrist out to him. He warily took it and inhaled her sweet scent. Never had he smelled blood more appealing than hers. Pushing aside his pesky worrying, he gently sank his teeth into her skin and drank. It was different than any blood he'd ever tasted, and it was almost addicting. He stopped himself before he took too much.

"Wow. It's different. A good different."

"So, what do you think of my idea?"

"I'll consider it. Now get back in this bed. I'm not done with you yet."

Lela laughed. "Oh really? You're taking this no holding back thing to heart, aren't you?"

"Completely. I love you, Mrs. D'Aubigne. I'm not letting you go ever again."

He waited for her wrist to heal then he tugged her close to him. He attempted to do a graceful shift but overcorrected and nearly sent them rolling off the bed. They both laughed and he could have sworn he felt his heart skip a beat. Every time she laughed, he became more hopeful for the future. As long as she had the ability to laugh, she would be fine. Losing Robin and her Uncle and Melody had been hard on her but she was strong and resilient.

After they made love again…and again, he held her with her back to him with a smile on his face. He lay with his head propped up by his fist and let his fingers trail over her in light strokes. She was so warm and he was convinced that being next to her had caused them to share warmth. The sun was starting to rise now. He couldn't believe the night was over. He wasn't ready for it to end. Then he remembered that it didn't have to.

He used to worry that their bond would be disconnected after she came back to life. He no longer felt the pull towards her or that link that had drawn them together years before. After sharing the night with her, he realized that their bond was even stronger now. Stronger than any pull or blood ties. Nothing could sever that.

Lela let out a content sigh. "Now do you know what I mean about magic hands?"

"I do." He slid his hand down her side and all the way to her knee. "I'm kind of captivated by your body."

"Oh really? Which part?"

"Hmm." His hand moved further down. "I would have to say your calves. They've always been impressive. Even though you are thinner than you were before you got sick, your calves are still that of a dedicated runner." He went back to stroking her side. "Your turn. What's your favorite part of me?"

"I'm not sure. I'd have to look at you again to find out."

She buried herself under the covers for a bit. She kept touching him until he thought he was going to go crazy then came back out so that she was laying on him with her arms crossed on his chest. She smiled her usual sneaky smile.

"I'm going to have to say your hands," she said.

"Really?"

"Yeah. They've always fascinated me. I used to like watching you do things; cook, repair kitchen appliances, patch up those ratty jeans you love so much. I loved watching you use your hands. I trusted your hands to never hurt me, and you always moved so gracefully and gently, no matter what you did."

Gallard stroked her cheek with the back of his hand. "*Mes main vous tiendront jamais*. My hands will hold you forever."

"You're a real Casanova, you know that?"

He kissed her lips. "What can I say? It's a D'Aubigne thing."

Gallard could see she was getting tired so he lay her back on her side and held her once more. Even he was feeling a bit lethargic. He decided to close his eyes for a bit. A few hours of sleep couldn't hurt. He no longer forced himself to in order to escape his reality. Lela was back in his arms, and the horrific nightmares had come to an end. With that thought in mind, he drifted off into a peaceful slumber.

Chapter Thirty-Six

Lucian awoke when he felt someone shaking him. His eyes shot open and on instinct, he grabbed the person pushed them to the ground. It took him a moment to realize it was only Aaron then he released his grip.

"You fool! Tis not wise to disturb me when I sleep!" he shouted.

"Sorry, Chris, but I had to! You've been asleep for three days. Your nightmares are causing earthquakes. Literally."

Lucian glanced around the room and saw that there were small cracks in the walls as well as pictures lying on the floor. He couldn't believe he'd caused this and wondered what sort of destruction he could create if he was awake and in control. His new powers fascinated as well as frightened him.

The evil inside of him was becoming more than he could bear. While he'd slept, he had visions; terrible visions of immortals slaughtering their families and wreaking havoc in fifty A.D. and beyond. It appeared that when Maximus gave him his power, along with it, he gave Lucian the memories of all the violence he'd witnessed over the course of two thousand years.

"Leave me, Sharmentino. Do not disturb me again. I care not about the earthquakes. You will have to deal with them."

"Leave and do what? We came here to party and now you won't even do that."

"Get out of here. I cannot think with you in my presence!"

Aaron rolled his eyes before getting up from the floor and leaving the room. Lucian secretly wished Aaron would leave. He was not useful in any way, besides fetching things for him and effectively sneaking in meals as well as disposing of them.

Lucian showered then changed into some day clothes, though it was the middle of the night, and poured himself a glass of vodka. He wanted to try and forget the nightmares he was having about Melody. She'd haunted his dreams since the night he learned of her death. He would have killed the spies himself for going against his orders, but Lela did that for him.

She is just so wonderful, isn't she?

Lucian stopped drinking then looked around. He hadn't heard voices in his head since he'd been dreaming. The voices were supposed to stop after he was awake. Why was he hearing them again? This was perfect. Not only did he have nightmares and visions, but he was hearing voices as well. He hated this and hated himself even more for allowing Maximus to force this upon him.

He poured more vodka then downed it as he waited for the voice to speak again. He figured if he could find out who it was, he could convince them to leave him be.

Father. Are you trying to get rid of me again?

When he realized who was speaking, he shook and set the wine glass down. There was no way he could be hearing her. She already haunted his dreams, and now she was appearing while he was awake.

"Melody. Daughter, why are you here?"

Melody began to laugh, and it echoed throughout the room, growing louder and louder until it clouded his senses.

"Stop!" he shouted. Instantly the laughing ceased. He wouldn't admit it, but hearing her voice rattled him.

"You sound like a crazy man, shouting to someone you can't

see," she said again, this time her voice was clearer; more close by.

Lucian quickly turned around and held his breath when he saw that Melody was standing in front of him. She appeared the way she had long ago, short sandy hair; almond eyes; her innocent smile. She was even dressed the way she had the day before the gypsies murdered her.

For a while, she didn't utter a word. She walked towards him, taking graceful steps as she moved in a zig-zag pattern. When she was close enough to touch, he reached out and took a lock of her hair in his hands. It felt real, she smelled real; like lavender, the scent she always used.

"What are you?" he asked.

"Do you not know? You were the one who summoned me."

Lucian had no idea what she was talking about. He didn't know how to summon anyone, and even if he did, he most certainly wouldn't summon her. The only other possibility was that he'd somehow brought her back to life. Maximus had that power, and now it was his. But how had she come here to New York?

He let go of her hair, backing away slowly. He couldn't handle having his daughter back. It made him feel guilt he didn't wish to have. If he had raised her from the dead subconsciously, he wanted to return her to the grave as soon as possible.

"You killed me, father. That was not very nice of you."

"I did not kill you. Twas a tragic misunderstanding."

Melody laughed again, but not as loudly as before. Whatever she was, she had the ability to mimic his daughter's melodic laugh.

"Your killings are not all I've heard about, my father. I also hear that you found a new obsession. Lela Sharmentino, is it? You would fall for a Sharmentino. You were always so easily influenced by Solomon."

"You cared about her too, am I right?"

"I know that you want her the way you used to want my mother. She is not good for you. It would be wise to stay away. You don't need her. You have me now."

Lucian forced himself to look at her once more and began to think through this whole encounter. Something was strange about the Melody before him. She wasn't completely the same as she had been. She may have had the same hair, eyes, gait, and laugh, but it wasn't her.

"You are not Melody. You're the one who tempted Maximus into gaining more power; the Devil."

"And you are smarter than I thought. Now that I have your attention, I can finally give you some advice."

Lucian chuckled. "Advice? Concerning what?"

"Leave Lela be. She will ruin you."

"How so? What could you know of it?"

"She is a threat to us, Lucian. She could ruin everything I've started. The only way to ensure our future is to eliminate her."

The specter smiled before approaching him once more and whispered into his ear. Lucian was somewhat unnerved by the frightening things it was saying. He wanted to know why it was so adamant that he stay away from Lela. Why it had taken the form of his dead daughter, he didn't know.

She finished speaking then he closed his eyes for a few moments and opened them to find the specter gone. He was thankful for this. He wasn't going to listen to this crazy voice. It didn't matter how long it would take him to pull it off. Lela would be his and he would finally have an adequate partner at his side.

For his plan to work, he needed to know where she was. Since Maximus had been connected to all immortals, he could use the connection to seek her out.

Lucian knocked on the door and one of his men came in. He didn't recognize him since he'd made too many to keep track. Lela had killed the man in charge of knowing who was who, so Lucian had to learn their names all over again.

"Who are you?" he asked the man.

"Alexander Mason, sir."

Lucian tried to decide what he would have him do. Alexander couldn't find Lela on his own, but Lucian couldn't search for her either without the risk of being caught. He needed to send someone who they didn't recognize.

Then he had an idea. It was like the power within him was giving him knowledge on how to use it. Without these voices whispering to him, he wouldn't have a clue what he was capable of.

He bit onto his thumb until it bled then held onto Alexander's arm so he couldn't move. Lucian smeared the blood onto Alexander's eyes and he began to cry out in pain.

"Ah! It burns!" he shouted. "Make it stop!"

"I cannot. I need you for something, and you will do as I say. From now on, you are my eyes until you are finished with your task."

Seconds later, Lucian lost his sight, and he waited for it to return. It needed to in order for this transfer to work. The darkness unnerved him greatly, but he did not panic. Soon, he began to see spots, then garbled colors, and finally everything was clear. He saw himself, which confused him, but he realized it was because he was now seeing everything from Alexander's perspective.

"Go find Lela Sharmentino," Lucian commanded. "I will lead you to her."

Jordan swooped down from the rooftop and landed on the sidewalk in the alley. The crowds of New Yorkers walking down the street allowed him to quickly disappear in their midst. He couldn't stand to watch another minute of the insanity that had occurred in Lucian's room. Very little frightened him, aside from Maximus and he hadn't felt this uneasy since the earthquake in the diner.

Something malevolent was going on with Lucian and Jordan had some ideas. How else could he cause his late daughter to appear in the room? Jordan questioned his eyes; whether they were deceiving him, but Melody had very much been in that room, speaking to Lucian and whispering things in his ear. Then as suddenly as she'd appeared, she was gone.

And the ritual with the blood. Lucian had said something about the day-walker becoming his eyes. That was when Jordan had enough of it and left to report back to Kevin. They'd been spying for a two nights and a day. He hadn't been able to hear what Melody, or the specter that looked like her, had said to Lucian, but he did have a bad feeling that Lela was in danger. The day-walker was sent to spy on Gallard and Lela and Jordan needed to get to them.

He dialed Kevin's number on his cell phone. Jordan didn't want to wait to retrieve him from their hideout, so instead he was going to let him know he was taking off to make sure Gallard and Lela were okay. Kevin would be safe here alone. Lucian still had no clue he was being watched and Kevin could handle his own very well.

"Hey, Kev. Something's come up, I need to fly down to Florida."

"Something like what? Is my sister in danger?"

"Not sure yet. Do you happen to know where she is?"

Kevin grew silent for a second then spoke again. "I found her last text. She said they were going to some place in Fort Lauderdale called the Gladiator Motel."

"Thanks. I shouldn't be long. I just want to check everything out."

"Cool. I'll hang around here I guess. Lela's probably still mad at me anyway. Don't worry, I won't be stupid and try to spy on my own."

Jordan chuckled. Though he'd been against it in the beginning, Kevin had turned out to be a great companion on this mission. He was glad he'd let Kevin stick around and he'd proven that he was useful. He'd even saved Jordan from being caught by warning him of Lucian's guards that he didn't see coming around.

"You're young. You're supposed to make stupid decisions," Jordan said.

"Not ones that could get me killed. I'll see you, Jay."

Jordan hung up then flew into the air as soon as he'd put his phone away. The trip would be long, but he would fly fast to speed it up. It was only ten in the morning, so he could possibly arrive in Tampa by nine that night.

While he traveled, he thought about what might be going on with Lucian. He was demonstrating abilities Jordan had only seen from one person; Maximus. Jordan had been led to believe Lucian couldn't be restored to his full power unless he drank Gallard's blood as well as Lela's and Solomon's, but Lucian hadn't fed on either. The only other possibility was that Maximus emptied the rest of his power into Lucian.

Jordan hoped that it wasn't the answer. Maximus needed his abilities in order to bring back Lydian and if he'd given away his power, she couldn't be raised from the dead. The only way he could find out was to either contact Maximus or get close enough to Lucian to witness the power for himself. More of it, anyway. He needed more back up if he was ever going to do that. Approaching Lucian alone would be idiotic and suicidal.

Around four, he stopped in Satesboro, Georgia to feed. He hadn't had much blood since he'd devoted his time and energy to spying. He could feel himself growing as obsessed with taking down Lucian as he had been four hundred years ago. When he wasn't spying, he was thinking about what his next move would be. Lydian's death no doubt was the cause for this. She'd given him perspective and kept him from being too involved. Now that she was gone and Lucian was rampant, he didn't have anything to keep him in check.

The Georgia weather was drastically different from New York. The humidity caused him to sweat even though it was late at night. He preferred the dry heat of Las Vegas. At least there it wasn't hard to breathe. He wanted to feed quickly so he could get out of there, check in on his family, and then hurry back to the perfect weather of Manhattan.

Jordan finally arrived in Tampa at the time he'd hoped and landed on the beach, not even caring who saw him He startled the people nearby, but they didn't pay attention to him for long. He took off his jacket, tossing it into the garbage then did the same with his shirt, only holding it in his hand. It was too hot for what he was wearing, and he would rather be bare-chested than bake in his black tank top.

He put his shirt back on when he got into town then took a taxi the rest of the way. Before they'd left for Miami from Vegas, Lela had gotten a cell phone, and they'd set up a plan so he could trace her location and vice versa. It was Gallard's idea so they could keep track of each other. He had trusted Jordan to take care of her if he was ever unable, and Jordan gladly accepted the responsibility.

His tracker indicated that she was about two miles away, so they should be close by. He thought about going in, but didn't want to risk running into them. He was supposed to be job hunting, not spying on Gallard and his sister-in-law.

THE RESURRECTION

Five minutes later, his phone beeped and he looked up as he approached the grand hotel. It would take too long to try and find out which room they were in, so he decided to do continuous sweeps of the place through the rest of the early morning. Lucian's spy was bound to be lurking nearby. He decided to stick around until he was sure no danger would come to them.

Chapter Thirty-Seven

I slipped out of my deep sleep, surrounded by warmth. The previous night had felt like one never-ending dream, and I had loved every moment of it. Imagining spending many nights like that with Gallard made me excited for our future. We were good together in more ways than one.

He was still close to me and had his arm around me, only it was over the blanket. I slipped my arm out so I could find his hand to hold in mine.

When I did find it, the smile left my face. I came into contact with warm skin. Gallard was never that warm. Sure he would be after getting out of a hot shower, but not like this. I let go of him, and my heart lurched in my chest.

Slowly, I twisted around so that I was facing him. I nearly shrieked but covered my mouth in time when I saw this stranger. There was a blonde man lying next to me, and his face was turned away. He wasn't just blonde; he was ice blonde. The color was nearly white compared to my golden hue. Whoever this was, I wanted to find out and quickly. Where was Gallard?

Trying not to wake him up, I removed myself from his embrace and slipped out of bed. I tiptoed to my suitcase and as quietly as I

THE RESURRECTION

could, put on some clothes. The man still hadn't woken up yet, so I decided to try and get a better look at him. I skirted the bed until I was next to him. He was definitely familiar. He had Gallard's physique and hair length. I noticed that Gallard's eye patch was on the nightstand.

The man moaned then sat up, and I backed away until I bumped into the door. He pushed his hair out of his face then looked at me. He definitely had Gallard's face. That's when I realized that this was Gallard. Something was very wrong.

"Good morning, Mrs. D'Aubigne," this strange blonde clone said. "Why on earth are you dressed?"

"You're...your hair!" I said, my voice shrill from shock and sleepiness. "What happened to your hair?"

He frowned. "What do you mean?"

He got up and clumsily tugged his pants on before attempting to run to the bathroom. He was moving very slowly, and he seemed as confused as I did. I followed him and watched as he stared and stared at his reflection. I did as well and noticed that not only was his hair different, but his left eye was no longer grey but baby blue.

Curious, I touched my hand to his neck and then his forehead. He was definitely warmer. Even warmer than me. Basically, he was at a normal body temperature.

"It's the blood," he said. "That's the only explanation. It has to be a reaction to your blood."

"How? I thought only your family's blood made you mortal!" My stomach turned. "Oh, God...we're not related are we?"

Gallard's shocked expression turned into a smile and he started laughing. I smacked his arm, shutting him right up.

"Ow! Careful. I'm mortal now, remember?"

"This isn't funny. We have to call Cherish. Maybe she'll know what's going on. We can't just ignore this, what if—"

"Hey!" he put his hands on my shoulders. "Breathe, babe. You're making me anxious just listening to you. Let's just take a deep breath and..." He inhaled through his nose and let the air escape his lips. He then chuckled. "I can breathe. Lela I can breathe!"

My anxiety was quickly turning into astonishment. I hadn't stopped to think about how pivotal this was for him. Gallard hadn't had a heartbeat nor had he drawn a breath in two hundred and fifty years. He was alive; really alive. While I was freaking out, he was in awe of this new development.

"Why are you blonde?" I asked, trying to take his advice and relax. "You never told me that you were blonde as a mortal."

"I guess it slipped my mind. I got my hair from my father's side. I'm sorry I didn't tell you. We can bond over our blondness."

I put my ear to his chest and listened in awe to his heartbeat. It was so strange since he hadn't had one for as long as I'd known him. I'd grown to appreciate my heartbeat since I'd lived without it for four years. I couldn't imagine living nearly three hundred years as he had with no vitals. No wonder he was so excited about this.

"What does this mean?" I asked. "Are you like David was?"

My mind raced with all the horrible things that could happen. I thought of my illness and how I had quickly started deteriorating within a month and a half. We had blood with us, but his situation was entirely different. It had taken me weeks to transition back into a mortal while he had changed within a matter of five hours.

"Only time can tell. I may be like him or…I may just be normal."

Normal. What I wouldn't give to be normal. It would make our lives so much simpler. Then again, normal for him was a wonderful thing while normal for me was complete dread. That would mean that in seventy years or less, he would be gone. We wouldn't have eternity like I thought. Like Melody, I would be forced to live on without the man I loved.

"What are you thinking about?" Gallard asked.

"The future." I looked up at him, my eyes brimming with tears. "How long we have."

He pulled me into his warm embrace and held me. I didn't cry, though. I had cried enough over the past several days. This was supposed to be a happy time. We had finally consummated our love and we were husband and wife. No sad tears were allowed on this honeymoon.

"Let's not worry about that right now," he said. "Let's enjoy our weekend and deal with the obstacles when they come." He pulled back and smiled. "Want to try out that huge bathtub?"

"Tempting, but you and I both know that if we did, we would never leave this hotel room."

THE RESURRECTION

"I suppose you're right. How about tonight instead?"

"It's a date."

I smiled then tugged him closer to me, kissing his neck while I held him. He chuckled, making no attempt to push me away. He lifted me up once more, and I giggled as he carried me to the bed. I knew our trip to town would be delayed. I sensed it was harder for him to carry me than usual but he never acted like he was straining. He got undressed more quickly than I did because I had on more layers.

As we came together, a long sigh escaped his lips. I hadn't expected it to be different, but it was. His mortality definitely made this all seem like a new experience. He was warmer and his temperature only continued to rise. I couldn't decide if it was better this way or just interesting. I would love doing this with him whether he was warm or not.

"This is so wonderful," he said. "I love you."

I let out a soft laugh. "Are you getting sappy on me, old man?"

"I'm not so old anymore. I'm back at twenty-five again."

"You'll always be an old man to me."

He pressed his lips to mine and steadied himself as he continued to move with me. I could tell he was losing steam and that was another thing I would never get used to. Him being tired. He would have to go from never sleeping to needing it every night to get him through the day. It would be a learning experience for both of us. For a moment, I forgot about the future and looked forward to what we would accomplish together.

As he had his release, his body trembled. At the same time, I felt a rush of heat that I hadn't experienced the night before. Suddenly, he stopped kissing me and looked into my eyes.

"I apologize," he said. He got off of me and went into the bathroom. I was going to question him when he came back with a towel and started cleaning me up. "I didn't know that would happen. I would have acted sooner or—"

"Gallard, hey." I put a hand over his to stop him. "What are you doing?"

He dropped the towel then sat on the edge of the bed with the sheet covering him. "That hasn't happened in nearly three hundred years."

"Really?" I sat up as well, unsure of what to say. I hadn't planned on addressing the situation. This was new to me, but I was well aware of human biology. What had happened was normal. A sign that he truly was mortal again. "Are you okay?"

"I'm fine." He turned to me. "Are you? Did I make you uncomfortable?"

I hugged him around his waist from behind. "You never make me uncomfortable. This is just a normal way of life. You don't have to be ashamed of it."

He kissed my cheek then rested his temple against mine.

This getaway was proving to be more exciting than I thought. I wasn't as worried as I was earlier and the more time I spent with him, the more I fell in love with him, if that was possible.

We finally found the strength to get away from each other, and I chose something comfortable and weather appropriate to wear. I showered first then sat on the bed with the TV on while Gallard had his turn. Nothing good was on, so I turned it to the news and pretended to be invested in what they were talking about.

Apparently, there had been a series of strange events occurring in Manhattan, like earthquakes and energy spikes picked up by the satellites in space. For a second I thought I was watching some sci-fi movie, but the story was so interesting that after a while, I wasn't pretending to watch anymore. I turned up the volume so I could hear better and listened to the theories the earthquake experts suggested.

Over the course of three days, there had been five earthquakes in Manhattan. They couldn't seem to locate the source, but they were starting to get worried. The quakes weren't too bad, though. Nothing was damaged, save for some cracks in the sidewalk and a few stores had shelves fall over. This didn't concern people any less. They were afraid that something was underneath the ground and some thought it was signs of the end times.

I found it oddly coincidental that these earthquakes began showing up around the same time I killed those night-walkers. But Manhattan was several miles away from Virginia. How could the two events be connected? Unless Lucian had something to do with it. If he did, how would he cause tectonic shifts in the earth? He didn't have that kind of power, did he?

I heard Gallard come out of the bathroom, and I shut the TV off.

THE RESURRECTION

I was supposed to be enjoying my new marriage, not worrying about crazy ol' Lucian. If he was causing mayhem somewhere, it wasn't our problem. We weren't responsible for every vampire that decided to be mischievous.

"Are you ready to go?" he asked.

"I am if you are."

I stood up and grabbed my purse and key before taking his hand He pushed down on the door handle but stopped before opening it.

"Do we really have to leave?" he asked. "We could have just as much of a good time in here."

"Yes we do, Casanova. You said it yourself; we need to start living a normal life and do normal things. Touring museums is what normal people do."

"The museums will still be there in two hours." He put his hands on the small of my back, pulling me closer to him. "You know what we could do?" He whispered in my ear then I gasped in surprise at what he'd suggested.

"Mr. D'Aubigne! You are naughtier than I thought."

"So, that's a no?"

His warm lips met mine, and I lost myself in his kiss. It didn't matter to me that he was mortal. Warm, cold; vampire or human, he was still my Gallard.

We were in danger of getting carried away, so I reluctantly ended our make-out session then we attempted to leave again when I noticed something move past the glass doors. By instinct, I ran across the room and onto the deck to see what it was. It couldn't be a bird. The shadow was way too big. It had to be a man.

I looked on both sides of the deck then up into the sky and sure enough, there was a bat flying away. I didn't have to see it up close to know it wasn't a normal bat. Someone definitely had been on our deck and whoever they were, probably spied on us.

"What is it?" Gallard asked when he joined me.

"Someone was just here, a vampire. I think they were watching us."

"Are you serious? Where did he go? Did you see him?"

"Only in animal form. Gallard, what if it was Lucian? What if he was watching us last night?"

Gallard looked like he was going to be sick; his expression showing how I felt. I didn't want to imagine Lucian acting as a peeping Tom. He'd invaded my private thoughts before, what would stop him from invading my privacy in the real world? The thought disturbed me and I shuddered at the idea. Why couldn't he leave me be? Why couldn't he be obsessed with someone who actually wanted to be at his side?

"Should we tell someone?" I asked.

"Maybe if we notice anything else suspicious. For now, let's try to forget about this. I don't really feel like staying in anymore."

"You and me both. Let's get out of here."

When he felt like he'd gotten the information he needed, Lucian commanded Alexander to leave and return to Manhattan. It had taken him all night to lead his vessel to Lela's location, and he'd only arrived that morning. He'd barely gotten away in time when Lela spotted him on the balcony.

There was no reason to stay longer anyway. He'd seen enough; heard enough to be filled with so much jealousy and confusion that he'd caused the very furniture in the room to levitate, or so he'd been told. His own sight hadn't been restored yet, and the only way he could block out Alexander's perspective was by closing his eyes.

He'd correctly directed his follower to Lela's location with the purpose of maybe trying another way of splitting her and Gallard apart. Their marriage had happened too quickly, and he was sure they would soon run into problems as a result. But when he'd seen her with this man; the blonde with the strange eye patch, he couldn't believe what he was seeing.

Though he knew it was wrong, he had Alexander stay and watch. Every second brought Lucian pain; when they laughed together, as she kissed him; made love to him. What Lucian wanted to know most of all was why she'd chosen this stranger and not him.

Why did he want her so badly? Before she'd come back, he'd felt attached to her and she fascinated him, though he never craved

THE RESURRECTION

her this way. It was as if he needed her, like she was the answer to his problems. He didn't like this obsession that he'd developed; he didn't want to need her or anyone for that matter. Yet, he couldn't bring himself to abandon her.

As if Alexander read Lucian's mind, he'd flown off from the balcony and began to soar over the beach. Lucian's spy had become nothing but a robot; a conduit for him. The longer he saw through Alexander's eyes, the more he'd learned how to control not just his vision, but his actions as well.

You must forget about her, the familiar voice said. *She will only bring you ruin.*

How? I want her and nothing will change that. I believe you are wrong. She belongs to me.

That shaman foresaw this. The man with hair of gold will be our undoing. He must die.

Lucian agreed. Whoever that stranger was, he was the one thing in the way of Lela being his. The man would die and then he could move on to his next plan.

Alexander was almost into the city when another bat slammed into him from the side. Lucian fell to the floor in the hotel as if he'd been struck himself. He got up then waited to see if the assailant would attack again, which it did. The bat flew at him once more then both Alexander and the other transformed, falling out of the sky and landing on the rough sand in their human forms.

"Did you think I'd let you get away with spying on my family?" the man snarled. Lucian stared at the man's face then it clicked who he was.

"Jordan. Well, well, it looks like you have secrets of your own!"

"I know you're really Lucian. I saw that whole creepy ritual with the blood on this man's eyes. What did you plan for him to do, huh?"

Lucian had Alexander grab onto Jordan's throat and begin to strangle him, but Jordan was stronger. He pried Alexander's hands off of him then broke his wrist. Lucian yelled, but realized he was only feeling his conduit's pain.

He is the other one, the voice whispered. *You stole his life.*
What do you mean?
Jordanes. His blood is your blood. He wants to kill you. You must kill

366

him first.

"Jordanes," Lucian said aloud. Jordan's eyes grew wide and he stood up, allowing Alexander to stand as well.

"How do you know that name?"

"Our creator sent you to kill me. Apparently, you are me. The real me, that is."

Jordan glared then grabbed Alexander by his shirt, shaking him violently.

"You spoke with Maximus? Where is he? Why did he reveal himself to you?"

These were all questions Lucian had, himself. He wanted to kill Maximus for forcing this evil power onto him. He wanted him to take it back so he could be of sound mind again; to think clearly and to be free of his dark desires for death, destruction; and for her.

"I do not know, Jordanes. He disappeared after we spoke."

"Whatever. What concerns me more is that you're still hanging around my sister-in-law like a creepy pervert. You need to get it through your thick skull that she doesn't want you. She never has and never will."

Lucian gave him a menacing smile. "Oh, Jordanes, you are very wrong. She will come to me. She's already left Gallard for that man she was with and soon she'll grow tired of him. And when she does, I will be waiting for her. And I will kill anyone who gets in my way. Including Gallard."

Jordan's face filled with a rage that Lucian didn't know was possible then Jordan began to tear Alexander's body apart, slowly killing him. Lucian's body tensed up and he writhed on the floor, trying to use his mind to end the connection.

Almost instantly, the pain ceased and the view of Jordan's wrathful expression disappeared before turning into the view of Lucian's hotel room. He had his sight back now that his conduit was dead and a breath of relief escaped
his lips.

Everything that had happened; his spying on Lela and her new lover; Jordan's threats; none of it swayed his original plans. Come Monday, everything would be in place and they wouldn't be prepared for what he had in store for them.

Chapter Thirty-Eight

Cherish groaned as the music on the phone began to play for the fifteenth time. She'd been on hold with the Blacksburg Police Department for a half an hour and was beginning to lose her patience. How hard could it be to locate her sister's body? There could only be so many people who were beheaded in the past week.

Now, she could believe it if Melody's death occurred in Chicago. It was the murder capital of America. Cherish had been groped, held at gun point, and nearly robbed within a two-hour span at one point and often wondered why she'd chosen such a place to live. Then she would remember it was because she could feed as much as she wanted without the deaths being suspicious. Nobody batted an eye to another body in the dumpster. It was a normal occurrence.

The music stopped then someone began to speak. Cherish wanted to complain to them about how long it took, but didn't want to waste any more time. The sooner she could bring Melody home, the better. She would be able to grieve her death better, knowing that she was buried in a cemetery instead of lying in a morgue.

"Miss Toffee, this is Detective Dean. I'm sorry for the wait. How can I help you?"

"It's Too-*fay*. Anyway, I'm calling to see if my sister's body can be released to me. Her name is Melody Davis. She was killed four days ago, and I was told that they would be done with the autopsy by this afternoon."

Cherish heard the detective clicking away at his keyboard. She'd hoped that the last person she'd spoken with had already talked to him about all of this so he would have the information ready by the time he got on the phone.

"Well, Miss...*Tophé*, it appears everything is ready to go. If you could just give me an address of your preferred funeral home, you sister can be sent there within the next couple of days."

"Thank you so much Detective, I appreciate your help."

She gave him the address then hung up, feeling relieved that this was taken care of. Solomon had gone back to Italy three days before, leaving her to do everything on her own. She had no idea how to plan a funeral or what needed to be done in regards to burying Melody.

As long as she'd lived, she'd never gone to a funeral, save for Melody's husband Theodore. That had been back when people made their own coffins and just buried them in the ground themselves. Funerals made her uneasy because they reminded her of when she'd dug herself out of
her own grave.

Cherish decided to text Solomon the good news. She knew he would be just as glad to know Melody was coming home as she was. He'd loved Melody like a daughter and could always get her to laugh. He didn't tell his funny jokes now, but Cherish was determined to get the old Solomon back; the one who wasn't so guilt-ridden and serious all the time.

The police are all done with the autopsy. Mel comes home in a few days, she texted.

Solomon responded: *That's wonderful news! I'll fly back this afternoon and help you with the arrangements.*

Giving her reply some thought, she smiled before texting again: *What are you wearing?*

Jeans and a crew neck. Why?

Don't you want to know what I'm wearing? He didn't reply, so she sent, *If you stay at my place tonight, you'll find out.*

Tempting, but I can't. There is something I want to discuss with you, though. I'll see you soon.

Pouting, she sent, *Tease.* She didn't see why he'd left when he was only going to come back soon. He'd claimed she tempted him too much. Oh, she was tempted, all right. Tempted to take his cardinal robes and burn them herself.

Since she was home alone, she decided to pass the time cleaning her apartment. It needed extensive tidying and she would rather clean than drive herself crazy sitting around and doing nothing. Now that she didn't have a job, she had too much free time on her hands. Solomon wasn't filling any of that free time, so cleaning was her only option.

Someone buzzed her just as she'd finished moving all the furniture. She hoped it wasn't Penelope showing up to see if she was still alive. Penelope was too nosy for her liking and only talked with her because she was one of the less annoying coworkers at her job. Like her father, Cherish didn't like to be around people that much. She preferred the comfort of her own home.

Cherish hit the button and said, "This is Charity, who is it?"

"It's Jordan. You busy?"

She hit the buzzer for him then waited for him to come up. She hadn't expected to hear from Jordan so soon, or at all. Everyone had gone their separate ways after giving up on Lucian. She'd thought everyone would disappear and not contact each other until Christmas or some other significant holiday.

He knocked two minutes later, and she opened the door to let him in. He looked like a mess; unshaven, wearing the same clothes he'd had on when they were in Virginia. Usually Jordan was more put together than this.

"Ever heard of a shower?" she asked.

"Later. I have something important you need to hear."

They went into the living room and sat on the couch. Jordan plopped down like he'd been on his feet for days. She could tell he hadn't been feeding enough by his lack of energy and she began to get concerned. Something was weighing on his mind, and it was affecting him physically and mentally. She could see it in his eyes.

"So what did you want to tell me?"

"Kevin and I have been spying on Lucian these past few days. Unlike everyone else, we didn't think he was done with us. We made the right choice because he isn't. I had a confrontation with him this morning. He said he wants to kill us all."

Cherish didn't say a word, but rested her head on the couch. This was just what she needed; her father getting all revenge crazy and wanting to go on a rampage. He'd always threatened to do this whenever someone made him angry. She'd heard him complain several times to Solomon about her mother or overhearing someone insulting him. Her father didn't know how to handle problems without violence.

"He'll get over it," she said. "He's done this before. He threatens to wreak havoc then once he's calmed down, everything goes back to normal."

"He's not happy. I caught him spying on Gallard and Lela in Florida. He really wants her, Cher. And he doesn't care what he has to do to get her."

Cherish's heart went out to Lela. She knew what it was like to be the object of her father's obsession. His attachment to her wasn't as creepy as his was to Lela, but he'd let his goal of making Cherish his protégé above everything else; even what she wanted.

"Do Gallard and Lela know about his creeping around?" she asked.

"I'm not sure. Sooner or later, we're going to have to inform them of this new development. I hate to interrupt their honeymoon, but they need to know they're in danger. At least Gallard is, anyway."

"Okay. We'll tell them tomorrow. But for now, you need a shower."

Cherish got up from the couch, and he followed her. She was glad he didn't protest or she would have sprayed him with the sink nozzle herself. She grabbed him a towel from the closet then gave it to him before pointing him in the direction of the bathroom.

"If I leave my clothes outside the door, could wash them?" he asked.

"Does this look like the Hilton? I'm not your maid."

"How about I cook for you in return? I can cook a mean steak."

He gave a sly smile then stripped down right in front of her, tossing his clothes on the floor before going into the bathroom. It happened so fast she didn't even have time to react. She'd always assumed Jordan was like Gallard, but she'd judged wrong. He was the complete opposite. Though as he walked away, she didn't hesitate to stare and she had to admit that she liked what she saw.

Trying to forget about what just happened, she went back to her cleaning after. She didn't do it as wholeheartedly as she'd planned to. Her mind was now on her father and his plan to massacre them. Why was he being so stubborn? If he would just act like a civilized human being, maybe she would have considered trying to build a healthier relationship with him. Instead, he had to be difficult and go after something he couldn't have, as always.

When she finished vacuuming, she went into the hall to grab Jordan's clothes then tossed them into the washer, accept for this jacket. It didn't look like it needed washing, so she hung it up on a hanger and returned to the kitchen to make lunch. Cleaning seemed pointless now that there was a possibility they would have to regroup and fight. She occasionally liked a good fight, but not right now. Cherish was starting to think that she was never going to fully have a free life. Her father would always be around to make sure of that.

She'd just taken the steak out of the fridge as Jordan came out of the bathroom. He'd shaved and looked a lot better than when he'd arrived. The only strange thing was that he was wearing her robe.

"I uh…didn't know what else to wear," he said. "I figured you wouldn't mind."

"No not at all. You've already barged in here, did a strip tease and ordered me to do your laundry. You might as well wear my clothes too," she said with blatant sarcasm.

As he'd promised, he started cooking the steak. She thought it was odd that a vampire knew how to cook so well, and then she remembered that Jordan had only been immortal for about a year and a half. He didn't act like the typical newbie, and she was impressed with his stealth. He'd shown up in the middle of the day. How had he managed that?

The more she looked at him, the more he seemed familiar. Besides the obvious fact that Jordan looked like Gallard's near-twin, something about him was strange. She would have remembered if she'd run into him in the past. Gallard once told her that Jordan used to farm somewhere in Wisconsin and she'd never been there before.

"This might seem like a weird question but…we've never met before this, right?" she asked.

"You're a very beautiful woman, Cherish. I would have remembered if we met."

She fought a smile then turned her face away so he wouldn't notice her blushing. Men didn't usually use the word beautiful when describing her. It was always seductive, sexy, sultry, or something along those lines.

"Did you spend any time in London at all?" she asked.

"I've only been immortal for a little while. How could we have met in London?"

"I don't know…It's just that you're always so quiet. Quiet people are usually the ones with all the secrets."

He turned the steak over then sprinkled some seasoning on it. His lack of reply started making her suspicious. What secrets could Jordan possibly have? He was a farmer. But Gallard had brought up that Jordan went missing for several hours after she'd left with her father.

"So um. Back in South Carolina; where did you go?" she asked nonchalantly.

"You heard about that? I was running an errand. I got caught up in traffic and everybody freaked out."

"What errand?" she asked, more boldly this time. "I'm curious, what was so important that you ditched Kevin and Robin without so much as texting him?"

Jordan set down the fork he was using to push the meat around then stared at her. She expected him to be angry or hostile, but instead he looked hesitant or reluctant about whatever he was thinking.

"Can I trust you?" he asked, almost whispering.

"Yes, I know how to keep a secret. I did manage to keep everyone thinking I was dead for the past four hundred years."

He slowly took her hand. She was surprised by how warm his touch was, and she realized that this was the first time he'd ever touched her. They hadn't even shaken hands when they'd met and she never hugged him. But what shocked her even more was that when he put her hand to his chest, she felt a flutter.

"Is that a heartbeat?" she asked him. He nodded then she bravely put her ear to his chest to see if it wasn't a trick. She heard it loud and clear, drumming at the same rate as any human. "I thought…didn't Gallard turn you?"

"Didn't Robin tell you? Gallard is magical." He chuckled. "I let him believe that he did. But I've been around a lot longer than he thinks. Even longer than you."

When she didn't reply he continued saying, "March twelfth, fifteen fifty-seven. It was Melody's birthday, and you danced with me. I tried to strike up a conversation, but you said my accent was too hard for you to understand. Then you said you didn't want to talk with me anyway. That's when you dragged me into the sitting room."

Cherish gasped in shock as it all started coming back to her. He was the foreign Earl that she'd lost her virginity to. He was different then; he'd had longer hair, a full beard, and if she recalled; brown eyes.

"Why did you sleep with me?" she asked. "Besides the obvious."

"I knew that if you got involved with me, your father would be furious. It was initially to make him mad, but then you chose Byron instead. It kind of ruined my plan."

"You knew my father? Why were you angry with him?"

"The same reason I'm still angry at him. He's a psycho."

He finished cooking her steak then they went into the living room to talk while she ate. He told her everything; his mistaken death, his plot to avenge his parents' murder. Cherish couldn't believe that the man she'd fought alongside with was more extraordinary than she could ever have imagined. Why he was telling her this now, she didn't know. She would have thought he would want to reveal this to Gallard. Maybe he was feeling as lonely as she was.

"Who else knows?" she asked once he was finished.

"Kevin. He figured it out when he found my contacts case. I got distracted and was caught. He's promised to keep it a secret…for now. Eventually I will tell everyone."

Part of the robe was hanging open, and she happened to glance at his chest. She hadn't exactly looked him over during their past two weeks on the road and never realized how ripped he was.

Honestly, she hadn't paid that much attention to him when they hooked up, plus it was dark and he'd kept his shirt on. Jordan had somehow managed to fade into the background on this mission. Until now.

"I noticed you had scars on your back. How did you get them?" she asked.

"The man who kidnapped me. He loved his rum, but he loved his whip even more. I was really defiant towards him and I often paid for it too. I forget they're there until someone brings them up." He looked at her with a sneaky smile. "Cherish, were you checking me out?" he asked, covering up like he was trying to be modest.

"Yes."

"Aren't you with Solomon?"

"No. He doesn't want to be with me because he's in the church. Solomon…he's like a pastry."

Jordan laughed. "A what?"

"A pastry! You know, like when your mother lets you try one and it's very delicious, but then when you go back for seconds, she says you have to wait until dinner." She looked at Jordan's face then sighed. "My goodness. What is it about you D'Aubigne men that make you pour out your heart when you don't want to?"

Jordan shrugged then leaned back on the couch. "It's the genes, I guess. So what I'm getting is that you and Solomon aren't…"

Cherish shook her head. She really didn't want to have this conversation with him, but she didn't have anyone else to confide in. Gallard had always given her good advice when they were friends and she figured Jordan might as well.

"He won't even kiss me anymore. I've come onto him so many times and he keeps rejecting me. He never specifically asked me to wait for him, so I don't know where he stands. What should I do?"

"Me. Think of me as a do over. We never really got to savor the moment back then. Not to mention that it was the most uncomfortable chair I've ever sat in. No strings attached, of course."

Now it was Cherish's turn to laugh. Jordan was definitely different than Gallard; more outspoken and not as noble. When she and Gallard had a tryst, he'd apologized several times, claiming that she was worth more than that. He even gave her flowers. She'd never received *Sorry I slept with you* gifts before. Gallard was one of a kind.

Jordan moved so that their faces were only two inches apart. Cherish knew she had to make a choice. She wasn't officially dating Solomon. It could be forever before he would officially leave the church. He'd never actually asked her to wait for him, so what if she did happen to hook up with someone? It wasn't like she was in love with Jordan. She could have a little fun with him.

He made the choice for her when he parted her lips with his, kissing her until she was dizzy. He was an amazing kisser, and she was surprised by how much she liked it. Jordan was not the reserved, quiet guy he'd appeared to be. She lost herself in the moment, not caring what he did to her, only focusing on him.

Jordan stopped for a moment and said, "Wait...I must warn you that I am like your father. I can father children."

"You didn't seem concerned back then."

"I was trying to knock you up back then."

"Wow, really? Whatever, it's not an issue for me anymore."

As she kissed him once more, he then lay her back on the couch. He pulled off her shirt then undid her jeans, tugging them of and tossing them to the side. She wrapped her legs around his waist and her arms around his neck. Somehow, her mind went back to his comment and she stopped them this time.

"Wait. You were trying to get me pregnant?"

"Yes...I don't see how that's confusing to you."

She gently pushed him away and sat up. Trying to go back nearly five hundred years, she mentally calculated the timing. It had always puzzled her how Byron had gotten her pregnant when he'd used protection every time. He didn't want an accidental child any more than she did. They had been seeing each other three months before she found out. Had she been pregnant that entire time?

"Jordan...I think you might have."

He laughed. "You can't be serious."

"Actually, I am." She looked at him. "The child I lost because of my accident could have been yours."

The teasing smile left his face and he blanched. This was the worst possible time to have this kind of epiphany. Now neither of them were in the mood. It wouldn't have changed anything for her. Byron was a scumbag no matter what and she still ached for the child she could have had. But the wound would be fresher for Jordan.

"This is messed up," he said. "That can't be right. It was Byron's."

"He always used protection, Jordan. I might be a slut but I'm a smart slut. I knew Lucian would kill me if I ever got knocked up. When we were together at that party, it was my first time, and I thought…I thought you couldn't get pregnant on your first time."

He smirked. "So much for being a smart slut."

She punched his arm. "Not helping! It doesn't matter now. I'm passed childbearing age and I can't contract diseases. My body fights them off before they manifest."

"Well, I never ceased to be able to produce sperm. But I use protection. As far as I know, Gallard is the only one left from my bloodline. I can't be a father right now. Not when I'm so obsessed with taking down Lucian. I neglected my children in the past because of my agenda and I wouldn't do that again. Being in Gallard's life is enough for me. He's like my brother and my son all at once. I can't really explain it. I feel protective of him."

Cherish smiled then leaned over and kissed him. She understood exactly how he felt. Gallard always felt the need to protect people and she always wondered who would protect him. She'd mentored him like an older sister. Now he had Lela, and they could look out for each other.

"Let's forget all this heavy stuff," she suggested. "If you're still up for it, I would like a redo of that night at the party."

Taking her advice, he tugged off the robe and they picked up where they left off. Afterwards, she lay there with his arms around her and she felt satisfied. He'd managed to make her forget all the loneliness and frustration she was feeling. Not to mention she'd had a good time. He was spectacular in more ways than one. It was ten times better than the first time they were together.

He began to massage her back and she sighed as her body began to relax. She then thought of what Melody had told her Lela said about Gallard and his magic hands and began to chuckle to herself.

"What is it?" Jordan asked.

"Magic hands must run in the family."

THE RESURRECTION

His hand moved onto her hip and then slid it over her stomach. He moved it lower and she pushed it away.

"No. No more," she said. "We'll never leave this couch."

"I wasn't even going there. I was just curious." His hand moved there once more. "What is that?"

Her eyes flew open and she realized he was talking about her scar.

"It's nothing," she said as she pushed his hand away again.

"Come on. I told you about mine. It's only fair that you tell me about yours."

Cherish hesitated before answering. As usual, his D'Aubigne charm was inspiring her to be honest. It was hard lying to Gallard in the past, let alone keeping her secret about her identity. And now it was hard to keep things from Jordan.

"After I confronted Byron about my carrying his child—"

"Possibly *our* child."

She groaned. "I can't even think about that. Anyway, I was kicked by a spooked horse. I was eight months pregnant at the time and went into early labor. The doctor knew my baby was in danger, so he had to cut it out. There wasn't even time for laudanum or any kind of numbing solution. I felt everything and it was the most painful experience of my life."

She closed her eyes, trying not to cry.

"They'd told my father of my condition, but he wouldn't come. He was still angry with me, so Solomon came instead. He stayed the entire time and didn't leave until I was fully recovered. He even..." now she could feel the tears coming, "He tried to convince the doctor to let me hold my stillborn son, though it wasn't customary to do so in those days. He wasn't able to, but I can't remember if I thanked him for trying."

That was when it hit; the overwhelming guilt. This reminisce on the past reminded her of all the things Solomon had done for her. He must have loved her. Why else would he have been so devoted? Now all she could picture was Solomon's face when he would find out that she'd gone behind his back. She'd told herself it wasn't cheating, but deep down she knew better.

"Are you okay?" Jordan asked, kissing her forehead.

"I'm fine. I just need a minute."

Cherish grabbed the robe that was draped around them; quickly slipping into it then ran to bathroom. She loathed herself to the point where she was going to be sick. She turned on the sink and filled a paper cup with water, drinking it down quickly then filled it again. She'd never loathed herself more than she did in this moment. She hated her own reflection in the mirror.

When she came back out, she stepped on something that was on the floor. She looked down and saw it was a piece of paper so she picked it up to see what it said. It was a letter from Jordan saying,

Thanks for listening to me. Don't worry about G and L. Will call them about the problem. As for Solomon, don't give up. He'll come around eventually. Lastly, even though we will never know if your child was mine, I am still sorry for your loss. I know what it's like to lose a child. If you ever need to talk to someone, you have my number. J

He was stealthy. She hadn't even heard him leave. Not to mention he had amazing penmanship. He wrote in calligraphy.

She spent the rest of the day curled up in her bed, wallowing in her intense guilt. She didn't even have the will to eat or get up. She'd only had the emotional energy to get dressed and put away her cleaning supplies.

The buzzer sounded again later that evening and it startled her. It had to be Solomon. He'd said he would be in by that night. How could she face him after what she'd done? She wanted to justify it by saying she didn't really trust that Solomon loved her, but that would be a lie. She knew he did, and she'd cheated on him for a few moments of pleasure that she truly wanted from him, alone.

Cherish never spoke to him and just hit the button to let him in instead. She had about a minute to build up the courage to be honest with him. There was no use waiting until later.

Solomon knocked and she opened the door, keeping her eyes cast down. If she made eye contact with him, she knew she would start blubbering. She needed to save the tears of guilt for after the big reveal.

"Hello, Solomon," she said. "How was your—"

THE RESURRECTION

"Before you continue, I have to say something. I was going to wait until after the funeral, but I feel compelled to get everything out right now."

Cherish grew quiet as he took her hands in his. He hadn't even said hello back, which meant whatever he had to say was important.

"I love you, *Accarezzare*. I always have and I always will. I have officially left the church." He chuckled. "I just...handed in my robes and said I was done. I did this for you because...I do want to be with you. I never want to leave your side again, and want to take care of you for the rest of our eternal existence."

She chewed on the inside of her mouth then forced herself to look at his face. He couldn't have picked a worse time to profess his love to her. If only he'd done this the last time he was here, then maybe she wouldn't have made a stupid mistake.

"Solomon...I have to tell you something." She let go of his hands. "Jordan was here today."

"Oh? Don't tell me Lucian is throwing another tantrum?"

Cherish nodded, folding her arms then walked away. There was no easy way to tell him this. She knew how he would feel because she'd felt the same way when she learned Byron was married. Would Solomon forgive her? He was a Cardinal after all. His profession was forgiving people of their sins in confession. Or was this indiscretion too terrible to forgive?

"What I want to tell you doesn't have to do with my father."

He turned her around and took her face in his hands, stroking her cheek with his thumb.

"You can tell me, *Accarezzare*."

Her eyes filled up with tears and she hung her head in shame. "Jordan and I...we...he was here and we were talking. And then...it just kind of happened, and I—"

Solomon dropped his hands, and his expression said it all. Cherish waited for him to start crying or to yell at her, or do something to show how angry he was with her. But he only stared at her with such pain.

"Was it because I won't touch you?" he asked. "Cherish, you don't understand this at all, do you?"

"Understand what?"

"I won't touch you *because* I love you. You have this idea that a man won't care about you if you don't give yourself to him, but that isn't true with me. I've lived the promiscuous life, and it was all meaningless. But I feel more with you by just holding you in my arms than I did with anyone from my past."

"You never asked me to wait for you. How was I supposed to know you wanted to be with me if you never said it?"

"There was my mistake. I thought you cared enough that I didn't have to ask. Clearly I was wrong and should have spoken up sooner." He closed his eyes, turning away from her. "You are more like your father than I thought. You've had this warped sense of love that was drilled into you for so long that you can't even see when someone cares about you."

She'd almost gotten hostile when he compared her to her father, but what he'd said made sense. She didn't know what real love was like. When Solomon came back into her life, she'd gotten a glimpse of what true devotion should be. And she'd tarnished it for a few moments of pleasure. If he ever forgave her, she would be shocked because she wouldn't if they were in each other's shoes.

"I suppose this threat is serious if Jordan made the trip here. I will call him and get more of the details. Maybe you should pack. I have a feeling we'll be making another trip."

Cherish nodded and went into her room to change as well as pack. All of this could have been prevented if she could only give up her bad habit of hurting those around her. Solomon was right; Cherish was like her father. She'd been betrayed and hurt those around her to save herself from being hurt by others. If she didn't stop doing this, she was going to end up like Lucian, and she would rather die again than let that happen.

Chapter Thirty-Nine

Gallard and Lela got back to their room really late that night. They kept finding more and more places to visit, and Gallard wanted to stop at every food stand they came across to try everything; hotdogs, donuts, even a hamburger whose patty had been cooked with bacon inside of it. Lela was afraid that he would keel over from a heart attack, but he only got a small case of heartburn.

While they were out, they didn't say anything about what had happened that morning. If they thought about Lucian's spying on them, they wouldn't have been able to enjoy their trip. As long as Lucian was doing just that; watching, they weren't going to worry, even though it was super creepy and disturbing.

Lela tossed her purse on the floor then flopped onto the bed and Gallard did the same. They were exhausted from all that walking and the fact that they didn't really sleep the night before didn't help matters either. He knew they'd agreed to try out the bathtub, but he could barely keep his eyes open.

"Can we postpone the romantic bathtub date for tomorrow?" he asked.

"What bathtub date? Oh right! Yeah…too tired."

She got up then started to take off his shoes and socks. He figured she wanted to help him out since he was probably more exhausted than she.

Lela was about to go look for some sweats in his bag when he grabbed her and pulled her on top of him. She laughed as he covered her face in kisses.

"You know, I'm suddenly not so tired anymore," he said.

"Oh, is that so?"

Gallard sat up, with her in his lap and smiled. He was sort of lying. He was so tired he could probably fall asleep anywhere. If they tried the tub tonight, he would definitely fall asleep and she would have to drag him out of it and carry him to the bed. It wouldn't be too difficult since she was three times as strong as he was, but she was tired as well and would probably drop him.

"Listen, about what I suggested earlier…I feel bad about it," he said.

"Really? Why?"

"Because! I know that this kind of relationship is new to you, and I don't want you to feel pressured by me just because we're married. And I promise I'm not into anything freaky. I guess I was just feeling frisky this morning and didn't stop to think."

Lela rested her head on his shoulder. He'd almost forgotten the conversation from that morning until they were back in the room. He'd always been so cautious around her before they were even together and was working on trying not to be that way. They were married now, and bonded for life. He wanted to be as comfortable around her as she was with him.

"I don't feel pressured at all. You're good to me, and I love you no matter what weirdo things you're into. But we must be clear that I am *not* swinging. I draw the line at that."

He laughed then began to kiss her, caressing her legs as he did. She had her eyes closed, but his remained on the glass doors. He suddenly remembered the man she'd seen hiding there and the uneasy feeling that came with his discovery. He wanted so badly to have peace of mind that the spying was a one-time thing, but he couldn't.

Gallard didn't want her to worry, so instead of voicing his concerns, he stood up and took her hand, leading her into the bathroom. If they were going to enjoy their alone time, it would

THE RESURRECTION

have to be somewhere no one could possibly see. The doors didn't have curtains, so their only other option was trying out the tub like he'd suggested.

The warm water was perfect for his tired leg muscles and the bubble bath that was provided had a relaxing scent. As he lay there with Lela resting against him, I was afraid she would fall asleep first. Gallard, however, decided to drink some coffee while she'd filled the tub and was more wired than he'd ever been in his life. He kept talking to her, trying to help her stay awake too.

"You want to know what I first realized that I loved you?" he asked her.

"It wasn't when you gazed at me while I cut your hair?"

"No. It was a few months before that." He held her left hand in his and stroked her wedding band. "It was when I saw Tyler's engagement ring on your finger. It hit me that you might be another man's wife, and I wasn't ready for how disappointed it made me feel. I had to decide whether I was going to let you go and lose you forever or if I was going to speak up."

Lela shifted so she was facing him. "But you didn't speak up. You tried to help me tell him the truth. Why?"

"I saw how happy you were when you were with him. I couldn't find it in me to ruin that. I do have to admit that when you two broke up, I wasn't completely sad about it. I hated that you were hurt by what he said to you, but then I knew I still had a chance. And it all worked out perfectly. All I had to do was wait and see if you felt the same way." He hugged her tightly then relaxed against the tub. "All right, new topic. I wanted to finish our conversation from before. About…children."

He waited to see how she would respond. She didn't say anything so he continued.

"I don't want to pressure you into something you don't want. However, I do hope we can agree to find some common ground. Would you be open to discuss it sometime in the future?"

Lela didn't say a word, and he decided to wait for her to give it some thought. He wasn't sure why he was pushing this. Bodoway's vision of Lucian and Lela with a child had scared him and he could barely think of anything else. If he couldn't stop it, he wanted Lela to know that no matter what happened, he would still love her and this possible child. Or maybe the vision meant something completely different. Maybe the child wasn't even hers. There were so many possible explanations it was making him dizzy.

"Ten years," she finally said. She turned around to face him. "We can discuss it in ten years."

He crooked his mouth. "How about…five?"

She shifted so that she was sitting on his legs and wrapped her arms around his neck.

"Eight years."

Resting his hands on her hips, he pulled her closer to him. He was determined to use any tactics he could to get her to change her mind. Like David, she was incredibly stubborn. It was always so funny watching her and David whenever they disagreed on something. Sometimes he would wonder how they were not related until he learned that they were.

"Six years," he said.

She pressed her lips together. "Seven.

His hand traveled over her the top of her thigh then traveled lower. She let out a small gasp as he began pleasuring her. He tried to focus on what he was doing while at the same time trying to persuade her into lowering her number. He had always been good at multitasking.

"Six and a half?" he whispered into her ear.

Her body trembled and she took a deep breath. "Six years…nine months."

"Six years, eight months."

He continued touching her, watching her slowly succumb to his spell. He quickly forgot what they were even talking about and got lost in the moment. Once she was spent, she rested her forehead on his shoulder and he switched to massaging her back the way she liked it.

"All right." She sat up and looked at him. "In six years and eight months I will consider adding a child to our family."

Gallard smiled and gave her a firm kiss. He knew he would be able to persuade her otherwise. Six years wasn't that long. He felt like those four years he spent with her had gone by quickly. For an immortal six years was nothing. Then again, he was no longer immortal.

THE RESURRECTION

Someone knocked on the door and they grew silent. Housekeeping had already stopped by when they were out, so it couldn't be them. He had a bad feeling about this, so he got out of the tub as quietly as possible, quickly pulled on the provided robe, and tiptoed out of the bathroom. Lela did the same, following behind him, and she stopped in front of the door. Thankfully there was a peephole, so he peeked out then let out sigh of relief. It was only Jordan.

He opened the door and gave Jordan an exasperated look. Gallard and she were supposed to be having alone time and Jordan's sudden visit was not welcome. Gallard wished Jordan would have waited until after this weekend to make an appearance.

"Oh *merde*, your hair!" Jordan said, without even greeting him. "It's bad enough that you're a Cyclops, but did you have to be blonde too?"

"Hey! What's wrong with being blonde?" Lela asked defensively.

Gallard and she got dressed in the bathroom before going back out to talk to him. Though Jordan's arrival was kind of inconvenient, Gallard knew that it had to be important. Jordan wasn't the type of person to hang around because he was lonely or bored. Gallard had a feeling it had something to do with the peeping Tom from last night.

"So what brings you here so late?" Gallard asked. He decided to keep the news of his mortality a secret and just let Jordan believe he'd dyed his hair for the time being.

"I know you don't want me here, and I tried to stay away, but you two aren't safe and I couldn't keep you in the dark. Lucian was here last night and he was spying from your balcony."

"I knew it!" Lela said. "I knew that sicko was watching us! Ugh, he's so disgusting!"

"That's not the worst of it," Jordan continued. "He didn't know that you were here with Gallard. He thinks you were with some stranger. He took it personally and it made him very mad. He wants all of us dead so he can have you to himself."

At this point Gallard was so done. Lucian was acting so childish and crazy that he couldn't handle it anymore. He was very tempted to just march on over to wherever Lucian was, give him a good lecture, possibly with a beating, and tell him to get out of their lives and to stay away from Lela. Gallard wasn't afraid of him at all; he was furious. Lucian needed to get over his deluded fantasies and realize Lela would never want him.

Bodoway's warning suddenly came to mind. He said that he saw Lela and Lucian and that they had a child together. There had to be an explanation for that because he was sure deep down in his bones that nothing would ever cause Lela to love a man that terrible, let alone have a child with him. Still, the worry kept building and building. Bodoway had never had a vision that didn't come true. Gallard would just have to end that streak.

"Okay, so what are we going to do?" Lela asked.

"Solomon and Cherish are flying in tonight. I told them to come here and we're going to come up with some kind of plan. No more deals, no more exchanges; he's going down."

This was great news. Gallard had been willing to give up this ludicrous mission before, but now that Lucian was taking back his promise of ending the feud, it changed everything. Gallard didn't care how they dealt with him, whether it was incapacitating him again or scaring him so badly he wouldn't think twice about coming after them in the future. The second one sounded fun, but the first option was probably the best.

However, he doubted Lela could bring herself to kill him. Not after what she'd done. She'd told him before that killing anyone for being out of control felt hypocritical now because of the men she'd killed. She had a taste of what Lucian's mindset was like and though she'd snapped out of it; she didn't feel comfortable killing anyone else unless it was in self-defense. He understood why she felt that way and completely supported her. At the same time, he wanted to do something to keep her safe.

Solomon and Cherish arrived a half hour later. With their arrival, Gallard sensed a strange awkwardness in the room between the two of them and Jordan. They never greeted each other, and the three of them avoided eye contact for several minutes.

Cherish stared with her mouth agape upon seeing Gallard's new appearance. She didn't say a word as he waited to hear what she had to say.

"What...happened?" she finally asked, saying what Gallard

knew the others wanted to ask but were afraid to.

"He fed on me," Lela explained. "And a few hours, we woke up and his hair was different and he had vitals. We think it has something to do with my blood."

"Your blood? That shouldn't have done anything; our blood has the same affects as human blood."

None of this was making any sense. Lela's transition from vampire to human had taken several weeks while it had only taken him a couple of hours. She wasn't any different than Melody and Cherish, so he shouldn't have reacted to her blood the way he had. He didn't even want to flirt with the possibility that we were related.

"Maybe it has something to do with…well, Lela. Let's face it; you are kind of an anomaly," Jordan said. "Not only were you fed Lucian's blood, but you were born from someone who had drunk it as well. When you died and came back, your DNA probably got extremely screwed up. Who knows what you're capable of."

"So you think the result of all this is that my blood is some kind of universal cure?"

"It's the only explanation that makes sense, unless Gallard is your second cousin twice removed on your mother's side and you just didn't know it." Cherish said. She looked at him again and laughed. "You know, you kind of look like my grandfather, Abraham. I never met the guy, but I've seen a painting."

"What are we going to do about this?" Solomon asked.

"Nothing," Gallard said. "I'm not worried, so you guys shouldn't be either. I'd rather focus on the bigger problem of Lucian for now."

Jordan gave Gallard and Lela a more in depth update about Lucian's plan. Apparently, Kevin did some more spying on his own and learned that Lucian planned to create an even bigger army than the one he'd sent after them in South Carolina. Fifty day-walkers. Gallard's idea to rattle Lucian felt foolish now. They wouldn't stand a chance against fifty. Not with only three day-walkers, two night-walkers, and one mortal on their side.

"Obviously, Gallard, you would have to sit out of this one," Solomon said. "I won't have you get killed because you tried to help."

"I have to do something. Can't I help Kevin be the getaway driver? I can't stay behind while all of you fight."

Lela took his hand, a sympathetic smile on her face. He'd almost forgotten that she'd been in his place not a year ago. Back then, he'd insisted she stay to be safe and here he was, fighting to be included just as she had. Unfortunately, he'd been right and Samil killed her. Lucian was angry at him the most right now, so Gallard's presence might endanger his own life.

"If you're as much like me as I know you are you'll probably follow us anyway. I guess you could stay with Kevin. He'll look out for you, but babe... *please* don't try to fight anyone. You're mortal. I would probably die if I lost you."

"Oh!" Cherish shouted, startling everyone. "Guys, I just thought of something!"

"Don't do that too often, you might hurt yourself," Gallard said.

She ignored his comment. "We could totally use the same concept! Lela, your blood makes vampires mortal. We could somehow give it to my father and make him weak. That way, one of us could easily take him out and he'll be dead."

Everyone exchanged glances then looked at her. The more Gallard thought about her suggestion, the more her plan sounded brilliant.

"Let's say this could work and Lela's blood can weaken him. How exactly are we going to slip it to him without knowing?" Solomon asked.

"One of us will have to trick him into thinking they're on his side. I could...I could try to play the part of the grieving daughter, claiming that I want to join his side because he's the only family I have left."

"Yeah, but he's not going to buy it," Lela said. "You told him you were going to seduce Gallard and you didn't, so he doesn't trust you."

"It was just an idea. If anyone has a better plan, please feel free to speak up."

The room grew silent as everyone tried to think of something more brilliant. Gallard had to admit that Cherish's idea was by far the best idea they'd had so far. Weakening Lucian would help their chances at taking him down and then they could worry about his army later, if they chose to continue the attack after their leader was destroyed.

He listened as everyone put in their two cents about what should go down and who should be the one to do it. They all wanted to be the one to kill Lucian since each had a personal vendetta. Gallard didn't even notice at first that Lela wasn't joining the discussion. She just sat on the bed, holding his hand in hers and stared at the floor. She looked like she was trying to pay attention, but was lost in her own thoughts.

Then she spoke up for the first time.

"I have an idea," she said, once it had gotten somewhat quieter. Everyone stopped talking and turned their attention to her.

"We're listening," Solomon said.

"Lucian is doing this because he wants me, right? What if we made him think that he was getting what he wants?"

"This sounds a bit sketchy," Cherish said. "What are you getting at?"

"He wants me. And I could use that to get close to him."

"So you think you can get close to him by, what? Talking over tea?" Jordan asked.

"Or I could try to seduce him," she said flatly. Everyone groaned in disgust and she rolled her eyes. "Obviously, I wouldn't...I just...it's the only way I could get close enough. I could somehow slip it into his drink when he isn't looking, or I could persuade him to feed on me. We'd be using his plan for Cherish against him."

"How about none of the above," Gallard said. "I don't want you going anywhere near that man."

"It wouldn't be real," Lela assured him. "You know that I love you and would never, *ever* be unfaithful to you. But if I can pretend to be interested in him, I'd get my blood to him faster."

"Guys, you have to admit. Her plan is kind of brilliant," Cherish said.

"Well, come and get us when you develop this *brilliant* idea because I don't want to stick around to hear it. I might
throw up," Jordan said, beginning to walk out of the room.

"Or why don't *you* seduce him, Jordan? Since you're so good at that," Solomon said.

"Maybe I will," Jordan jabbed. "I'm not celibate, so I can do whatever and *whomever* I want."

Gallard stared at the two men. He had a feeling that there was some hostility between them, but never imagined it was because of Cherish. That had to be what Solomon was hinting at.

"Could you two fight downstairs?" Cherish asked. "We have planning to do."

Solomon nodded in agreement and followed after Jordan. Gallard stood up as well and Lela held onto his hand tighter.

"You're leaving?" she asked. He looked at Cherish and she headed for the door.

"I'll give you guys a minute," Cherish said.

Once they were alone, Gallard sat down once more. This whole plan made him extremely uncomfortable, especially after Lucian spied on them and the thought of Lela being near him, flirting with him; made him sick. He did trust her, though. If she said she could pull it off, he would have faith in her.

"You really think the best plan is pretending to seduce Lucian?" he asked.

"Like I said, it wouldn't be real. I would sooner swallow nails and eat my own liver before getting involved with him. It wouldn't go too far. I just need him to…bite me."

He fell back on the bed and covered his face with his hands. "I am not okay with this," he said, his voice muffled. He felt her lay down next to him.

"Neither am I. I'm as conflicted as you are. If it doesn't have to come to flattering him, then I would be thrilled. Maybe I could just get him to bite me for experimental purposes. He's probably curious to know what I taste like as much anyone else. There's no one else like Cherish and me. I could try my best to keep everything civil and p-g."

Gallard uncovered his face and looked at her. "I'm married to you for a week, and I already have to worry about sharing you, even if it is an act."

Lela moved closer and kissed him. He hated that she had to go through this. If there was a better idea, he would be thrilled, but unfortunately there wasn't. He had to hope that it would work and that she would quickly return to him; to his arms where she would remain for all of eternity.

"Wanna fool around until Cherish gets back," he asked, smiling.

"Can't, sorry. We need to make a plan as soon as we can and since you guys don't want to help, it's up to the two of us to put our heads together and make sure this works."

He gave her a pathetic look of disappointment and she laughed. There had been a time when she had to push him to express his feelings, and now he didn't want to stay away from her. It didn't help that they had to spend the rest of their honeymoon on a dangerous mission when all he wanted was to get away and be alone with her for longer than a few days. He would have to settle for spending time with her in short segments until this was all over.

"It's because he has two eyes, isn't? That's why you think he's sexy."

She rolled her eyes. "Get out of here, blondie."

Gallard laughed then got up and left the room. Cherish, who had been waiting outside, came in and rubbed her hands together deviously. He heard what she said and it made his stomach turn.

"All righty! Operation Seducin' Lucian has now commenced."

Chapter Forty

We spent the next two hours collaborating ideas for how I would go about tricking Lucian. My stomach was in knots the whole time, but I didn't want Cherish to know I was nervous. I was determined to make this work and I needed her to have faith in me that I could go through with it. One wrong move and Lucian would kill me and then finish off the rest of the group.

I was the worst flirt ever. Something I learned from Cherish. We'd done some silly, yet necessary practice scenarios for what I would say to him and I failed miserably.

Cherish also gave me a brief history of what her father was like. The parts that I didn't know about. Unlike him, I hadn't fished through all of his memories because I hadn't the need to do so. I may have been in his head, but I barely knew anything about him.

"My father likes strong women," she explained. "That's why he went after my mother. He must have cared about her at first, but she turned out to be just another selfish bitch who cared about nothing except herself. She screwed every immortal on the east side of London and didn't even try to hide it. But once a woman submits themselves to him, he loses interest because the challenge is gone."

"So...you want me to play hard to get?"

"Exactly! See you got this! You just need to work on your seduction skills."

"Well, I'm not completely clueless. I've had some practice."

"Oh please, Gallard isn't that hard to seduce."

"Uh, yes he was. We've had several opportunities to be together in the past and we've just now accomplished that. Also it took a year of flirting before he finally admitted that he had feelings for me."

Cherish gave me a sneaky smile. "So, how was it? Did he blow your mind?"

"He blew something, alright."

"Lela Sharmentino!" She shoved me, and I laughed. "You dirty birdy. I'm a bad influence on you."

I smiled to myself as I replayed our honeymoon in my mind. It had been worth the wait and I couldn't have imagined my first time with him being any better. Each time was better than the last, and I loved being with him.

"So educate me," I said. "How do I get Lucian to think that I like him?" I asked.

"You have to come off as innocent. My father likes to manipulate people to give him what he wants. He plays the sympathy card. But at the same time, he doesn't like it when they're *too* easy. He likes a challenge."

This all seemed more difficult than I thought. I had to act like I was stringing him along so he would want me more, only try to give in to his charms at the same time. It was so confusing to me and felt nearly impossible to act both ways at once. I wasn't a manipulative person and this was new territory to me. This was different than when I'd gotten a John to give me a ride in Vegas. Lucian was unpredictable and super obsessed.

"You look overwhelmed. Why don't we take a break," she said. "And by the way, I need your advice on something."

"Really? What words of wisdom could I possibly have for someone five hundred years older than me?"

Cherish suddenly became more solemn and my stomach tightened. I had a feeling what she was about to tell had something to do with why she and Solomon were acting so strange around each other. The last time I'd seen them, they were all cozy and affectionate. Now they were distant and barely even looked at one another.

"I messed up bad, Lela. I did something horrible and now Solomon probably hates me."

"What did you do?"

She looked down, avoiding eye contact and said, "I slept with Jordan."

"What!" I shouted. So that's why Jordan and Solomon were at odds. I couldn't believe what I was hearing. After all that pining and tension between her and Solomon over the past few weeks I'd thought she was going to stick with Solomon and try to start a relationship with him.

"I could slap you again!" I continued. I picked up one of the pillows and hit her with it. She didn't retaliate but opened her mouth in surprise "How could you? With *Jordan*? Why Jordan?"

"I don't know! Because he was listening to my problems and he's sexy and has an awesome body. Did I mention he's an amazing kisser? It wasn't like I invited him over to hook up, it just happened!"

"But what about poor Solomon? He loves you and you know it. How could you do that to him? He's spent four hundred years trying to deal with his guilt over your death, and you throw it all in his face by sleeping with Jordan?"

Cherish started crying, but I didn't feel bad. I was glad she felt terrible. Solomon had done so much for my family and though I'd been angry before because he'd refused to help us in the past, I'd seen his heart. He was kind, devoted, and willing to do anything for his family. In a way, he was like Gallard, only in a more Catholic sense.

Because of what happened between my mother and David, infidelity was a touchy subject for me. I couldn't stand cheating, married or unmarried because I'd seen the damage it could cause, emotionally. My family was completely dysfunctional because of my mother's affair and I needed to help Cherish to keep her from ruining her relationship.

"How do I fix this?" she asked.

My anger slightly softened and I gave her a hug.

"Do you love Solomon?"

She shrugged. "I don't know. I think it's too soon to use the L word, but I definitely feel something for him. If I didn't, I wouldn't hate myself so much right now."

"Then tell him that, Cher! Take a chance with this man who obviously adores you. The two of you finally have a chance to be together. Don't let that second chance pass you by."

She released me from the hug and I got up to get her some tissues. I came back then handed them to her and she wiped her eyes before forcing a smile.

"So, in the past...you've never thought about banging Jordan?" she asked.

"Ew, no! I love Jordan to death, but I see him as my brother, and now he sort of is."

"You should have. Every woman should spend one night that man. I'm telling you—"

"Hey! What happened to being monogamous?"

"Oh, right. Damn, I need more help than I thought."

The group arrived in New York the following day. Gallard had probably been extremely clingy towards Lela during the flight, but he couldn't help it. He was dreading the moment when he would have to let her go and deceive Lucian.

It helped that Cherish and Solomon would be keeping an eye on her, but he wouldn't feel at peace unless he was the one doing the watching. They wouldn't let him because of his mortality.

Cherish and Lela went shopping right after they landed and when Lela returned, she looked like a new woman. She was wearing a tight red dress with black heels that were at least four inches. He couldn't keep his eyes off of her and that bothered him because it meant Lucian would probably feel the same way.

To try and get a closer look at what was going on they booked a room next door to where Lucian was staying. Solomon specifically requested a room that was directly across from Lucians. They could even see it through the window, though his curtains were closed.

While Cherish, Jordan, and Solomon were downstairs discussing who would be where and what they would do in case the plan failed, he kept Lela company while she paced around the room.

He could tell that she was nervous and he wanted to help somehow. It was a lot of responsibility on her shoulders because if she didn't succeed their entire group could be in danger.

Gallard hugged her from behind as she stood in front of the window and he could feel some of her anxiety leave her body.

"What's going through that head of yours?" he asked.

"I can't do this, Gallard." She turned around to face him and he kept his arms around her. "I'm not...Lydian. I'm not Cherish. I have no idea what I'm doing. I don't know how to be flirtatious or sexy. Lucian will see right through me the moment I open my mouth. I'm not—"

"Lela you can do this! You are an extraordinary person. You fought off the first vampire who ever attacked you and you won a fight with one while you were mortal. You've been attacked countless times and survived. You were killed and death didn't stop you. You're here now because you're strong. I have more confidence in you than anyone, and I know you will succeed. And when you do, we'll be ready to back you up."

Lela smiled, and he was glad that he might have boosted her morale. What he really wanted was to take her and fly out there without telling anyone, but he couldn't. They had spent too much time running from their problems. This time, they would go in with a plan.

"I have to tell you something funny," he continued. "It has to do with what I talked with Bodoway about a few days ago."

"What did he say?"

"Remember how he told you about the blonde man with blue eyes? Well, I think he predicted my turning mortal again. He said that when he hugged you, he saw the man again. At first, I thought he meant some other guy was going to come along, but now I realize he'd seen me."

Lela laughed. "Gallard. Do you really think I could ever leave you for someone else? Nothing; no one could stop me from loving you."

THE RESURRECTION

He thought back to what Bodoway told him he'd seen. That was the main reason why he was against this. He doubted Lela would suddenly fall for Lucian in one night, but he couldn't shake the feeling that something might happen. Bodoway saw Lela and Lucian and they had a child. What could possibly occur that would push Lela into Lucian's arms?

As for the blonde man thing, he was glad one vision had been cleared up.

"I know. I feel foolish now that I was so worried about it. I guess it was meant to be, right?"

Lela pulled him close to her and kissed him. Her lips were extremely soft and she tasted like raspberry. Cherish must have put some flavored lipstick on her.

"What do you mean you don't know how to be sexy?" he asked, chuckling. "I'm finding you pretty irresistible myself in that dress. I like you better in blue, but red…wow."

"How irresistible?" she asked, giving him a sly smile.

Gallard kissed her again, and she slowly walked backwards, taking him with her and they fell on the bed, their lips moving in softly in sync. Eventually they got under the covers and she pulled off his shirt then he helped her get out of the dress. His body began to get warmer and it concerned him.

"Is the heater on?" he asked. She stared at him to as if to see if he was being serious then laughed.

"No. You're just hot."

He was confused at first but when he got her joke he laughed. He was going to take things further when she rolled him over onto his back and he looked into her eyes. He was going to ask what she was doing when she silenced him with a kiss and pulled him so that he was sitting up. She straddled him, steadying herself by holding onto his shoulders. He was surprised by her actions but as they came together, surprise turned into euphoria.

Every movement they made validated that they were designed for each other. He lost himself in the ecstasy of their bond, never wanting it to end. He imagined it being like this every day; every decade that they would spend together.

Gallard then lay on his back and she kissed his cheek before moving away from him and lay on her side with her head resting on the pillow. This hotel was probably twice as expensive as the place they'd stayed in since it was New York and it showed. The bed was more comfortable than any he'd ever been in.

"Wow," he said. "That was…amazing."

"Well, it was your idea for me to be on top. Or did your mortal brain give you Alzheimer's?"

He chuckled then eased himself up with his elbow. "It's different now. I haven't experienced this as a mortal in so long that I've forgotten what it's like." He smiled. "And it's not just that. I love being with you because I love you."

Her cheeks flushed as if she were embarrassed but she didn't stop smiling at him with such love. This woman never failed to surprise him, and he knew she always would, no matter how long they had together.

"I love you too," she said. "And I'm going to come back to you. I promise you that. Whether I fail or succeed, we'll find our way back to each other. Just like you promised me all those years ago."

"I remember that." He pulled her closer to him and she rested her head on his shoulder. "I don't know if this is the best time for this, but I have an idea for our future."

"Any time is perfect to plan our future. What did you have in mind?"

"Texas. I've never felt more at home than when I lived there with you and I know it was hard for you to leave Arlington and I thought—"

"We should totally move there!" She sounded truly excited. "I loved Texas, though I may have some sad memories there. But I don't have any tragic ones like I do in Florida."

"Then it's settled. After we make Lucian mortal and take him down, we'll move there."

She began kissing him again and he rolled over so that he was on top this time, and she laughed.

"We are so going to get caught in here," she said.

"That's okay. If I had a dollar for every time I caught Jordan and Lydian fooling around in my room, I could afford two of these hotel rooms."

He laced his fingers through hers and kissed her once more, his lips moving from her lips to her neck, and he basked in the moment. They quickly got carried away again, but he didn't care. He would

THE RESURRECTION

keep her there with him forever if he could. For now, he was going to savor what few moments he had left before she would go into the war zone.

Chapter Forty-One

Though we didn't want to, we had to get up in case Solomon, Jordan, or Cherish decided to check on us. Cherish had done a lot of work putting makeup on me and doing my hair. My hair was all right, but not as nice as before Gallard and I had our moment...or several.

He zipped up my dress for me, and I walked over to the mirror to assess my appearance. I looked fine, for the most part. I knew Cherish would know something happened since my curls were less defined. Unless I blamed it on my hair texture, which wasn't completely a lie. They would have fallen flat anyway.

We then left the room to go find the others, Gallard's hand in mine. In a way, what happened between us gave me more confidence. If I could get that reaction from him, then maybe it wouldn't be so hard to flatter Lucian since he was already obsessed with me, for whatever reason that was.

Jordan left to retrieve Kevin from their hiding place while Solomon, Gallard and Cherish prepared to send me off to the hotel next door. When Jordan told us that Lucian had taken residence at my parents' time share we had some pretty good ideas how. Aaron was the only one who knew about it besides us, and Cherish swore

THE RESURRECTION

that she'd never mentioned it. I couldn't decide if I was glad about the possibility that he was still alive or angry that he'd switched sides.

We remained inside so that no one would see us. Lucian had quite a few people on the lookout, so hanging around the front wasn't an option. I wasn't looking forward to walking in heels, but it was a necessary pain to endure. I stopped in front of the lobby door and leaned against the side, taking a few seconds of mental preparation.

"You're going to be fine," Gallard said, massaging my arm reassuringly. "And if you're in danger, Solomon and Cherish will be nearby."

I wrapped my arms around his waist, holding him tightly. I wished that he could be the one watching out for me instead, but it wasn't safe for him because he was still mortal. He planned to join Kevin and Jordan on a stakeout across the street later in the evening, but that wouldn't be for another couple hours.

"I love you," I said to him. "Whatever happens, remember that."

"Just hurry back to me, Lela."

I moved my head from his chest so that I could see his face. "What? No nickname today?"

"Maybe when the situation is less dire."

I stroked his blonde hair and smiled at him. Though he looked like a completely different person, he was still my Gallard. My best friend.

"It's getting late," he said. "I should let you go. I don't want to, but I want to get this over with."

"She's going to be fine," Cherish said. "Go for it, Lela. We've got your back."

I parted with the group and headed down the street and into the hotel. Since the bar was open to the public, I decided to sit and wait there until I found someone who could direct me to Lucian. Hardly anyone was around, which was nice. I needed some space to get my thoughts together.

To calm my nerves, I ordered a scotch, which I downed in two gulps. My history with alcohol wasn't all that great, but I hoped that it would loosen me up and help with my inhibition.

Twenty minutes passed, and I still didn't see any immortals. Either they were all holed up in the room or he didn't have as many guards as we'd thought. I was starting to get bored, and slightly buzzed. I'd ordered two more scotches, finishing them equally as quickly as the first. I stopped ordering them after that since I didn't want to become the babbling mess I'd been the last time I'd had too much to drink.

Cherish said that Lucian was turned off by drunkenness, so slightly buzzed was the way to go. It was enough to loosen me up but not enough to make me babble like an idiot or talk like Yoda.

I heard someone come through the door, so I turned around to see who it was. We met gazes and I groaned.

"Aaron. I *knew* you were here, you little traitor," I said. He came over to me and set the bags that he had in his hands on the floor, taking the seat next to mine. "Please don't tell me you left us so you could go shopping."

"Don't tell me *you* left the group so you could get drunk." He took my empty glass and put it to his nose. "Scotch. You must really be depressed. Did you have a fight with the hubby?"

He didn't know it, but this was actually part of my cover story. I was to tell Lucian that we'd gotten in a fight over what happened to Robin and the other men, saying that he'd strongly disagreed with my decision. It was a harsh story, but it had to be something that would hurt me enough to leave.

"Bingo," I said, taking my glass back. In order to keep up the act, I ordered another scotch. I didn't drink it as fast as the other, but took a small sip.

"What about? I can't imagine Gallard making you mad enough to risk your safety."

"He didn't make me mad, it was the other way around." I set the glass down. "Aaron, something happened after you left."

"If you're confessing to killing Lucian's followers, I already know that. I didn't realize what a badass you were until I heard you took on ten night-walkers." He looked at what I was wearing and whistled. "That dress...damn. When did you start dressing all sexy like that?"

I shoved him and he laughed.

"You're disgusting. Keep it to yourself next time."

"Fine by me. So what is this terrible thing that happened?"

THE RESURRECTION

I had to just tell him. He deserved to know what happened to our sister, and though I was still furious at him for what he did, I knew he loved her just as much as I did. He'd turned her because he didn't want to lose her, and I killed her because I loved her enough to save her from the immortal life.

"Robin's dead, Aaron. I couldn't let her be like us. It would be cruel and unfair for her. I did what I thought was best."

Aaron hung his head. I could tell that he was pretending he wasn't as upset as he really was. He was trying to be this tough, macho guy, acting like he didn't care about anything, but I could see right through him.

"You killed her?" he asked. I didn't answer but took another sip from my glass. "And...you left them?"

"I finally see things the way you do. Too many people have died, and I'm tired of running."

"Did you come here to join Lucian?"

"I'm not sure why I came here. I just left." I looked at his face to see if he was buying it. He didn't show any sign of suspicion, so I kept going. "Is Lucian here? I'd like to talk to him."

"Yeah he's here. He's been nagging me to try and get the two of you to meet."

"If you wouldn't mind, could you go and get him?"

Aaron nodded then got up, taking the bags with him. After he was gone, my heart rate picked up, causing me to down the rest of the scotch against my better judgment. I thought maybe being drunk would help me loosen up and have more confidence.

Ten minutes later, I looked up to see him walking towards me. It was so strange seeing him in the flesh up close. He was completely different from the long-haired, sixteenth century Englishman that I remembered. He'd cut his hair shorter and was wearing black fitted jeans, a white collared shirt, and a dark grey cardigan. He either had good taste, or someone had helped him out because he looked rather nice.

He smiled as he stood next to me then took my hand and kissed it. His touch was very warm, and I could hear his heart racing. Was he nervous? Why would he be nervous? If he was, we were both equally as uneasy about this meeting.

"Hello, darling," he greeted me. "Tis a pleasure to finally meet you in corporeal form."

I didn't know what else to say so I said, "It's nice to meet you as well."

He sat down next to me but didn't order anything. He smelled good, like very expensive cologne. What was even weirder was the color of his eyes. I remembered them being a cyan blue, and now they were a somewhat luminescent lime green. I couldn't have mistaken his eye color. It was too drastic of a difference.

"I have wanted to see you for some time now," he said. "You have made it easier by coming to me instead. Tell me; what brings you here?"

"I left Gallard," I said flatly. This was the hardest part. Lying about our relationship. I had to keep reminding myself that I shouldn't feel bad because it was an act. Still, it was hard saying the words out loud.

"But you were just married not too long ago, am I correct?"

"Biggest mistake I've ever made. We rushed into it and we've done nothing but argue ever since. And after I—" For some reason, my tears were trying to make an appearance just when I needed them to. Crying would help my case even more.

Lucian took my hand and held it in both of his. "You cheated on him, didn't you?"

So far, the plan was working. He still thought that I'd cheated and this was the big part of my story that he needed to believe.

"Where did you hear that?" I asked.

"I will not lie to you, darling. I had spies watching over you. They saw you and a blonde man with one eye in a hotel a few days ago. Your relationship must have really been terrible."

"Yeah, um...after we had a fight, I had a one-night stand with some guy I met at a bar. Gallard found out and we ended things for good."

"So you do not love him anymore?" Lucian asked. I looked down, preparing for what I would say next then slowly my eyes met his.

"No," I lied. "He berated me for killing your men and said I was no better than you. He believes that when I came back from the dead, I came back...wrong; screwed up. He says I am not the same woman he used to love. In a way I guess he's right."

"I am very sorry, darling. People can be so closed minded.

Sometimes we make decisions that others do not agree with and they act all high and mighty as if they have not made mistakes themselves."

Lucian let go of my hand then ordered a drink. Scotch, just like I had, so I asked for another one. For a while, he didn't look at me. I used this as an opportunity to study him. Up close, he looked very young. I remembered it was mentioned that he was twenty when he'd stopped aging. He was the same age as me.

"What are your plans, long term?" I asked. "What will you do in the future?"

He took a drink before answering. "It depends. Would you be interested in being part of my future?"

"What do you have in mind?"

His fingers stroked along my arm. "Why don't you come upstairs and find out?"

This guy moved fast. I'd barely talked to him for ten minutes and he was already propositioning me. Something was strange about him, more so than just his eyes. The Lucian I knew hated the idea of me being with any man. He would have scolded me for the one night stand and I doubted he would try to sleep with me after only a short time. It was like he'd made a complete personality switch.

I wasn't about to make it *that* easy for him. Cherish said that he liked a challenge, and it was a challenge he was going to get.

I gave him a flirtatious smile, resting my hand on his leg and leaned closer to him until my lips were practically touching his ear. "I'm still a married woman, Mr. Christophe. It just wouldn't be right."

"You gave yourself to a man you only knew for one night. Why not give yourself to me? You have known me longer than anyone."

"That was a mistake. I don't usually behave that way, I was upset. I'm not a one-night stand kind of girl. But you already know that, don't you?"

He stopped stroking my arm and changed to stroking my cheek. "You are not making this easy for me, darling. You never have. That is why you fascinate me so much. How long ago were you married?"

"Six days. Before everything imploded." This was half true. Not ten hours after the ceremony, tragedy struck and we'd barely been able to recover from it.

"Bugger. I should have sent for you instead of Cherish that day. The marriage never would have happened, and you would be mine."

A prickle went up my back. His voice sounded even more possessive than it had when he was in my head. In the past, I had gotten the sense that he was into me, but I thought I was being paranoid. He always got very quiet if I ever accused him of flirting with me. Now he wasn't being shy about stating what he wanted. He wanted me and he would be fine if we just went upstairs and did the deed after only having a five-minute conversation.

He stood up, taking my hand. "Come with me. If we cannot stay in, then we should go out." He led me to the doors and I let him, curious to know where he planned on taking me. We went outside and took a right down the street, traffic sound blaring all around us. The crowds on the sidewalk were huge, and we had to push our way past them. He kept a firm grip on my hand so that we wouldn't be separated.

In the crowd I noticed a man with a baseball cap wink at me, and I had to do a double take to realize who it was. It was Kevin, so I smiled back, instantly feeling better. They were keeping an eye on me as promised. Wherever Lucian was taking me, I wasn't going to be alone.

We got to a less populated area and Lucian switched from holding my hand to linking his arm through mine. He was so old fashioned that I began to silently make fun of him. Unlike Gallard, who had only come around about hundred years after him, Lucian jumped from being in the fifteen hundreds to the millennium. It had to have been a major culture shock for him.

Lucian stopped in front of a building that looked a bit sketchy. Some people in shiny and tight outfits were going in the door and I stopped walking. Puzzled, he stopped as well and looked at me.

"What is this place?" I asked.

"Tis a night club. Aaron took me here a few days ago and—"

"Wait, *Aaron* brought you here?" I should have known that he was behind this. He knew I didn't like to dance and that large groups of people stressed me out. This had to have been some kind of plot to embarrass the both of us.

THE RESURRECTION

"You do not like to dance," he assessed. "Quite all right. Why don't I take you to dinner instead?"

This night was getting weirder and weirder by the minute. First, Lucian tried to get me into his hotel room and now he was trying to turn this into a date. If he wanted me to join his side, he was sure trying very hard. Maybe too hard. But this meant I was on his good side, so I decided to play along.

"Have you ever had Mexican?" I asked.

"Mexican? Oh, right. The country below the southern border. I hear they are struggling economically. Why would we go there?"

His random spouting of facts made me chuckle. I was impressed, though. He'd gotten fairly up to date on the issues of modern times. "We don't have to go there to eat their food. We passed a restaurant about a block before this one."

I then turned us around and we walked back in the direction that we came. It didn't take long for us to find it and we went inside. We were seated within five minutes. This was convenient because I'd been craving Mexican food for a while. I hadn't eaten much food lately besides the meals I'd shared with the Shepherd's. Fortunately, I'd gotten blood from Solomon before this since Gallard was still mortal. I was worried that his mortality wasn't going to wear off and hoped that in a matter of time he would change back. We needed his strength in this fight in case my plan didn't work.

I picked what I wanted and watched as Lucian struggled to read the menu. I couldn't read Spanish, but the food names were universally known. I didn't know if he was fluent in any other language besides English.

"I cannot read this. It reminds me of Italian, but I never learned it. I only know Aramaic and English."

"You should order the *Arroz con pollo*. It's just chicken and rice. It's pretty good."

He set the menu down. "I will trust you."

"Wait...how do you know Aramaic of all languages?"

"Tis the language of Christ, darling. I thought you would know since you are Catholic."

The way he said *Christ* and *Catholic* was with such hostility, like he was spitting out poison. I knew he had an aversion to the

Church, but the way he was acting was as if the very subject made him sick. I decided not to ask any more questions.

We ate our meal mostly in silence. What was there to talk about? Who did you kill lately? How's the immortal life going for you? I'd already used all of the flirting tips that Cherish so graciously had spent hours teaching me. I was running out of things to say.

Like a gentleman, he paid for the meal with his gold card. How he'd acquired money, I had no clue. He must have had money stashed somewhere all these years and had just now been able to retrieve it. Unless he'd just killed some poor guy and stole his wallet.

After we left the restaurant, we went for a walk, taking in all the sights of Manhattan. The city seemed to never end and the buildings were so tall. Even for the time, there were still tons of people everywhere. It truly was the city that never sleeps. The perfect city for immortals, really.

We came across another long string of night clubs, some for dancing and others for different purposes. Some creeps started whistling at us and Lucian looked mortified. He'd obviously never been hit on by a guy before, let alone one that was dressed as a woman. Thankfully no one got in our face so we were able to pass through unscathed.

My feet began to hurt after a while. The ridiculous heels Cherish had picked weren't exactly made for walking. I waited until we were in an area that didn't look so dirty before taking them off and held them in my free hand. Lucian had kept our arms linked for the entire walk. He even offered to carry my shoes at one point and I let him.

We'd walked for almost an hour before we were both tired and stopped when we got to City Hall Park. It had a beautiful fountain and amazing landscape. The setting was very intimate, especially since it was dark and I wished that I could have been there with Gallard instead. But I was here to make sure that we would have more time together. If Lucian was weakened, then our chances of surviving the feud would be higher and we could finally begin our lives together.

Sitting at the edge of the fountain, I put my feet in to sooth the soreness from the shoes. The dress was tight, making it awkward to sit and it made me regret not helping Cherish pick out a more comfortable one.

"How is my Cherish," Lucian asked. "She must hate me even more after what transpired a few nights ago."

"Can you blame her? She lost her sister. The one person in her life that she loved. She's devastated."

"She brought it upon herself. She failed to follow through with our agreement and she paid for it."

"You mean *Melody* paid for it. She didn't deserve to die like that. She was a wonderful and selfless person. She wasn't like—" I was getting into hostile territory. If I got on his bad side, then everything would fall flat. "She wasn't like your wife. She wasn't a nag or promiscuous. She may have looked like Florence, but she was the exact opposite."

Lucian chewed on the inside of his mouth. A habit that I noticed Cherish had also. Lucian and Cherish looked more like twins than father and daughter. And they'd both suffered from betrayal by people they'd loved. Lucian from his parents and Cherish from the man she'd once cared for.

The only difference was that Cherish was slowly learning to forgive while Lucian was still hardened by his experience. Solomon may have been the one he was targeting, but I had the feeling that he was channeling his hatred toward his parent into something else. I knew this all too well from when I'd projected my problems into eating disorders. It all came down to our immortality and how much it had ruined our lives.

"Why are you here, Lela? Is it to try and reform me, as you so dearly suggested that you do?"

I'd forgotten that I'd mentioned that to Gallard. It had been when we were on the beach, just before I'd been taken by Samil. I'd been joking at the time, but now that he brought it up, I wondered if it would be possible.

"I'm here because…you get me. We've both gotten revenge for being betrayed and we've become outcasts because of our choices. We've been in each other's heads; no one knows me like you do."

Inwardly I was cringing. This was the sappiest thing I'd ever said in my life, and for some reason, I didn't stop there.

"You know all my secrets; my inward thoughts, my darkest moments; all my desires. And I've seen yours as well." I wanted to gag. If Cherish and Solomon were listening, they were probably as repulsed by what I was saying as me. "You've been so consumed by hate that you've forgotten how to love. That's your biggest regret, and you wish that you'd been a better father, and a better man."

I was done talking now. If I continued, I would start dry heaving. Instead, I waited to see how Lucian would respond. He hadn't said a word to interrupt me, so he must have been giving me his full attention and genuinely taking to heart what I had to say.

Lucian took my hands and pulled me to a standing position. I held my breath, dreading what might come next. It had to have been the last of the alcohol talking before, and now I would rely on my own merits to get through the rest of the night.

"Dance with me," he said. I rolled my eyes, sensing a cliché moment about to happen.

"Oh please, let me guess; we don't need music, we're going to *feel* the music, right?"

He shook his head and took an iPod touch out of his pocket, hit play, and *Hero* by Enrique Iglesias came through the tiny speaker. He put it in the pocket of his cardigan so that we could still hear it then tugged me closer to him into dancing position.

"You have an iTouch?" I asked as we moved from side to side.

"No, I stole it from one of my guards. I have not the slightest idea what dancing music is this day. I picked a category called, '*For My Girl.*'"

I happened to look to my left and saw movement. Cherish came out from behind a bush, pretended to slit her own throat then went back into hiding. I had to fight a laugh.

"Did he dance with you?" he asked.

"What?"

"Did Gallard dance with you on your wedding night?"

We hadn't, but it wasn't because he'd been inconsiderate. We'd just had other things on our agenda, like being together for the first time, though it never happened that night. Besides, we weren't exactly a traditional couple, which was why we were so good together. I figured that eventually we would have our first dance, but it wasn't the most important thing on our list.

"No, he didn't," I said, trying to sound as disappointed as possible.

THE RESURRECTION

"Good. Now I can say that I have danced with you and he has not."

Did he seriously just make this a competition?

"Lucian, why are you so set on being with me? Ever since we met, you've been saying that I belong to you. What is it about me that fascinates you?"

Lucian stopped dancing. "Like you said. You get me," he mumbled into my ear. I felt his lips on my neck and I froze. This was my chance. If he was ever going to taste my blood, there was no better time than when he was near the temptation. Gallard had said that I tasted good, so if I brought up the subject, Lucian might take me up on my offer.

He continued kissing my neck while I continued to pretend like I was okay with it. It made me sick. I felt so uncomfortable that I was shaking. I needed to speak up before he could take it any further.

"You can try it if you want," I said. "I've been told that my blood is unlike anything anyone has ever tasted."

Lucian stopped kissing me for a second then inhaled deeply, taking in my scent. "You smell…incredible."

"Go ahead. Try it," I coaxed him.

He looked at my face and I waited impatiently to see what he would do. I was dangling my blood right in front of him, and he wasn't taking the bait. Instead, he drew closer to me until our lips were only inches apart. Then for some reason he stopped.

"I want to show you something," he said. He took my hand, leading me over to a small garden on the other side of the fountain then knelt down. At first, I thought he was going to pick me a flower, which would have been weird and kind of corny.

But he did something else. He held his other hand over the flowers, closing his eyes, and my breath caught in my throat as I watched the plants begin to shrivel up and die. The once vibrant garden was now dead.

"How…did you do that?" I asked.

"Do you know the story of how we came to be? How the immortals first appeared on the earth?"

I nodded. Gallard had told me the story of the man from biblical times who made a deal with the Devil so he could bring people back to life. I'd nearly forgotten about it and wondered what it had to do with Lucian and his new ability."

"Well, darling, I met our creator a few days ago. He was the one that brought me back to life when I was but a baby and he offered me his power. I accepted and now I am stronger than I could ever imagine. I can do things; healing, teleporting, even killing with just a thought."

"Lucian, why did you do this? Did you *really* want to be filled with pure and unadulterated evil? This guy is the reason we are all in this situation in the first place! How could you do that to yourself? Now everything that's left of your humanity could be gone!"

"Careful, darling. It almost sounds like you care about my soul."

"No it's...listen, think about this. He said that you died as an infant. But you came back. You're here, and you're not as evil as you think you are. You're just lost. You've never known anything but hate and betrayal. You have some good in you and—"

"You think I have *good* in me? Oh, Lela, you have it all wrong. Just because I have spent this whole night talking and dancing with you...and because I find you fascinating does *not* mean I've changed my mind about killing your family. Nothing will change that. If Maximus' power can help me finish the job faster, then I am willing to take on what comes with it. Do you even know why Solomon killed me?"

I shook my head. I'd always assumed it was because he'd been a careless hunter and that he'd messed with the wrong people.

"Just a week before it happened, two children went missing. The son and daughter of a count. One day, when the gardener was digging in the flower bed just next to the fence of my house, he came across two bodies. The missing children. That night, I had Solomon help me move the bodies to another location. I swore to him that I was not responsible, but he did not believe me. He promised to keep the incident a secret, and he did, but dealt with it himself. I was killed ten days later."

"Who killed them then?" I asked, nearly whispering.

"The night they were murdered I had just arrived from a long night of feeding. I heard something in the garden and thinking it was a thief, I crept up on them to see who it was. That was when I saw Melody. She was digging a hole and dumping two bodies into it. One girl and one boy. I did not say a word, but watched until she had done the job. I did not plan to tell Solomon, but he thought I was responsible. That is why he killed me."

His confession was beyond what I'd imagined he was going to say. Melody killed two innocent children while she was still mortal. She never said a word about any of this when we'd talked. Then I remembered. She'd probably been about to tell me that day in the hotel, only she'd stopped for some reason. But I knew why she'd done it.

"You didn't tell Solomon? Why?" I asked.

"Because I was proud of her for the first time since she'd been born. Not only did I have one daughter to carry on my legacy, but two. I was glad that she did it. But when I saw them for the first time since coming back, I knew that they had lost the part of them I had worked so hard to instill. Both of them failed me, and I blame Solomon for that."

I had to come up with something to say to him that would appeal to his humanity, whatever was left. If I could talk him out of killing those I loved and not have to give him my blood, I was willing to try. Only this time, it wouldn't be some fake sappy speech. The lives of my friends depended on it.

"All of that is in the past, Lucian," I argued. "If you're as far gone as you say you are then...why did you promise to save my sister? And why did you kill Matthew after he tried to assault me?" I had to think back to what I remembered from when I was in his head. "Why did you encourage me to fight for my life when Samil was trying to kill me? Why did you sing to Robin when she'd woken up from a nightmare? By the way, *Highway to Hell* is the worst song to sing to a scared child."

"Why are you trying to stop me? It cannot be because you still care about your family because you told me that you were through with them, so why? Why are you so set on saving my soul?"

I had to choose my words carefully. This wasn't about trying to seduce him anymore; this was a serious attempt to keep him from making a mistake and hurting those I cared about.

"All right, fine. I care. I've been inside your head long enough to know that you weren't always bad. In a way, you helped me get through my childhood. You were the one I confided in about Mark and my mother's depression. You tried to give me good advice, and though sometimes it was annoying, you were right."

"How much do you care?" he asked, getting closer to me. I wanted to back away; to stop with the whole charade and be done with this, but people's lives depended on it. Who knew how many would die if Lucian used this new power of his.

I had to do something that I didn't want to. I was desperate to stop him. I took a few seconds to prepare myself and then I took his face in my hands and kissed him. I did it for Kevin. I did it for Cherish and Solomon. I did it for Jordan. And I did it for Gallard. Though I hated every second of it, I had to think of who I was saving. They were depending on me to stop him, and if that meant kissing someone I loathed, then I would do it.

As I kissed him, I felt myself grow lighter, and when I finally ended it, I saw that we were floating. We were a good fifty feet from the ground, and I was worried I would fall, but he held onto me tightly.

"Lela, I did this so we would be unstoppable. No one would ever think to cross us again. With this new power, we would be feared by everyone. We would never be killed, or betrayed. We would be gods on earth. You and I were made for this."

THE RESURRECTION

Chapter Forty-Two

Jordan watched Gallard pace back and forth in their hiding place. After Lela and Lucian had left the hotel, Kevin went to stay with the car in case he needed to rush them to a different location while Solomon and Cherish followed the two of them down the street. Jordan and Gallard were in charge of keeping an eye on Lucian's followers to watch for any signs that they were going to leave and prepare for an attack.

He studied Gallard's features as he continued to nervously walk around. With his blonde hair and blue eye, he resembled his father, Abraham. He also somewhat reminded him of his son, though Gallard was more like a brother than a descendant.

A secret he'd carried with him for the past few years was that he hadn't met Gallard for the first time in Las Vegas. It had actually been nearly three hundred years before that in Ohio. Gallard had been sixteen at the time, and Jordan had found his family because he was curious. Gallard was attacked by a lone wolf and Jordan saved him, but not before Gallard's leg was wounded terribly. Since Gallard's father was away at war, he'd stayed and nursed Gallard back to health when the wound had gotten infected.

As what had happened before, his demons caught up with him and he left without explanation. He'd felt himself gaining a paternal connection to Gallard and that scared him. He could never stay in the same place for more than a few months.

All these years later, and he was changed. The thought of leaving Gallard made him sick and Jordan vowed to never desert him again.

Jordan hated that he'd lied to him about who he really was. Soon, the truth would have to come out and now seemed like as good a time as ever.

"Hey, relax! Lela is smart, she'll get through this and she'll be okay," Jordan assured him.

Gallard stopped pacing and leaned against one of the trees.

"Why did I agree to this?"

"Because you know it's a good plan. If we can make Lucian mortal, we can kill him."

"This was a terrible plan. Nothing good is going to come of this. Bodoway..."

Jordan stepped away from the tree he was leaning on. "Bodoway what?" There was no answer. "Gallard, what did Bodoway see?"

"He saw Lela and Lucian together, all right!" Gallard raked his hands his hair. "He saw them together....and they were happy. Now tell me that everything will be all right."

This put a real synch in the situation. Because of Maximus' gifts, Jordan never doubted Bodoway's abilities for a second. Gallard heavily relied on the man for advice and Jordan respected him. If he saw something, it meant it was going to happen.

"Like hell they will," Jordan said, though he doubted his own words. "We're going to kill the son-of-a-bitch tonight and Lela is returning to you. I guarantee that."

Jordan felt his phone buzz and he looked down to see who it was. Maximus was texting him. Why? He never contacted him so close together in time. Jordan thought that he wouldn't hear from him again until Lucian was dead. Something must have changed.

The message said that he wanted to meet somewhere in Manhattan. This wasn't the best time for him to make a quick disappearance. The group needed him to help Gallard with the stake out, especially since Gallard wasn't as strong as he used to be.

THE RESURRECTION

Jordan wanted to stay close to him in case it got ugly. Gallard was his priority, and then Lela. They were the only family he had left and he wasn't going to let anything happen to the two of them.

Maximus texted him again, pleading with him to hurry. Jordan knew he couldn't get out of this. Maximus scared the hell out of him, and he was afraid that if he ignored him, there would be painful consequences.

He had no choice but to listen and explain to Gallard what was going on. He messaged back that he would be there as soon as possible then put his phone back in his pocket.

"We have to go," he said. He walked out from their hiding place with Gallard following close behind. Maximus said he was inside the hotel, which meant it was a risk to meet him. They could be seen by Lucian's followers, but Jordan was confident that he could fight them off if needed.

"Did something happen?" Gallard asked.

"No, but I have to speak with someone. It's an old acquaintance and I think he wants to help us."

"Wait, what old acquaintance? I thought I was your only friend. I guess I am now that Solomon is mad at you. Sleeping with Cherish was a dick move, bro. If I were him, I would have thrown you out the window."

Jordan laughed then stopped walking before turning around. This was it. The moment where he might lose the person he cared about most. If he kept Gallard in the dark, then he would find out eventually. Maximus would make sure of that.

"Gallard, do you trust me?"

Gallard gave him a puzzled look and folded his arms. "Yes. With my life. What is this about?"

Jordan tried to think of how to approach his revelation. Blurting it out would probably put him in shock, which was easier now that he had a heartbeat. And beating around the bush would only waste time.

"Five hundred years ago, Abraham and Emma Christophe adopted Lucian because their son was believed to have drowned."

"Is that how it happened? How do you know this?"

"I know this because…I was that son. I didn't drown, I was taken."

Gallard let out a nervous laugh then went silent for several moments. Jordan couldn't tell if he believed him or if Gallard thought he was crazy.

"Are you serious?" Gallard finally said.

Jordan nodded. He then explained to him how he was not a descendant of Gaspard as he'd claimed, but that Gallard was *his* descendant. He tried to fit in as much information as he could and Gallard grew more and more shocked by the minute. He lowered himself down until he was sitting on the curb of the sidewalk. When Jordan finished speaking, he sat next to him and they sat in silence. He wanted to give Gallard a chance to react.

"Why did you keep this from me?" Gallard asked.

"Maximus ordered me to hide my real identity. He didn't want anyone to know about him and he's controlled me with threats my entire life. He can't kill Lucian because he's not powerful enough. He's immortal, but doesn't have the strength that we do because he isn't a vampire. He asked me to use you so I could get close to him."

"But...you were sick. In Las Vegas, you were dying. You had cancer, and I tried to take care of you. How did you pull that off?"

"I stopped feeding for a month. My body began to shut down, so I didn't have to pretend to be ill. I was in agony. The only way to get healthy again was to get you to think you were turning me so I could drink blood."

Gallard stood up again, resting his hands on the back of his neck then let them drop. So far, he wasn't yelling, which was a good sign. Jordan had only seen him yell once and it hadn't been pretty.

"So...I'm a *Christophe*, not a D'Aubigne? That means I'm...*we're* the true descendants of Lucian's adopted parents. Does that also mean we're not French?"

"You are, I'm not. My wife was French, and my children married into French families, so—"

"You had children?

"Well, yeah. You had to get here somehow, right?"

"This is insane. It's like I don't even know you."

Someone came out of the hotel and Jordan stood up as well. It was a short man with curly brown hair and brown eyes. He seemed familiar, but Jordan didn't recognize him.

"Jordanes, you said you would meet me ten minutes ago. When

I ask you to meet me, I expect you to—" Maximus stared at Gallard. "You...you're one of them."

"I'm one of who?" Gallard asked.

"The brothers. His undoing. You and the Almighty's appointed one will be his undoing. The shaman foresaw this."

"Shaman?" Gallard's eyes grew wide. "Bodoway! You spoke with Bodoway?"

"Maximus? Why are you mortal?" Jordan asked, interrupting yet another one of his soap box speeches. He didn't need to ask questions. He knew that Maximus had given someone his powers. If he'd done this, Jordan already knew who it was. "What. Happened?" he asked through clenched teeth.

"You were not making progress so I took matters into my own hands. But, Jordanes, you must listen to me. This man—"

Jordan grabbed onto his shoulders. "Enough with your stupid ramblings. What did you do? I swear, if you gave him your power I'll—"

"Yes. I gave Lucian my power. In doing so, I made myself mortal again. Now I can finally die."

Jordan threw Maximus on the ground, hard enough to knock the wind out of him. For the first time, he wasn't afraid of Maximus. He was mortal and no longer had the power to hurt him. But this also meant that he no longer had the power to follow through with his promise.

"Jordan what are you doing?" Gallard asked. "He might have important information!"

Jordan ignored him and continued questioning Maximus.

"And what of Lydian? You said that you would bring her back if I killed him!" Jordan shouted. Maximus coughed then hoisted himself up onto his elbows.

"I said I would help you get her back, Jordanes, not that I would do it myself. But...if you can find it within yourself—"

"Find it within myself to what? Forgive you? I hope you burn in hell for everything you've done to me! I will never forgive you!"

Jordan was overcome with grief and fell to his knees. He'd given over five hundred years of his life in service to Maximus, buying into his empty promises and hanging onto a false hope that one day it would all be over. That it was worth the blood and sweat.

He didn't have anything to hang onto until Lydian came along. She gave him something to fight for, but now that she was gone, he felt cheated. He'd jumped at the chance of getting her back, only to be deceived again.

"Jordanes, you must hear me out. If you do not do exactly as I say, everything will—"

He pinched Maximus' nose while covering his mouth with the palm of his hand, blocking off all air. Maximus writhed a bit, trying to get air, but he didn't fight. Jordan then realized that Maximus wanted to die; that killing Maximus was exactly what he wanted.

"Jordan, stop!" Gallard said. "He's not a threat to us anymore. Just let him live with whatever he's done to wrong you."

There was another way. A way to make him suffer a fate even worse than death. He removed his hand, allowing Maximus to breath then tore his wrist open.

"You may not go to hell, but I can make your life hell on earth," Jordan said. Maximus' eyes filled with fear and before he could try to get away, Jordan pressed his wrist to Maximus' mouth, forcing the blood down his throat. Maximus cried out in protest, trying to push Jordan away, but he was too weak. His human strength was no match for Jordan.

Suddenly, Maximus touched his chest and a surge of energy coursed through him. The act caused Jordan to fall backwards and knocked the breath out of his lungs. He struggled to sit up and watched as Maximus writhed in pain, either from the transformation or the agony of not getting his wish and dying.

The transformation finished and Jordan stood up, leaving Maximus to fend for himself.

"Gallard, go find Kevin. I'm going to find Lucian."

"You can't fight him alone. Wait for backup."

Jordan put an assuring hand on Gallard's shoulder. He was grateful that despite everything he'd just told him, Gallard was still concerned with his safety. It showed that their bond was real, even if it had been created under a lie.

"I will never get Lydian back, but I swear to you that I will do everything to keep Lela safe. Now go to the car and I'm going to see if she's made progress."

Chapter Forty-Three

"It is almost time for me to finish this. Tonight is the night the feud will end," Lucian said.

After he'd made his speech about what he planned to do and how I fit into his plan, I started to panic. He wasn't getting any closer to drinking my blood, and my lecture about preserving his humanity hadn't worked.

The trick with the dead flowers and the whole levitation thing had frightened me. I didn't want to know what else he was capable of. But I knew that as long as I appeared to be on his side, he wouldn't hurt me. I was safe, for now. I just wished that this could be over and done with.

That stupid kiss I'd given him made him even more smitten than I wanted. As he continued to speak of his plans for our future, he kept his arm around my waist, assuring that I was close to him at all times. Though his touch wasn't forceful, he frightened me more than ever. His words were that of a crazy man and everything he said was so over the top that I had to often look at him and see if he was for real. He hadn't seemed that fanatical before.

"What do you think, darling?" he asked once he was finished. I forced myself to smile at him and put my own arm around his waist. Flattering him wasn't as hard as I thought it would be. All I had to do was touch him and his expression would fill with satisfaction.

"I think you are brilliant and I don't know why I didn't team up with you sooner."

He smiled then began playing with my hair. "As my new partner, I would like to give you a gift." He turned me around, keeping his hands on me and I looked for whatever he wanted to show me. I knew that this gift probably wasn't going to be something I would like.

When I saw what he wanted to show me, I nearly crumbled to the ground. A person was walking towards us from the other side of the park. Someone who had died and I thought I would never see again. My father, David.

"How is this possible?" I asked Lucian. He lightly pushed me forward and I began to walk towards the figure. David didn't look how he had when I'd last seen him. He was younger; the age he'd been when I met him in Orlando.

"Hello, Lela," David said. "I've missed you, sweetheart. How are you?"

I couldn't answer him. I felt my eyes tear up, and I backed away. It wasn't real and I didn't want to pretend that it was. David was gone, for good. He'd died in Italy and seeing him again only made it hurt more.

"No. I don't want to do this. Make him...make it go away," I pleaded.

"Darling, I thought you would want to say goodbye. You never had the chance."

"Please, Lucian."

He put his arms around me in attempt to comfort me. I didn't want him to. I wanted to run away from there; from his evil presence and frightening abilities. I was in over my head and didn't want to do this anymore.

I looked back one more time and saw that the figure had disappeared. I hated that he'd been able to get to me like that. I didn't care that he'd done it to be kind. It only hurt, knowing that David could never come back.

"Get away from her, Lucian," I heard a voice say. I recognized it and turned around, relieved that Jordan was there. What confused me was why. This wasn't part of the plan. Nobody was supposed to make an appearance until I'd given Lucian my blood.

"Jordanes. Why are you here?" Lucian asked.

"I've come to kill you," Jordan said. "Maximus told me that he gave you his power and I had to get here before you hurt anyone."

"So, you are the real Lucian Christophe. I do not know why I could not see it before. You look like our mother, Emma." Lucian moved away from me then stopped directly in front of him, cocking his head to the right. "You are hiding. There is no need for that anymore."

Jordan began to moan in pain, covering his eyes and blinking to try and get it to stop. It intensified to a point where it was unbearable, so he forced his eyes open with his fingers and peeled off the contact lenses, revealing that he had dark brown eyes, just as he had when I'd first met him.

I didn't know how to react to this. Jordan was the real Lucian? This entire time he'd lied to us about who he was and now he and the fake Lucian were going to have a fight.

"Jordan...how is this possible?" I asked. "You're a night walker!"

He shook his head. "I'm not. I told you, I'm a really good actor. If only you knew just how good."

"So all of this...finding Gallard and helping us find Lucian...was all just part of your plan to kill him?"

"No! There is one thing I never lied about and that is how I feel about you. I care about you, Lela. All of this I've done to take care of Gallard and you. If you don't believe anything, believe that."

I looked over to the bushes where I'd last seen Cherish, hoping that she would make another appearance. I had a bad feeling about this and I didn't want to be caught in the middle of their fight. Something was off. I couldn't sense the others nearby, almost as if they'd completely left the area. I couldn't have felt more alone if I had been in a room with no one else around.

The feeling came simultaneously with Jordan's arrival, and I wondered if they were experiencing the same thing. The whole atmosphere changed from safe and serene to evil and desolate.

"I don't know what to believe," I said. Of course this wasn't true. Jordan owed me answers, yes, but I didn't doubt that he truly cared about me the way I did him. I needed Lucian to think that I was on his side. "We were just pawns in your game! That's why it was so easy for you to help Aaron hurt Robin, wasn't it?"

Lucian gave a sinister smile then laughed. "You see, darling. They are not on your side. I am the only one who you can trust." He turned around with his hand in his pocket and pulled out a cell phone, handing it to me. I didn't what was weirder, that he was giving it to me or that the fact that he had one in the first place.

"Call Aaron, tell him where we are and have him send the others. All fifty of them. It is time for this war to begin."

I had to stay in character, though it was difficult now that Jordan had arrived unplanned and threatened my cover. I didn't know how strong he was compared to Lucian now that I knew about his new powers and I didn't want to risk Jordan's life or mine.

"How did you have enough blood to make fifty vampires?"

"I am more powerful than you can imagine. Anyway, darling, please make the call."

I nodded and began to move away to make the call when he grabbed my arm and tugged me closer to him until his lips were on mine. It happened so fast that I didn't even have time to protest or be repulsed. It didn't last long, though and he ended it saying, "Hurry."

I shuddered as I walked away then dialed Aarons number. I was about to hit the call button when something stopped me. I wanted to know where my people were first before calling in Lucian's small battalion. I erased the number then dialed Cherish's, putting the phone to my ear. I tapped the heel of my foot nervously as I waited for her to answer.

"Lucian, if you've done something with her I'll—"

"Hey, it's me!" I interrupted her. I didn't address her by name in case Lucian was listening in. Chances were that he wasn't since he was talking with Jordan.

"Lela, thank God! Where the hell are you?"

"What do you mean? I'm in the same place I was five minutes ago."

"No…you're not. I'm standing next to the fountain. Solomon and I have been looking everywhere in this park."

"Cherish, this isn't a time for jokes. *I'm* standing next to the fountain." I looked around to see if she was nearby, but the only

THE RESURRECTION

other people around were Lucian and Jordan. Could it be possible that Lucian was somehow hiding us from everyone else? If so, he had to be very powerful, and very dangerous.

"Your father, he's...something's happened. I'm getting a very bad vibe. You need to get Gallard and Kevin here. I'll text you if my location changes."

Without waiting for a reply, I hung up and quickly dialed Aaron's number. He answered on the third ring and I gave him a brief summary of what was going on. He promised that everyone would show up within the next ten minutes then we both hung up.

"Enough with the magic tricks, Lucian," Jordan said. "You want to hurt me, hurt me. But don't fight like a coward."

Lucian glared then shoved him backwards, causing Jordan to fly several feet away. He collided with the fountain, causing major damage to it and the water started pouring out more profusely than ever. He recovered then started running towards Lucian, but was stopped by some invisible force, which sent him sliding back until he hit a tree.

"Come on, Jordanes. Fight back!" Lucian taunted. "Avenge your family!"

Jordan slowly stood up, preparing himself for Lucian's next blow. I'd never seen him fight before, but he'd probably held back in the past since he was stronger than I was led to believe.

He ran full speed at Lucian, tackling him like a linebacker, only with the force of a locomotive. The two of them went crashing through the park, passed the sidewalk and into the street, barely missing the traffic.

Cars honked, swerving around them, they paid no attention. Their only focus was killing each other. I followed them to make sure Jordan was okay. I still couldn't find Cherish or Solomon, nor did I know if they could see all of this happening.

Lucian struck Jordan with punches that would normally shatter a human being's bones, but barely fazed him, and Jordan hit back twice as hard. Lucian was definitely strong. But not undefeated. He'd been stopped once and I had to believe it could be done again.

Together, they damaged everything they came in contact with, and even as the police lights surrounded them, they continued fighting. Jordan slammed Lucian against a car, breaking all the glass and the people inside screamed. Lucian kicked him backwards, severely denting another vehicle. Lucian then pulled the car door off and flinging it at Jordan, who ducked just in time to miss it.

"You will not succumb to my force. I should try a new approach," Lucian said. He held up his hand and a few second later, Jordan's body tensed up. By his expression, I knew he was in a lot of pain. Whatever Lucian was doing to him, I had to stop it. I ran in front of him, hoping it would somehow block his power.

"Stop! Don't do this!" I shouted.

"And why not, darling? I thought you were through with him. With all of them!"

"Lela, get out of here!" Jordan urged. "Go find Gallard!"

Lucian let out a loud cackle that made my spine tingle. Almost like two voices were speaking at once, one guttural and one his.

"Oh, Jordanes. Did Lela not tell you? She is with me now." He wrapped his arms around my waist from behind. "You see, she has always been mine from the second she was born. We are one and the same. I am her and she is me, do you understand?"

Jordan smirked. "I don't think her husband will be happy this."

"He does not have to. He just has to accept it." Lucian turned me around to face him. "I think that now is as good a time as ever to tell him, don't you? And while we are there, I can take care of Solomon at the same time."

Lucian grabbed onto my hand, and before Jordan could stop us, we disappeared at a quick speed. I had no idea what was coming next, but I was comforted knowing that Jordan wasn't in danger anymore.

With Lela's hand in his, they teleported across the city. His plan was going better than he'd ever dreamed. Not only had he successfully persuaded Lela to join his side, but he'd accessed more power beyond his imagination.

He felt a new strength. He was aware of everything around him from the rustle of leaves a mile away to the very heartbeat of the woman next to him. He always knew that she would come to him. They had bonded, like she'd said and no matter what she'd had with Gallard, nothing could change that.

At one point, they'd existed as one person. They were both betrayed by people they trusted and they were both outcasts, judged for the decisions they had made. She was better than Florence or Cherish ever could have been.

Lucian spotted his followers gathered in the middle of Times Square. Aaron was at the front of the flank. Police and other armed forces surrounded the area in huge trucks and a few helicopters were flying above. He hadn't planned to cause this big of a scene, but there was nothing he could do about it. The battle was going to happen whether they liked it or not.

They landed on the top floor of the tallest apartment complex. Lela had to take a moment to adjust to their stop and stood next to him. The view of Manhattan was amazing from there. He could see everything; every movement, every person that walked below. His eyes swept over everything as he looked for someone in particular. Solomon had to be down there, and the others not too far.

He couldn't find them, so he glanced over at Lela who was clinging to the steel railing as though she were afraid she would fall. He knew she wasn't afraid of heights. Something else was putting her on edge.

"What is the matter, darling? Are you afraid?" She didn't meet his gaze but continued staring down at the street. She was shaking, very subtly yet enough for him to notice. Was she afraid of *him*? If so, he needed to show her that he wasn't a threat to her. "I will not hurt you. You are my—"

"What? I'm your *what*?" she asked, somewhat harshly.

"Have I angered you in some way? Is it because I wanted to kill Jordanes?"

She turned her body towards him, but kept her eyes on the ground. "Yes."

"He is no longer your concern, Lela. Those imbeciles down there need to learn that we will not be trifled with. They cannot control us anymore, and with this new power, we can be sure that they never do so again."

"How many more have to die to get your point across?"

He pushed a lock of her hair behind her ear.

"Only a few darling. Only a few."

Lucian looked down once more to try and spot Solomon. Either he was lost in the crowd or he wasn't even there at all. He had to be somewhere nearby since they had run into Jordan.

A familiar face stood out to him and he recognized the young man as Kevin. He was tempted to strike him down where he was, but that would take all the fun out of it. He would rather his army kill the Sharmentino boy.

"Kevin!" He shouted out in his loudest voice. It sounded deeper than usual; not his usual tone. Everyone stopped what they were doing and looked up to see who had spoken. He made eye contact with the boy and smiled. "Where are the rest of your friends?"

The light from one of the helicopters shined in their direction, and someone inside with a gun aimed at Lucian. He fixed his eyes on the officer and within seconds, the man was pulled by an invisible force out of the chopper and fell a hundred feet below. The man flying the helicopter took off without even hesitating, taking the chopper into the opposite direction.

"Ask me again once you've let my sister go!" Kevin shouted back up.

Lucian lips curled into a smirk as he placed his hand over Lela's, which was still resting on the railing.

"She is not my prisoner, young man. Ask her. She will tell you herself."

Lela trembled even more and he interlocked his fingers with hers. He noticed that she still had her wedding ring on, to his vexation. If she truly was through with Gallard, she shouldn't be wearing it anymore, unless she'd just
forgotten.

"He's right, Kev," she struggled to say. She then formed a smile on her face while putting an arm around Lucian. "I am with him...willingly."

Lucian glanced at the ring again. It was bothering him more than it should. Something needed to be done about it. "Throw down your ring," he commanded. Her eyes filled with a silent horror. "Tis the only way they will believe you. Throw it down."

He let go of her hand and watched as she slowly pulled it off. She then held up, staring at it with a sadness he didn't understand.

THE RESURRECTION

A full thirty seconds went by before she held it over the railing and let it drop three stories down.

"Thank you, darling," he said. He returned his attention back to Kevin. "It appears that you and your group are outnumbered. Since you have given *me* the gift of Lela's partnership, I will do you a favor and even the odds."

Lucian closed his eyes, drawing all of his power from within and placed his focus on his followers below. He wasn't exactly sure what he was doing since this was all new to him, but somehow it came naturally.

Horrifying yells flooded the streets and he opened his eyes to see what was happening. Several of the immortals he'd created were crouched on the ground, holding their heads and writhing in pain as blood poured from their eyes, ears, nostrils and mouths. They were bleeding out, gradually but enough to cause them extreme discomfort.

Soon, about ten of them were dead, leaving about forty left, including Aaron. The police below had surrounded the area, holding their guns on the remaining immortals. None of them moved and Lucian wondered if they would do anything at all. It didn't matter. They would lose.

"What are you waiting for?" he shouted to the survivors. "Kill him."

Chapter Forty-Four

Cherish ran into the street towards the flashing lights. What she'd witnessed in the park was more terrifying than anything she'd ever experienced. The fountain burst open, causing damage by seemingly invisible forces. She still couldn't find Lela and she was beginning to panic. She'd promised Gallard she would watch out for her and now Lela had disappeared with her father.

Solomon came up behind her, and at the same time, she spotted Jordan. He looked beaten and tired. Had he been in a fight? Was it him and her father that had caused the damage to the park. If so, how had she not seen it? How had they made themselves hidden from her and Solomon? The bigger question she had was where Lela and her father were now.

"Jordan what happened?" Solomon asked. He stood up from the ground, wincing as he did and leaned against the damaged taxi cab he was next to.

"Lucian took her. He has...abilities. He overpowered me then ran off, taking Lela with him."

THE RESURRECTION

"What do you mean, Jordan?" Cherish asked. "What sort of abilities?"

"There's no time to explain. Lucian has his army ready to attack. Gallard and Kevin are on their own out there. They won't survive a second against them."

The three of them returned to Times Square just as Lucian's army closed in to attack. They needed to find Gallard and Kevin, if it wasn't already too late. The police began trying to stop the fight and the helicopters hovered, occasionally shining a light on different parts of the street.

She searched for Kevin, hoping that he was all right. He could hold his own, but still she worried. And she worried for Gallard, who was the weakest of them all. He would need someone to watch his back.

"Hey, you three need to stay back. There's some gang-related activity going on and we are asking all citizens to go a different route," said an officer.

"Yeah, we would but, we're gang members so…if you could let us pass, that would be helpful!" she said. The officer reached for his gun, resting his hand on the holster.

"Then you could answer some questions. Could you tell me what the hell is going on?"

Jordan sighed with exasperation and she folded her arms, equally annoyed. She didn't have time to explain everything to the police. They didn't have a need to know. The people weren't the ones that were in danger, it was her friends. Mortals weren't even supposed to know about vampires, but Lucian hadn't done anything to be discreet and now Manhattan was about to witness a full on vampire war.

"I can't tell you everything, but I can say this. Unless you let us by, this mob isn't going to break up. This war isn't a threat to civilians…not as long as they stay far away. We can't stop all hell from breaking lose until we can join our friends and stop the threat," Solomon said.

The officer loosened his grip on the gun before letting his hand drop completely.

"They're so strong," he murmured. "What are they?"

"We are abominations," said a person behind them. She turned to see a strange man standing not too far away. "The filth of the earth. God destroyed the Nephilim in the flood and then I created these...animals. They can't be stopped. Not unless—"

"Maximus, this isn't the time for a soliloquy," Jordan snapped. "You either help us, or stay out of the way. I would prefer the latter since you've done such a good job of it."

Cherish wondered if this was the man Jordan told her about. By the way they spoke, she sensed hostility between them. What had he meant that he'd created them? Surely, he couldn't be the one that she'd heard about in the legends. What was he doing here and what was his connection to all that was happening here?

There was no time for questions, so the three of them walked past the officer, and he didn't try to stop them. They walked over the cop cars and sped by the SWAT vans unnoticed until they got to the midst of the fighting. Unlike the first battle, there were less of them. Four to be exact and the group was struggling.

None of Lucian's followers had been killed, and the chaos had gone on for a good half an hour. Either the morale was down, or everyone was just tired. Cherish wasn't up to her full potential since she hadn't fed in a while, but she was holding her own. Kevin was actually an adequate fighter, despite being a night-walker. He wasn't going to give up anytime soon.

The group wasn't the only one trying to take down the army. Several of the police and SWAT teams were attempting to stop them as well. They were using shields and batons to fight them off, but they didn't stand a chance against the immortals. The group was spending more time trying to save the officers than anything else. All the chaos and confusion was working to their advantage. If some of the attention was on the officers, then the group could use the distraction to stay alive longer.

Kevin was lying on the ground, being kicked over and over by two men, and Cherish rushed over to intervene. She jumped onto the back of one of them and tore out his throat with her teeth, causing him to fall to the ground instantly. The other one went after her but she ducked out of the way and Kevin handed her a baton from one of the dead officers and she beat the guy with it until she'd broken most of his bones then pressed on his neck with her foot until his head separated from his body.

"Where's Gallard?" she asked Kevin as she stepped over the

dead man.

"Didn't you see him? He's out there somewhere. I lost him in the crowd."

"You *what*? He's mortal and you got separated from him?"

"I did my best. It's hard to watch someone when fifty vamps are coming at you."

She looked over to see Solomon and Jordan trying to fend off five that had surrounded them then she and Kevin went to help. The men were almost gaining the upper hand when a scared officer tossed three canisters of tear gas in their direction, enveloping the area in a disorienting fog and then men stopped fighting and Lucian's army scattered.

Cherish felt blindly for a way out of the street. The tear gas didn't affect her, but she couldn't see past the fog. She nearly tripped upon finding the curb and as the fog began to dissipate, she spotted Aaron, watching from sidelines. She wondered why he wasn't fighting. Either he was still conflicted over which side he was on or he was just enjoying the view. Upon seeing her, he started backing away, but she sped up next to him before he could make a run for it.

"Hey, Aaron. How's the traitor life for you?"

"You're one to talk, Cherish. Weren't you the one plotting to seduce Gallard not a week ago?"

She punched him in the gut and he coughed. "At least I didn't follow through. I stayed on the good side." She grabbed him by his jacket, shoving him against a newspaper stand. "Where's Lela? I know Lucian left with her, and since you're his new lap dog, I'm guessing that you have special knowledge."

He gave a mischievous smile. "Oh, she's with him all right. You should have seen how cozy they were up on that balcony. She's all but forgotten Gallard."

"Have you ever considered the possibility that she's, I don't know, faking?"

"She's not faking. I have proof." He dug in his pocket a bit then pulled his hand out, opening his fist and in the middle of his palm was a tiny, gold ring. She knew whose it was because she'd been there when Gallard bought it.

"Where did you get that?" she asked, loosening her grip on his jacket.

"She dropped it. Tossed it over the railing like it was nothing. Don't know why I grabbed it, though."

A blast went off and the remnants of the explosion flew in their direction. The helicopter had returned and accidently blew up a car, which then blew up another. A piece of shrapnel flew in her direction and imbedded in her side. Aaron was unharmed, so he ran off before she could recover.

One man came running at her and she pulled out the shrapnel and stood. This immortal was big; about six foot-five at least and he was built like a lumberjack. She took a swing at him, but it didn't gain a reaction. He slapped her across the face, knocking her ten feet away and into a wall.

She tried to get up, but the guy was already on her, kicking her repeatedly. She finally got a chance to grab his leg and bit onto it, tearing violently at his skin. He failed at getting her to release her grip and pulled a long sword from the sheath strapped to his back.

He raised it into the air, preparing to run it through her when an SUV came out of nowhere and crashed into the man, sending him flying several feet. The driver rolled down the window and she smiled when she saw it was Gallard.

"Whoops! Sorry. Guess I'm a bad a driver," he said. He parked the car then got out just as the others came running over.

Solomon helped Cherish up from the ground, and to her surprise, he kissed her. It wasn't a quick kiss either. It lasted for quite a while, and he held onto her as she kissed him back. In that moment, she knew that Lela had been right. Solomon loved her. She promised herself she would never doubt his feelings again.

"You all right?" he asked.

"I am now." She turned to Gallard and shoved him. "Where the hell were you? Kevin said you disappeared and, I thought you were killed!"

"I'm sorry. I got lost in a crowd of police officers and did my best to stay out of the way. It appears I showed up just in time."

Cherish looked over to see Kevin coming towards them. So far, there were no casualties, but Aaron had disappeared again. They hadn't killed all of Lucian's followers, though the police had them fairly distracted, allowing for the group to duck out and escape the mob.

"Hmm...nice sword," Gallard said, picking it up off the ground. "But it's of no use to us."

Solomon looked at the sword in Gallard's hands and furrowed his eyebrow. "I've seen it before. That's the one that vamp used to kill Melody."

Gallard put the sword back in its sheath then slung it over his shoulder. "Then we'll take it. I think it's fitting that Lucian die by the same sword that killed his daughter."

"So everyone's okay?" Cherish asked.

"We're a bit bruised and aside from some internal bleeding, I think we're good," Kevin said.

"We need to find Lela," Gallard said. "Lucian left with her after the fighting started. Do you know where he might have taken her?"

"He kept going on and on about Lela being his or some creepy nonsense like that," Jordan said. "Maybe...he might have taken her back to the hotel."

Gallard kicked the newspaper stand. "I should never have let her go after him again. If he touches her—"

"He won't!" Cherish assured him. "My father may be many things, but he's *never* taken advantage of anyone in that way. Besides, Lela wouldn't take it that far. She's obviously earned his trust or he would have killed her by now."

"Kevin, take Gallard to the hotel," Solomon said. "The rest of us are going to try and help these poor officers fend off Lucian's army. They aren't equipped to handle them. It wouldn't be right if we left them to clean up this mess."

Kevin quickly got into the driver's seat while Gallard ran around to get in on the other side.

"Hey!" Jordan called to Gallard before he got in. "Don't do anything stupid. You may have a sword, but you are mortal. Scope out the area and wait for me."

"I can't promise you that."

"Gallard—"

"That's my wife out there, Jordan! You can't ask me not to act. I can promise not to be stupid, but I refuse to promise not to do anything."

Gallard then got into the into the car and Kevin drove off. Cherish wished she could along with them, but she her strength was needed in the field. She could only hope that Lela would somehow get her blood to her father before Gallard and Kevin would arrive.

Chapter Forty-Five

I was somewhat glad when Lucian suggested we go back to the hotel. After he'd given the order for his army to attack, I'd looked away, unable to watch. My group was perfectly capable of handling themselves in a fight, but still I didn't want to see it in case they ended up losing.

I sat on the bed, trying to stay comfortable despite my tight dress while he stared out the window. He'd barely said a word the entire way there and he'd been in the same place for the past ten minutes. He must have been waiting for something, a message about how the fight ended.

There was no way I could focus on him. I was scared to the point of sickness, and I had to use what strength I had left to keep from vomiting. If I showed any sign of fear, he would know that I was deceiving him. Throwing my ring down had been hard enough, but now that we were alone, I needed to be extra careful.

Someone burst through the door, and I flinched then relaxed when I saw that it was only Aaron. He looked tired, physically and emotionally. Though I knew it would never happen, I wanted him to comfort me. I felt so alone in that room with just Lucian and I needed my brother. Not the Aaron that betrayed me or the Aaron that turned our sister, but the Aaron that I loved.

"What are you doing here, Sharmentino?" Lucian asked him. Aaron glanced at me then back at him.

"I came to give you an update. I left the scene about five minutes ago. Two of them are dead."

"Which two?" I asked. Aaron swallowed, keeping his attention on Lucian.

"Cherish...and Solomon." His eyes shifted a bit and I frowned. I'd seen that look before. He'd done that same thing with his eyes when he'd promised Mark we wouldn't have a party while they were out of town. He was lying. He had to be.

"And what of Gallard and Jordan?" Lucian asked.

"I'm not sure. The police got involved in the fight and it's utter chaos out there. Cars are blowing up, guns going off, and tear gas. I was lucky to get out of there. They could be headed here, or they ran off. I left before I saw what happened to them."

"Thank you, Sharmentino. I only have one last request of you."

"And what is that, my master?" Aaron asked in a patronizing tone.

Lucian smiled at me. "I need you to kill that blonde whom your sister slept with. The one with the eyepatch. My spies told me he was lurking outside of the hotel earlier. Find him and slit his throat from ear to ear. And then I want you to kill Gallard. Divorce is a long, messy process. Death is quicker."

Aaron seemed confused but did a good job at hiding it. I knew him better than Lucian did, so he couldn't fake it with me.

"It shall be done."

"Good answer. You have earned your immunity. Once he is dead, Take your brother and leave my sight. I would like to be alone with your sister."

Aaron looked at me again, and I pleaded with my eyes for him not to leave. I was surprised when he came over to me, and he dropped something in my hand then left the room, closing the door behind him.

I opened my fist. A tear escaped my eye when I saw what he'd given me. I'd thought the ring had been lost, falling into a gutter or rolling somewhere never to be found again. The ring gave me hope. Hope that my friends were still alive and that they would protect

THE RESURRECTION

Gallard. I didn't trust Aaron to defy Lucian's orders.

After Aaron left, Lucian sat on the bed next to me and smiled. I couldn't understand how he'd gotten attached to me so quickly. We'd barely spent four hours together in the flesh and he was acting like we were soul mates. Why was this so? We'd fought so much in the past that the idea of us being together seemed absurd. He had obsessive tendencies that were borderline delusional.

"Soon, Gallard will be dead. That means you are no longer married to him. Til death do you part, right?"

"Yes," I struggled to say. "Til death."

"Now there is nothing standing in the way of us being together."

He moved closer to me and I didn't move a muscle. I'd been willing to flatter him, pretend to be on his side, and even kiss him. But nothing more. I drew the line at sleeping with him; even if there was a chance that Gallard was dead. I had a strong feeling that he wasn't. I would know if he was.

"You don't except us to get married, do you?" I asked.

"Of course not. We have both been through that before, and look how those marriages turned out. Besides, our connection is beyond that of marriage. We are bonded by blood and nothing can destroy that."

"But...I thought you said that you liked that I was pure and good or whatever. What changed?"

"Forget everything I said. I want you, and I only want you to be with me from now on."

Lucian began kissing me with appalling presumption, and I did nothing but sit there, wondering why this always happened to me. I was always the object of my enemies' advances. First with Simeon, then Matthew, and now Lucian. For too long had I let this happen to me. Lydian would never let a guy get close to her if she didn't want them to and neither would Cherish.

Curtis' words at the party came back to me. Though it was nearly six years ago, I remembered them clearly. *"Lela, you're so innocent, it's adorable."* Was that my problem? I appeared so innocent that men felt they could take advantage of me? If that was so, I needed to take a new approach.

Cherish told me that Lucian almost always got what he wanted.

And if I had to make him think that he'd won me, then that was what I would do, only *I* would be the one in charge.

Without warning, I flipped him over onto his back and straddled him. He chuckled at my unexpected move and then I kissed him back, only to bide my time. I needed him to be under *my* submission so that I could persuade him to feed off me. This was the only plan we hadn't tried yet and if the others were on their way, I needed to weaken him before they arrived.

He unzipped my dress, and I let him take it off. In a way, it was nice because now I could move around better. To keep up the façade, I unbuttoned his suit vest and threw it to the floor then did the same to his shirt. I was disgusted the entire time, but I needed to be believable.

When he started to unhook my bra, I stopped kissing him and said, "Not so fast, my redheaded monster. You haven't tasted me yet. And I think it's only fair since I've tasted you."

He chuckled, sitting up as well, resting his hands on my waist. "You really know how to lead a man on, don't you?" His lips touched my throat, and I waited impatiently for him to do what I wanted. "But if you insist, I will accept your offer."

Finally, he bit my carotid artery and began to drink. I winced at the pain, but endured it. He was greedy, though, taking more than I expected him to. I felt myself growing weaker and weaker the more he drank. I guess Gallard hadn't been lying when he'd said I tasted good. Only he'd had the self-control to stop.

Suddenly, he pushed me away and starting choking. He looked terrible, like he was being poisoned or something. If my blood was the cause of this sudden illness, then it was working a lot faster than it had on Gallard. I watched as he clutched at his throat, falling off the bed and onto the floor.

"What have you done to me?" he asked, his voice forming a deep, guttural tone. His eyes turned black and so did his hair. I got up from the bed, dressing myself once more, and cowered over him, not letting his changes frighten me.

"Funny, I said the same thing the night I drank *your* blood!" I jeered. He tried to crawl towards me and grab my leg, but he wasn't fast enough. "I was only fourteen when I turned. *Fourteen*! I was all alone in my room, suffering the excruciating pain of the transformation. I thought I was dying. And I did it because I trusted you. You *told* me to do it and I obeyed. But I'm not listening to you anymore. *I'm* calling the shots now!"

As he continued coming towards me, the room began to shake. I remembered the news reports about the earthquakes and realized my hunch had been right; he'd been behind them this whole time. It was so bad that I lost balance and fell backwards. The dining table across the room snapped in half and I had to roll out of the way as the chandeliers came crashing to the ground, shattering on impact.

I moved away from the glass, but then the floor began to drift apart and I nearly fell into the crack. The split went all the way up to the ceiling, breaking the window and knocking everything off the walls.

The shelves toppled over then the Jacuzzi broke as well, causing all three hundred gallons to come pouring out and I was pushed against the wall by the force of the water. The level didn't stay high for long because of the cracks in the floor and slowly the water seeped down into them.

Then everything came to a stop. The shaking ceased and all that was left was the carnage it had created. Lucian had given up trying to come after me and lay on the floor, convulsing. His appearance started going back to normal, only this time his hair kept getting lighter and lighter until it was red and. The convulsing stopped, allowing him to be relieved of some discomfort.

He sat up and I prepared to run away when he began to speak, stopping me in my tracks.

"What's going on?" he asked. I stared at him for a moment to see if he was faking it. He looked genuinely confused and kept looking around the room like he was lost. I noticed that his eyes were blue again instead of lime green.

"What's going on? You're crazy is what's going on!" I said, slowly inching my way towards the door. He finally stood up and looked at me.

"How did I get here? The last thing I remember was…the night club. Aaron and I were there all night and I…had a terrible hangover. The rest is…gone."

I stopped moving away and suddenly found myself moving closer to him. Had Maximus' power really corrupted his mind so badly that he wasn't in control? I thought that he was just this maniac who had finally lost it completely, but now it seemed like something more was going on with him.

"You really don't remember the past two weeks?" I asked him.

"Darling, I can't even remember the past few days. All I know is that Melody is dead and…your sister—" he stopped speaking for a moment then his eyes grew wide as if he were suddenly recalling everything. I waited to see what he would say.

"Maximus! He forced his power on me…I remember now. And…" he looked at me, "You! I wanted you so badly that I couldn't think straight. That's all I know."

"Well, Lucian. I hope that's over now because I can't take any more of this craziness. I'm going now. I have to help my friends fight off the men that *you* sent!"

"Wait! Lela. Please listen to what I have to say!"

"Why should I? After everything you've done, you're asking me to listen to you?"

Lucian pleaded to me with his eyes, and I frowned. Something was different about him. He didn't have the crazy eyes I'd seen from earlier. He seemed calmer; saner.

"I understand now; why I craved you; why I felt like I needed you more than air. Something within me must have known your blood would free me of this."

He stepped closer to me, but I didn't move. I wasn't going to let him get too close, though I did want to know what else he was going to say. I wished he would hurry so I could go check on the rest of my group. I didn't believe any of them were dead.

"How could you know when I didn't even know?" I asked.

"I do not know, darling. I'm not the expert when it comes to this."

I rolled my eyes then walked passed him. I didn't have time for cryptic discussion. I didn't even care why my blood had taken away his power. He was no longer a threat and now I needed to stop the chaos he'd started.

I heard footsteps beside me in the hall and realized he was following me.

"What are you doing?" I asked.

"I want to see what damage I have done. Maybe I can get my memory back and—"

"I think you've done enough, Lucian. Just stay out of my way.

THE RESURRECTION

Besides, you're mortal now. And don't think I would try to save your—"

I stopped as I saw two of his followers enter the hallway. They must have been his personal guards since they weren't with the others.

"Those are the men who killed Melody," Lucian whispered. "I thought you killed them."

"So did I."

"I replenished my army, you said?"

"You made fifty day-walkers after your other followers were killed. You sent them after us."

"*Fifty*? I barely wanted to turn my wife, let alone a stranger. Why would I do that?"

I ignored his question as they both charged at me and saw this as an opportunity to strengthen up from Lucian's overzealous sample he'd taken. The man on the left attacked first, and though I wasn't as fast as I usually was, I managed to dodge him then jumped on his back, sinking my teeth into his neck.

He slammed into the wall, smashing me into it and I fell to the ground. I hadn't taken as much as I wanted to, but I was stronger. I head-butt him and he staggered back into the other guy. His partner pushed him aside quickly then began an attack of his own. I kicked him backwards and then they both came at me again, rushing at full speed this time.

"Enough!" Lucian shouted. The men stopped, turning to him. "She is with me. Harm her no more."

"Hey, Lucian," the man said. "Remember us? You recruited me then you let them kill my girlfriend."

The first man, who was taller than the other, was about to walk away when he stopped and took in a deep breath through his nose. That was when I knew Lucian's pretense had failed. They smelled his mortal blood and there was no way he could hide it.

"You're human," the man said. He began to laugh and nudged his partner. "Looks like our so called great leader is not so great anymore."

He grabbed Lucian around the throat and shoved him against the wall. I had no idea what I was supposed to do. In a normal situation, I would have been grateful that these night-walkers were going to end him. I wasn't supposed to want to save his life. Yet here I was, contemplating whether I should let them kill Lucian or try to talk them out of it. There was that pesky compassion again.

"Let him go," I said, calmly but also firmly. "He's not worth it."

"Not worth it?" asked the second man. "He let his daughter kill my sister. My only family is dead because of him!"

"Oh yeah? Don't think I don't remember you. You dropped my sister from the top balcony and now she's dead. You deserve worse than what she suffered."

The other man lunged at me, throwing me to the ground. "You must remember me as well. I killed that friend of yours and I think you deserve to die too."

"Sure, that sounds like a great idea. Let's just kill everyone!" I heard someone shout.

I turned my head in the direction of the voice then smiled when I saw who it was. Gallard had finally come. His arrival was bittersweet, though. He was now in danger and I didn't know if I had the strength to protect him from two night-walkers. Not while I was still weak from Lucian feeding on me.

Gallard came towards us until he was standing about thirty feet away. I wanted to go to him, but the second man held me down on the floor with his foot on my throat.

"Perfect," the first man said. "Just the person I want to see. Aaron called it quits and passed off the task of gutting you to yours, truly. It was stupid of you to come here."

"Well, I did come here with the hope that I could kick Lucian's scrawny, British ass, but if you want to, no one's stopping you," Gallard said.

"Why are you blonde?" Lucian said, his voice raspy since the man's hand was squeezing his throat.

"Same reason you are mortal," Gallard said. "Feels great to be truly alive, doesn't it?"

Lucian tried to get away, but the man holding him tightened his grip.

"No one is going anywhere. You are going to die." He then turned to Gallard. "And you…you get to be my dinner."

I tried to fight off the one holding me down, but he kicked me in the side of the head, disorienting me so that I couldn't stand up without the room spinning. My vision blurred, and I could only see garbled shapes, swiftly moving around. I smelled blood and by the time I could see clearly again, I found that Gallard had sliced the first vampire in half.

The second man let go of Lucian then went after Gallard, throwing him against the wall. There wasn't much space to move around since the floor had huge cracks caused by Lucian's earthquake. The impact of the fall caused Gallard to drop the sword and the man picked it up. I saw where this was going so I stood up, running to Gallard's aid.

The next few seconds all seemed to mesh together. Everything happened so fast that I couldn't have done anything to prevent it. This moment was very similar to the night Melody died; so many things happening at once that I couldn't react. The man prepared to stab the sword through Gallard but then someone jumped in the way. The blade pierced Lucian in the chest.

"Well, well," the vamp said. "You've just made my job easier. Now I can kill two birds with one stone."

He shoved the sword deeper into Lucian, and in the process, he ended up stabbing Gallard as well. He then pulled it out and both men fell to the floor.

"No!" I yelled in fury.

The vamp then turned his attention to me, and I stopped moving. He was going to try and come after me, and he was the one thing standing in my way to get to Gallard. I got up and went after the man, twisting the sword out of his hands then beheaded him, just as he had Melody. She was finally avenged.

I then turned around to check on Gallard and Lucian. Both were still conscious, but bleeding very badly. I helped Gallard move so that he was leaning against the wall then tried to press on his wound to slow it down. It was no use, though. The sword had gone all the way through and he was bleed from both ends of the wound.

"How much pain are you in?" I asked.

"Compared to losing you for a year, this is nothing."

"Oh, please," Lucian said. "Try being hung upside-down and having your blood drained into—"

"Shut up, Lucian!" Gallard and I shouted at the same time.

As much as I wanted this to be a private conversation, we had to accept that until the others arrived to help we would have to talk with Lucian next to us.

Gallard laced his fingers through mine the same way he'd done before so that our rings touched. I was glad that Aaron had found mine and given it back to me.

"*Je t'aime*," he said.

I smiled and replied, "*Tu es l'amour de ma vie.*"

"Where did you learn that?"

"Jordan. I asked him to teach me a few phrases when you weren't around. Like the one at the end of my wedding vows."

He grimaced and closed his eyes. He was growing paler and paler as he continued to bleed.

"No, Gallard. Stay awake! Help will be here soon!"

I moved back over by Lucian and started digging in his pockets. He must have known what I was looking for because he reached into the one on his vest and handed me the phone. I took it from him then began to dial.

"Why did you try to save him?" I questioned.

"Redemption, darling," he coughed. "Because of me, you lost your parents, your biological father, your friend. Then by my hand, your uncle. I failed at protecting Robin even though I swore to you I would save her. I wanted..." He grimaced. "I wanted to save him for you. You must know..." He looked over at Gallard for a second. "He is not the only one who loves you."

The way he'd said that was different. It didn't sound crazy or possessive like when he'd kept saying I was his and how we were bonded. It sounded genuine. Before I could answer, I saw the door open and turned to see Jordan come into the room. His eyes grew large as he saw the horrific scene and he hugged me.

"It's okay, Lela. We're here now," he said. I nodded then stepped out of the way as Solomon, and Cherish entered the room as well. But my focus wasn't on them. It was on the large pool of blood that was forming underneath Gallard.

"What happened?" Cherish asked. I explained everything to her, starting from his drinking my blood and ending with the unexpected double-crossing of Lucian's lackey's. I was even honest about his not remembering the past few weeks, though I doubted they would believe it.

To my surprise, she looked at Lucian then knelt down so that she was sitting on her knees at his side. I saw her wipe away a tear

THE RESURRECTION

as she took his hand and held it in both of hers. This was the first time I'd ever seen her show any warmth towards him.

"Cherish, daughter. Why are you crying? I thought I was already dead to you."

"Lucian. For years I've hated and resented you for what you'd done to me as a child. You passed your coldness and distrust of others onto me, and now that I'm finally breaking from that, I have nothing but pity towards you. You raised me to be a monster, and it took me almost a lifetime to realize that I am not who you tried to create me to be. It may be too late for you, but it's not too late for me." She let go of his hand and lightly pressed her lips to his forehead. "I forgive you, father."

She then twisted his neck, breaking it with one flick of her wrists and he went silent. Just like that, it was over. Lucian was dead. I knew she'd done it because he was dying anyway. The sword had pierced an artery and he didn't have much time left. She'd put him out of his misery.

Cherish began to tremble and Solomon helped her up from the floor, pulling her into a comforting embrace. The initial shock of what she'd done wore off, and I started shaking Gallard, noticing that he'd lost consciousness. He was whiter than usual and covered in blood. I'd never seen him so still and I was beginning to panic

"Gallard, wake up! You *need* to wake up!" I pleaded with him. "Please. I'll…I'll rethink our agreement. You want children now? I'll do it. We'll adopt all the children you want. Have a huge family. Live in a two story house with a big back yard."

I took his hand. "We'll get a dog. One that's good with kids and will look out for them when they go out to play. They'll grow up with Gabby's girls and we'll continue the tradition of spending The Fourth of July with them. I'll stay by your side until you're old and grey. I'll help you when you can't do things by yourself anymore. You won't go into a nursing home because I'll take care of you until you draw your last breath."

He didn't respond. He couldn't be dead. I refused to give up on him since I'd already lost so many people. My parents were gone; all three of them, as well as my uncle. I'd lost Lydian, Melody, and Robin. Their deaths culminated into me nearly shutting down, but now that there was a chance I was losing the love of my life, the tears came flowing freely.

"Solomon, Jordan; one of you need to change him!"

Jordan stepped forward first and cut open his wrist, holding it over Gallard's mouth. The blood did nothing but drip down the sides, and held his head up to try and get it to drain down his throat. It didn't work. Nothing worked.

Just a year ago, our places had been reversed. He'd held me in his arms, begging me to wake up only to be left hanging. An entire year had gone by before I'd been able to wake up and finally return to him. But he was stronger than me. I couldn't survive without him.

I kissed him and held onto him while I listened as his heartbeat grew slower and slower; his breathing shallow and uneven. Finally, his heart beat one last time and he drew his last breath. I heard Cherish begin to sob as Solomon held her. Jordan pressed his back against the wall and slid down to the floor next to me.

"No!" I shouted, finding my voice. "No, no, no, no! Come back! Please come back!" I called out to the heavens. "God, please give him back to me!"

Jordan took one of my hands, squeezing it while I held Gallard's in the other. This wasn't like when I'd blacked out before or became blind with rage. This was complete and utter heartbreak. I hadn't felt this empty since I'd been dead.

I gazed at Gallard's face and stroked his hair. I thought back to a few days before when I'd accidently made him mortal. If only I hadn't given him my blood, he would have overpowered those men. A sword to the chest wouldn't have been able to kill him.

I felt partially responsible for this, though I hadn't hurt him, myself. This had to be what Bodoway had seen. On our honeymoon, Gallard had said everything was ripped away from him just when he had a glimpse of happiness. He probably felt that way because he knew he was going to die.

Then, I felt movement. It was subtle at first, and I didn't address it because I thought it was just my own body shaking with grief, but as the movement grew stronger and I heard gasps from the others, I looked up. His hair began to change from blonde to black and as he opened his uncovered eye, I saw that it was grey again. He looked puzzled as if he was unaware of his surroundings and then he spoke.

THE RESURRECTION

"Lela," he murmured. I held onto him tighter and he put his arms around me. I began to sob as the others let out sighs of relief. Jordan squeezed Gallard's shoulder.

"You really got us there, bro. We thought you were a gonner."

"It must have worn off," Solomon said. "The effects of Lela's blood must have gone away in time to save him."

Gallard began to stand up, and I helped him since he was weak from the blood loss. He looked around until his gaze fell on me. He gave a half smile, reaching up to touch my face.

"What happened?"

I stood on my tip toes, my lips meeting his then said, "It doesn't matter. You're here now. And I love you."

Chapter Forty-Six

As we walked down the hall, a swarm of firemen flooded the area. They must have showed up because of the earthquake. The rest of hotel had suffered some major damage. The room was severely trashed and there was blood everywhere, though we'd wrapped Lucian's body in a sheet. No maid service was going to be able to clean that mess up.

The firemen held their axes up as we stopped in front of them. We must have looked terrifying, our clothes covered in blood and our pale complexions. We didn't even try to fight them. We'd taken enough lives for one night. Instead, we rushed off in the opposite direction, disappearing around the corner then exited the building out of a window.

Outside, the night was filled with emergency response vehicles and fire trucks. Some more firemen were outside, spraying the hotel with hoses and trying to put out a fire that had erupted on the fifth floor. The earthquake had not only cracked the entire left side of the building but also severely ruptured the pavement and the street as well as knocked down a few trees.

All the glass from the cars parked on the road was shattered. Red and blue lights reflected off everything and the air was smoky. There were people watching from afar to try and get a glimpse of the action. There probably hadn't been this much police attention since nine-eleven. The battle of immortals had exposed our kind unintentionally, which meant that it wasn't safe for us to stay for much longer. After remaining relatively hidden for so long, all hell broke loose in one night.

I noticed someone running towards us and I met him half way, throwing my arms around him. Kevin had survived, making the night so much better. Aaron had been lying as I'd suspected. He would never let anything happen to our little brother.

"You're alive!" I said, no other phrase coming to mind.

"Nobody messes with the Sharmentinos. How else would I have lasted this long?"

I held his hand as we walked back to the rest of the group. "Have you seen Aaron? He was here not too long ago. I kind of owe him for not following through with his orders to kill Gallard."

Kevin shook his head. "No. If he was here, he's probably long gone."

I stopped at the edge of the street, and I could feel a sense of peace that I hadn't experienced in a long time. Five and a half long years of running, fighting, dying, and coming back to life and the threat was finally gone. There was no one who wanted our blood. No one who wanted us dead. No one who wanted to possess any of us. We were free.

Of everyone in the crowd of bystanders, one person stood out. He turned to look at us then broke from the crowd to join us. Jordan stepped forward, and we curiously watched, wondering what would go down between them.

"Have you destroyed him, Jordanes?" the man asked, his voice weary.

Jordan, who was carrying Lucian's body, moved the sheet to show Maximus Lucian's face.

"And...what of his power? Did it die with him?"

The power. I'd almost forgotten about that. He had been

displaying some wild abilities; killing a large portion of the immortals, making David appear, creating earthquakes. But when he'd drunk my blood, the power had left him. I'd explained it to the group after it was all over, and no one had an explanation for it, not even Jordan.

"I am the last of those you created, yourself. Other than that, the power is gone."

Maximus looked over at Gallard. "It isn't over."

"Oh, it's over," Jordan said. "I'm done following your commands. From now on, I'm living my own life."

Maximus clung to Jordan's shirt, falling to his knees and tears fell from his eyes. He then whispered something into Jordan's ear. When he was finished he stared up at him.

"You cannot ignore this."

Jordan pushed him away and Maximus crumbled to the ground weeping in utter desperation. My heart went out to him, even if he'd been the cause of all of our problems. If he hadn't created Lucian, Solomon never would have killed him, and I never would have drunk the blood, which then drew me to Gallard and David and Lydian. None of us would have ever met each other, save for my brothers. All the people I cared about had come into my life because of Maximus' choice.

For whatever reason, Jordan was not going to give him what he asked. I must have been elsewhere when their feud had been explained. Still, I felt moved to help the poor man. He didn't want to be immortal anymore. Everything he'd done had been in attempt to be released from this life.

I let go of Kevin's hand and walked over to Maximus, kneeling down to his level. I used my finger to lift his face up by his chin and he looked at me with the saddest eyes I'd ever seen.

"Since tonight is a night of forgiveness, I want to help you," I said. "I'm speaking on behalf of my friends and family. There's been enough betrayal and cruelty in our lives."

I took the knife David had given me out of my bra. It had been in my pocket when I'd woken up in the coffin and I'd had to come up with tricky ways to carry it with me. I cut my wrist and held it to him.

"My blood has the ability to make vampires temporarily mortal. I don't know why, but there are several mysteries in this world that we'll never know the answers to."

"No," he said, pushing my hand away. "I cannot. I do not deserve such a gift."

I smiled and reoffered it to him. "Who does, really? None of us are completely innocent. That's why we can't blame you for what happened to us. We *all* made choices that effected our lives one way or another. Take it, Maximus. I insist."

He smiled then kissed both of my cheeks, saying, "Blessed are you among women."

I chuckled nervously. "Thanks."

"You truly are." He looked at Gallard again. "He must live, dear one. Protect him at all costs. Swear it."

His tone was so serious that I couldn't be amused by him anymore. He seemed so truly worried about Gallard's safety.

"I swear," I said.

Maximus then bit onto my wrist, drinking only a little of my blood. About as much as Gallard had taken before. When he released me, his eyes displayed the same peace that I was feeling. He stood up and without another word, walked away, disappearing into the crowd.

Solomon put the comforter containing Lucian's remains into the trunk of the SUV then we drove off. We all agreed that draining Lucian of the rest of his blood and disposing of it was the best thing to do before burying him. That way, no one else could try to bring him back. It was probably a little much, but we wanted to be thorough.

Before we did anything, we changed into some clean clothes, disposing of our torn and bloody ones. We didn't want to risk getting pulled over looking like we'd stepped out of a slasher movie.

Jordan was at the wheel and Kevin, in animal form, was in the pouch behind the seat while Solomon and Cherish sat next to each other in the middle and Gallard and I were in the back. The sun was coming up by then, and the sunrise never looked so beautiful. We didn't say a single word as we arrived at our first destination and sat in the car with a comfortable silence.

Cherish got out first and the rest of us followed, with me holding Kevin under Jordan's jacket. We walked up to the railing and looked down below. The sight was breathtaking and I could see why so many people would want to visit there for their honeymoon.

If Gallard and I had been normal, we probably would have gone there. But we weren't normal, and we'd spent our honeymoon fighting off an army of immortals and nearly dying.

"Well, who would like to do the honors?" Solomon asked. Nobody made an effort to volunteer.

"I'll do it," Jordan said. "He was me in another life, after all. Burying him could be symbolic of reclaiming it." He took the wrapped up body from Solomon and began to dig in the ground. Why we'd chosen Niagara Falls as the place to leave him, I had no idea. Maybe everyone wanted to get rid of him as soon as possible.

"There. It's done," he said, wiping his hands on his pant after shoveling the last bit of dirt.

"Does this mean we should start calling *you* Lucian?" I asked.

"Don't even think about it."

Gallard walked over to the railing next to Jordan. "What about Jordanes? I think it is a good name. You should stick with it. It sounds more…regal than Jordan."

"And what about you?" I asked. "You're really a Christophe. Your whole life is a lie!"

"Once a D'Aubigne, always a D'Aubigne. Right, *Jordanes?*"

Jordan rolled his eyes. "Oh, *merde.* I'm never escaping that name, am I?"

We stayed at Niagara Falls for another half an hour. There was nothing pressuring us to leave, so we were taking our time. For once, there was no agenda, nowhere we needed to be in a hurry. Just the anticipation of living a life free of conflict.

Solomon and Cherish, holding hands. walked over to Gallard and me, glowing with the joy of young love, though they weren't really young at all. After all these years, and they'd finally found their way to each other.

"What do you guys plan to do after this?" I asked them. They exchanged glances then looked back at us.

"I'm returning to the Vatican to turn in my robes," Solomon said. "I'm not entirely proud of the way I left. I owe my fellow brethren an explanation. I don't know what this girl is doing."

Cherish playfully shoved him. "I'm coming with you, of course.

THE RESURRECTION

Unless…you haven't forgiven me yet."

"I'm working on it, my *Accarezzare*. It takes a while to resign, so until then, we will work on building trust."

She smiled at him then looked at us. "What about you and Gallard. You going back to Florida?"

Jordan cut in before we could answer. "Actually, they are coming with me to London. The Christophe house is just sitting there, unused and I think we should crash it. It is my house, after all."

Gallard looked at me, but I said nothing. He didn't seem against the idea at all.

"Really? You want to put up with us some more?" I asked. Jordan smiled.

"You two are the only family I have left." He stood up straighter. "I don't know if you knew this fact, but my father was a duke. That makes me the heir to his title and estate. The Christophe family built that house and real Christophes should live there. Besides, it's just going to waste. Think of the parties we could throw!"

Everyone started getting into the car, and Gallard handed Kevin to Jordan. I wanted a moment alone with Gallard so I could appreciate his being alive. He had his arms wrapped around me from behind and we continued to stare out across the water fall as the sun rose above it.

"You've been really quiet," I said. "Are you okay?"

He rested my chin on my shoulder. "When I thought I was dead, there were…no words for how I felt when I opened my eyes and found that I was still alive. That I have more time with you."

I turned around to face him and smiled. "That's exactly how I felt when I first woke up. We survived this, and now we have all the time in the world."

Gallard leaned down and softly kissed me before I hugged him close to me. I could feel the love in his embrace and it brought me so much comfort.

Maximus' words were still haunting me, and I wanted so badly to pretend I wasn't worried. He'd told Jordan that it wasn't over and had made me swear on my life that I would protect Gallard. I had a feeling that he wasn't bluffing. Whatever was in store for us in the future, I knew we would face it together.

THE RESURRECTION

Epilogue

Two weeks later...

Evelyn woke up from her nightmare and stared into the darkness. For a moment, she forgot where she was. After flying to Texas for Jeff's funeral, Simeon had flown her back to Orlando. She had been staying with Sharon for the past month. It had been a wise idea instead of staying in Texas. She'd been able to heal here.

The room she was in was very homey. The queen size bed had a lovely diamond tufted headboard covered in lavender cloth, and the bedspread was a dark violet with beautiful designs. The curtains were also violet and had a lavender sheer underneath. The dressers had more than enough room for the few clothes she had. It was the kind of room she'd always wanted as a young girl.

No longer wanting to sleep, she got up and took a shower. A cold one to assure she would wake up. She couldn't believe how much she'd been through during the past several weeks. She kept telling herself that she would leave in a few days and yet here she was. Still at Sharon's. Secretly, she was hoping that Lela, Kevin, and Aaron would show up so she could have some of her family with her. Then she would remember that Lela had lied to her and that something strange was going on with her nephews.

While she got dressed, she heard voices downstairs. Usually Sharon was in bed at this time, or at least Evelyn thought she was. Since she was already up, she decided to go and see what she was doing. She stepped into the hallway and just as she did, she bumped into a strong pillar.

"Oh!" her eyes adjusted and she saw it was Simeon. "I didn't know you were in town!"

"I wanted to surprise you." He leaned forward and smelled her hair. "You took a shower?"

"It was relaxing." She looked around. "Is Sharon up?"

"Yes, but she's otherwise occupied. I guess she's expecting a visitor tonight."

"Then we're alone?"

Without further ado, he crushed his mouth to hers. She kissed him back with equal intensity, and he lifted her into his arms, carrying her into the room. After she'd left with him, both of them had bonded over their recent losses of their spouses. What started as an innocent friendship soon turned into a full blown affair.

While she enjoyed Simeon's company, it was all physical. A way to forget the pain she had from losing Jeff. When she was with Simeon, she would pretend it was her husband. The two men were complete opposites in personality, but she found it easy to fantasize that her husband was still alive. That he was the one she was making love to and not her brother's college friend.

Simeon was in the middle of undressing her when the door opened, and Evelyn quickly sat up. Sharon was standing there in her robe. She was giving Simeon a look that Evelyn didn't understand.

"Honestly, Simms? You could at least wait until my sheets were cold before jumping to the next bed."

Evelyn sat up and smiled. "You could join us if you want."

Simeon chuckled then kissed the back of her neck. "My wild woman. Look what we've done to her, Shar."

Sharon came into the room and lay on the bed. Evelyn tugged off her robe and started kissing her. In the past, she never would have done something like this; have a threesome. The old her was a proper, law-abiding Catholic. With her husband gone, she felt she had nothing left to live for but herself. She was done playing by the

THE RESURRECTION

rules.

"As hot as this is, we don't have the time," Simeon said.

Evelyn stopped kissing Sharon and pouted. "Why not?"

"Tonight's the night. I know you've wanted answers about what happened to Mark and Sheila. You will get them."

The doorbell rang and the three of them grew quiet. Evelyn was disappointed that their fun time was cut short, but she was curious about what they wanted to tell her. She couldn't pass up the opportunity to get answers. Sharon kept telling her that some things in life would never be explained. In her heart, she knew there was more to the story but was afraid that they would just lie to her like her niece and nephews had.

Sharon put her robe back on then took Evelyn's hand, leading her down the stairs. She told Evelyn to wait in the kitchen then Evelyn stood quietly and listened. Sharon opened the door and started speaking to the visitor.

"Junior, you're back early," she said.

Junior? Evelyn had never heard Sharon talk about someone by that name before. Whoever it was, she'd spoken to him with an intimate voice. It had to be one of Sharon's many lovers. Sheila often told Evelyn about how Sharon went through men like a person went through toilet paper.

"You sound disappointed, Sharon," the guest said. "Should I go away and come back later?"

Evelyn put a hand to her mouth in shock. She knew this voice. It was her nephew, Aaron. Unable to hide any longer, she peeked around the corner so she could see. Sure enough, Aaron was standing in the doorway. Sharon leaned forward, kissing him, and began pulling him inside when he stopped her.

"Wait. I have a present for you," he said.

"Oooh, a present? I never get presents."

She grabbed a jacket from the door hook, wrapping it around her shoulders then followed him outside. Evelyn's blood began to boil. Of all the men in the world, Sharon had to get her hooks into Aaron. Evelyn knew Sharon had a thing for Mark and was probably using his son as a substitute.

Someone came up behind her and she turned around to see Simeon in the kitchen. He got out two wine glasses then proceeded to pour some very aged wine into them. She wasn't in the mood to speak with him just yet. She wanted answers and she wanted them now.

"What is going on, Simeon?" She asked. "Why is Aaron here?"

"We will explain in time." He held a glass out to her and when she didn't take it, he drank a sip from it. "Your life is about to change, Evie. Once you find out what we've been up to, you won't want to run away."

"What makes you so sure?"

He set the glass down then took her hand, leading her out of the kitchen. She wanted to recoil but somehow he still had a spell over her despite how much the secrets infuriated her. Jeff would be ashamed if he could see her now. The woman that had married him would never do half the vile things she'd done with Simeon and Sharon. Jeff's death had altered her.

Simeon stopped in front of one of Sharon's many closets and opened it. He motioned for her to go in first so she did and held her hands out so she wouldn't run into anything. Thankfully, he turned a light on and she looked around. She was confused about why she was there when she saw it.

There were two portraits hanging on the wall. One was of a man with the reddest hair she'd ever seen and eerie blue eyes. He shared the same characteristics as the woman who had come by their house.

But that wasn't what caught her attention the most. The man was without a doubt the same man who ran them off the road and tried to strangle her.

"That's the man who killed Jeff," she said, her voice trembling. "I...I don't understand. Why does Sharon have a painting of him?"

"Because he is no ordinary man." He pointed to the left wall. "I think you will recognize him as well."

Evelyn studied the portrait and gasped. The painting was of Solomon Schaech. The private investigator who had watched out for them the past year.

"Start talking," she said. "Who are these men? How do you know them?"

"The man with the dark hair is the same man you know, but his last name isn't Schaech. It's Sharmentino. He's an ancestor of yours and the reason the other man wanted you dead. The crimes against your family are the result of an age old feud between two immortals."

"Immortals? Simeon what the hell are you talking about? You make this sound like some sort of fairy tale!"

"I assure you, this is very real."

He stepped closer to her and she was suddenly filled with fear. He had never given her reason to be afraid of him, but the look in his eyes terrified her. She had nowhere to run and she wouldn't be able to escape. He was twice her size.

"What are you?" she asked.

Before Simeon could answer, Sharon appeared behind him.

"He's here," she said. "I've explained everything to Aaron and he's on board. Our boss wants to see Evelyn."

Simeon turned to her and smiled. "You ready, Evie?"

"For what? You promised me answers, and I expect you to give them to me. What is all this about immortals? How do you have a portrait of the man who killed my husband?" Tears were stinging her eyes now. "Are you going to kill me?"

"No. We are going to recruit you." He held his hand out. "Come."

Not having any other choice, she took his hand again and let him lead her out. They went through the kitchen with Sharon in front and Evelyn had trouble walking. Her knees were shaking and Simeon had to keep her from falling over. She heard Aaron was speaking with someone. She saw the man's back and waited to see who it was.

"She's ready," Sharon said to the man.

When he turned around, Evelyn's knees gave out. He reached forward and helped Simeon steady her and she started hyperventilating.

"You?" she said in a soft voice. "How?"

"Simeon is not the only one good at keeping secrets, Evelyn."

Her stomach turned and she tried to back away. This was too much for her. She didn't have an ounce of trust for any of these people. Not even the man before her whom she had much respect for. This night was turning into one huge nightmare.

"Let me go," she said. "Please, I don't want any part of this madness!"

"Evelyn—"

"No! There are no vampires or people who live forever. I refuse to believe this. I refuse!"

Sharon took her by her arms and shook her.

"You need to believe this because it's happening. Nothing you say or do will change anything. We need you, Evie. We're forming this alliance so we can avenge those who have been wronged. Sheila, Jeff, Robin, your brother. We can't do this without you."

Evelyn sobbed, covering her face with her hands. She was so tired and full of grief that she didn't even push Simeon away as he tried to console her. Then someone reached forward and pulled her into a hug. It was their so called boss, as Sharon referred to him. How he had gotten that title was a mystery to her. One she was willing to listen to. They were right; they were all she had.

"Now that you know about your heritage, it's time that you know everything. Starting from the beginning. But first, I must know for certain that you are willing to be a part of this. I know you're really doubting yourself right now and I don't blame you."

She forced herself to look at him. "Does Lela know about you?"

He shook his head. "The less I say the better. I've had my secrets for a very long time, and I thought it best that neither she nor Kevin knew. Thanks to Aaron, he nearly blew our cover by telling Gabriella about what he was."

Aaron scoffed. "Please, you really think I'm the one who told her?" His glance slid over to Simeon. "I think you should ask the father of her children."

Evelyn held her breath. There were a lot of secrets coming out and she didn't think she could handle more.

"We have an arrangement," Simeon said. "She sticks to the college boyfriend story, and I leave her be. Besides, she's too close to Lela to ever join us."

"Just so we're clear, you still owe me for that," the *boss* said. "Statutory rape is a serious charge. Especially when it involves someone close to me. Gabriella is to be left alone. No questions asked." He turned to Evelyn. "As I was saying. Recent events have convinced me to come forward. What we do is dangerous, but I guarantee it will be worth the risk." His gaze became serious. "So, are you in?"

Wiping away the last of her tears, she stood up. Ever since she got the phone call that her brother was murdered, she'd been spiraling into a pit of despair. If she continued, she was going to end up like her sister-in-law. Or worse, dead. Whatever they had planned to avenge those who had died, she wanted in on it. She had nothing else to lose.

"Yes," she said. "I'm in."

He smiled. "Good. We should begin initiation immediately. The sooner the better. Then, we can finally begin." He stood back and put one arm around Aaron and another around Sharon. "Welcome to the Ladies and Gentleman Society."

Made in the USA
San Bernardino, CA
21 September 2016